ÆRENDEN
THE REAPER RISES

Kristen Taber

sean tigh
press

For my second pink bundle of joy,
who has quickly taught me that greatest creations
are not limited to one.

ACKNOWLEDGMENTS

Huge thanks to those who dredged the swamps of my insanity in search of errant toads (a.k.a. thank you to my beta readers), Edward Booker, Marci Bookman, Bekki Fahrer, Rebecca Glogower, Brigid Gorry-Hines, Trish Hanson, Jo Reed, Cheri Schueller, and Sabine Veasey. Extra special thanks to my early beta readers, those brave souls who read the roughest of drafts in an effort to help build the best book possible (yet somehow did not strangle me), Karen Giera, Catherine Taber, and Kimberly Whitehead. And, of course, my unending gratitude to my editor, Jessica Davis Lux.

Prepare the way, the sign doth show, beginning to the end
Upon the loss of child's heart, freedom doth depend
Beware the words of troubled times, beware the truths of old
The answer hides in buried lies, the **Reaper** *now will sow*

—*The Aurean Prophecy, Verse Four*

PROLOGUE

As a child, someone had told Meaghan what death would feel like. It was a neighbor. A friend, maybe. A teacher. The details no longer mattered. The words did. *"Your life flashes before your eyes. In a second, you remember everything."*

They had lied. Meaghan could recall only the last moment before she went over the cliff, the split-second when Garon's vilest monster had clamped his bony fingers around her wrist. Stilgan's menacing smile, the stretch of pleasure over his webbed Mardróch mouth, filled every inch of her vision as her body twisted, weightless in the air. Even after he had let her go and his body tore away from her sight, she saw that smile.

The rocky crag of the cliff face flew past her, a blur of red and brown, melting in the warmth of the day's sunlight. She could not breathe, and then breathing no longer mattered. Nothing did, except the horror squeezing her chest when she realized Cal's massive form had tumbled after her.

She watched his beard streak through the air, gray and black smoke billowing over his shoulder, and she closed her eyes against the truth of what had happened.

Meaghan had expected to die on her mission to Zeiihbu. Too many prophecies had warned of her fate. She had not expected to take Cal with her. She had never wanted to take him away from his wife and unborn son.

Her arms jerked away from her body as she fell. Wind roared in her ears. It enveloped her, a blanket both suffocating and warm.

"Give me your hand!"

Meaghan yanked open her eyes at the sound of Cal's voice.

"Now!"

Meaghan forced her hand through the wall of wind and met Cal's fingers. With one hard tug, he twisted her around and pulled her on top of him.

The ground cascaded toward her, a brown sea swelling upward, reaching for them. Stilgan had already met that sea. His broken limbs pointed in grotesque angles toward the rivers of dirt flowing away from his body.

Meaghan squeezed her eyes tight again.

"Brace yourself," Cal said, though she wondered why he would bother. No amount of bracing would change the ground's impact.

The wind roared louder, whipping Cal's cloak around them, and Meaghan started to slip from his arms. He tightened his grip and her eyes sprang open with understanding.

No amount of bracing would help in a normal fall, but if this had been a normal fall, they would be dead by now. The wind had slowed them, or more to the point, Cal's control over it might have saved them.

"5...4...3," Cal counted down before Meaghan lost his voice within the hurricane that filled her ears. He let out a strangled breath, and then silence followed.

CHAPTER ONE

SCREAMS ECHOED down the streets, bouncing from wooden house to wooden house before escaping into the noonday sky. A pair of blue birds scattered at the noise. A pebble mouse dove under the stairs where Nick sat, but none of the villagers reacted. They continued with their business, repairing houses, handing out baked goods, making small talk as if Neiszhe's suffering over the last two days held little more concern than the pain of a child's stubbed toe.

Neiszhe's cries ceased. Nick glanced up at the window to his mother's house, counting down the seconds to her next wave. Clear glass winked back at him in the sun. A cart squeaked as it passed.

"A flower for your mother?" an elderly man's voice broke through Nick's concentration. The man selected a blue daisy from a bucket on his arm and extended it forward.

"She's too busy for that right now," Nick said, his annoyance turning his words more sharp than he had intended. The man shrugged and kept moving, disappearing into the crowd milling along the cobblestone streets.

Nick studied the weary faces of the men and women as another scream erupted from behind him. Not a single pair of eyes sought the Healer's house in curiosity or concern. Nick's people had grown numb to pain. That frightened him more than he wanted to admit.

In the months since he had lost Meaghan, they had worked hard to establish new villages. He had hoped trading the bleakness of cave living for sun-lined streets would bring normalcy back into their lives. So far, they only pretended. They shared conversation alongside suspicion, looking for the traitor who lived within the protection of one of the new villages. They rebuilt schoolhouses and trade shops, but they could not believe they would stay long enough to enjoy them. They were too afraid to step out of the boundaries of the protection spell, too jaded to believe Garon had forgotten about the villages he had destroyed a decade before.

It did not help that they lived with the ghosts of their fifteen-year war. Nearly every building flaunted grisly scars. Some of the structures had succumbed to nature. Vines grew around them or tore them apart, plank by crumbling plank. Others needed repairs, though they still offered comfort. In the months since Nick and the Elders had reestablished this village, they had reclaimed dozens of houses, clearing away brambles and painting the walls and doors in cheerful colors. They had tried to make the village feel like "home," yet Nick could not shake the feeling they were playing another game of pretend.

He tore his eyes from a yellow house to seek out several fire-ravaged structures lining the edge of town. No amount of fresh paint could hide their darkness. People had died here. Weeds had cradled naked skeletons, caressed skulls, and blanketed hands outstretched in prayer. The nameless victims still haunted Nick's dreams long after he had overseen their burials. They begged someone to avenge them. He closed his eyes to chase away their voices, and then jumped to his feet when a door creaked open behind him.

Nick hoped his mother would emerge from the house, victorious. Mycale stepped through the doorway instead. The younger Healer ran a hand tinged with blood through his thick, red curls.

"When I apprenticed with Neiszhe, I never imagined she would be my patient someday," he said, grimacing. The expression did not harden his near-cherubic face. "It feels wrong somehow."

"Is she...?" Nick started to ask, then swallowed hard, afraid to finish his question.

Mycale shook his head. "We had a few scary moments, but May refused to give up. She's managed to stop Neiszhe's bleeding."

"And the baby?"

"Still coming. We couldn't stop her labor. Can you find Emma for me? This will be a good lesson for her."

A lesson about birth or death? Nick wondered, though he did not ask the question aloud. He had assisted his mother with dozens of deliveries over the years. She had rarely lost a baby, though the few times her determination had failed her had been in situations similar to this. Neiszhe would be delivering seven weeks early.

Nick took the shortest route through the village, cutting down dusty roads and narrow passageways until he reached a house close to the edge of the village. He knocked on the front door and waited. A reply came from outside the house.

"She's in the back yard."

Nick turned to find Faillen standing close by, a trowel in his hand. Dirt speckled his knees, a regular side effect of the garden he and his sons tended in their free time.

"Emma, I mean," Faillen continued. "Unless you're here to see me?"

Nick shook his head. "My mother needs her. Neiszhe's baby is coming."

"I see." Faillen's eyebrow twitched, the only indication he had caught the fear in Nick's voice. "Her son will be okay. He has four talented Healers ready to help him."

Nick wanted to embrace the hope that brightened Faillen's flint-colored eyes. He looked away instead.

"You're too afraid to believe it, aren't you?" Faillen asked. When Nick did not respond, Faillen stepped closer. "I know what you're going through. I saw only shadows after I lost Ree, but you can't let that darkness overwhelm you. You can't let death swallow your life."

"Death controls all our lives," Nick said, and glanced toward the field that marked the eastern boundary for the protection spell. Faillen understood Nick's pain well enough, but he did not know his anguish. Ree had never betrayed him. "I've grown accustomed to it."

"Nick—"

"Send Emma to my mother's house," he told Faillen, and disappeared into an alley.

Although Nick's wandering had aim, he avoided rushing to his destination. He did not want to draw attention or questions, and he certainly did not want the false sympathy he received every time he wanted to be alone.

At the outskirts of town, alongside the field he had seen from Faillen's house, the remains of an old barn welcomed him as a friend. Swatches of red paint peeked through black charcoal on the back half of the building. On the front, two broad doors waited for someone to throw them open again and fulfill their purpose.

Next to those doors, weeds and tall grass filled in a raised bed that had once held a flower garden. He approached it, and waved his hand through the air. "*Illusion lifts, as sight I gift. For all who hear, let truth appear.*"

The grass shimmered, and then disappeared to reveal a knee-high gray stone. Large pits had marked its edges and weather had sanded down its sharp points, but the words etched into each of its five sides looked freshly chiseled.

Nick had discovered it a few days after his arrival in the village and had recognized the prophecy almost immediately. Now an invisibility spell kept it safe from prying eyes. He smiled, remembering how Aunt Vivian had taught him the spell "just in case." Her seer power had helped him once again.

"I still don't understand why you're hiding that from the Elders."

Nick suppressed a sigh before turning around, unsurprised to find Max standing behind him. His friend had made a habit of sneaking up on him.

"They have a right to know what you found."

Nick pressed his lips together in agitation, but did not respond. They had already had this debate one more time than he felt necessary. "Did Faillen send you?" he asked instead.

Max shrugged. "Who else? He's concerned about you. There are plenty of people who know what you're going through, but you won't talk to any of us about it."

"Talking doesn't help."

"If it keeps you from turning into a blood asp, it helps. You're our king, Nick. You should be putting us first. Stop being so selfish."

Humor shone behind Max's blue eyes. It irritated Nick more than Max's comment had. "Don't you have someplace else to be?"

"Nope." Max tossed a hand through his wavy blonde hair. "What are you doing out here, anyway? I thought you were keeping vigil at your mom's house."

Nick turned back to the stone. He traced a finger down one weathered edge. Since Cal's death, grief had worn him down too, though it had done little to soften his anger. Max moved to his side.

"He should be here," Nick said.

"A lot of people should be here for a lot of things," Max responded. "He died making sure Garon didn't get his hands on a Spellmaster. That should count for something."

"We shouldn't have to choose, Max."

"No, we shouldn't." The levity disappeared from Max's voice and Nick looked at him again. Shadows painted the skin under his eyes. "Cal should still be here. So should Cissy. But sometimes we have to sacrifice those we love for the greater good."

"Sometimes," Nick said, only because he did not want to argue with Max. His friend dealt with the loss of his wife in the best way he could—by pretending it would someday serve a larger purpose. Nick could not fault that. He did not feel the need to agree with it either.

"It's not Cal you're thinking about though," Max said. "Is it?"

"Don't start."

"They might both be alive, you know. The Writer's book—"

"Is useless. If they'd survived, Cal would be here by now."

"You don't know that," Max said. "Or is this about you feeling responsible?"

Nick glared at him. "I am not to blame for his death, Max. Meaghan is. If she hadn't gone behind my back, he'd be here."

"So would she," Max said. "And you'd be dead in her place."

A fate Nick would welcome gladly. It would be better than the pain threatening to swallow him whole with every breath.

"I should check on Neiszhe," he said and he recited the spell to hide the stone once more. It did him no good to keep revisiting these words. The prophecy did not matter. Not the first four verses he had heard when the gildonae appeared, sealing Meaghan's pact with Faillen. And not the last verse he had recently discovered.

None of it mattered because it had been about Meaghan. She no longer lived to fulfill it.

CHAPTER TWO

"AND TO think, I actually *wanted* to learn how to hunt."

No one responded. No one ever did. Meaghan plodded onward through a muddy field in search of dinner, though she doubted she would have much luck. Only one creature would be crazy enough to wander around in a storm, and that person now talked to herself.

A bush to her right rustled and she stopped, tightening her fingers around her makeshift spear in anticipation. Nick and Cal had made hunting seem like fun. She could not understand why. She loathed everything about it. It took too long to find enough for a meal and preparing the food had been much harder than she had expected. She had mangled a dozen roasts learning how to carve them, and the first time she had skinned a bat-wing squirrel, she had lost her appetite for two days.

A rabbit burst out from beneath the bush and sped away from her. Meaghan planted her feet and took aim, throwing her spear when she felt confident in her aim. The weapon sank into the soft dirt inches behind the disappearing cottontail. Meaghan cursed. Two months she had been in this wilderness. In that time, she had failed to master another weapon as well as she had her battle knives.

She collected the spear and examined it. This weapon, like the bow and arrows she had made before it, bent in several places. She had not been able to find a single straight limb since she had been here. Every tree seemed to have grown within a wind tunnel. Even the bushes curled into each other, as if trying to escape an invisible attacker.

A black-speckled hen dropped down from a tree ahead of her and Meaghan readied a knife, trading practice time for a quick kill. Cal would awaken soon and she needed to have his meat cooked before then.

The bird hopped from one foot to the other, then leaped forward. It acted like an easy target, but Meaghan had learned the hard way it could outrun her in a matter of seconds. This bird was young by its gray spots, and she hoped its age would translate into carelessness. She exhaled a silent breath and let her blade fly. It hit its mark.

Although the hen would not provide enough meat for two people, it would work well enough for one. Meaghan would eat berries. For the third day in a row.

She choked back a sigh and tried to stay grateful. At least she would not starve to death while she went insane.

§

CAL'S EYES fluttered open, and as he always did at this time, he howled in pain. A minute passed before Meaghan forced a wedge of jicab root between his teeth and another went by before his wails halted. She had expected him to pepper her with questions while she spoon-fed him. Instead, he blinked at her several times, then pushed his burly body up to sitting and grabbed the plate out of her hands.

"How long's it been?" he asked between bites.

Meaghan studied him for any sign of confusion. The usual clouds had cleared from his pale blue eyes. "What do you mean?"

"I mean how long's it been since I've been in a coma. Stop watching me like a wide-eyed tree mole. Blink or something. It's disturbing."

"I can't help it. You're...lucid?"

He chuckled. "At least one of us is. How long?"

"Eight weeks, I think. Nine? I lost count somewhere along the way. What's the last thing you remember?"

"You mean after the whole falling off the cliff, breaking my leg, and getting poisoned thing?"

"Yes."

"Not a lot. We found the sickle herb and the cave. I went to sleep and here we are. Speaking of which, where'd you put the herb? I don't taste it."

Meaghan inclined her head toward the hen as he took another large bite. "I've been soaking it in spice berry juice. I thought it would mask the bitterness."

"That it did. You could've taken some of the bird for yourself before you laced it though. I notice you're not eating."

"There isn't enough. You need to keep up your strength to heal."

"I'm not going to heal, Meg. That's the point of the sickle herb. It puts me in stasis so nothing advances. Not my leg and most importantly, not the nettlebarb poison. We talked about this."

"Right. I'm supposed to get help at all costs. I'm supposed to leave you with a stash of sickle herb to take every day when you wake up."

"So why didn't you follow my instructions?"

"Because every day you wake up screaming from the poison, and every time you ask me what you're doing here. At least you did, until today. You wouldn't have remembered to take the herb."

Cal grunted and trailed his fingers down his black and gray beard, bringing them together where the bristles ended at his chest. "I can see your dilemma. I didn't expect the herb's memory loss side effect to last so long." He shrugged. "That's really beside the point. You should've gone anyway."

Meaghan rolled her eyes. *The queen's life at all costs*, Cal had told her before he fell asleep the first time. She had followed the decree, just not the way he had imagined it. She still lived.

"I've mapped the area," she told him and picked up a piece of dried bark from the ground at her side. On the back of it, she had drawn the terrain using a piece of charcoal she had found in a riverbank. "I'm hoping you can help me figure out where we are. I don't think we're in Zeiihbu any longer."

"We're not. And we're not quite in the Barren either. The cliffs here form a natural barrier. You won't be able climb them, but if my memory serves me right, you should be able to cross back into Zeiihbu a few days north of here."

"I won't leave you. When you're strong enough, you can use your power to reach Faillen's village, carry a message along the wind—"

"I'm not going to be strong enough for that. There aren't any other options. You have to leave me."

"No." She slapped the map back down and stood. "I won't exchange your life for mine. We've come too close to that happening already."

"It's my job to protect you, Meg, not the other way around."

"Not any longer." Retrieving a bladder of water from a rock by the cave entrance, Meaghan handed it to Cal. "Eat your meal. You have about ten more minutes before the herb kicks in. If you still want to argue tomorrow, so be it. We're done talking today."

Cal sighed. "At least eat more. You look terrible."

"I'll see what I can do," she promised, allowing him the small concession because she could not deny his statement. She had lost too much weight over the past few weeks. Berries had not sustained her as well as she had hoped and she did not know enough about the local vegetation to eat much of it. Her near-black hair had taken on a dull sheen. Her olive skin had started to turn a sickly-yellow. And the last time she had caught her reflection in a pool of stagnant water, she had been shocked to see dark shadows circling her copper eyes. She looked more sick than tired and that scared her, though she refused to admit it to anyone, least of all Cal.

"Good," Cal said, then finished the hen without uttering another word.

CHAPTER THREE

A SWOLLEN moon skulked low across the horizon. Red tinged its bulging edges and Meaghan could not shake the sensation it would burst before morning came. She shuddered at the thought of blood pouring from a gaping hole in the sky, then cursed when her foot sank ankle deep in a thick puddle of black sludge. After today's storm, blood could not make the ground any worse.

She debated heading back to the cave. She already felt vulnerable, without mud slowing her down. The razor beasts common to this area left her alone, thanks to Faillen's foresight. He had commanded their leader, the ghoul Anissa, to stop hunting humans. The rest of the animals had no such code of conduct and they were far better at hunting than she was.

Rubbing a hand across her forearm, Meaghan grimaced when a thick scar tickled her palm. The white bear that had left the mark had become dinner, but his surprise attack had almost reversed their fates. The prospect chilled her, as did the realization that each day could bring another attack with a different outcome. Each night could be her last.

Several saplings rustled up ahead, their leaves swaying back and forth wildly, and Meaghan loosened a knife from its sheath. Only one animal would be stupid enough to make its path known. A silver-backed swine stepped onto the trail. It burrowed its snout into the dirt and she threw her blade. Her kill-strike hit the animal between the eyes. It dropped to the ground without uttering a sound.

She retrieved her knife, and then nudged the animal's side with her boot. The sow had enjoyed a healthy winter. It easily weighed thirty pounds, which meant Meaghan's hunt could end for the night.

Bending over to pick up the animal, she froze when a whiff of rotten trash floated through the woods. *Mardróch.* This time, panic gripped her as she shoved the animal under a bush, and sought cover within a cluster of trees a few yards away.

Although she had not had the chance to focus her empath power since her cliff dive, she kept it active at all times. Lately, she had been grateful for that decision. This was the third time in a week a Mardróch had almost stumbled upon her.

"I don't see how it matters so much to Garon," a guttural voice carried past Meaghan's hiding place. She shrunk into the shadows.

"Me neither," a second, rougher voice said.

The smell of rotten trash grew overwhelming and Meaghan fought to keep down what little dinner she had eaten. It appeared her empath power translated Mardróch frustration into garbage.

"They don't belong here," the first Mardróch whined.

"The villagers or the female Mardróch?"

"Both. Why Garon felt the need to establish a village out here is beyond me, but it's worse with those female guards. They give me the creeps."

The second voice cackled. "Only because they won't have you."

"Yeah, because I want my head to explode after mating. I don't think so. I get having them at the castle, but nothing happens in this wasteland."

"Does it matter? Garon can do whatever he wants. I'm not about to ask questions."

"That's wise, I suppose," the first Mardróch said. "Hello. What's this?"

Meaghan caught her breath and held it, hoping he had not discovered her pig. When the sound of rustling leaves followed, she slid her fingers over one of her knives.

"Dinner?" the second Mardróch asked.

Meaghan shifted away from the tree.

"Not an animal's though," the first Mardróch said. "That's a knife mark if I ever saw one."

Meaghan stepped out of her hiding spot. One Mardróch knelt over the carcass of the swine. The other stood behind him.

"You're welcome to examine the blade up close, if you'd like," she said.

Both Mardróch turned to face her. Neither of them seemed worried as they stretched their bone-like hands in front of them. Blue lightning crackled at their fingertips.

"Prey," the first Mardróch said. The noise escaping his web-like mouth sounded almost happy and Meaghan's power translated the emotion into rotten eggs. His gray skin looked like dry leather in the moonlight. "I've been itching for a good fight."

"You have one," she told him.

The second Mardróch wiggled his fingers. Electricity arced into the air. "Run," he said. "I'll give you a head start."

Meaghan attacked instead. The air sizzled as she slid into the second Mardróch's legs. He hit the ground with a groan. She thrust one of her knives into the opening of his hood before he had the chance to recover, and then rolled to the side. A bolt hit the dead Mardróch's body, blackening his clothes. Meaghan jumped to her feet and faced his companion.

"You'll regret that," he growled.

"I doubt it," she said, then dove out of the way when he gestured toward her. Lightning hit the ground where she had been standing.

Grabbing a knife from her belt, she swung it wide. It bounced off the Mardróch's impervious cloak. He retaliated by casting another bolt in her direction. She felt the heat of it as it singed her hair, and then attacked again. This time, her blade traced a red gash along the back of the monster's gray hand. He howled and lashed out, grabbing her neck and driving her into a tree.

The Mardróch's lips parted into a webbed smile. He forced her chin up with his bony fingers so that her eyes met his red gaze. The smell of rotting flesh overwhelmed her senses, rather than the fear his freezing power should have emitted.

"You'll watch as I torture you," he said. "You'll feel agony beyond anything you've ever imagined and I'll enjoy knowing that you can do nothing about it."

"I don't think so," Meaghan said and swung her blade up over his arm, aiming for one hideous, red pupil. It exploded in a gush of clear fluid.

Everyone else froze under that red stare, overwhelmed by supernatural fear. Everyone, that was, except the queen. She hoped that thought crossed his mind before his last breath left him.

She reclaimed her knives and cleaned them, then turned to find a razor beast sniffing her white-backed swine.

"That's mine," she warned.

The animal looked up at her. Though it resembled a lion-sized house cat, a swish of its barbed tail warned that its tame appearance hid more than a foul temperament. It extended its blade-like claws, drawing deep grooves in the dirt in challenge.

"You have bigger game to eat," Meaghan said, gesturing toward the Mardróch. The beast's golden eyes trailed toward the dead monsters. It approached, bypassing her in a wide circle, and then sniffed at one of the Mardróch's hoods. She knew the minute the razor beast had accepted her offer. It looked toward the trees and two dark forms appeared among the shadows.

Cold crept down her spine when she realized the beasts had been watching her. She chased the fear from her mind and picked up her pig. At some point, Faillen's command would no longer overcome their animal instincts. She had no desire to be around when that happened.

She turned away, and then hesitated when a fourth cat slipped out of the forest. She watched it saunter around her. When she had first seen the razor beasts in this wasteland, she had attempted to get a message to Faillen through them. They had ignored her attempts at communicating and she had vowed not to waste her time trying again, but her conversation with Cal had left her feeling desperate. Desperation had no use for embarrassment.

"Can any of you understand me?" she asked. The first beast looked up at her and she forced herself to continue. "Tell Anissa to deliver a message to Faillen. Tell him the queen and her Guardian are still alive."

The beast returned to his meal. Meaghan sighed. At least tonight's hunt had been a success. She had food for Cal and tomorrow, she had one more move to make. The Mardróch had spoken of a village. It might belong to Garon, but it might also be her only hope.

CHAPTER FOUR

"I DON'T know how much longer she can hold out," Mycale whispered, worry etching creases in his forehead.

Nick worked to hold back a smile. "You haven't been through many births, have you?" he asked.

"Not really," Mycale admitted. "I assisted Neiszhe once, but I spent more time corralling the woman's three other kids than helping with the delivery. I don't remember it taking this long."

"Usually the first child takes the longest. If that was the woman's fourth—"

"You're *not* helping," Nick's mother growled from across the room. Nick's attention snapped to her. She sat at the foot of Neiszhe's labor bed, her cheeks nearly as red as her hair. Her eyes crackled with anger.

"Sorry, May," Mycale said. "I didn't realize you could hear."

"It's not me you should be concerned about," May said and nodded toward their patient. Neiszhe sucked in a short breath and blew it out as another contraction hit. Her screams had grown closer together, indicating her son would arrive soon. When this one ended, she dropped her head back to her pillow. A strand of jet-black hair escaped from a bun at the nape of her neck. It clung to her flushed cheek as a bead of sweat trickled down her face and landed on her blue birthing gown. She struggled through a breath, then her smoke-colored eyes widened.

"Mycale," May said. "Nick. Time to get to work."

Nick sat next to Neiszhe's bed and took her hand, then gritted his teeth through her crushing grip. Mycale moved to her side. He slid an arm under her lower back and a moment later, Neiszhe's fingers relaxed. Mycale had numbed her pain with his power. Nick had seen his mother perform the same technique many times, and because he had witnessed it before, he knew Neiszhe could still feel some of the contraction. She inhaled, and then huffed out a breath beside him. He wondered if he could manage labor with the same strength.

Neiszhe went limp, and then tensed a second later.

"It's time," May said. "Are you ready to push?"

Neiszhe managed a nod and Nick had no doubt she felt more than ready. The end of her torture grew near and the reward for it would be her son.

With each subsequent contraction, Mycale glanced toward May. Worry blossomed over his face. Nick counted the minutes. This, too, took more time than most people expected.

When the baby finally entered the world, he stared at Nick with clear blue eyes, then bunched up his fists, opened his mouth and wailed.

Nick had never heard a more perfect sound.

§

"**HE LOOKS** so much like his father," Neiszhe said as she cradled her newborn son in her arms.

Nick had to agree with her. The baby's broad forehead and round face seemed like a carbon copy of Cal's. He even had the same wide shoulders as his father. Nick's eyes filled with tears and he looked away, afraid Neiszhe would see his grief.

Neiszhe tucked a hand under the baby's bunting and warmed him with her healing power. The boy had not gained enough weight to regulate his body temperature, but he had managed to avoid the more serious issues that could have accompanied his early arrival. Although Mycale had gone home to rest, the Healers intended to watch the child in shifts for at least the first week of his life.

"Step outside with me," May said, and Nick followed his mother into the street. She stopped at the eastern corner of the house and leaned against it. Nick waited. Lines had deepened in his mother's face over the last few days. She passed a hand over her forehead.

"I was worried," she confessed. "I wasn't sure if I'd have enough time."

Nick waited for her to say more. She continued to stare at him and he took her arm. "You need sleep, Mom. You're not making much sense."

"No, I guess not," she said. "But I can't leave yet. When Mycale returns, I will. I trust him. Neiszhe did a good job with training him. And that girl, um…" Her brows pinched together over her nose.

"Emma," Nick offered.

"Yes. She has a lot of potential, but I need to be harder on her.

She's too timid."

Or afraid of you, Nick thought. Most Healers feared his mother at first. He did not blame them. Her skill had no equal in the kingdom. Neither did her temper.

His mother slipped a handful of red berries from a pocket attached to her belt and tossed them into her mouth. The muddleberries had been an increasing habit of hers over the last few days. Although their energizing properties would revive her soon, she could not live on them for much longer. He needed to ensure Emma and Mycale took double shifts so she could rest.

When her green eyes brightened, he continued the conversation.

"What did you have enough time for?"

"Strengthening the baby's lungs," she said. "If he'd come earlier, I couldn't have saved him."

"He didn't," Nick said. "He'll be okay."

"I believe so. I need to talk to you about something that isn't related to Neiszhe. You can't tell anyone you heard it from me."

"What is it?"

She looked up and down the street. When no one returned her gaze, she pulled Nick into the alley separating her house from the larger home next to it. "Listen, Nick, the Elders are trying to protect you. I think they're wrong to do so, but I've been outvoted."

"About what?"

"The traitor."

Despite the warmth of the late afternoon sun, Nick's blood ran cold. "They've discovered who it is," he guessed.

May shook her head. "Not yet, but it does seem breaking up the villagers helped us keep the traitor away from you. Artair sent a messenger. He found a commcrystal earlier this week. You know what that means, don't you?"

Nick frowned. His mother's question had been rhetorical. The Elders had outlawed commcrystals in the new villages. Only their enemies would be brazen enough to use them. The Shadow Guard had returned.

"That's impossible," he said. "Their only purpose was to kill Meaghan. She's dead. They should have disbanded."

"Possible or not, the crystal was there. Artair said it had turned black."

"That means the traitor has his assignment already. It's the only reason the Shadow Guard would have destroyed the crystal's power."

His mother nodded. "I know. The Elders—"

"You're an Elder, Mom."

She sighed. "Miles and Sam then. They feel the Shadow Guard should be gone now, too. They think it's a trap. They want to wait and see what happens."

Leaving Artair and Talea vulnerable if the commcrystal had been a true warning. Nick gritted his teeth. "Not a chance. I'll take care of it."

"The Elders won't appreciate—"

"Tell them to pound sand."

"What's that supposed to mean?"

Nick turned and walked away, not bothering to explain the Earth expression or the other more vulgar ones he feared he would use if he continued their conversation.

His mother huffed loudly enough for Nick to hear, but he could not find the interest to care about her anger. She and the other Elders had already sacrificed too many people through their inability to act. Nick would not allow it to happen again. Not even if it meant turning them into his enemies.

CHAPTER FIVE

"**HAVE SOME** jicab tea," Caide offered. He set a stoneware mug down on an end table next to Emma before taking a seat in the straight back chair across from her.

She smiled and his stomach warmed. It had been too long since they had been able to talk. The last time Caide could recall, they were living in the caves. Since then, Emma's apprenticeship with May had monopolized most of her time. She had been excited to learn under one of the kingdom's best Healers. Caide wondered if she still felt the same way after months of non-stop work.

Emma's dark brown eyes drifted half-closed as she took a sip of the tea, then a grimace creased the dimples in her cheeks. "This stuff is horrible," she said. "Don't we have any petal firewater?"

Caide laughed, nearly choking on his own tea, and Emma's eyes twinkled. "Remember the batch Stippell made for the Eastern Star Festival?" she asked.

"How could I forget? What was that? Four years ago?"

"Five. He used so many petals that it practically glowed when we tapped the barrel. I don't think I've ever seen a color of orange that bright before."

"No one could drink it," Caide added, grinning. "I snuck a sip when Dat wasn't looking and burned the inside of my mouth. I couldn't taste anything for almost a week."

"Serves you right," Emma said. "You shouldn't have disobeyed your father."

Caide raised an eyebrow. Emma had never been wild in school, but she also had not been a stickler for rules. Before he had the chance to ask her if she was joking, a hand squeezed Caide's shoulder. The strong grip left no question as to its owner's identity. His father used the affectionate gesture often.

"Emma's a wise woman," his father said, sitting in an armchair next to Caide. "You should listen to her."

Caide had always suspected his parents had known about the incident. The humor tilting one corner of his father's mouth confirmed that belief.

Emma laughed, and then her gaze drifted to the door as the other reason Caide and Emma had had little time together strode into the room. Mycale dropped down next to Emma on the couch and reached up to pull her ponytail.

"Drink your tea, kid," he said. "You'll need it. You and I have the next shift with L.J."

Emma wrinkled her nose. "Don't call me kid."

"Emalía then?"

Her frown deepened.

Mycale chuckled. "C'mon, Em, don't give me that look. It'll be a long night with you glaring at me."

"Then stop teasing me," she said, though her reprimand held little punch. A smile crested her face and Caide had to check his impulse to leave the room. He hated the way Mycale and Emma flirted, but he also knew he had no hope with her. She and Mycale shared a power and a rare bond as the only two non-Guardian Healers in existence. Emma and Caide shared a month's worth of torturous experiences at the hands of Garon's worst Mardróch and a heritage as Zeiihbuans. The former had brought them together in some ways, but Caide did not find that connection pleasant. Their heritage gave him some advantage over Mycale, but even that had its limitations. Emma's dark olive skin, equally dark eyes, and black hair marked her as a pure Zeiihbuan. Caide showed the effects of his mother's Æerenden heritage through lighter skin, strawberry-blonde hair, and bright green eyes.

He looked more like his mother than his father and the thought paralyzed him for a moment—not because of what his lineage might mean to Emma, but because the reality of his mother's death hit him once more. The memory of her face brought tears to his vision and he pressed his chin to his fists as he fought to control his grief.

The reaction gained attention from the last person he wanted to notice. Mycale narrowed his eyes. His green irises turned to dark emerald, and Caide shifted in his seat. The Healer had subjected him to that same look after the battle in Zeiihbu, when he had used his healing power to sense for injury.

In this case, Caide suspected Micah searched for physical strain. Caide's emotions would be safe, but he felt unsettled by the intrusion anyway. He cleared his throat. "Who's L.J.?"

"It's short for little James," Emma said. "Neiszhe named her son James after Cal's brother. We understand that James raised Queen Meaghan, so we thought it would be easier for her if the baby had a nickname."

"So you think she survived?" Caide asked. "How is that possible? The drop alone would kill anyone, and that's if they didn't hit any of the outcroppings on the way—"

Caide's father silenced him with a hand to the knee. "Careful, Caide," Faillen said. "I don't want Nick overhearing."

"Why not?"

Caide's stomach twisted at the king's voice. Nick stood in the doorway. His blonde hair looked rumpled, as did his shirt, and his blue eyes appeared stormy as they fixed on Caide. Caide shrank down in his seat.

"Why shouldn't Caide speak the truth?" Nick asked, trailing his hard gaze to Faillen. "Do you think I can't handle it?"

Faillen met Nick's accusation with calm. "Do you really want to discuss this now?"

"Maybe." Nick said and turned his attention to Mycale. "Mom needs a break. I want you and Emma to relieve her. While you're there, don't refer to Neiszhe's son as L.J. You devalue my uncle's memory by denying him his namesake."

Mycale frowned. "You know I didn't mean it that way."

"What I know is you've overstepped your bounds, just like you did in Neiszhe's village when Meaghan's power overwhelmed her. You seem to think you know what's right for everyone."

"That's not fair. I didn't know you were her Guardian then. I was only trying to—"

"This isn't about you, Mycale," Faillen interrupted. "Go help May."

Nick's cheeks flashed red. "I'll say who it's about and who it isn't. Mycale—"

"Isn't Meaghan," Faillen said. He waved a hand toward the door. "Go, Mycale."

Mycale disappeared from the room. Emma followed on his heels.

"You have a right to be furious with Meaghan," Faillen told Nick. "You don't have a right to take your anger out on everyone else."

"*Don't* forget who you're talking to," Nick growled. "You may be in line to lead Zeiihbu, but I'm still your king."

Faillen settled back into his chair. "Fortunately for you, I haven't forgotten. We're friends, Nick. If I felt differently, that comment would've earned you a reminder of who *you're* addressing. Sit."

Nick did not move.

"Sit, Nick. This isn't a territorial dispute. We don't have to battle over everything like our uneducated ancestors."

Nick held Faillen's gaze a moment longer, then crossed the room and took the spot Emma had vacated. He pressed his forehead into his hands and crumpled forward.

"When's the last time you had a good night's sleep?" Faillen asked.

"I don't know." Nick dragged his fingers down his face. "A few days ago, I think. I keep dreaming about what it must have been like for her to die that way. You saw it all, didn't you? You watched

Meaghan and Cal go over the cliff."

Faillen nodded.

"How did it happen? I need to know exactly. I need every detail."

"For what purpose?"

Nick's gaze trailed to Caide. His eyes appeared haunted, though the command in them still held firm. Caide fought not to squirm.

"Does he know about the book?" Nick asked.

Faillen pressed his lips together. Caide looked at his hands. Nick had kept the Writer's book a secret from most people, but Caide had overheard Nick and his father talking about it after their arrival in the village. The book delivered its readers directly into a story, as if they lived within it. More importantly, Nick's book had the power to divulge tales as needed, and make those same tales disappear as quickly.

"Never mind." Nick said. "Caide's face answered for you. I need to know everything because Vivian's words are still there. I look at that book every night hoping they'll be gone. They never leave."

"So you think if you know all the details, you might be able to figure out if Vivian was right about Cal surviving?"

"Yeah." Nick dropped his hands. "Now that I hear that out loud, I realize how stupid it sounds. Caide said it, didn't he? There's no way they could have survived."

"No way that we know of," Faillen conceded. "It's a long way down."

"Then I guess that settles it." Nick stood. "I came for another reason. I need Caide for a few days."

"Me?" Caide asked. "Why?"

"For the same reason I don't mind that you know about the Writer's book. I can trust you."

"To do what?" Faillen asked.

"I'll share that information once we've left the village." He addressed Caide again. "For now, what do you say? Are you ready for your first mission?"

CHAPTER SIX

"HE'S A boy. Why are we bringing him along?"

Nick glanced at Caide. The *boy*, as Max had called him, walked a few paces behind them. He stared at the ground, acting as if he had not heard anything. Nick knew better. Only a deaf man could have missed Max's complaining. Neither of them was so lucky.

"He's going to get hurt," Max continued.

"Knock it off, Max."

"Knock what off? I'm serious."

"He's stronger than both of us combined. You know that."

Max turned around, keeping pace as he walked backward. "Are you?" he asked Caide. "I know a Spellmaster is strong, but I've never been told how strong."

Caide shrugged. "My power's stronger than Nick's. I don't know about yours. What is it?"

"I weaken powers."

"So if you wanted, you could make mine weaker than yours."

"Maybe. I've never tried. I imagine it wouldn't be an issue. You're no more than a child, really. What are you? Twelve?"

This time, a smile tugged at the corners of Max's mouth and Nick realized his friend was trying to rile Caide. Most likely because he had grown bored. A year ago, Nick would have enjoyed Max's joking. Today, it irritated him.

"Fifteen," Caide said, his voice stiff. "But age doesn't define maturity."

"Sure it does. I bet you haven't even kissed a girl yet."

Caide's cheeks flared red. Nick punched Max in the arm.

"I said cut it out."

"Ow," Max protested, and rubbed his bicep. "That actually hurt."

"It was supposed to. Caide is more than suited for the job and I'd appreciate it if you didn't second guess my judgment."

"Fine." Max turned back around and glared at Nick. "Who put stinging nettles in your cloak this morning?"

Nick stared ahead. "I'm not wearing a cloak."

"*I'm not wearing a cloak,*" Max mocked. "Geez, Nick, it's an *expression.* You weren't on Earth long enough to forget that."

Nick had not forgotten. He had intended for the remark to irritate Max. When his friend pushed his shoulders forward and shoved his hands into his pockets, Nick controlled a small smile. Other than a short growl of annoyance, Max remained quiet as they continued their trudge onward.

The silence suited Nick. This part of the kingdom, though still forested in spots, gave way to flat lands too often. Nick did not want their conversation traveling in front of them in case Mardróch searched the area for victims.

As the day waned, the occasional field yielded to thicker forests and then to evenly spaced rows of trees. Each green and brown giant filed in line behind one another, an army waiting to march after their commanders. No one would be coming for them. Dozens of similar forests had dotted this area of the kingdom prior to Garon's reign. Seven close-knit villages and half a dozen strong Gardeners had replenished and maintained the trees. Now one farm remained, though its unkempt appearance barely hinted at the glory of its former days.

Nick detoured left. Neat paths between the trees had succumbed to underbrush. He pushed onward, leading Max and Caide to a destination only he could see. His friends slowed and then stopped.

"Nick—" Max started.

Nick held up his hand. "I know. You can't move."

Max's brow wrinkled. "It's clear there's a protection spell here, but I thought these villages were beyond repair."

"Most were." Nick took Caide's hand in his. "You are welcome here," he said, and then moved to Max and lifted the spell by reciting the same words.

"Wow," Caide said, and Nick realized the village had appeared for him, shimmering into view through an illusion of trees. Brightly colored houses flanked perfectly straight streets, their order a memorial for the people who had once lived here. This village held twice as many people as Nick's current village. It touched a smile to his face to see it.

"The Village at Shadow Forest was abandoned, not destroyed," Nick told Max. "Garon's army never discovered it."

That made it the perfect place to hide, until recently.

Nick's flash of joy dissolved. He ushered Caide and Max through the last of the forest and onto the dirt roads, looking for a bright red cottage at the end of the main thoroughfare.

The sun glinted behind the home's roofline as it disappeared with the last of the day. Nick knocked once, then again when no one answered. When a third knock echoed around them, worry blossomed in the pit of his stomach.

Not a single person had greeted them as they walked through the village. At first, he had credited their silent passage to dinnertime. Now he had his doubts. He pounded on the door. When that effort netted no results, he stepped back to study the village more critically.

Primary-colored houses stared back at him, their windows sparkling in the receding sun and their curtains hanging motionless. Curiosity often plagued villagers confined too long in one place. If they did not watch from the secrecy of their houses, they waved from their doorways, hoping for gossip.

Nick scanned a row of brick chimneys jutting into the sky. The absence of gray smoke disturbed him. No smoke meant no fire and no food. At least one of them should have been emitting tantalizing scents of tonight's meal. Streetlights hung dark overhead, though they should have begun flickering by now. Children should have been playing outside.

Nick shuffled a foot and frowned when a pebble skidded down the street in front of him.

"Where is everyone?" Max whispered, his face holding none of its usual humor. Worry etched lines in the center of his forehead.

"Let's get inside," Nick said. He tried the door first, not surprised to find it locked, then skirted the outside of the house to the backyard. A birdbath sat next to the door. A small golden jay perched on its rim.

As Nick drew closer, the bird did not move. Its wings reached wide. Its beak searched for water, but it had frozen a half inch from its goal.

Caide reached out to touch it. Nick grabbed his arm. "Don't. We don't know what this is."

"Do you think it's contagious?" Caide asked.

"I don't want to find out."

Nick skirted around the birdbath. A green snake lay in the grass, motionless as he tested the locked back door. Max managed to shove open a window and they climbed inside.

Shadows welcomed them into a kitchen. Nick had been inside Talea and Artair's home before. He knew the layout, so he stepped into the center of the room and allowed his eyes to adjust to the dim light before tiptoeing down the hallway. An open door revealed an empty bedroom to the right. He bypassed it and exited the hall into a large living room.

Drapes covered the front windows. To his right, a staircase stretched into the black shadows of a second floor. A couch remained empty on the far side of the room, as did a chair next to the coffee table. Talea sat in a rocking chair in front of the fireplace, a blanket stretched across her lap. Beside her, Artair knelt on the floor, his eyes fixed on an unmoving fire within the hearth. The flames seemed to swallow light instead of casting it.

Max disappeared down the hallway, returning several minutes later with a candle. Nick expected the flame to freeze like the fireplace, but it continued to dance in oblivious joy. Max set the candle on the mantel.

"Whatever spell this is, it isn't covering the kitchen," Max said. "I was able to start a fire in the stove." He moved to Talea's side. Despite Nick's earlier warning, he drew his fingers to her forehead, and brushed several curls of her auburn hair to the side.

"Come on, Talea," he said, waving a hand in front of her vacant green eyes. He grabbed her arms and shook her. "Wake *up*."

Nick placed a hand on Max's arm to stop him. "That's enough."

"He's warm," Caide said from the floor. Nick looked down at him. He sat beside Artair, his hand an oddly dark contrast against Artair's pale cheek. "He has a pulse. I've never seen anything like this before."

Nick crouched next to Caide and tried not to notice Artair's soulless stare or his stiff black ponytail as it brushed against his hand. He held his breath and counted heartbeats instead.

"Ten a minute, maybe," he said. "Faint, but there."

Max sat down on the other side of Talea's chair and covered her hand with his own. For the first time since Max's wife died, Nick saw tears sparkle in his friend's eyes.

"I can't believe Garon got to her," Max said. "First Talis and now this. Do you remember the day we met them?"

Nick nodded. He, Max, and Cissy had been playing stinkball when they stumbled upon Talea and Talis doing the same. It had not taken long for the five of them to become inseparable. Now Cissy and Talis had fallen to Garon's war and Talea did not appear to be far behind.

"Talis caught the ball last," Max continued. "It exploded in his hands. He looked like he'd fallen into a vat of bright pink paint."

"As if reeking of moldberries wasn't bad enough," Nick said and stood. "Come on. We don't have much light left."

"Where are we going?" Caide asked.

"To search the village for something that will help. Talea isn't gone yet and I refuse to let her die without a fight."

§

BY THE time Nick, Max, and Caide had broken into their fiftieth house, Nick stopped caring about leaving evidence behind. He tossed a heavy rock through the pane window of a vibrant yellow cottage and reached through the newly created opening to unlatch the front door.

It swung inward with a soft creak. No other noises followed. The occupants of every house on this block and the blocks they had searched before it were as frozen as Talea and Artair. They had even found a child's pet rabbit balanced on its hind legs as it reached for a treat.

As soon as Nick crossed the threshold, a stench knocked him backward. He covered his nose. "It smells like something—"

"Died," Caide said and stepped around him. He kept his voice low and Nick wondered if he did so out of awe or respect for the deceased. "I've run into carcasses in the woods that didn't smell much better."

"I think it's coming from this way," Max said and turned toward a flight of stairs, leading them to the second floor. Within the largest bedroom, they found the source of the smell. Sprawled out on a narrow bed, a man lay in rest, though his body had started to swell and his skin had turned green beneath dark bruises. He stared at the ceiling, his eyes as dark as the long crystal he clutched tightly between his hands. Dozens of flies stood like tiny statues on his arms and face.

"He died before the town froze," Nick realized. "The flies were caught in the spell."

Max approached the side of the bed. He reached for the crystal, and then hesitated, grabbing a blanket from the floor and using it to complete the task instead of his bare hands. The commcrystal slid from the dead man's grasp. Skin clung to it and Max used the blanket to wipe the crystal clean.

"I thought those things were forbidden," Caide said.

"They are." Nick took the crystal from Max and slipped it into his pocket. Max and Caide would need to know why they had come to this village, but he could not tell them here. "Let's check the rest of the houses. Something tells me we don't want to be here overnight."

They rushed through the rest of the buildings. When black had eclipsed the sky, Mardróch fires joined it, dotting the horizon in orange pinpoints of light. Nick caught a glimpse of them from the second story bedroom of a cobbler's house.

"There are at least a dozen," he said. "Too few for an army."

"And too many to allow safe passage," Caide responded. "We're stuck here for the night."

"Looks like it." Nick turned from the window to face the dismal scene in the room behind him. Three children huddled together next to an empty bed, frozen in a circling embrace. Caide felt for life while Max searched the house for some sign of the children's parents.

Caide stood. "Their heartbeats are fainter than Artair's. How long do you think they've been like this?"

"Too long," Nick said. "But less than a week. Artair contacted the Elders about five days ago. He didn't mention this at the time, so it must have happened after."

"Why did he contact them?" Max asked from the doorway. His face looked pale, his eyes dark and shadowed, and Nick did not have to ask if Max had found the children's mother and father. Like a handful of other people, this strange spell had claimed their lives. All of the victims had been on this end of town and Nick suspected whatever froze the villagers had done so in stages. These children would not be far behind their parents if he could not find a way to break the curse.

"He found the same commcrystal we did," Nick answered Max's question. "He suspected the dead man was a traitor."

Max frowned. "That doesn't make any sense."

"No, it doesn't. Let's head back to Artair's place. We'll talk about it there."

They threaded their way through the darkened streets, using the faint moon to guide them. The sounds of their shuffling feet along the dirt road seemed unnaturally loud in the oppressive silence of the village. Nick held his breath several times on the journey and felt no safer once he stood in Artair and Talea's living room. His friends' blank stares reminded him that he, Max, and Caide could be in the same position by morning.

Max lit the candle on the mantel again. Nick placed the commcrystal on the coffee table and sat down on the couch. Max settled into a chair opposite him. Caide chose to kneel on the floor next to Artair.

Max picked up the crystal and flipped it over in his hands. "I understand Artair's suspicion. That guy shouldn't have had one of these, but if he was using it to contact Garon, the Mardróch would be swarming the village by now, not camping out in the forest. I'm sure they'd love to eliminate Talea's and Artair's powers."

"Garon isn't our only threat."

Max's brows knit together as he looked up at Nick. Caide showed no surprise.

"Someone from the Shadow Guard is here," Caide guessed. "My father told me about them."

"No one told me," Max said. "What's the Shadow Guard?"

"It's a rogue group of Guardians," Nick said. "They think Meaghan is a threat, so they've been working with Garon to kill her."

"One of them was on the mission to rescue me," Caide added. "The rescue party figured out who he was because he was using a commcrystal."

"Like this one." Max set the crystal back down. "Meaghan is dead, so why are they here?"

"I don't know," Nick admitted. "Do you think they know about Vivian's prediction?"

"If they do, then that means there's a traitor in our village," Max said. "Who knows about it?"

"Only a handful of people. The Elders, you, Faillen—"

"More people than you realize," Caide told him. "Emma and Mycale heard you talking about it at the same time I did. They discuss it sometimes."

"Which means anyone could have overheard them," Max said. He stood and approached Talea, though he did not touch her. "If the Shadow Guard member who had the crystal is dead, who froze the village?"

"Maybe a second Shadow Guard member," Nick guessed. "Before all of this happened, I hoped Caide would be able to create a truth spell to compel the traitor into talking. There's no point in attempting that now."

"No, but…" Caide hesitated. "Something else might work. It would be temporary, but it's worth a try."

Max raised an eyebrow. "What's worth a try?"

Rather than answer, Caide started reciting. *"Strip the power from this room. Erase all magic of create and doom. I command the nature for one and all, be banished for now from these walls."*

Flames flared up in the fireplace. A fly buzzed overhead. Nick watched the confused creature as it zoomed from window to window and understood its panic. Nick felt hollow. He recognized the sensation from months before when Angus had stolen his powers with the Reaper Stone. Nick snapped his attention to Caide, but all questions died on his lips when a groan rose from the floor.

Artair lifted a hand to his head, and then fell backward into Caide's waiting arms.

CHAPTER SEVEN

TALEA SCREAMED. She pitched forward and Nick dropped to his knees, catching her a second before she hit the floor. He searched for her pulse, relieved to find it normal again.

Max spun around to glare at Caide. "You idiot! Do you have any idea what you did?"

"I blocked magic from the room," Caide said. "I thought it would help."

"Help," Max scoffed. "You made us vulnerable. How do you think—?"

"Max, shut up," Nick said and held Max's hot gaze long enough to convey command. When Max nodded, Nick brought his attention back to Caide. The young Zeiihbuan appeared pale. His hand shook as he pressed it to Artair's shoulder. "This is the first time you've been without your power, isn't it?" Nick asked him.

"Yeah." Caide grimaced. "It feels wrong somehow."

"That's because it is. Are you sure it's temporary?"

Caide nodded. "Cal told me once that no one could stop magic for long. It would be like killing the world. Since I can't write a counterspell for a spell I don't know, I thought I could try shutting off its source."

"Smart thinking." The words came from the floor and it took Nick a moment to recognize them, let alone the voice that had croaked them. He stared down at Artair. This time, Artair's dark green eyes met his. "Water," he whispered.

Caide jumped to his feet and disappeared down the hallway, returning a minute later with two glasses. He handed one to Artair. When the glass slipped from Artair's grasp, Caide helped guide it to his lips.

"Talea," Artair managed in a stronger voice after a few gulps. Talea remained motionless in Nick's arms. Artair lifted her onto his lap. "Come on," he said, stroking her forehead. "You have to fight this."

Talea coughed. Nick took the other glass of water from Caide and pressed it to her lips. Liquid cascaded down her chin, wetting her shirt. Her throat constricted and soon the glass emptied. Talea's eyelids fluttered closed. She passed a hand over them. "What happened?"

"You don't remember?" Max asked.

Talea shook her head.

"She was one of the first to freeze," Artair said.

"Freeze," Talea repeated, and shifted her focus to the far side of the room. "That's right."

"We don't have much time," Caide warned.

Warmth blossomed around Nick's heart. Caide's spell was already starting to fail. "Will they freeze again?" he asked.

"I don't know," Caide said. "It depends on how the spell was written."

"It's not a spell," Artair told him. "It's a power."

"The traitor's?" Max asked. "We found a black crystal. It looked like the guy who had it died a while ago."

"He did. Someone killed him before I sent a messenger to the Elders. People started freezing after that."

Several flames within the fireplace stopped dancing and Nick frowned at them. "Give us the short version. Time's almost up."

"She's still here," Artair said.

"Who?"

"I don't know. She didn't look familiar."

"She has red hair," Talea whispered and pointed where she had been staring. "She stood there. She swept her hand around the room and that's when I...froze."

"We didn't see anyone with red hair in any of the houses," Max said. "She could be long gone."

"She's still here. Her power—" Artair said, and then his lips froze partway across his teeth. Talea's gaze drew back to him. She reached out for his hand, then her movement also ceased.

The fly fell from the air. It bounced on the floor at Nick's side. A moment later, the fireplace dimmed, leaving only the glow of the candle on the mantel. Nothing about this made sense. Even if the Shadow Guard believed Meaghan still lived, why had they attacked this village and why now?

"Check upstairs," Nick told Max. His friend nodded and dashed up the stairs to the second floor. His footsteps echoed overhead as he went room to room. Nick held his breath until he saw Max's feet touch the top step.

"There's nothing up there," Max said when he stood in the living room once more. "Unless she can transform into piles of dust and broken furniture."

"It doesn't matter, does it?" Caide asked. "She might not be here, but if Artair's right about her…"

Caide's voice trailed away. Nick understood his worry. If the redhead hid somewhere in the village, she had already seen them.

They would not be safe through the night.

§

HE SHOULD have brought a commcrystal. Despite Nick's anger with his mother and the Elders, he should have brought a way to communicate in case of an emergency.

"Hindsight and all that," he muttered. The Earth expression had its merits. He strained his hearing, listening for any sign of the enemy, and then dashed out from his hiding place under an evergreen when he heard none. He crossed over two rows of trees, sought the cover of another large trunk, and waited. Several Mardróch ate a raw feast by the glow of a fire several hundred yards away. He could hear the crunch of bones as they chopped apart whatever animal they had captured. Noise traveled too well within the neat rows of trees. Each footstep could give away his location. Every swaying branch or rustling bush could bring Garon's evil minions to his side.

Better the enemy he knew, rather than the one who could starve him to death. At least death by the Mardróch's hands would be quick.

A shadow moved several yards to Nick's left, a black outline against semi-black air and Nick held his breath until Max found refuge behind a sweetspur tree. Caide followed in his lead, but pasted his body against the closest trunk when shuffling echoed a row of trees in front of him.

"I'm bored with swine and rabbits," a Mardróch growled. "Why can't we catch anything bigger?"

"Because we're too close to the castle," a second voice said. This one did not sound gruff, and Nick realized it came from one of Garon's soldiers. "Garon's spell to kill edible food means animals don't have anything to eat either."

"Some stuff grows," the Mardróch said. "I saw a brickleberry bush back there."

"Only birds eat brickleberries. Do you really want to eat a bird?"

Their footsteps moved away from Nick and he exhaled. Lifting a hand, he waved, signaling for Caide to continue.

They leapfrogged several more times before the sound of a twig snapping shot through the still air. Max, mid-way to another tree, dropped down to the ground with a light thud.

"What was that?" the soldier's voice came from behind Nick's tree.

Nick bit back a curse.

"I didn't hear anything," the Mardróch said.

"You wouldn't hear a screech wren if it was sitting on your shoulder. Go check over there."

The Mardróch's deep growl broadcast his anger. A few seconds later, wool brushed against Nick's arm as the monster's cloak swirled past. Nick tightened his fingers around the hilt of his sword, prepared for battle, but the Mardróch kept moving. His outline pushed down the row, away from where Max lay prone within the tall grass. The soldier's footsteps followed the same direction, deeper into the forest.

When they had moved out of earshot, Max rose to his feet and sought the protection of a large spruce. Caide pushed forward again. He raced along the line of trees, stopping a row away from Max and flattened his back against another trunk. Nick sought out his next target, prepared to run, then froze when movement caught his attention several feet down from Caide.

They had missed another enemy. The unnatural height of the shadow that bled from the tree made the identity of Caide's attacker unmistakable.

Blue lightning crackled to life between the shadow's hands, cascading an eerie glow into the darkness and brightening the Mardróch's red eyes. They sparked with pleasure as the monster fixated on Caide.

Max vaulted out of his hiding place. Nick yanked his sword from its scabbard and followed in Max's wake, though he knew neither of them would get to Caide in time. It would be up to the young Zeiihbuan to fight. He had his spellmaster power and if he could not think of a spell fast enough, Nick had given him a set of Meaghan's practice knives for this mission.

The Mardróch raised his hands in threat. Caide straightened his back, but he did not reach for his blades. Nor did he utter any spells.

He simply stared at the Mardróch, as if the monster's red eyes had already frozen him.

Blue light cascaded over Caide's features. Lightning struck the ground to his right. The Mardróch laughed, a sound similar to rocks striking metal, and another bolt landed to Caide's left.

"Run!" Nick commanded.

Caide did not move. A third bolt splintered the tree above Caide's head, illuminating the white pallor of his skin and his wide, unblinking eyes, and Nick realized it would be up to him and Max to save Caide.

He launched at the Mardróch. His sword bounced off the monster's impenetrable cloak, as he had expected. It also did exactly as he had hoped. The Mardróch spun around and shot a bolt in Nick's direction. A blue streak crackled close enough to singe Nick's shirt, then dissolved before making full contact.

The Mardróch growled and attempted another strike, but that one failed, too.

In the shadows, the monster could not see Max nodding, but Nick could. Each nearly indistinguishable gesture had corresponded with a failed lightning bolt. A fourth and fifth attack sizzled into smoke and the Mardróch wailed. His call echoed through the forest, loud and shrill. Crashes followed as the closest Mardróch answered the beckon. Minutes, at best, separated Nick, Caide, and Max from death.

Max snatched a knife from his belt and drove it into the Mardróch's hood. "Let's go," he barked, turning from the crumpling body before it hit the ground.

Nick dug his fingers into Caide's arm and yanked him away from the tree. They ran in the only direction they could—back toward the village where darkness would hide their escape, and back into a house where a redhead would have the rest of the night to hunt them at her leisure.

CHAPTER EIGHT

"DO YOU want to tell me what happened?"

Caide peered up at Max and swallowed, trying hard to control the bile charging up his throat. He doubted he would be able to manage it for long. His hands felt distant to him, as if they belonged on someone else's body. He watched them shake.

Max grabbed Caide's shoulders, his fingers sharp as talons. He dragged Caide to his feet. "Answer me! You nearly got us all killed. You might as well be a traitor for what you—"

"Max, let him go."

The fire in Max's eyes shot from Caide to Nick at the king's request. "Why? He's dangerous."

"He's not. Let him go."

"I disagree," Max said, but released his grip. Caide fought the urge to slide back down to the couch. Max turned and walked to the fireplace across the room. Talea and Artair still held each other's hands in the center of the floor. Caide brought his focus to Nick. The king regarded him with a look that disturbed Caide more than

Max's ever could. Pity softened his face, and kindness kept his gaze unblinking and unafraid.

"You panicked," Nick said.

Caide closed his eyes. Darkness enveloped his vision and within it, the outline of a Mardróch appeared. He yanked his eyes back open.

"Is this the first time you've seen a Mardróch since…?" Nick hesitated, but Caide knew what he wanted to ask. Since Stilgan had kidnapped him. Since Garon's worst Mardróch commander had tortured him for over a month. Caide sat down.

Nick sighed. "Look, Caide, there's no shame in it. I can't even begin to imagine what you went through, but I can assure you, I've seen grown men break under less stress."

"I didn't," Caide protested, though his voice came out as little more than a whisper. "I'm not broken."

"Aren't you?" Max asked. He leaned against the mantel. "You can shut off magic, Caide, yet you couldn't help us when it mattered most. Why not?"

Caide glanced down at his hands. They had stopped shaking, so he clutched them together. He could have annihilated their attackers, if he had found the right words. If he could have found any words at all. He had seen the monster's red eyes and suddenly, he had lost his mind to the past. His attacker's face had turned into something darker. It had twisted into Stilgan's. Caide had seen the branding iron in the Mardróch leader's hand as it seared into his flesh and he had felt the pain of it all over again. The puckered scar on his shoulder throbbed and he shifted his arm to ease the ache.

Maybe he had broken after all.

"I saw Stilgan," he confessed. "I didn't know what to do. I just..." He pushed out a breath. "I couldn't move."

Nick sat down next to him. "Don't let Max intimidate you. We have a long night in front of us."

"And two powers to worry about," Max said. "The one causing this," he nodded toward Talea's frozen form, "and Caide's."

"Max," Nick warned.

Max shoved his hands into his pockets. "It's a valid concern, Nick. He's powerful and we can't rely on his sanity. What happens next time? What happens if he can't tell the difference between us and them?" He pressed his lips together and studied Caide. "Is it true what people say? Did you refuse to be fully healed?"

Nick stood. "Max, that's enough. This isn't helping—"

"It's okay," Caide interrupted. When Nick looked down at him, Caide gestured for him to sit back down. "I'll answer his questions. I'd be concerned in his place, too."

Max nodded. "So it's true."

"Yeah, it's true. Emma wasn't able to heal my burn all the way and when Mycale healed me after my rescue, I asked him to leave it."

"Why?" The question came from Nick. Shock tightened his voice. "Caide, why would you want that?"

Caide pressed a hand over the scar. "To remember," he said, and realized how absurd he sounded. He could never forget what Stilgan had done to him. Every detail filled his dreams and haunted the quiet moments in his days. Skepticism shadowed Max's face and Caide squirmed beneath the silent judgment.

"We don't have Healers in Zeiihbu," Caide explained. "Emma's the first. We have scars. You know, from battles, hunting—marks of honor. I just thought, well…" He shrugged.

"You wanted to remember that you survived," Nick said.

Caide nodded. "I didn't think I would. I lost hope at the end, but this," he pointed to his shoulder, "reminds me not to do that again. It reminds me of what I need to focus on in this war."

"And what's that?" Max asked.

"Garon," Caide said and the name filled his throat, a hard stone that threatened to choke him. He swallowed around it. "Revenge."

A dangerous endeavor, one his father had warned could bring out a Mardróch in even the strongest warriors, but Caide would not lie. Not to those interrogating him now and never to himself. Emotions had more control when ignored. By naming them, he could manage them. His mother had taught him that.

Although Caide's mother would have agreed with his father in this situation, Caide did not see the harm in bringing justice to a ruler as despicable as Garon.

Nick pinched his lips together and Caide realized the king also sided with Caide's father, but he did not voice that opinion. He stood and crossed the room to the candle.

"Let's get some sleep," he said. "I'll take the first shift watching for our mystery woman."

Max nodded in acceptance and Nick blew out the flame. Darkness surrounded Caide like a blanket, the shelter of it welcome, though it did nothing to silence the gruff whisper of Stilgan's taunting voice.

§

MAX STOOD guard after Nick. Caide watched his dark form as he paced across the living room, from the fireplace to the couch, then the door to the chair and back to the fireplace. His feet made only the slightest shuffling sound and soon Nick's heavy breathing drowned out the soft noise. Caide did not understand how either of them could sleep. Max had started snoring within seconds of Nick snuffing out the candle and Nick had taken less than a minute to stretch out on the couch and close his eyes.

Caide tightened his fists, released them, and then tightened them once more to ease the anxiety coursing through him. The redhead could be here at any moment. Talea's power had a near instantaneous effect, turning the brains of her targets into liquid with the slightest gesture, yet she had not had time to destroy the redhead before succumbing to her freezing power. Caide had a hard time believing they could do any better, even if Max had enough time to warn them.

He turned on his side, shifted as the hardwood floor numbed his arm, and then focused his gaze on Talea's outline. She and Artair had seen their attacker. They knew about the woman's power. If Caide could wake them again, maybe they could share enough information to save them all.

The heat of his power surged through him like lava as he whispered the words to his spell. He held his breath, and then let it out in a disappointed sigh when nothing happened.

A second attempt, a third, and a fourth netted the same results. He cursed under his breath.

Max's legs crossed his line of sight. "Is everything all right?" he asked.

Caide did not reply. He hoped Max would assume he had fallen asleep. The Guardian nudged him with a foot instead.

"I know you're awake. Might as well talk to me."

Caide sat up. "I tried to revive them again."

"And?"

"The spell didn't work. I'm not sure what I'm doing wrong. My power seems to be dissipating as soon as I let it go."

"Ah, okay."

Although Max had uttered the words with nonchalance, Caide detected a note of suspicion. He frowned. "I haven't gone insane. I can control my power."

"Maybe," Max said. "But seeing as how you can't cast the same spell twice, I'm not sure that's entirely true."

Caide wanted to snap back, to fight until Max admitted he was wrong, but a voice in the back of his mind wondered if Max's fear might be valid. Caide clenched his fingers into his palms and remained silent.

Max sat on the floor next to him. "Look, Caide, I know I'm being hard on you, but you have to see this from my perspective. You're creating dangerous spells without thinking about their consequences. Don't you think it's possible you might have been influenced a little by your experiences in Zeiihbu?"

"The spell isn't that dangerous," Caide said. "It won't last more than a few minutes. Besides, we wouldn't know anything about the woman without it. We needed the help."

"That's usually the first excuse someone uses when they're about to do something wrong. Shutting off magic can have unforeseen consequences, particularly if that spell got into the wrong hands."

Caide opened his mouth to argue, and then closed it again when rustling came from the couch. Nick rolled over, still asleep, and Caide thought back to another Guardian who had protected Caide's family when they first moved to Ærenden.

Cal had been Caide's friend and his guide while he tried to make sense of a power that had turned him into an outcast in his homeland. Cal also had been Caide's teacher. At the beginning of each lesson, they had repeated a single mantra: *Analyze each spell three times before using it.* When had he stopped following that advice?

Sometime during one of Stilgan's torture sessions, Caide realized. He had begun to react, rather than think, to behave like the trapped animal Stilgan had made him.

Stilgan no longer caged him, but he had not shaken that instinct. The spell Caide had created might only work for a short time, but it would be enough to leave someone vulnerable to a surprise attack. And plenty of people had strong enough powers to use the spell, Max included.

Caide frowned as Max's exact power trickled into his memory. "You prevented me from completing the spell, didn't you?"

Max did not respond, and that was answer enough for Caide.

"I can't write the spell down," he reminded Max. "My power isn't strong enough. If I can't write it down and infuse it with my power, no one else can use it."

"Not now, perhaps, but you'll get there someday. Soon, I think, and then what? What happens if these dangerous spells become second nature to you?"

Caide believed he would do the right thing, but he understood Max's point. Once danger became a habit, it ceased to feel dangerous. Caide nodded. "Okay. I get it, but if you didn't agree with the spell, why didn't you just say something to me? You didn't have to use your power."

"Sure I did. Stubborn people always learn lessons the hard way. Trust me. I'm one of those people." Max stood. "Get some sleep. We'll find a better way to get out of this mess tomorrow."

Caide hoped so, though he spent the rest of the night wondering if he had already cost them their one chance for escape.

CHAPTER NINE

"I DON'T know why you're still hanging around here."

Meaghan did not respond to Cal's complaint or the disapproval she saw on his face. She pressed the tip of her knife into the roast hanging on her crude spit. Clear juice trickled down the boar leg, and sizzled when it splashed into the fire.

"I get why you didn't leave before, but it's been days since I last woke up confused. I can manage taking the herb without you. And it's not like I couldn't stand to lose more weight." Cal patted his stomach. He had lost several pounds since their ordeal had first started, yet his arms still looked like solid logs. Only his beard appeared different. More gray streaked the wayward bristles now. "It's better for both of us if you find help," he continued. "This poison isn't going to stay in stasis forever."

Meaghan cut several hunks of meat from the roast. She piled them on a strip of bark, next to the bright orange root vegetables she had fished from the ashes of the fire.

"C'mon, lass, you can't keep ignoring this conversation."

"I'm not leaving you."

"You won't have much of a choice soon."

She sprinkled the roast with pale green sickle herb and brought it to Cal. He refused to take it from her.

"Fine, if you won't pay attention to me, pay attention to this." He yanked up his left pant leg. Beneath it, his skin had turned gray. Tendrils of fluorescent green pulsed up his calf.

The sight of the poison twisted Meaghan's stomach and she sank to her knees. Placing Cal's meal in her lap, she stared at his leg for a minute before gingerly pressing an index finger over one of the tendrils. It burned to her touch.

"It's grown," she whispered.

Cal grunted and pulled his pant leg back down. "A few inches, yeah. At this rate it'll take less than a couple of weeks to reach my heart."

She nodded and handed him the makeshift plate. "I'll go the day after tomorrow. That should give me enough time to gather food. I won't leave you to starve while I'm gone."

"Works for me," Cal agreed and shoveled a large piece of boar into his mouth.

Meaghan filled Cal's plate twice more. Once he had fallen asleep with a wedge of orange potato in his mouth, she eased him back against a rock, tucked their tattered sack into her waistband, and left the cave and his dismal prognosis behind. At least she tried to, but the image of his leg consumed her mind. Soon she could no longer focus enough to hunt.

In the last few days, she had searched as far from the cave as time would allow. She had found no trace of Garon's village. She sat down on a large boulder, feeling defeated for the umpteenth time since she had been stranded here.

Even if she could find the village's location, she did not know how it would help. She doubted Garon's people would have sympathy for her plight, and stealing shelf-stable rations might keep Cal fed while she went into Zeiihbu, but at the rate his poison had spread, he would not live until she returned.

A cliff loomed in the distance, as tall as a Manhattan skyscraper and no less intimidating. Ragged rock faces cut dark rivers into its surface, each crevice wielding sharp knives, rather than footholds. She had tried to scale the cliff every day for two weeks and bore the scars for her efforts. Curling her fingers over one red line dissecting her palm, she banished the idea of trying once more. Where weather had not worn the rock into razors, it had bullied it into submission. Ledges that looked promising had crumbled under her weight. Falls from five and ten feet off the ground had left only bruises. Those from higher up would not be so kind.

A gust of wind swept past her, brushing her hair from her shoulders, and with it, the scent of wild strawberries awakened a growl in her stomach.

She had lost her appetite after seeing Cal's leg. Now it resurged with the tenacity of a hibernating beast. Pressing a hand to the ache beneath her breastbone, she rose to follow the tantalizing smell.

In this section of wilderness, grasslands and rocky dirt stretched in three directions. A small patch of woods commandeered the fourth. Around the bend to her right, the cliff that had nearly claimed her life two months ago would dominate the sky. Each time she saw it, guilt squeezed her heart and shame tormented her for the decision she had made that day. Her plan to kill Stilgan had worked. When she closed her eyes, she could still see his bloody and crumpled body in the dirt below the cliff, though his minions had long since collected his remains. Despite that victory, her carelessness and inability to let Cal and Faillen help had cost too much.

Their families and friends would have mourned Meaghan's and Cal's deaths and moved to a new location, a new cave somewhere underground where Meaghan might not be able to find them. Worse, Cal's son would grow up not knowing his father, the hero who had jumped off the cliff to save his queen.

His foolish and selfish queen.

Meaghan turned away from the bend. Fresh strawberries would not be worth the reminder of her failure.

She wandered toward the stream to check her traps. One contained a rabbit. The other three sat empty, the leaves over them as still as they had been every day during this last week. Lately, she had found better luck south of the caves. This area had not seen rain for weeks and the river had begun to disappear, taking the wildlife with it.

The rabbit would serve well enough for Cal's meal tomorrow, as would a few more pounds of the root vegetables she had fed him this afternoon.

Sunlight yielded to shade as she crossed into the wooded area. It covered only a few city blocks by her old measurement standards, but size mattered little when it came to the forests in this section of the wilderness. Thick overgrowth made the ground treacherous. Weeds and moss made it uniform. More than once, she had gotten lost, turning circles until she found her way back to the field.

Fifty paces past the tree line, a patch of purple grass marked the wild vegetables Cal enjoyed. She dug up a dozen orange potatoes and a handful of red sweetroots, then tied them together with a shriveled vine and slung them over her shoulder, alongside the sack containing Cal's rabbit.

An owl hooted in the distance and Meaghan decided to return to the cave. She wanted plenty of sleep before her early morning hunt. She rose to her feet, and then grabbed a tree branch as her world turned black around the edges.

When had she eaten last? Yesterday. At breakfast, maybe, or the day before. She could not remember. She considered eating the rabbit, but she could not risk lighting a fire and attracting Mardróch. Even the root vegetables needed to be cooked. They would break her teeth if she tried to eat them raw.

Her head thrummed. A sharp ache started behind her temples. She would have to find food soon or she would be useless against large game in the morning—if she made it to morning. She might be weak and underweight, but most animals were not so fussy. Even the scrawniest waif would be a feast during a drought.

Taking a deep breath, Meaghan forced her feet to move forward. She had explored this area a week or two ago. If her memory still served her, she would find several brassberry bushes in the darkest section of the forest. Although the copper-colored fruit looked similar to blackberries, it tasted closer to sour vinegar than the sweet fruit she had known on Earth.

She reached a grassy clearing on the other side of the trees and doubled back. After several passes that ended on the far side of the forest, she cursed. She had missed the bushes. Lightning flashed overhead, followed by heavy rumbling. While she had been searching in the woods for the berries, the sky had turned black.

She ran at full speed back the way she had come, avoiding roots and underbrush by luck more than skill. Halfway to the patch of vegetables, rain broke through the leafy canopy and pelted her shoulders. Wind soon joined it, howling alongside her like a pack of rabid wolves. Steps from the field, darkness billowed over her sight and she skidded to a stop. Reaching for the closest tree, she worked to control her panic.

She would never make it back to Cal in this storm. She had to find closer shelter. A small cave faced the cliff area she had so recently avoided. She would be able to make it there safely, if she hurried.

Gritting her teeth, she raced into the field. Rain banded together like a blanket, swallowing the ground in silver. Lightning brightened the clouds. She tore across the grass and around the bend with as much strength as she could muster, then dropped to her knees in the dirt and crawled into the cave. Her hair streamed rivers. Mud squished between her fingers. She shook with tension and adrenaline, but she was safe.

She tucked her knees under her chin and wrapped her arms around her legs. Her pants suctioned to her thighs. She ignored them and the chill that soaked into her bones.

Lightning struck the ground outside. She scurried backward, and then recited the spell to create a ball of light. An orb blossomed in front of her, cascading pale yellow beams into the shadows of the cave. Mud caked her knees. She brushed off what she could before wiping her hands down her shirt. Weeks of wearing the same clothes had left her feeling dirty, despite regular river baths, but this had to be the worst she had ever felt.

Shivering, she turned her gaze toward the entrance for the cave. A few raindrops found their way inside. They bounced off the dark stone, and then rolled back out, following a natural incline Meaghan had failed to notice on her way inside.

Her stomach grumbled loudly, its urgency turning into a vicious bite. Meaghan pressed the palm of her hand to the ache, and then moved her fingers upward, searching for the hard circle of her mother's amulet. She traced it through her thin cotton shirt. Each delicate metal flower edging the necklace welcomed her fingertips like a cold caress. In the center of those flowers, a false amethyst pushed back against her skin, its beauty belying true danger.

She tugged on the chain, lifting its weight off the back of her neck. It had grown heavy since she took Stilgan's power. She wanted to take it off, but she was afraid to lose it. If her cousin, Angus, managed to get ahold of the Reaper Stone protected beneath the glass, the kingdom would be at his mercy.

Her light orb fizzled out, swallowed by the cave, and she recited the spell a second time. When that orb also died, she gave up. She did not have the energy to keep the spell going.

Rumbling thunder filled the cave and Meaghan closed her eyes, letting its symphony wash over her. Cal's poison faded from her memory, as did the endless days she had lived in this nowhere land, hungry, tired, and afraid. Each heavy hour had eaten away at her resolve, her strength, until she had to struggle to believe she could leave here alive.

Eighteen. The number echoed hollowly in her mind. She would die at eighteen, though she felt a hundred years older now.

She took one deep breath, then another. Dirt and musk greeted her. The rain pushed in its own, almost salty air, and beneath it, the sweet smell of ripe fruit tickled her awareness. She inhaled more deeply, disbelieving her sanity. When the aroma came again—a delicate blend of red raspberries mixed with apples and honey—her eyes popped open.

She stood and felt along the walls of the cave, brushing her fingertips across jagged rock until the texture changed. Gritty sand and hard stone gave way to tacky slime. She recoiled at first, and then the strawberry scent grew stronger. It drove her onward. The slime turned into fine strands of silk-like hair. It threaded through her fingers as smoothly as water, warming to her touch and dissolving the chill from her skin. When it trailed to an end, something brushed her knees.

Thunder rolled outside again, followed by a quick succession of lightning strikes. A blue glow filled the cave long enough for Meaghan to make out a lush, green bush. Fruit clusters hung low on its branches and she gasped with recognition. Each cluster contained a half-dozen blueberry-sized gemfruit, and each gemfruit had a distinct flavor and aroma based on its color. Pink gemfruit tasted of strawberries, green ones were similar to granny smith apples, and tan berries oozed thick syrup as sweet as honey. She reached for one, reveling in the sticky fluid that rolled over her tongue. A trickle escaped from the corner of her mouth. She wiped it away with her thumb, and then continued eating, stripping the bush each time lightning brightened the sky.

When she licked the last of the apple-strawberry liquid from her fingers, light began to fill the cave, emanating from the slime-coated wall. At first, it glowed white. Then it deepened to blue and began to pulse, a slow rhythm that became a dizzying strobe. She backed away from it, retreating to the entrance of the cave where she had left her food. Grabbing the sack and vegetables, she dashed out into the rain.

Ice-cold pellets prickled her shoulders. The cave now glowed so brightly it illuminated the ground. Fear overwhelmed Meaghan and drove her onward. Her fingers shook. Her lips trembled. She ran as if a Mardróch chased her, though she did not understand her own reaction. She forced her feet to stop and her lungs to take a deep breath. She could not control the frantic pounding of her heart. When the sky rumbled in anger, she fled from its vengeful call.

Terror turned each mouth of air into an agonizing gulp and each thought into a prediction of death. A massive oak loomed to her left. No sooner had she cleared its shadow than lightning shot from the sky, splitting the oak in two. Wind ripped two more trees from their roots, and then another crashed to the ground in front of her, knocking her over with a bone-shaking roar.

Scrambling to her feet, Meaghan raced away from the woods, toward the one place she had tried to avoid all day—the cliff that had almost killed her and Cal.

It stood in the distance as an impenetrable rock wall shattering the sky. She barreled toward it. Her breath stalled within her throat. The cliff grew farther away with each pounding step, and then it suddenly appeared as a giant in her path.

The sky cleared, and she skidded to a halt. Behind her, the storm still clashed with the land in an epic battle, lightning inflicting its powerful will on the ground as dirt exploded into the sky. But here, a sunny oasis warmed her skin and dried her clothes. She dropped the food, and stared at her hand. Her knuckles had turned white. Blood dripped from her palms where her nails had dug deep slivers into her skin.

The sack unfurled, spilling its contents at her feet. It grew and knitted together, forming the outline of Cal's cloak. The garment appeared pristine, not ragged as it had after they had fallen over the cliff. Meaghan knelt beside it and ran her hand down the wool fiber. She had finished shredding it with her own hands, tied it tight so she could use it for hunting. It should not look like this. It *could* not…

Her fingers bumped something hard. She flipped open the cloak and gasped when she found a tattered brown book inside. It had no title, no defining marks, but she had memorized every scratch and worn edge. There could be no mistake. This was her Writer's book.

It should not be here either. It had been in her pillow when she had last seen it, not in Cal's cloak. She backed away. This had to be a trick, a spell Garon had used to get her to divulge the secrets she had learned from its pages.

The book disintegrated and with it, her confusion swayed. She was hallucinating. She knew it with the same certainty she knew the rain had not subsided. Her clothes looked dry, yet they felt heavy. Her hair stuck to her face instead of blowing in the breeze. If she squinted, she could see storm clouds outlined within the blue sky.

A guttural scream echoed across the field. The scream came again and she snapped her gaze upward. A dark figure plunged over the cliff, a black ant that turned into a Mardróch as it grew closer. Air pushed the monster's cloak behind him like a kite, and Meaghan ran. She tried to fight the terror surging through her and failed. Instinct drove her. She had to escape. She could not be here when he hit the ground.

She heard a sickening thud and risked a glance over her shoulder. Stilgan's vacant eyes stared back at her. He reached out a hand, his arm impossibly long, elastic as it stretched the distance between them. His bony fingers circled her wrist and he tugged her forward. Instead of the hard ground slamming into her face, air rushed around her as she plummeted over the cliff.

She tried to scream, tried to make sense of what had happened. The muscular form of a familiar body rushed toward her, and she realized nothing could stop her descent. Stilgan's touch had launched her into the past. Cal had jumped off the cliff after her, just as he had done the day of Stilgan's death. And just like that day, the wind grew stronger until he caught up to her.

"Give me your hand!"

Once again, Meaghan forced her hand through the wall of wind to meet his fingers. When his palm met hers, she lost her grip on the present. The past consumed her as Cal twisted her around and pulled her on top of him.

"5…4…3," Cal counted down, and then let out a strangled breath when he hit the ground. The impact of it reverberated through him, rattling Meaghan's own skeleton. She also felt him breathing and knew they had both survived.

She started to roll off him and he shoved her in the opposite direction. Rocks scraped her palms when she skidded to a stop. She drew up to her knees and stared back at him, and then she saw his leg. Bone protruded from a gash in his shin. Next to it, a blood-splattered rock peeked through a tangle of barbed vines. One of them curled around Cal's leg. She scrambled toward him to remove it.

"Don't," Cal commanded. "It's poison."

Meaghan's gaze shot to the vine again. It looked as harmless as the lush, green ivy that had grown alongside her childhood swing set. Cal used the edge of his cloak to unwrap the vine from his leg.

"We have to get out of here," he said. "Other Mardróch will come for Stilgan."

Meaghan glanced back at the twisted body of the Mardróch leader, grimaced at the blood pooling under his head, then yanked a knife from her belt when a Mardróch appeared out of nowhere to tower over his fallen master.

Not nowhere, she realized. He had come from Faillen's village. He had teleported down to collect Stilgan, but now that he had found her, he would not return without his prize. His excitement triggered her empath power. The smell of rotten eggs overwhelmed her nostrils.

She hurled the knife toward the Mardróch's head. He caught it in midair, and then threw it back in her direction. She spun to the side. The weapon ripped along her forearm, drawing blood. The Mardróch's laughter rattled as he drew a sword from a scabbard on his back.

Meaghan grabbed another knife and blocked his strike, then slipped her last weapon from her belt, cursing when she realized she had lost one during her fight with Stilgan. Three would be enough. It would have to be.

Ignoring the pain searing through her arm and the warm blood slicking the hilt of her blade, she thrust it forward. A pig-like squeal escaped from the Mardróch's hood before he collapsed to the ground.

She turned back to Cal, her weapons raised and ready to protect him, but he was gone.

"Meaghan!" he called to her, his voice muffled by the raging storm. She turned to see his bulky outline approaching through the heavy raindrops. "This way. The Mardróch."

She looked in the direction he pointed and saw at least ten monstrous shadows coming from her right. They ran, nearly floating as Mardróch did when they used their supernatural speed.

They had to be another hallucination. This was not how that day had happened. She had braced Cal as they escaped from the cliff moments after she had killed the single Mardróch who had tried to claim his master's body. If others had come that day, she had not seen them. She and Cal had been safe.

As safe as two people who had fallen off a cliff into an unknown land could be, anyway.

They had limped toward their cave, finding the sickle herb along the way, and then devised a plan to save Cal's life. He had not been able to walk on his own, let alone run as he did now.

She shook her head to clear it.

"Meaghan!" Cal hollered again as he grew closer. A thick tree branch had been bound to his shin with two withered vines. It served as a brace.

The sun dissolved within a wash of rain. Rotting flesh overwhelmed her power, her senses, as the Mardróch drew their swords. Her focus snapped back to Cal and she fled.

Cal changed direction as she tore past him. His heavy breathing labored behind her, and then he raced at her side. His pain assaulted her power, stronger than the Mardróch's scent and somehow she knew this was real. He had run through agony to find her. And she had nearly gotten them both killed.

Fear took over again, accompanied by a panic stronger than any she had ever known. The Mardróch's scent disappeared as she and Cal dove into the woods, losing them within the darkness. She pushed onward until she found the protection of their cave. She expected to see Cal asleep on the floor, caught in a sickle herb-induced coma. He was not where she had left him. He huffed into the cave entrance, his face red with exhaustion and shiny with raindrops.

"How did you—?" she started to ask.

"Jicab," he answered and shoved a sprig of dried sickle herb into her hand. "Eat this."

She stared down at the pale green leaves before turning her attention to the cave floor and the last small scrap of jicab that remained. There had been a full chunk of root this morning. A dose that large should have killed him. She shook her head. "I don't understand."

"Eat it!" he barked. Her fear surged again and she shoved it into her mouth, not bothering to strip the herb from its stem. As she lay down, she saw him swallow a handful of the same leaves.

She wondered who would wake up first.

Then somewhere in the back of her mind, as confusion pushed past the fear, she wondered if maybe they would not wake up at all.

CHAPTER TEN

"WHY HASN'T she come after us?"

Nick flopped down on the couch in Artair and Talea's living room and shook his head, not certain how to answer Max's question. They were the only moving targets among a village of statues, yet the redhead had not come for them. Adding to their frustration, they had double-checked every building, every shed, every crawl space and ditch, and they had found no trace of her.

"Maybe she left after all," Caide said. He stood at the fireplace, staring into the low flames. A candle cast a dim yellow glow over his face. "Is it possible Artair was wrong? Maybe her power continues after she's gone."

Nick glanced down at the frozen couple in the middle of the floor. Max slept beside them. Nick never understood how his friend could sleep through anything. Even a whelk horn to the ear would not wake him. Nick had tried it more than once when they were children.

"Let's hope Artair is correct. Otherwise we have no hope of

breaking her hold over them."

Caide nodded. Silence eclipsed the room for a few minutes until Max started snoring. His whistling sounded like a freight train in the still air. Nick almost said as much, until he realized explaining a train to Caide would be close to impossible.

Caide danced his fingers over the candle, back and forth. The flame flickered from his movement. A frown crested the young man's face and for the briefest moment, Nick caught shadows drawing dark circles under his eyes. Although Caide's skin was lighter than his father's, a result of his mother's Ærenden heritage, his darker olive tinge had hidden the evidence of his grief until now. Or perhaps the Zeühbuan had done a remarkable job at keeping it a secret. Too often, those bred to be leaders learned not to show any weakness.

"Caide," Nick said. "How are you doing these days?"

Caide dropped his hand back to the mantel. "You mean am I holding on to my sanity?"

"No, I mean how are you doing with your mother's death? I've been there. I know it's hard to talk about. I lost my father when I was young."

"Dat told me," Caide said and turned to face Nick. "We mourn too many people. It isn't right."

"No, it isn't."

"Don't you ever get...I don't know. Angry?"

Nick raised an eyebrow. "Sometimes, sure. Do you?"

"All the time." Caide pushed his hands into his pockets. "At Garon mostly, but at Mata sometimes. That anger scares me. She doesn't deserve it. It's not her fault she died."

"Yet she left you," Nick said. "I felt the same way about my dad."

Caide tilted his head to the side, his gaze searching. "What about Meaghan? Are you mad at her? You've been acting like it. I know I shouldn't say that, with you being the king and all, but..." He shrugged.

"But it's true," Nick said. "I *am* angry with her for so many reasons. I miss her more. So much of what I feel has to do with what I didn't say to her when I had the chance." His mind wandered back to the day she had kissed him on Earth. What would have happened if he had followed his heart, as Aunt Vivian had told him to do? He would never know now. "There's so much I wish I'd done," he admitted.

"Too much of grief comes from guilt," Caide said. "And maybe that guilt feeds our anger."

"Maybe," Nick said. "Those are wise words for someone your age."

"Zeiihbuans are considered men at fifteen. Besides, I'm not much younger than you."

"Six years can be a lot."

Caide shrugged. "I guess. My people believe that at the core of us, we have a spirit that's reborn into a new body at the end of each life. Our spirit's experiences create wisdom." The shadows returned to his eyes and he passed a hand over them. "Not all spirits move on though. We're not sure why. Maybe a spirit misses its family or maybe the person died too early, but we see them sometimes."

"Have you seen your mother?" Nick asked.

"No." Caide sighed. "I keep looking for her. I keep thinking I'll find her, but she's gone." His focus returned to the mantel. He flicked a bubble of dried wax from the wood. "You know, Nick, I never want to overstep my bounds with you."

Caide's unspoken "but…" hung in the air and Nick realized Caide feared the same reprimand Mycale had received. Nick felt a pang of shame for it. Mycale had not deserved his anger that day, as few people had since Meaghan's death.

"We have to trust each other," Nick said. "One day you'll rule Zeiihbu and we have to be honest with each other if we want to work together."

"I know, but—"

"Just say whatever's on your mind, Caide."

Caide swallowed hard, and nodded. "If Cal survived, do you think it's possible Meaghan did too? The prophecy's still in the book, right? Doesn't that mean there's a chance?"

"I don't know." Nick pushed deeper into the couch, suddenly more tired than he cared to admit. "I wish I did. We should get some sleep. I'll keep watch first."

"Sure. Okay." Caide claimed a spot on the floor next to Max and his heavy breathing soon joined Max's whistling. Nick crossed the room to their travel bags. Inside the ratty backpack he and Meaghan had carried with them from Earth, he found a simple brown book and brought it to the couch.

Aside from the one small prophecy Aunt Vivian had written in the back of the Writer's book, the pages had remained stark white since the day Faillen had brought it back from Zeiihbu. Meaghan's parents had remained eerily silent. Disappearing and reappearing stories had refused to share their lessons with him. Just one verse taunted him. He turned to it, frustrated by its familiar handwriting once more.

Tell Neiszhe not to despair. Keep a fire burning.

He tossed the book aside, and then searched the room for something to help him pass the time. The titles on Artair and Talea's bookshelves made him sleepy just from reading them. Artair preferred history books. Talea liked to revisit her textbooks from school.

Nick would rather keep company with a dranx monkey. He crossed the room to the couch and picked up the Writer's book once again. Although he rarely missed Earth, he would give anything for a magazine or a movie right now.

He flipped to the front of the book and frowned when a pristine page greeted him. Every page that followed treated him with the same blank stare. Frustrated, he moved to slam the book shut, then paused when color shifted in front of his eyes. Words bled from the color, coasting across the pages under his fingertips. Before he had time to register what he saw or to look away, the book pulled him into its magic. He no longer sat in the living room, on guard as he had promised. He now lived within the story written on the pages.

§

ED'S SWORD slammed into his faceless enemy's weapon. The clash of hard allestone against allestone resonated through his bones and into the pit of his stomach, serving as a testament of life, a reminder of death, and an echo of slaughter and anger. He pushed off, shoved downward and the soldier spiraled out of his grasp, fleet-footed and agile as his training required.

Another enemy attacked from the left, a third from his right. Ed had no Guardian to protect him, no magic to keep him safe. He preferred his fights this way, open and honest. This was bare truth, his life at stake and humbled.

One man appeared a foot taller than the others did, though Ed suspected the fighter on his right would prove a more worthy opponent. That man's muscular physique hinted at a soldier accustomed to battle.

The three men circled. Ed shoved a strand of dark hair from one of his eyes, and swung his sword in invitation. The taller man lunged.

Ed ducked underneath his sword, evading the clumsy attempt with ease before blocking a strike from the second man. He grunted with the unexpected force, but recovered fast enough to side-step a third attack as their friend rejoined the fray. Ed lost track of all but his enemies' weapons. Each allestone sword sparkled menacingly in the sunlight. With little more than the instinct to survive, Ed parried swipes, pushed back against overhead arcs, and danced away from lunges. His opponents wore black masks. Ed could not strike at their faces, nor could his sword pierce leather armor covering their bodies. Stopping his attackers permanently would not be an option. That did not rule out a well-placed maiming.

Ed struck the tallest man, his blade swift and piercing as a howling scorpion's tail. A gash opened down the length of his enemy's arm, from elbow to wrist. With a quick scream, the opponent dropped his weapon and retreated, though Ed knew he would not stay away for long.

The stockier enemy's next strike kept Ed from dwelling too long on his injured foe. He blocked the sword with a graceful arc, reversed to block another, and missed a third.

Blood seeped across his white shirt, though the dull pain in his side told him the hit had not been serious. He rebounded, casting off another attack, then swept low, taking his enemy's legs from beneath him.

The man landed on his back with a loud groan. Ed scurried to his side and ripped the mask away. Before he had the chance to see his enemy's face, a blast of light filled his vision. The faint smell of mint lilies wafted past his nose, and darkness descended over him like nightfall. Terror closed his throat, but another groan reminded him that he did not have time for panic. Without sight, he would have to rely on his hearing to save him. He strained his ears and tightened his grip on his sword.

Heavy footsteps thudded in the dirt behind him. He spun around. A man grunted close by and Ed thrust forward, taking the offensive. The footsteps circled out of his reach, their pace unconcerned and Ed knew his strike had not come close. Heavy breathing quickened to his right. Ed changed directions, thrusting his blade upward—and missed.

Pain seared through his shoulder. Warm blood flowed down his arm. This time, the wound felt severe. He gritted his teeth and fought through it. If he did not figure out how to fight without his vision, the injury would be the least of his problems.

A sword whooshed through the air and Ed swung his blade wide.

He braced for impact. None came. The rasp of two weapons striking each other met his ears and he realized someone else had taken up his fight. He did not have to use much imagination to figure out his savior's identity.

Sizzling came from in front of him. Smoke filled his nostrils, and his blindness dissolved.

Dark brown eyes he did not recognize stared back at him. They moved away once a familiar voice spoke.

"That was a valiant try."

Ed did his best to ignore the smirk on Cal's face. "Trying doesn't count in battle," he said. "There's succeeding, and there's dead."

Cal chuckled. "All right. That was a valiant *death* then."

"One you should have allowed me to earn. Why did you intervene?"

"You need to be healed. I don't mind these sparring matches. I want you in top form if we ever have to fight together again, but I don't see the point in getting myself hurt in the process."

"How would my battle get you hurt?"

"You mean aside from you knocking the wind out of me?"

"Rightly deserved. You weren't supposed to be one of my attackers."

Cal shrugged. "You'll have a hard time keeping me out of a fight. But I'm less concerned about getting hurt sparring with you than I am about bringing you back to Adelina close to death again. She'd have me exiled. Or worse, hand me over to May."

Ed turned to regard the men who had so recently served as his enemies. Without their hoods, he recognized the tallest man as a gate guard named Darian. Although his gregarious smile whenever Ed passed into the courtyard had always made the man stand out, the shock of white hair curled tightly against his head had made him memorable. The man next to him, the first who had attacked, stared back at Ed with owlish eyes so dark, the brown within them could be mistaken for black. He had been the one who had revived Ed's sight. And likely, he had been the one who had blinded him.

He stood only to Ed's shoulder, but his agility in battle had proven him a worthy soldier.

"What's your name?"

"Atton."

"So what was that you threw at me?" Ed asked. "Some sort of potion?"

"It's my power." Atton snapped his fingers and a white ball, no bigger than the pit of a plum, hovered over his hand. "When this explodes, it releases a scent that removes sight. The smoke from this," he twisted his hand in the air and the ball burst into red flames, "returns it. If the person isn't dead, of course."

"I imagine you're not returning a lot of sight in battle."

Atton's grin spoke the truth in that statement.

"He was one of my most valuable men on the front lines of the War," Cal said. "Come on, we have to get you to a Healer. You're starting to look a little white."

Although Ed had not quite forgotten about his wound—the pain of it would not allow such a lapse— he had grown adept at hiding his ailments in the presence of his subjects. He had tucked his hand into his pocket to keep blood from dripping off his arm onto the ground, but he suspected the blood soaking his pants would not hide much. Nor would fainting, which would not be a distant occurrence if he did not stop his bleeding.

He followed Cal into the castle. Although he still had not gotten used to the pain of a Healer's touch, he could not argue against the value of it. Even when an apprentice filled the role, as was the case today.

"Elliana," the young woman introduced herself while Ed settled into a cushioned chair in the infirmary. She knotted her blonde hair at the base of her neck, and then placed her hands below the gash in Ed's shoulder. "Just relax, okay? This won't take long. A few hours, maybe."

"Even five minutes is too long," Ed said.

The young woman's brows pinched together as she turned a puzzled look on Cal. "Do you want me to accelerate this?"

Cal snorted. "Not a chance. He'll complain more. Where's May? I thought she was on duty today."

"She was. Nick broke his leg this morning. I can send for her if you want."

"No need. The king usually prefers her bedside manner, that's all."

Ed coughed, barely containing a laugh for Cal's veiled threat. May's ire for his "schoolboy fighting," as she often called it, meant intentionally painful healing sessions. This could certainly be worse.

Of course, Ed could not fault May for his punishment. He had the option to spar using the same spells as the Guardian army, ones that would prevent injury and extra work for the Healers, but those battles were never much fun.

Elliana shook her head in confusion and moved her fingers to the edges of Ed's wound. Pain surged through him with the impact of her power. He closed his eyes and did his best to focus on more pleasant thoughts.

The cherubic face of his infant daughter did the trick. Despite the burning heat ripping down his arm, the memory of Meaghan's cheerful coos over breakfast this morning still brought a smile to his face.

That smile faded when an unwelcome voice filled the room.

"Again?"

Ed opened his eyes and swallowed a groan when his advisor walked through the door. By all accounts and actions, Garon had been a good advisor during Adelina's rule. He could be contentious at times, but his duties included providing counterpoints in debates. Ed recognized his importance, yet something about Garon made Ed want to strangle him just for the pleasure of it. Perhaps it was the near emotionless way he delivered his words, or the smug smile that always hovered on the corners of his mouth. Or perhaps he simply brought out the worst in Ed. His personality seemed to be as smooth as a barbed dahlia bush and it prickled Ed in a similar way.

Garon arched a manicured eyebrow over a bright blue eye and Ed stifled the urge to punch the arrogant smile off his advisor's face. He did not want to have to start the healing process all over again.

"You really need to control your charge better," Garon said to Cal. "You're one of the best Guardians in the kingdom. Ed doesn't make you look like it."

Although a growl rumbled in the base of Cal's throat, he said nothing. Ed's fights with Garon belonged solely to Ed and everyone knew it.

"No one controls me," Ed said with no hint of the fury he felt.

"Including yourself," Garon said, leaning against a wall. He ran a hand along his jaw, a pondering gesture that irritated Ed. It seemed a lecture always followed the move. "If you want to keep playing your battle games, that's fine. Just try not to let them interfere with your duties. You're supposed to be in a meeting with the Elders in fifteen minutes. I'm guessing I'll have to cancel that now."

"A bonus," Ed said and dropped his head back against the chair. "That's not why you're here though, is it? Adelina prefers to meet with the Elders alone. I'm not needed nor welcome in their meetings."

"An opinion only you hold," Garon said. "You'd go a long way toward repairing your relationship with them if you at least tried to show some respect."

"Respect is earned," Ed said. "And they don't earn mine by using their ability to revoke my title at the slightest argument. What do you want, Garon? I'm not in the mood for a debate."

"Then how about a candid discussion. Alone."

"Cal's privy to anything you have to say."

"And the girl?" Garon gestured toward the young Healer, who had yet to look up from her work.

Ed sighed. "Fine. Elliana, would you mind leaving the room?"

"Only for a few minutes," she said. "I wouldn't go longer than that with this injury."

He nodded and she disappeared into the hallway.

"You heard her," Cal said. "Keep it brief."

"I'll try," Garon said. "But that depends on Ed. It's about Adelina."

"What about her?" Ed asked.

"I need you to talk to her."

"I talk to her every day."

Garon narrowed his eyes. "Try to be serious for once. I need you to talk some sense into her regarding the Zeiihbuans. It's been several years since the Zeiihbu War. We're not making any progress with them. There are still skirmishes along the border."

"And?"

"We have to protect our people."

"The Zeiihbuans are also our people, Garon."

"Not really. They're savages, blights on our kingdom and our ancestry. Adelina would see that if she wasn't wed to…" Garon hesitated.

"To someone with skin almost as dark as the Zeiihbuans?" Ed ventured a guess. This time he did not keep the anger from his voice. Garon straightened up and stiffened his shoulders. "Someone who doesn't have a connection with Zeiihbuan ancestry?"

"You said it. I didn't."

"You implied it," Cal growled.

"She needs to see them for the danger they are," Garon continued. "The only way she'll do that is if Ed convinces her."

"And why would he want to do that?"

"Because he's king. It's best for his people. We need to send in the army and take control."

"That's against our treaty," Ed reminded him.

"Do you really think they'll hesitate to break the treaty the first chance they get? We'll be at war with them again within five years and then what? We barely beat them the first time. I'm not sure we can do that twice."

"Then what exactly do you propose?" Cal asked. "The Zeiihbuans wiped out a large part of our army. We're still training new forces. I doubt attacking them would give us much of an advantage."

"A secret weapon would. There's a woman in the Pit who has a unique power. She can freeze people, animals, anything she wants. If she goes with the army, she can freeze the Zeiihbuan villages. Her power doesn't have a long range, but if we collect the leaders and the strongest warriors, we can put them all in one village and freeze them indefinitely."

"Why haven't I heard of her before?" Ed asked.

"Because she predates all of us. She's been in the Pit for decades. I understand her power has the side effect of slowing her aging. She still looks twenty."

"If she's been down there that long, she's bound to be insane," Cal said. "Why would she help us?"

"She's sentenced to life. I imagine spending the next hundred or so years guarding a Zeiihbuan village would be a much kinder alternative than the Pit, don't you?"

Cal raised an eyebrow. "I'd say. Even spending a hundred years stuck in a tar swamp would be better than the Pit."

"Either way, it's out of the question," Ed said. "We're not

attacking Zeiihbu. Adelina's arranged to meet with Cadell next week. We'll work this out diplomatically."

Garon frowned. "You'll die trying."

"I'd rather die early in a life I can be proud of than live a long life of shame," Ed said. "Is there anything else?"

"No, my king." Garon inclined his head in a show of respect Ed had no doubt he meant sarcastically, and left the room.

"I don't know how anyone can stand that guy," Ed muttered.

"The years have made him surly," Cal said. "He hasn't always been like this."

"I'll take your word for it."

One corner of Cal's mouth tipped up. "He means well. I'll talk to him after I get the Healer."

"Thanks. When you're done, let's look into this woman he mentioned."

"The one in the Pit?"

"Yeah, her. Adelina said prisoners aren't held there long-term. I have a feeling there's more to her story than Garon's telling us."

"Yes, my king," Cal said, inclining his head, then fled from the room seconds before the shoe Ed launched at him would have hit its target.

CHAPTER ELEVEN

THE CASTLE faded from Nick's sight. A moment later, the words he had been reading turned pale gray and then disappeared, leaving white pages behind. He blinked several times, unsure of what had happened, and shut the book. He had never had a story come and go so quickly before. He would have liked to read it at least a second time.

He stood, intending to cross the room to put away the Writer's book, but managed only half a step before he saw her—the redheaded woman. A white gown swirled around her as she descended the staircase from the second floor and Nick had to stare hard to see her over the pictures hanging on the wall. Each one distorted the near-vapor appearance of her body when she passed.

"Max, Caide," Nick commanded. "Get up. We have to move!"

No one responded. Nick turned from the ethereal vision in front of him and shook Max. His friend remained asleep on the floor. Nick cursed and shifted his weight to place a hand on Caide's shoulder, then realized why Max had not moved.

Caide stared at him, unblinking, an arm propped under his head. She had already gotten to them. If Nick did not run, he would be her next victim.

He glanced over his shoulder. The woman blocked the door to the front of the house, so he charged toward the back exit. If Talea had been right and the redhead could activate her power by waving her hand, Nick would not stand a chance.

She lifted an arm. He tensed, expecting the worst, and then his muscles exploded. He raced down the hallway with a speed he had never known he possessed. Survival filled his mind, moving his body with precision and instinct. He was the prey, and the hunter owned a swift arrow.

Black engulfed his vision as he fled into the kitchen. He smashed his shin on a stool, cursed, and pushed forward. The pain dulled with an onrush of adrenaline. Dim light shone through the curtain next to the back door, a beacon for his panic. Five steps. Four. Three. He reached out a hand and by some miracle, grasped the handle and yanked. His sight opened up to a bright moon and he stumbled over the stoop, landing in the flower garden with a dull thud.

Jumping up, he kept moving, running into the street and dodging down small alleyways until he faced a red brick wall. He turned, half-expecting to find his pursuer a step behind him. Only the silent windows of the closest houses watched him. Overhead, dozens of pinpoint stars twinkled against a clear, black sky. The illusion of a face winked at him from the low moon, but nothing else signaled life in this village.

He was alone, stalked by a near immortal woman sentenced at

least half a century before for a heinous crime that had earned her a long-term booking in the castle's dungeon. And she had escaped, or worse, Garon had convinced her to do his bidding as he had once proposed.

Nick looked down at the book still clutched in his left hand. What had Cal and King Edáire found out about this woman? Nick leaned against the wall as he worked to catch his breath and flipped to the section of the book that had contained the story. Nothing appeared. The next page stared blankly as did the one after that and the one following. In disgust, he snapped the book closed again.

"You won't find anything to help you."

Nick tore his focus from the book's plain brown cover. The redheaded woman stood a few feet in front of him. She had made no sound as she approached.

He scanned the alley behind her. He could not escape, not unless he could find a way to distract her.

"Do you know what this is?" he asked.

Her smile flashed white, barely a contrast to her pale skin. "Do *you*?"

Nick did not answer.

She laughed, her voice soft as wind. "Whose Writer's book is it? I have learned of many in my long life. Some are history. Some are fiction. The trouble is telling the difference."

Nick tucked the book under his arm. She had the option to freeze him, but she had not done so yet.

She faded, her body a near whisper to the night, then turned semi-solid again. The cobblestones forming the ground behind her drew lines through her white dress.

"This is too difficult," she said. "I'd hoped to talk to you before I did this."

"You don't have to do anything," Nick said. "We can talk as long—"

She swept her hand in front of her. Ice rushed through Nick's veins, and then frigid air filled his lungs. The houses around him swayed. White bled into black and brown until only a haze remained. It swirled, forming a tunnel that taunted him with a village at an end too far to reach. He wanted to race down it, to escape. His limbs refused to move.

The woman walked down the center of the tunnel toward him, her saunter purposeful and carefree. When she stood in front of him, her body had taken on solid form. She smiled at him, her silver eyes dancing with life, and this time, her face radiated. As Garon had said, she appeared to be no older than twenty.

"We can talk best this way," she said. "Though I hope doing so doesn't kill you."

Nick wanted to shake his head, to argue against his death. No words came to him.

The redhead pressed her fingers to his lips. Warmth returned to them.

"Who are you?" he asked, both surprised and relieved that his voice worked. "What have you done?"

"Ella," she said. "I've brought you into my realm."

Realm. The word made little sense.

"I thought you froze people," he said.

"I suppose it looks that way. Some people I bring fully into my realm, like you. Your body no longer resides on the land of your birth. Other people I bring into a half-realm, one where they reside in stasis until I need them."

"Like Talea and Artair," Nick said, his words finding certainty as his body adjusted to the unnatural feeling of wherever she had brought him. "But you froze the insects, the birds, even the fire in their living room. What do you need of those things?"

"Companionship. Warmth. I like the beauty nature provides. I like entertainment, too," she said, and reached for the Writer's book. Nick whipped it behind him before she could touch the cover. Her smile shook as her hand fell beside her. "I can't reside for long outside my realm, so I drift between both places. I explained this to your friend. The man, Artair."

"I thought you were in the Pit."

Ella's face stiffened. "So that's the history in your book? My crimes?"

"Not quite. Garon spoke of you to King Ed."

"Ah," she whispered. "The king tried to help me. He failed."

"Why? What happened?"

She cocked her head to the side to study him. "I'm a murderer," she said. "A weapon. Garon didn't want to lose control over me, so he convinced the Spellmaster to lie about his skill."

"The king believed Farrow couldn't help," Nick said and frowned. The Spellmaster had once tried to kill Ed's tribe with a curse that mimicked a plague. The king would have had to be desperate to ask for his help. "What could he have done for you?"

"Cure me," Ella said. "Save me. Remove my power so I could accept my true punishment. I belonged in exile for my crimes. The Elders locked me in a power-binding cell of the Pit instead. They were afraid of what I could do. My power took many lives."

"You control your power," Nick said. "Not the other way around."

"I get lonely. I can't survive without human contact."

And she used her power to bring people into her reality, to talk to them. Nick wanted to argue that it was still her choice, but he had a feeling decades of despairing loneliness would take a toll on anyone's morals.

"So Garon let you out to kill us," he said.

"So little you know."

"Educate me."

She shook her head. "That's not up to me."

"Then what is up to you?" he snapped. Her silver eyes flashed. He pushed forward anyway. If she intended to kill him, he wanted her to make his death fast. He had no desire to play the part of a child's toy during his last moments. "Why are we having this conversation?"

"There are some powers that should never be allowed to survive," Ella said. "Mine isn't the only one and it's certainly not the worst. I understand what it's like to feel the darkness my power creates. I'll do whatever it takes to save others from this fate."

"You're working with the Shadow Guard," Nick realized. "You're after Meaghan."

"The Shadow Guard saved me from the Pit, but I'm not a

Guardian so I can't be one of them."

"I see. So the member who died…"

"Gave me my assignment. Not everyone can tolerate crossing realms. He took the risk willingly."

"What exactly is your assignment?"

"Getting you to come to me and bring the boy. The Shadow Guard knew that putting your friend's village in stasis would ensure that happened."

The ice returned to Nick's spine. He had walked into a trap. "Why?" he asked. "What do you want from me?"

"Nothing you haven't already given me."

"I don't understand."

"You don't need to. Just understand that you can't win. You can't protect her. If the Shadow Guard doesn't kill her, her power will."

Meaghan's powers could never hurt anyone. Nick fought the urge to argue, to convince Ella of that fact, because he knew it would be useless. The Shadow Guard had saved her from the misery of the Pit. She would believe whatever lies they spouted.

Ella waved a hand in front of Nick and the world exploded back into colorful existence. Ella became half-shadow once more. Without a word, she turned and walked down the alley.

"You have what you came for," he called after her. "Let the people here go."

She did not respond. Nick pulled a knife from his belt and chased after her, though he did not know what he would do if he caught her. He only knew he had to stop her power at all costs. Even if it meant stabbing her in the back as she retreated from him. The thought halted his feet. He could not resort to murder. She had killed and deserved trial, but he would not become her executioner. He had to figure out how to unfreeze the town another way.

He reached the end of the alley and turned. Ella had already disappeared. A small slip of paper lay on the ground where he had last seen her. Messy handwriting stretched across the yellowing paper in three sections, each more unreadable than the last. He tucked it into his pocket to examine later.

For now, he had a more pressing matter. He directed his attention toward the trees and counted seven fires flaring in the distance. Two more sprang up, and then a tenth blaze danced within the dark recess of the night.

The Mardróch army had grown.

CHAPTER TWELVE

NICK STEPPED back into the blinding dark of Talea and Artair's kitchen. A floorboard squeaked and he held his breath, listening for the slightest movement. When only the rush of his own blood met his ears, he took a tentative step forward, his muscles tense and ready to spring into action.

He remembered the stool and sidestepped it, skirting down the hallway with the same grace and silence as a hunting ambercat.

A glow still radiated from the living room, though it had grown dim and Nick realized the candle would be close to a nub by now. He would have to find another if he intended to stay up all night.

He flattened his back against a wall as a groan drifted past. Another followed it. The familiar baritone of a third, wordless complaint brought a smile to Nick's face and he snuck a glance around the corner.

Max sat up in the middle of the floor, his head cradled in his hands. Beside him, Caide stirred, and then rolled onto his side.

"What happened?" Caide asked when he spotted Nick.

"It's a long story." Nick crossed the room to Talea. Though she had not moved, her heart raced when he pressed his fingers to her neck. "Bring some food and water," he commanded of no one in particular.

Max obeyed the order. He climbed to his feet, unsteadily at first, and moved down the hallway toward the kitchen. He returned a moment later with salted crackers and slices of white cheese. Artair shifted at Nick's side. Caide helped Nick pull him into a seated position.

"She let us go," Artair whispered.

"Why?" Caide asked.

Artair shook his head. He slid a hand across the floor to wrap Talea's fingers in his own.

"Bring the food here," Nick instructed Max, then broke a piece of cheese in half and handed it to Artair. "Eat. Talea will wake up soon enough."

Artair tore off small pieces of the cheese with his teeth, though the effort seemed slow and difficult. Nick offered him a glass of water. It shook within Artair's grip, but he managed to lift it on his own this time.

"Tell us what happened," Max said, sitting down next to Talea. "I remember waking up and seeing the redhead. I wasn't able to say anything before she…" He hesitated. "I'm not sure what she did. We weren't quite frozen, were we?"

"No, we weren't," Nick said. "She brought us into another realm. Like I said, it's a long story."

"I think we're safe now," Artair said. "Why don't you tell it to us?"

Nick crossed the room and hid the Writer's book in his bag so Artair would not ask about it, then filled the group in on the details of his conversation with Ella and the paper he had found. Halfway through his retelling, Talea woke and helped finish the cheese and crackers.

"So she never told you what she wanted?" Talea asked. "I don't get it. She had the chance to kill you and Caide. Why didn't she? It certainly would've helped Garon."

"Maybe she's not trying to help him," Caide said. "She wanted me here, right?" Nick nodded. "Let me see that paper."

Nick slipped it from his pocket. Caide examined it for a minute, and then his face paled.

Max raised an eyebrow. "Do you know what it is?"

"Not exactly," Caide said, running his fingers down the verses. "It's a spell, or at least the start of one. I can't make out any of the words."

"If you can't read it, how do you know?" Artair asked.

"Because my power recognizes it. It's hard to explain. A new spell thumps against it, kind of like a heartbeat. I'm pretty sure Farrow wrote it. His name flashed through my mind when I first touched it."

Talea frowned. "Farrow? You mean the last Spellmaster?"

"Yes." Caide held up the paper. "Can I keep this for a while?"

Nick nodded. "Come to me immediately if you learn anything new. Whatever you do, don't try to cast the spell. It could still be a trap. Just because the Shadow Guard says they're after Meaghan doesn't mean they don't have ulterior motives."

"Got it." Caide folded up the paper and tucked it into his pocket. "So what now? Even if Ella's gone, we're still trapped."

"For now, you rest," Nick said. "We'll come up with a plan tomorrow. I'll check on everyone else in the village and make sure they're awake."

"I should come with you," Artair said. "Talea and I are responsible for them."

Max stood. "You're too weak to do anyone any good. I'll help Nick. Let's plan on reconvening at sunrise."

No one argued. Nick followed Max out the front door. As he turned his gaze toward the firelight in the distance, he wondered what a handful of hours would gain them, besides a bunch of frail villagers ripe for the Mardróch's picking.

CHAPTER THIRTEEN

BY MORNING, the villagers had gathered in the town square. Some had fared better than others, but it would be days before most of them gained their strength back. Still weak, Talea sat on the steps of her house while Artair stood and addressed the crowd. His hands shook as he raised them in a request for silence. Once he had given them an abridged version of what had happened, an elderly man stepped forward from the front of the crowd.

"Did she bring the Mardróch?" he asked. "That woman—"

"Ella," Artair said.

"Yes. Is that why they're here?"

"If she had, we'd all be dead."

"How did she get in?" a blonde-haired woman asked. She turned her piercing amber eyes on Nick. "I thought only certain people could invite others past the protection."

"Varuth could," Artair answered and the blonde's gaze flicked back to him. "He's no longer a threat, but that doesn't help us with our current situation. We think the army's position here is simply bad luck. We're within range of the castle. We knew this would be a risk when we took over the village."

A tall woman stepped forward. A toddler propped on her hip played with her black braid. "How long can we outlast them?" she asked.

"Our provisions are low," Talea said. "As you know, we bring soil in from another village to counterbalance the spell that prevents food from growing. It has to be replenished every so often and we're due for another delivery soon."

"What happens if it doesn't come?"

"Our plants will die. We'll pick what we can before then, but we won't have enough for more than a few weeks."

"We can fight," a man said from the back of the crowd. "A Mardróch lightning bolt seems like a better death than starving."

"It might come to that," Artair said. "We need time to recover first."

"We can hide out in the open," Talea said, her voice soft, though the certainty in it commanded everyone's attention. "What about that spell Meaghan used to sneak everyone into Caide's village? It could work for us, couldn't it?"

"I don't know all of it," Artair said. "Do you?"

Talea shook her head.

"I do," Caide told her. "But if the Mardróch discovered us, we'd be slaughtered."

"It's a risk we'll have to take," Nick told him. "Only a few of us need to go. We can get the Elders and rescue those who remain."

"I guess it's us then," Max said and clapped Nick on the back.

"Let's hope this time goes better than the last."

§

THEY DECIDED to wait for nightfall, hoping the Mardróch's dinner would keep them distracted if the spell failed. Out of the three of them, only Caide had seen the spell used and none of them knew exactly how it worked, or if it would work at all. It did not help that they could see each other. Caide said that was intentional. Nick felt as if he were walking directly into the enemy camp, hands up in surrender as a sacrifice for their feast.

Stepping outside the boundary of the village's protection spell, Nick gestured for Caide and Max to wait for his signal. The closest fire flickered orange and yellow against the trees twenty paces away. Although he saw no Mardróch, they would be close by at this time of night, tearing into the raw flesh of whatever hapless animal had wandered into their path.

He tiptoed toward the flame, hiding as best he could among the shadows of the taller trees. Each footfall stopped his heart. Every twig that moved as he passed halted his breathing. When he finally emerged into the circle of light the fire cast, he skirted to the backside of a tree, away from the three Mardróch standing in the opposite side of the circle. They huddled around the body of a pink-backed boar, their webbed mouths dripping with bits of flesh and blood as they took turns tearing large chunks from the carcass. One Mardróch tore off a leg. The sound of crunching echoed between the trees as he chewed through flesh and bone.

Nick pressed his hand to his mouth to keep from getting sick. He wanted to run, but he had to test if they could see him. He had to get closer.

The dying scream of another animal pierced the night sky, freezing Nick to his spot. Cowardice had never been part of his vocabulary before. Today, he mulled over every definition for one he could live with. He felt insane for even attempting this plan. Forcing his legs to move, he stepped around the tree. One Mardróch raised his head. His red gaze swept over Nick, along the tree line, then returned to the carcass.

Nick pushed out a breath to calm his galloping heart. After a minute elapsed without the Mardróch sounding an alarm, Nick retreated into the shadows. When he stood within eyesight of the village again, he signaled Max and Caide to move. They followed him as he threaded his way through the woods, avoiding each Mardróch camp for his own peace of mind. Halfway to safety, two Mardróch marched close enough so Nick could smell rotten flesh on their breath. He pressed his back tight against the closest tree. Caide took the same position beside him. Max dashed behind another tree a row away.

"Isn't it about time?" the second Mardróch in line asked.

"I think it must be," the first agreed. "I still don't know why we have to keep doing this."

"Because Garon said so. Isn't that reason enough?"

The first Mardróch shrugged. "I guess. Why don't you do it? I keep forgetting all the words."

"Yeah, all right."

The Mardróch's voice faded as he and his comrade moved farther way. Nick could no longer make out his words, though their rhythm reminded him of a spell. Caide grabbed Nick's arm.

"We need to move," he hissed under his breath. "Quickly."

"What's wrong?"

"It's the counterspell."

"Where'd he come from?" the guttural voice of a Mardróch boomed from several rows over. Nick snapped his head around in time to see one of Garon's monsters pointing at Max.

"Get him!" another Mardróch shouted.

Max tore away from his hiding place and streaked past Nick, his face white with terror. Nick and Caide followed close behind.

Underbrush blocked their path, slowing them down as they raced through row after row of tall evergreens. Mardróch voices shouted in the distance, and then moved closer. Out of the corner of his eye, Nick saw a brown cloak flicker through the air. One of the Mardróch had caught up with them.

Nick pushed forward, harder than before, though he might as well have been fighting a fire with a thimble of water. No human could outrun the Mardróch. He banked hard to the left. A second Mardróch joined the first. Up ahead, more monsters lined up next to the trees, blocking the path for escape.

Nick changed direction again. A cackle greeted him, and the bony hand of a Mardróch clamped down on his arm. He tore out of the chilling grasp, but managed less than two steps before an arm wrapped around his waist.

Nick flew through the air, and then slammed back onto the ground. The impact forced the breath from his lungs. A rock dug into his shoulder. Another bruised his right knee. His head throbbed.

He rolled over. Skeletal fingers circled his ankles and dragged him backward.

Caide yelled. At first, Nick could not see him. Then the Zeiihbuan landed on the path up ahead, motionless. Max sparred with a Mardróch a few feet beyond him.

Nick thrashed, attempting to kick the Mardróch away. His attacker growled and flipped him around. Nick grabbed his sword from its sheath, launched it through the air, and prayed it would hit its target.

His luck held. The Mardróch dropped with a groan. Nick jumped up and raced toward Caide. He grabbed the Zeiihbuan's arm and yanked him to his feet. A lightning bolt struck the ground to their side. Caide returned the Mardróch's fire with an attack of his own, a spell Nick had heard first after Caide's younger brother invented it. The Mardróch turned into a statue, his lightning bolt a hard, gray line in the night.

Caide turned another monster to stone, then a third. Max managed to take out his attacker with a knife strike to the face, and Nick felt renewed hope.

Until he turned around.

Dozens of Mardróch advanced through the woods. The closest monster raised his hands. Lightning crackled between his fingers. A Mardróch to his side did the same, then another and another. Soon, the air filled with an eerie blue glow. Caide would never be able to turn them all into stone in time.

Nick retrieved his sword from the dead Mardróch and held it in front of him, prepared to fight to the death. Beside him, Max stood his ground. Caide joined them. The Mardróch cast their bolts. Nick sucked in one last breath as a wall of blue descended toward them.

Then it stopped, and exploded upward.

CHAPTER FOURTEEN

THE MARDRÓCH fired again. When this attack met the same resistance, they pulled their weapons from scabbards and sheaths, and charged forward. The first wave of the Mardróch army crashed into the air. A second wave slammed into the same nothingness. Glancing around in confusion, the remaining Mardróch backed away. Some turned and fled. They did not get far before they met a more daunting force. Villagers swarmed them from behind. A few faces Nick recognized. Mycale took down a Mardróch using a scythe with the same ease as Sam used his hunting knife. Faillen shot arrows into the pack of monsters, sending one after another to the ground.

Nick held his own weapon in front of him, ready to fight. The invisible shield stayed in place. Several Mardróch hacked away at it, their blows useless. Miles approached, one hand held in front of him as his power projected the shield. The other hand hung at his side, an allestone sword held in a relaxed grip. The Head Elder's dark gray eyes sparked in anger, a harsh contrast to his soft face. Even the waves in his salt-and-pepper hair seemed tight against his head. He stood at Nick's height, though Nick felt smaller under his glaring scrutiny.

"I don't relish having to rescue my charge from Mardróch," he said. "Particularly when that charge is the king."

"You're not my Guardian," Nick responded, keeping both anger and shame out of his voice. "Although I do appreciate your help."

"Your mother is watching over Neiszhe, so we transferred your Guardianship for the time being. Believe me, I considered leaving you here to suffer the consequences of your decision. Faillen convinced me otherwise. He reminded me you brought a Spellmaster with you."

"Your heroism astounds me."

Miles pressed his lips together. "You shouldn't have come, Nick. We knew this would be a trap."

"What else was I supposed to do?" Nick snapped. "You left the villagers to die, rather than come up with a plan to rescue them."

"It doesn't look like you had a plan either."

Nick clenched his jaw.

"You directly disobeyed an order from the Elders," Miles continued. "You put us all in danger."

"I don't report to the Elders any longer," Nick reminded him. "But you didn't come here to argue did you?"

"No, I didn't." Miles raised his sword. "Are you ready?"

Nick nodded. Miles dropped his hand and the Mardróch held back by the Elder's power surged forward. Miles veered to the right to chase after a few who tried to escape. Nick charged forward, taking the tallest one head on and stabbing him through the opening in his hood before he could do more than form the beginning sparks of lightning. A second Mardróch went down with the same speed as the first. A third proved a more worthy enemy. Nick dodged a lightning bolt, and spun around to face the monster again. Electricity crackled on the Mardróch's fingertips. Instead of discharging it at Nick, he threw it to the side, taking down another Mardróch who had been trying to sneak up on Nick.

"Mine," the Mardróch hissed. Several Mardróch close enough to hear backed away. "You'll know true pain before you die, king."

Nick did not doubt the threat. He also did not intend to let the Mardróch prove it. The Mardróch cast another bolt in Nick's direction. Nick dove to the ground, and the shot missed, though he had expected no less. The Mardróch had meant it as a warning. Killing Nick with electricity would be too easy.

Rolling up onto his knees, Nick caught the outline of a body a few feet away. Blonde hair trailed along the ground, intertwining with weeds and leaves, and Nick chased away the immediate grief that struck him. Ellice had been the village's best baker. Now she had lost her life because of his foolishness. Miles was right about one thing. Nick should have had a better plan before coming here.

At least he had one now. The Mardróch charged toward him, his sword held high. Nick jumped to his feet and ran toward Ellice. By her side, he had seen metal glinting in the moonlight. She had preferred to fight with a small hand axe, and tonight, Nick did, too.

He claimed her weapon a second before the Mardróch's sword descended toward his head, then fended off the attack with the sharp scrape of metal hitting allestone. The Mardróch hissed in frustration.

Nick's anger charged up to match it. He was tired of fighting these monsters, tired of Garon claiming people he loved, of having to say good-bye and burying those who mattered to him.

And he was tired of losing this war.

He shoved the Mardróch back with the strength of his hatred, and then flew forward, his metal and allestone weapons flashing in the starlight.

"For my father," Nick declared with the first strike. "For Adelina. For Ed." His voice grew stronger, his blows harder. "For Neiszhe's village," he barked and his sword sliced halfway through the Mardróch's left hand. The monster howled and shoved his own blade toward Nick's stomach.

Nick twisted to the side to avoid the lunge, and then arced the axe backward, gashing the Mardróch's exposed forearm. Nick's breath came in quick bursts hot with fury.

"For Cal," he shouted. "For Ellice." He blocked another strike and pushed hard against the Mardróch's sword. "And most importantly, for Meaghan!"

With one powerful kick, he knocked the Mardróch to his knees. Nick thought he saw fear reflected within the monster's red eyes. He wanted the satisfaction of staring directly into that gaze, but he could not risk being frozen.

The Mardróch struggled to rise again. Nick planted a foot on his shoulder and shoved him back down. Blue crackled in his palm.

"Tell Garon I'll see him soon," Nick commanded and drove his sword through the Mardróch's hood. His enemy crumpled, diminished to a pile of gray skin and brown wool.

"It's going to be hard for a dead guy to tell Garon anything," Max said from beside him.

Nick worked to catch his breath as he turned to face his friend. Blood speckled Max's cheek and stained his blonde hair in spots. Otherwise, he appeared to have escaped the fight without a mark.

"I doubt he would've gotten the message right anyway," Nick said. "Who's next?"

"I'm afraid no one, though I hate having to end your fun." Max swept his hand outward, indicating the forest. A few Mardróch remained standing. Those villagers converging on them would make short work of their lives. One monster tried to sneak off through the trees. A blue orb streaked through the sky and exploded in his face.

"I guess Artair is feeling better," Nick said.

Max chuckled. "It seems so. Come with me, you need to see something."

Nick followed Max toward the village. Close to the fire where Nick had watched the Mardróch tearing apart their dinner, Nick saw a small party of men clustered around a body. At first, he could not see beyond the human wall that Faillen, Caide, Miles, and Sam had created. When they parted to let Nick through, he realized why they had gathered here. Vacant silver eyes stared up at him from a pale face he had seen only hours before. A scythe parted her red hair, making her body solid for all time.

"Well, that's one enemy we don't have to worry about any longer," Caide said. "I wish I knew who to thank."

Faillen reached down to close Ella's eyes. "A life should always be mourned, son. Don't ever forget that."

Caide's cheeks flashed red.

"I know who she is," Faillen continued. "I saw her once. Queen Adelina had sought my father's help in finding a cure for her."

"A cure?" Max asked. "I don't understand."

"Her power drove her insane. It's happened before, to someone in Zeiihbu. Our stories speak of a man who went crazy, shifting through realms until there was nothing left of him but vapor. Adelina hoped we had found a way to save him, but we couldn't help."

"Cures are for diseases," Nick said. "Not for this."

"The king is most wise," a female voice purred from behind them.

Nick turned. A woman stared back at him with light red eyes. Though she held no weapon, he raised his sword. He did not know if her unblinking gaze or the almost feline way in which she moved, willowy and silent, had made him more uneasy. He did not care. He would not let his guard down again tonight.

"Some powers are harder to control," the woman continued. "She never learned the trick to hers and it drove her insane. The cure, as you say, was within her."

"You've seen this power before?" Faillen asked.

The woman inclined her head. Thick brown hair striped with gray cascaded over her shoulder. Her face appeared long and graceful, much like her fingers. She had filed her nails into sharp, claw-like points.

"Yes." The word left her mouth as a gentle hum. A smile warmed her face, though it spoke more of her familiarity with Faillen than her kindness. "Those who learned to control it became powerful beings."

"And what sort of being are you?" Nick asked.

One corner of Anissa's lips twitched in irritation. Her hard gaze trailed to Faillen. "Do you not speak of me?"

"Not as fondly as you'd like," Faillen said. "Nick, this is Anissa."

"Oh, yes. The ghoul who can transform into a razor beast." Anissa hissed at the description. Nick ignored the reaction and sheathed his sword. "What is she doing here? I thought you sent her back to Zeiihbu."

"He did," Anissa said and bowed low. "I did not want to miss my opportunity to meet the new king."

"Don't play games," Faillen said. "What are you really doing here?"

"Delivering a message. I have been tracking your scent for a week, but your village's protection forced me away. Forgive me for taking so long. This is the first opportunity you have given me to speak."

"You're forgiven," Faillen said. "What does my father need?"

Anissa's brows knit together. "Your father? No. I have not spoken to him since we rescued your cub."

"Then who is the message from?"

She nodded at Nick. "His mate."

For a moment, Nick's heart stopped beating, and then his blood rushed forward, thundering within his ears. He knew he should not believe her, but the possibility still brought joy.

"Do you wish to speak in private?" Anissa asked. "Or do you give me permission to—"

"Just deliver the damn message," Nick barked.

Anissa's eyes widened. Her gaze snapped from Faillen to Nick and back again. "Have I displeased you?"

Faillen laid a hand on Nick's arm to calm him. "No, Anissa, please continue. We can speak openly here."

She nodded and tucked her hands together in front of her. "His mate has spoken with one of my pack leaders several times since our battle, though I am afraid he has a short memory. Only recently has he come forth with her message."

"And what message is that?" Faillen asked.

"The queen and her Guardian still live."

"That's all he said?"

Anissa nodded.

Nick cursed. "That doesn't help us. We need to know more. We need to know where she is."

Faillen tightened his grip on Nick's arm, and Nick obeyed the silent command. He stepped back, leaving the ghoul to Faillen.

"Where were your razor beasts when they received Meaghan's message?" Faillen asked.

"In the lands below your village," she told him. "The last time my pack mates saw her, she hunted a half-night's prowl from the base of the cliff."

"In which direction?"

"Toward the rising moon. There are Mardróch there. Armies of them."

"That's okay," Faillen said. "I have armies of my own."

"What's your plan?" Miles asked.

"If the razor beasts are telling the truth—"

"They are," Anissa said.

"Then my father is closest to Meaghan and Cal. He and an army of my people can find them. If I send Scree to deliver the message, her gildonae powers should help her reach Dat by morning."

"Do it," Miles said. "Let us know if there's anything you need."

Faillen nodded and walked way.

Nick's hand shook as he ran it through his hair. Vivian had been right. Meaghan and Cal were still alive. Or at least, they had been a few weeks ago. By tomorrow, the note Faillen's bird carried would start their rescue mission. Nick hoped the Zeiihbuans could find Cal and Meaghan before the Mardróch did.

A log popped in the fire pit beside Nick. He cast his gaze toward the waning flames, mesmerized by the dimming yellow flicker before Vivian's words came back to him, as clear in his mind as they had been in the Writer's book earlier tonight.

For once, Vivian's message had been literal.

"Faillen, wait," Nick called out. Faillen turned. "I know how to find them. Tell your father to keep a fire burning."

CHAPTER FIFTEEN

MEAGHAN GROANED, opened her eyes, then shut them again when dim light filled her with pain. She felt the dirt and stone of a rough floor and knew she had found her way back to the cave, though she could not remember how.

"How're you feeling?" Cal's voice boomed from close by.

She winced and he chuckled. "You had a bit of a rough day yesterday. Not sure if you remember any of it."

"Not really. I remember hunting, and there was a storm. That's it. I had the weirdest dream."

"I'd wager it wasn't a dream. You nearly handed yourself over to a pack of Mardróch."

"I...what? Wait. That was real?" Meaghan yanked her eyes open, and squinted when the light assaulted her again. A fire roared in the distance. It appeared hazy. So did Cal. She knew him from the outline of his bushy beard, but could make out nothing more of his features. "What happened?"

"You tell me. I'd almost forgotten I was your Guardian until your fear yanked me out of my coma. It must've been intense. I've never been able to sense anyone from that distance before."

"Where was I?"

"By Faillen's cliff. Is it coming back to you now?"

"Sort of." She pressed her fingers to her temples in an attempt to kill the throbbing behind them. "I thought we were falling again. It seemed so real."

"What else do you remember?"

"Not much. I found a rabbit, some root vegetables." She cursed. "I left them behind. I lost our sack."

"It's all right. Your life is more important than my old cloak. What happened next?"

"When the storm came, I hid in a cave. I found what I thought was gemfruit. Since everything became weird soon after I ate it, I'm guessing I was wrong."

"Not likely. It's hard to mistake. What else was in the cave?"

"Some sort of moss. I didn't eat it though."

"Ah, that explains it. You touched it. That's enough. I'm sure you have a doozy of a headache right now, too."

"Enough for what?" Meaghan stared down at her hands. They appeared blurry. Soon her eyesight sharpened and fingers grew from the haze. "Are you saying the moss has something to do with the way I'm feeling?"

"Yup. It even explains your fear. You found Vision Moss. The Zeiihbuans use it in some of their ceremonies, so they warned me about it."

"And you didn't think to tell me?"

"I didn't think you'd run into any. It's not easy to find. And frankly, it's been twenty years since I last heard about it. My memory isn't exactly what it used to be. You hungry?"

Despite the headache exploding between her ears, her stomach still rumbled with need. She nodded.

Cal rose and crossed the room to the fire. He returned a moment later, a piece of bark in his hand. A leafy-green vegetable formed a messy pile on top of it. She raised an eyebrow.

"Serace weed," Cal said and pointed to several prawn-like fish next to it. "These are river bugs. You have to dig down into the banks to get them. Eat up."

Meaghan shoveled a handful of the weed into her mouth. Chewing became an afterthought as her next bite followed quickly after the first, then the third blended into a fourth. Somewhere in between bites, her headache subsided. She cleaned her makeshift plate in minutes. Cal refilled it and brought it back to her.

Halfway through inhaling her second helping, she slowed her pace, taking the time to glance at Cal between mouthfuls. His breath came in shallow bursts as he leaned against the rock wall, one leg propped up on a boulder. His skin appeared yellow in the low light. When he leaned forward to roll up his pant leg, she understood why. Little of his skin remained untouched by bright red and purple blotches, some of the color from bruising and some from blood. Streaked through it, fluorescent green tendrils stretched up to his knee, though they did not stop where his pant leg started.

Within the depths of her foggy mind, she remembered him running, his leg braced, though she knew the pain from his break would have been severe.

She set the bark and the rest of her food aside. "Cal," she whispered. "How far has the poison gone?"

Instead of answering, Cal lifted his shirt. His skin had turned gray, the same color his leg had been before the bruising, and interlaced through the gray, green tendrils reached the bottom of his rib cage. They circled his stomach in elaborate, crisscrossing marks.

"I have a few days left," he told her, lowering his shirt. "If I'm lucky."

"What about the herb?" Meaghan asked. "Can't we use it to slow the spread again?"

"Maybe by a day or so. It's not enough time."

"No." She shook her head to keep her tears from falling. Her carelessness had cost him again, and this time he would have no escape. "Cal, I'm so—"

"Don't you dare apologize," Cal interrupted. "It's not your fault."

"It is," she insisted. "The moss—"

He waved his hand, dismissing her protest. "It's not like you went looking for it. Besides, I'm still your Guardian."

"I've told you before, I can protect myself. You can't keep putting your life in jeopardy for me."

As soon as the words left her mouth, Meaghan expected Cal to point out the absurdity of them. Clearly, she had needed him yesterday. If he had not come, she would be in the hands of the Mardróch right now.

He said none of that. Instead, he gestured toward her leftovers. "You done with that?"

She pushed the makeshift plate over to him. He ate in silence, then set the bark down and closed his eyes. Another few minutes elapsed before he spoke again, his voice a mournful breath that dissolved into the high ceiling of the cave. "Your father used to say that to me."

Meaghan tucked her knees under her chin and waited.

"He liked having me around as a friend, but he hated having a protector. I let him believe he had his way. I left the room when he requested it, always certain I could spot danger if I needed to. I was cocky then, and wrong."

"Is that what happened the day he died?"

"Not exactly. The Elders asked me to help fight the uprising at the perimeter of the castle grounds. I could have turned down the request. I didn't because I knew your father would have insisted I go. I can't help thinking that he'd still be alive if I'd stayed by his side."

"More likely you'd be dead, too."

"I'd gladly sacrifice my life to save a charge."

Meaghan tilted her head to the side as she studied Cal's face. Beneath his stiff lips and the tight draw of his brow, she saw the stoic truth to his statement. Dying while protecting her would be more than duty. He would consider it an honor. And within the tears wetting his eyes, she saw something more.

"Your guilt is keeping your grief alive," she told him. "It's not warranted."

"I hate when you use your empath power on me."

"I don't need to, Cal. I know you." She moved to his side and took his hand. "When Nick first told me that he was my Guardian, I didn't really know what that meant. On Earth, people hire bodyguards to protect them in dangerous situations. The guards on Earth are detached, usually, and kept that way on purpose so they can react without emotion while under fire."

Cal sighed. "That's what we're supposed to be. May and I both screwed up. We became friends with your mother and father. In the end, that cost us."

"Yet you still encouraged Nick in his feelings for me. If you really believed you were wrong for befriending my father, you wouldn't have done that."

Cal shrugged. "I was just following Vivian's prophecy."

"And when you came to help us at the cabin or offered to take Nick's place on our mission? Was that all about Vivian? It wasn't even about duty, was it?"

"I did it because I love Nick, and I loved your father. I haven't really learned from my mistakes, have I?"

"That's because they aren't mistakes. I had to love Nick to trust him. If my father was anything like me, you were the only Guardian he truly trusted, because you were the only one he cared about. You never would have been his Guardian otherwise." She stood. "You were the perfect Guardian, whether or not you realized it. Take the herb and sleep. Keep taking it as soon as you wake up. Don't stop to eat. Don't look for me."

Cal raised an eyebrow. "Where do you think you're going?"

"If there's one thing I've learned from the Writer's book, it's that my father would have done anything to save your life, too. I intend to do the same."

CHAPTER SIXTEEN

NIGHT DROPPED a cloak over Meaghan's eyes, eclipsing her sight before the moon sliced through her blindness with silver light. A cloud overcame the moon once more, and Meaghan stuck her tongue into her cheek, fighting the urge to hide until morning returned. She had never liked traveling at night. Although Nick preferred the secrecy darkness offered, she always felt vulnerable. Every noise seemed to broadcast her location, a barge horn echoing across the quiet ocean of a sleeping world. Every animal's scurry made her feel as if an enemy hid in the shadows, waiting for her to walk into its outstretched claws.

A lizard scurried up a tree beside her, and she tensed, reaching for her knife before she realized it posed no threat. Its tail changed from brown to green as it disappeared among the leaves. She held her breath, and then let it go. Disappointment rolled through her.

For once, she wanted the enemy to be close. She strained her senses, searching for the heavy footfalls of a careless soldier or the rotten scent of a Mardróch as the monster's vile emotions overwhelmed her power. Only the distant twitter of a bird and the scent of wet dirt greeted her.

Tracing her fingers over her battle knives, she counted them for comfort. She had four now, not three as she had thought the day she fell off the cliff. Cal had grabbed the one she had dropped before he dove after her. He always thought ahead. It was a talent she never seemed to master.

Her tension began to ease once the sun broke the horizon, shattering the deep navy sky with shards of red and gold. Over the last two months, she had explored the areas beyond the cave, avoiding the cliffs at all costs. The farther she wandered, the fewer Mardróch she had seen. But when she had mistakenly returned to the cliffs, she had run into a small army of Garon's monsters.

She hoped that meant Garon's village lay on the other side of those cliffs. Cal's life depended on it. A mouse squeaked at her from under a nearby bush and she slipped a knife from its sheath for no other reason than to feel its weight in her hand. Curling her hand around its hilt, she held the blade up, watching as it caught a ray of sunlight. White dots sparkled within the dark stone.

A fool's errand. That was what her adoptive father would have called this mission. She had little hope of finding the village and even if she could, what exactly did she expect? She would be able to convince someone to take pity on Cal and help him? She scoffed and put her weapon away. She would be lucky to utter five words before they killed her.

Still, she had no other choice. She had to save Cal. Or she had to try, anyway. She repeated the mantra with every step, every sore muscle, and with each hour that passed. When morning turned into afternoon, and afternoon into evening, she began to lose her focus and confidence. She had not seen a Mardróch all day.

A cluster of trees loomed up ahead and she decided to make the oasis her stopping point. She hated to take the break. Even a few precious hours of sleep could cost Cal his life, but attacking an enemy while exhausted would not help Cal either. Dead people did not make good heroes.

She crossed into the shadows of the woods, and then wrinkled her nose as the smell of rotten garbage wafted toward her. She dashed behind an ancient red oak before a line of six Mardróch marched past, their feet muted thuds on the soft earth. Meaghan waited until their odor subsided before moving again, this time with more care, using bushes and trees as her companions while she tiptoed through the forest. Another pack of Mardróch skirted her hiding place a few hundred yards away, then two more, and a cluster of three. When she counted more brown cloaks than trees, she crouched behind a brickleberry bush and recited the invisibility spell her aunt had taught her.

Meaghan hated using it. Despite the fact that only those with a true need could see her, she felt too vulnerable to rely on it. Yet she had no other choice.

She was growing tired of running out of options.

Pushing out a breath, she worked to control her panic as another Mardróch sauntered close enough to rustle her bush with his cloak. She stood. A Mardróch rounded a tree. He stared directly at her hiding place and she bolted in the other direction.

The Mardróch did not follow. The spell had worked.

As more Mardróch swarmed the forest, she pushed on, sprinting past trees, jumping over bushes, and weaving around her enemies with a precision dictated by adrenaline. Each breath hurt. Her eyes stung. Her mind screamed with primal instinct.

She burst from the forest into a valley lush with purple and yellow wildflowers, and then skidded to a stop. A battle stretched out in front of her. Hundreds of Mardróch fought with soldiers, their brown cloaks billowing like capes behind them, their electricity blasting craters into the ground and decimating plants. A blue lightning bolt knocked a balding man to the ground. Smoke snaked up from a hole in his stomach, and then dissolved as his injury disappeared. He climbed to his feet and launched a magical bomb at the Mardróch who had attacked him. The monster exploded. Meaghan sucked in a breath. When he rematerialized a moment later, she realized magic protected the battle. Garon's army fought for practice.

Her gaze trailed beyond the army to the reason for their victimless fight. A massive village rose into the sky, its bright, two-story houses a deceptively beautiful contrast to the advancing night. Among the taller buildings, several traditional huts dotted the streets, evidence that the Ærenden people and Zeiihbuans had once coexisted here in peace.

A Mardróch lightning bolt struck the ground several feet to her right and she gave the battle a wider berth, circling to approach the village from behind.

By the time she stepped onto the first gravel-lined road,

streetlights twinkled in front of the houses. She watched a man open a hanging lantern and blow into it, inciting a magical glow, and she followed him, using his steady gait as a guide.

One wide road cut through the center of town, providing a straight view to the opposite end of the village. Although the well-maintained houses sported fresh paint, the Zeiihbuan huts had begun to crumble beneath the weight of time, their moldy walls and caving roofs evidence of Garon's hatred for their former owners. If he hoped to annihilate what he considered Ærenden's blight, he would never give equal status to them by using their handiwork. The huts served one purpose here. They reminded the villagers that they had not yet won the war.

She focused her empath power in front, then to the sides and behind, sweeping it like a beacon to prevent the villagers' emotions from overwhelming her. Nothing sinister raised any alarms. She expected as much. They could not see her, nor did they have any reason to suspect she was here.

In the field surrounding the village, Meaghan had counted ten Mardróch for every soldier. Here, less than a dozen brown cloaks dotted the crowds. Neighbors gathered around porches, chatting and laughing. Children played with balls and sticks in the streets. A baker handed out loaves of bread from a waist-high basket on wheels. For dinner, Meaghan guessed, though it turned her stomach to imagine these people living normal lives, eating meals around the family table, and laughing at each other's stories and jokes. Laughing as if they did not follow a man who had wanted to annihilate every Zeiihbuan for the simple fact they were different, who had claimed his seat on the throne by murdering Ærenden's former king and queen.

Meaghan clenched her teeth and stepped into the shadows of an alley to avoid bumping into the baker when he walked past. Greed, self-righteousness, racism—they had been the hallmarks of nearly every war she had studied in school. This might be a different world than the one of her childhood, but Earth and Ærenden still had one thing in common. Humans had populated both, and inherently, humanity was flawed.

A couple strolled by Meaghan's hiding place wearing the wistful looks of budding love. The young man stopped, glanced around, and then pulled on his companion's hand to lead her into the alley.

"I never thought we'd get time alone," he whispered, pressing his lips to her neck. She leaned against the wall, and he angled his body against hers. "Your parents have been way too strict lately."

The young woman giggled. A lock of straw-colored hair fell forward and she dashed it away with a quick flick of her hand. "You didn't come down here to talk, did you, Myrel?" she asked.

Myrel's hands snaked up her shirt. Meaghan looked away. The woman giggled again and Meaghan suppressed a tortured sigh. Listening to someone else's make-out session had not been on her checklist for today, but the couple blocked most of the alley. She did not see how she could escape without brushing them as she passed.

Several minutes went by before the sounds of longing groans subsided. When Meaghan dared to look back at the couple, she found them still fully clothed, to her relief.

The woman wrapped her arms around her lover's neck. "I liked it better when I could sneak you into the house. Wonder how long it will be before Dad stops locking the doors?"

"A few weeks, I'd imagine," Myrel said and ran a hand down the length of her hair. "I guess I can't be too upset with him, though. He's just trying to look out for you."

"It's not like anyone's going to attack us here."

"We're at war, Sabie. We don't know what can happen. No one expected the insurgents to kill an entire Mardróch army."

"I wish Garon would just squash them already. If they hadn't been working with the Zeiihbuans to overthrow the king and queen, none of us would be in this mess."

"Yeah, maybe. I don't know anymore. What do you make of that guy claiming to be king? The Mayor told my parents that the imposter fought in that battle."

"*Shut up.*" Sabie swatted at his arm. "Don't talk like that, Myrel. Garon's here. What if he overheard you?"

"What would he overhear? I didn't really say anything."

"I don't think he'd see it that way. Besides, the insurgents lie. We all know that. I'm sure the guy claiming to be king has no more right to the throne than a fireworm."

"Yeah, I guess you're right. We should head back. If it gets any later, your dad will turn *me* into a fireworm."

The couple exited the alley and rushed down the main road. Meaghan followed them, and then paused when deception surged through her empath power. At first, she thought the emotion had come from two men arguing on a stoop, but soon she realized it came from their left. A cloaked figure too short to be a Mardróch turned down a side street and the emotion fizzled as quickly as it had come. Meaghan frowned, though she dismissed her paranoia. She did not have time for distractions. Besides, if the cloaked villager had spotted her, he would have sounded an alarm and she would be dead now.

She quickened her pace, scanning the buildings for the one she needed. As with the other villages in Ærenden, shops were marked with wooden shingles advertising their services. The baker's sign depicted a loaf of bread. The house beside it had a shoe, and the one opposite showed the cloak of a tailor. Near the end of town and down a small side street, Meaghan found the sign she needed. It did not use a picture to advertise its resident, but a single word in block print: *Healer*.

This house had been painted brick red. A pale yellow glow emanated from its bay window. Meaghan debated abandoning her mission, then Cal's face flashed in her mind and she pushed forward.

No one occupied the front room, so Meaghan snuck inside. She closed the door behind her and counted to five, waiting for someone to come running. When she heard only silence, she crossed the room to a bookshelf. She had planned to force a Healer to come back with her at knifepoint, but if she could find a cure instead, she would prefer it. She doubted her original plan had a high rate of survival for her or Cal.

A battered, red spine caught her attention first. She pulled the book off the shelf and flipped it open. *Herbs* the title page declared. She did not get a chance to read more before the front door burst open. Meaghan dropped the book, its thud on the hardwood flooring masked by the door slamming shut.

The man who had entered wore a heavy, gray cloak. He pulled down his hood and swept near-black eyes around the room. She held her breath. A member of the Lignaerius tribe could not be here, not unless he had suicide on his mind.

Yet the skin of a Zeiihbuan native was unmistakable, as was the broad nose and long, black hair of a man she had met before, when he stood alongside her father's people. He had made the boats that had carried her and Faillen across the river into Zeiihbu.

He looked straight at her. "Garon's coming," he said.

Meaghan did not respond, certain she had misunderstood.

"Don't pretend you didn't hear me." Laegoli crossed the room and grabbed her arm. "He'll be here any minute."

"I don't understand. What—?"

"Quiet," he said, and started reciting. It only took a few words for her to recognize the invisibility counterspell, but the implication of it took less time to understand.

Garon was heading her way, and Laegoli had made sure her enemy would find her.

CHAPTER SEVENTEEN

"WHAT DO you think you're doing?" Meaghan demanded and took a step back to rid her arm of his grasp.

"There's no time to explain."

"Make time."

"Just trust me," Laegoli said, and grabbed her again. He swung her around, then pinned her against him with a bear hug. His chest pressed into her shoulder blades. His labored breath warmed her ear. "Whatever you do, don't move, or we're both dead."

"Let me go—" she started to protest, then the door opened and she clenched her jaw shut. Laegoli recited another spell. Meaghan's vision shimmered before steadying again.

"They can't see us now," he whispered.

Meaghan pinched her brow in confusion, but quelled the urge to ask what he had done when two men stepped into the room.

The first man shuffled across the floor to an adjacent wall. His face had no defining features. His cheekbones were flat, his chin melted into his face, and his mousy hair lay flaccid against his head.

Even his wide-set eyes seemed as dull as a blue denim shirt faded by the sun. In one hand, he held a terracotta plant pot. A leafy green vine snaked up from the dirt to curl around his wrist. He rocked it back and forth, the movement slow and hypnotic, then he smiled and stroked the strange plant with an index finger.

Behind him, the second man moved to the side. His caramel skin tone hinted at heritage beyond the lands of Ærenden and Zeiihbu, as did his black hair, cut to within an inch of his head. He scanned the room with brown eyes framed in dark shadows, then picked up the book Meaghan had dropped.

"Odd," he said, then shelved it without another word. He returned to the door, taking a position beside it. A third man entered. He wore a brown cloak, but lowered his hood as soon as the second man closed the door behind him.

Meaghan bit her tongue to keep from gasping. She had never seen a man quite so grotesque. His pale gray skin looked as if it writhed in places. Where it did not, it stuck to his bones, giving him an emaciated appearance. He rubbed at a black spot on his cheek with skeletal fingers. The spot began to ooze green blood. He blinked twice at the sticky substance on his fingers and frowned, then turned pale red eyes on the darker-skinned man.

"You're late with my potion, Aristos," he said in a voice almost as brusque as a Mardróch's.

"It's ready," Aristos said, lowering his head. "Would you like me to get it?"

"Of course, idiot. Do you think I enjoy pain?"

Aristos hurried to a cabinet above the fireplace. He removed a small vial of red fluid and brought it to the malformed man. "Here, Lord Garon."

Garon snatched the vial from Aristos's hand and tipped it to his lips. After taking a first, slow sip, he gulped the remaining fluid. Both Aristos and the man with the plant took a step back from him.

With a howl, Garon collapsed. His screams echoed around the room, each louder and more agonized than the last. His limbs jerked in different directions as he thrashed against the floor. Minutes passed before his seizure subsided, then a few more elapsed before he stopped screaming. Aristos stepped forward again to help Garon to his feet.

This time, Meaghan did gasp. The man standing in the center of the room looked nothing like the one who had fallen to the floor. Lush blonde hair fell to his shoulders. His skin appeared smooth and pale peach, instead of the sallow gray that had coated him before. It no longer moved or collapsed against his bones. Even his red eyes had turned sapphire blue. He seemed not much older than Nick, though Meaghan knew that could not be possible. He had grown up with Nick's mother.

Aristos glanced in her direction. "Bracken, get a chair," he said and the other man left the room, returning a moment later with a high-backed wooden chair. Garon settled into it.

"Did you recite the counterspell?" Garon asked, his voice now a smooth tenor.

"Not yet, my lord," Bracken responded.

"How many times do I have to tell you? Recite the spell every time you enter a room. The traitors could be anywhere. Do you want to wind up a fool like Stilgan?"

"No, my king."

"Then do it," Garon said, waving his hand in a dismissive gesture. Bracken recited the invisibility counterspell and Meaghan bit her lip. Laegoli had known, somehow, and had saved her life.

"No one is here," Aristos said. "Can I get you food or drink, my lord?"

"Neither. I don't wish to stay in your presence longer than necessary."

Aristos nodded. He knelt in front of Garon. "I wish you would let me work on a cure for you. I hate to see you go through so much pain every month."

"And lose this lovely power?" Garon asked, raising his hand. Blue electricity crackled along his fingertips. Aristos winced. "I don't think so. Bracken, come here."

Bracken's steps were tentative as he moved across the room and knelt beside Aristos. His shoulders shook. Meaghan held her breath, expecting to witness his murder. Garon closed his fist instead, dissolving the lightning.

"That will be the last time you forget," Garon warned.

"Yes, my lord," Bracken whimpered. He kept his eyes glued to the floor.

"Good," Garon said. "Now how are your new pets coming along?"

"Beautiful." A smile split Bracken's face as he lifted the plant entwined around his hand. A tendril crawled forward. When Garon extended a finger to touch it, the vine jumped into the air. A head formed from its end and large teeth snapped at Garon's finger.

Bracken snatched the plant away, his eyes twice their size from fear. Rather than punish him, Garon roared with laughter.

"You are truly a gifted Gardener," he said. "Release it into the forest. Start in the area where the insurgents slaughtered my Mardróch. That should make them think twice about their actions."

Bracken snickered. "It will be my pleasure."

"Leave me now. I want to speak with Aristos in private."

Bracken slid from the room, shutting the front door behind him. Garon turned a hard gaze on Aristos. "You disappoint me."

Aristos dropped lower to the floor. Meaghan turned her empath power loose in the room. She half-expected Garon's emotions to translate as odors, just as the Mardróch's vile feelings did. What she sensed from him seemed far worse. Though his eyes broadcast anger and his smile at Aristos's genuflection spoke of pleasure, she felt neither from Garon. Cold indifference replaced those emotions.

Garon rose and circled Aristos. Fear emanated from Aristos in waves. He did not show it when he looked up at the self-appointed king.

"Your ineptitude is an embarrassment," Garon said. "Your father never would have allowed my disease to progress as far as you did today."

"I'm sorry, my lord."

"Is that all you have to say?"

"Your disease is progressing faster each time. If you would just allow me to cure you—"

"Enough!" Garon shot a lightning bolt into the floor at Aristos's side. Splinters flew into the air, leaving black scarring behind in the wood. "I did not allow your father to experiment on me so that you could undo his work. No one can cure a Mardróch, as I'm sure he told you. Containing one, though," a crooked smile split Garon's face, "that was truly a stroke of genius. If I could figure out how to rid Finnil of his insanity, I would be done with you."

Electricity crackled in Garon's palm. This time, anger surged across Meaghan's power. Aristos dropped his gaze to the floor.

"I warned your father of claiming a lesser breed."

"I can't help how I was born," Aristos said. His voice shook at first, but he soon controlled it. "I trained well under my father. You won't find a better Healer."

"Unfortunately, that's true," Garon said. "I keep you around for that reason. Don't mistake my tolerance for trust, and don't mistake my generosity for benevolence. A man can suffer a lot without succumbing to death."

Aristos nodded, though Garon did not see the motion. He had already stormed from the house. Aristos sighed and rose to his feet.

"His charm has no equal," he muttered, then crossed the room to the bookshelf and removed the book Meaghan had been reading. "I'm not sure what you were looking for, but I doubt this was it. The strongest herb in this book wouldn't cure a headache."

Meaghan sucked in a breath and held it.

"I know you're here," Aristos continued. "You shouldn't have left the book out. Show yourself or I'll get the Mardróch."

Laegoli cursed, and then recited what Meaghan assumed was a counterspell. Surprise lifted Aristos's eyebrows.

"Clearly you're both either brave or foolish to enter Garon's village," Aristos said. "What would make a Zeiihbuan and his companion risk their lives to come here?"

Meaghan grabbed a knife in each hand and brandished them in front of her. "I'll kill you before you have the chance to call for Garon."

"Twice in one day," Aristos said. One side of his mouth twitched into a half-smile. "I'm not usually lucky enough to have my life threatened once, let alone twice. I must be making quite an impression."

"I'm not joking," Meaghan warned.

"I have no doubt," Aristos said. "Do you want to share your name with me, or should I guess?"

Meaghan stepped forward and lifted one of her blades.

"I'll guess then. A Zeiihbuan and a lone female brave enough to enter Garon's village with a weak invisibility spell. Many in Ærenden still hate Zeiihbuans, despite the dead king and queen's love for them—"

Meaghan hissed. Aristos narrowed his eyes. His smile grew. "So you're Meaghan. I'd heard of your bravery, and your foolishness. Clearly the last part is true, or you wouldn't have come here without a Guardian."

"Enough," Laegoli barked.

"I've also heard about your aim, Meaghan," Aristos continued as if Laegoli had not spoken. "I don't take your threat to kill me lightly. I also know I'm safe as long as you need me, just like I am with Garon."

Meaghan tightened her grip on her knives. "I don't necessarily need you."

Aristos shrugged. "You haven't killed me yet, have you?"

She could not argue with his logic, nor could she ignore the fact he had not called for help. Although she did not understand why he hesitated, she could not sense malice or deception in him. She sheathed her weapons, but kept her hands perched on her hips, close enough to grab the blades again if she needed them.

"That's better," Aristos said and nodded at Laegoli. "Does your protector have a name?"

"He's not my protector."

"Then who is he? You know Garon will skin him if he's caught, don't you? The last Zeiihbuan felt that pain alive."

Meaghan's stomach rolled. Laegoli's voice held no fear when he responded. "I'm a friend of her mother."

"Is that supposed to mean something to me?"

"She had a weird hobby," Laegoli said. "She collected invisibility spells."

Meaghan suppressed a smile at the lie. She understood Laegoli's message. Vivian, the woman who had raised her on Earth, had visited him before she had died. Like so many other times, her seer power had given her the chance to save Meaghan. She had given Laegoli the second invisibility spell and instructions on when to use it.

Aristos shook his head. "So your Zeiihbuan friend is here to keep you out of trouble. Why did you come? What ailment couldn't your own Healers cure?"

"Poison," she answered, not bothering to correct his assumption that she was not in the area alone. "Nettlebarb to be exact. Do you know it?"

"I do. I can heal it for you, but I have to be honest. Your Healers need better training if they can't take care of that. Where's the patient?"

Meaghan hesitated. She had pictured bringing Garon's Healer to Cal at knifepoint, blindfolded and under protest. The last thing she had expected was having him volunteer. Although she still sensed no deception in him, his ease at helping her made her question her empath power.

"You'll find out when we get there," she said. "You'll wear a blindfold—"

"And the Mardróch will kill all three of us before we get ten steps into the field. We can't use the invisibility spell you used with Stilgan. Garon requires everyone to recite the counterspell at least once an hour. And your spell," he waved a hand toward Laegoli, "isn't worth much. I heard you a couple of times. Fortunately, Garon's love of toying with nature has dulled his hearing and Bracken is as dumb as a barn bat. Did Meaghan's mother collect any other spells?"

Laegoli did not respond.

"I didn't think so. You'll just have to trust me to get you out of here."

"Why would we do that?" Meaghan asked.

"For the same reason I didn't call for a Mardróch the second I realized your identity. I'm on your side."

CHAPTER EIGHTEEN

"**YOU MUST** think we're stupid to believe that," Laegoli said. "Especially after you offered to cure Garon."

"True. You also heard him mention my father, Finnil. Do you know who he is?"

"No," Meaghan said, though somehow she felt she should. His name pulled on her memory as if she had heard it before.

Laegoli smirked. "Why would I know the name of one of Garon's minions?"

"He was a traitor," Aristos said. "He killed his entire family."

"Clearly not everyone," Laegoli scoffed.

"He's too young," Meaghan said as the details shifted into place. The Writer's book had revealed Finnil's trial to Meaghan within the story of her parents' wedding. Finnil had gone insane after testing a new potion he had intended to use on the king and queen. In his rampage, he had killed his family and nine other villagers. "It happened when my mother was a teenager. Finnil was exiled."

"A common punishment for most of Garon's favorite minions, as your friend so succinctly described them. Not long after my father's exile, he met my mother and forced her to…keep him company."

Although Aristos spoke his words without emotion, Meaghan sensed the anger raging beneath them, strong and fresh. Meaghan suspected Finnil had done more than rape Aristos's mother.

"About a decade later, he found out I'd inherited his power and came back to claim me. He killed her, sliced her open in front of me. I've been planning my revenge since."

"He's trained you since you were ten?" Laegoli asked.

Aristos nodded.

"So you learned from the best," Laegoli said, sarcasm lacing his tone. "But you're not a boy anymore, so that tells us everything."

"What do you think it tells you?"

Laegoli crossed his arms over his chest. "You learned more than just his skill. You learned how to serve your *lord*, to become his lackey and confidante."

Aristos's anger surged. He tightened his grip on the tattered red book Meaghan had forgotten he held. "My father's sanity came in waves for decades. Do you really think his insanity is permanent now by coincidence?"

Laegoli narrowed his eyes. "Displacing your father doesn't prove your allegiance. If anything, it shows how well you fit in with Garon's people. Curing Garon without your father taking the credit would bring you plenty of reward."

"That *cure* you keep focusing on is a poison."

"Then why not slip it into his potion?"

"Because he doesn't trust me. My skin is a constant reminder of my lowly stature in his eyes. The first small sip he takes of the potion is to test it, to test *me*. He knows the flavor of the potion. He'll know if I've tampered with it. He needs to drink the whole thing for the poison to work."

"But a new potion, a so-called cure, might get past his distrust," Meaghan guessed.

"Exactly."

"I don't believe you," Laegoli said. "Like you told Garon, a man can't help how he's born. You were born to a liar and a traitor. I'm sure you're no different."

Meaghan honed her empath power, trying to decipher Aristos's intent. If he had any emotions aside from anger, she could not tell.

Aristos slammed the book down on a table. His eyes sizzled before his rage exploded. The emotion seared hot through Meaghan's mind. She hissed from the force of it.

"I meant what I said," Aristos snapped. "A man may not be able to help how he's born, but he *can* help what sort of person he becomes. I know I'll die in my mission. I intend to die making my mother proud."

"What do you propose?" Meaghan asked.

"Let me help you. You could use a spy in one of Garon's villages. After all, he has enough of them in yours."

§

MEAGHAN SNAKED down back alleys and side streets, tracking her companions by the moonlight. She held her breath more times than she could count, each time seeking out her knife in anticipation of a fight. Despite her reluctance to trust a man whose consuming anger made his other emotions impossible to read, no Mardróch hid around the corners and they reached the border of the village without triggering any alarms.

When she scanned the sleeping army littering the open field, she almost ran for the woods. It would be easy to leave Aristos behind in the night-darkened forest. Almost as easy as Cal would die without the Healer's help.

She hoped they would not all be dead because of it.

Aristos led Laegoli around the impromptu camp, threading between a few outlying soldiers, and Meaghan followed. A pale quarter-moon pierced the dark sky. A wolf howled in the distance. No one stood guard over the houses that harbored Garon's elite.

The thought struck her at the same moment she heard rustling coming from the trees to her left.

"Get down," Aristos whispered. He dropped to the ground and tucked his arms under his head, mimicking the posture of the sleeping soldiers closest to them. Meaghan followed his lead, taking the vacant spot a row behind him. Laegoli did the same to her right. Two voices broke free from the forest before Meaghan could make out their sources. They sounded gravelly, similar to the guttural tone she had come to expect of Mardróch, yet higher pitched than she had heard before. *Female Mardróch*, she realized, and tightened her hands into fists to keep calm.

"We were supposed to be guarding the village," the first Mardróch said.

"You didn't have to go with me," the second responded.

"What else was I supposed to do, Valia? You're my cousin."

"Then stop complaining."

"I'm just looking out for you. Bellan will be furious when he finds out you ate his goat. He killed another Mardróch last night for mentioning how good it looked."

"What's he going to do, Fillessa?" Valia asked. "He can't get within ten feet of me without risking his head exploding."

"Lightning can travel farther than ten feet."

"And Garon's reach is a lot farther than that. Do you know what he'd do to Bellan if he tried to kill me? You worry too much."

Two pairs of black boots marched by Meaghan's head. Meaghan glanced up and saw the stiff woven legs of drab brown pants. One of the Mardróch kicked Meaghan's arm and she squeezed her eyes shut. By the time she risked another look, the Mardróch had continued their trek toward the village. Each wore brown shirts that matched their pants, and each had a long, black braid down the center of their backs.

"Besides," Vallia continued. "Male Mardróch are idiots by nature. He probably wouldn't figure out it was me if I ate a goat leg in front of him."

Fillessa laughed. Behind them, a Mardróch rose from his bed in the field. Lightning sparked blue within one hand. When the female Mardróch moved a few more steps beyond him, he fired. His bolt hit Fillessa square in the back, disintegrating her braid in fire before she fell to the ground.

Vallia turned and hissed. She pressed her fingers to her temple. Rather than fight, the male Mardóch raised his hands in surrender.

"Astasia sent me to kill her," he said. "She was tired of Fillessa's constant worrying."

Meaghan bit her lip in recognition of the name. Astasia had been the last Spellmaster's sister, the woman who had betrayed her brother in order to earn Garon's favor.

"A Mardróch must never show emotion," Vallia said, lowering her hands. Fang-like teeth flashed through the webbing covering her mouth. Everything about the female Mardróch looked similar to her male counterpart. They were both unnaturally tall. They had the same hollow cheeks and deathly gray skin that clung to their skeletal bodies. Their noses collapsed in, becoming mounds of unrecognizable flesh. And their uniquely colored eyes announced unusual powers, though the female Mardróch's were not red, like the male's. She stared at him with ice blue irises that glinted sharp in the moonlight. With a quick movement, the Mardróch pressed her hands to her temple again. Her eyes flashed white and the male Mardróch exploded. His head burst first, scattering blood, skin, and dark matter Meaghan did not want to recognize over his sleeping comrades. The rest of his body followed, piece by piece. The sounds of heavy rain echoed after each muted pop.

"Astasia only sends assassins she wants dead," Vallia said, then turned and strode toward the village.

A cricket chirped in the distance. Another responded from across the field. None of the soldiers stirred. Meaghan turned her head to the other side to search for Aristos's instruction. A Mardróch's red gaze caught her attention first. He lay on the ground a few feet away from her. She snapped her eyes shut, then remembered what Artair had told her the day she had met him. Mardróch did not sleep. She opened her eyes. The Mardróch grinned at her, and her heart sank. The escape attempt had been a trap.

"Run!" she commanded.

Laegoli cursed and jumped to his feet a step behind her. Monsters and soldiers writhed in their makeshift beds, and then rose in chase. Fear pushed Meaghan's legs and lungs beyond their limits, and she burst across the tree line with almost inhuman speed.

A Mardróch blocked her path. She grabbed a knife and cast it toward him, hitting her mark with a satisfying thud. Two more Mardróch materialized in front of Meaghan. The closest one arced blue lightning between his fingers. He raised his hand, and then howled when Meaghan tackled him to the ground. She rolled off him, grabbed another knife and plunged it into the opening of his hood.

"Look out!" Laegoli yelled. Meaghan dove to the side as lightning charged through the air overhead. Yanking her blade from the Mardróch's body, she spun around, prepared to attack. Laegoli beat her to the remaining monster, landing a kill strike with a metal blade he pulled from his belt.

Aristos appeared between her and Laegoli. Before she could warn the Zeiihbuan, Aristos grabbed him and the two men disappeared.

Hollering echoed across the field as waves of soldiers and Mardróch barreled toward the forest. Meaghan cursed. She collected her first blade and took off running again, though she had no hope of making it back to the cave alive. She had too far to go and an entire army at her heels.

An arrow sank into a tree trunk next to her head. Another hit the ground by her feet. She skirted behind an oak and pressed her back to it. A quick glance behind her revealed two archers in pursuit. She yanked another knife from her belt, and then yelped when a hand dropped down onto her shoulder. Before she could fight back, her world dissolved.

A moment later her sight returned, though rocks replaced grass and trees had turned into flowers. Aristos stood close by and she lunged, aiming for his heart with her blade. Long fingers grabbed her wrist a breath before her weapon made contact.

Her gaze moved from the hand grasping her to Laegoli. He stood next to her, though she had failed to see him before. He let go of her wrist.

"You still need him," he reminded her.

"It was a trap," she said, then directed her anger at Garon's Healer. "You set us up."

"If I set you up, why aren't you still in the forest?"

Meaghan stepped forward, squaring off with him. She tightened her grip on her knife. "You tell me. Mardróch don't sleep, yet you led us straight through a nest of them."

"They don't *have* to sleep," Aristos said. "They choose to sometimes, particularly after one of their play battles. I thought we were safe."

"Bullshit."

Aristos's eyebrows knit together. "What?"

"Forget it. Let's just say I don't believe you."

"Fine. Believe this, then. I can't go back there now, thanks to you."

Meaghan raised her blade and pointed it at him. Aristos pulled a knife from his own belt. She stepped forward, tensed for a fight. Aristos spun to the left and threw his blade between her and Laegoli. A howl erupted behind her. Her attention snapped to the noise. Two Mardróch advanced across the field. A third appeared from nowhere. All three of them stepped over the body of the Mardróch Aristos had killed.

"They traced your teleportation trail," Meaghan said. "We have to get out of here."

"Not before we dispatch them," Laegoli told her. "Or we won't make it far. The one on the right is mine. Aristos, you take the one on the left."

That made the stockiest Mardróch Meaghan's responsibility. She eyed the creature and advanced, expecting lightning to fly before she got close. The monster chuckled.

"I know who you are. I'll enjoy this."

In response, Meaghan rolled her eyes and tossed a knife in his direction. It sailed past his hood.

Electricity crackled at the Mardróch's fingertips. "Shame. I expected better of you."

She cast a second knife. It sailed far to his left. Lightning blasted a hole in the ground at the Mardróch's feet and he swung his attention toward the source of the discharge. One of his Mardróch friends lay sprawled on the ground, the bolt his last accidental act.

Meaghan's stocky Mardróch growled and spun to his right, hissing when he saw his other comrade on the ground, Meaghan's first knife protruding from the opening in his hood.

"Is that more what you expected?" Meaghan asked, and then threw her last knife. The monster fell. She turned in time to meet Aristos's wide-eyed stare. "You had better not be lying to me."

His throat constricted as he swallowed. He nodded.

"We should hurry," Laegoli said. "There'll be others coming. Which way do we go from here?"

Meaghan reclaimed her weapons, and then recited the invisibility spell, covering the three of them. Although she knew the Mardróch might remove the spell at any moment, she still felt safer than traveling in the open. She led them back the way she had come. They moved single file, with Aristos second and Laegoli taking up the rear. The few times she glanced over her shoulder at them, Laegoli had his blade ready in his hand. His trust for Aristos matched hers.

The first warm rays of morning touched the green landscape, turning it gold, before she saw the cave. Several razor beasts milled in front of it and she raced toward them, pulling her knives to scare them away. They sauntered a few yards outside of her range, and then circled in the grass and lay down, stretching their forelegs in a clear gesture of boredom.

"Mangy cats," she muttered before ducking into the cave entrance.

The fire had burned out, leaving the cavern dark and musty. She paused long enough to allow her eyes to adjust. On the far side, she could make out the shape of Cal's bulky form. A bear-like snore erupted from him. She sighed in relief, then moved to the fire pit to build a new flame. It sprang to life with hues of red and yellow that danced shadows along the wall.

When she turned again, Laegoli guarded the entrance, his blade still in his grip, and Aristos knelt over Cal. Meaghan rushed to his side, her own knife tight within her fingers. If Aristos had any tricks in mind, she hoped her immediate presence, and the not so subtle threat, would cause him to think twice. As added insurance, she focused her empath power on him, hoping she could sense if his intent turned malicious.

Aristos traced his hands down Cal's body, using his power to sense for injury. He hesitated over Cal's broken leg before moving back up to his head.

"What's he been taking?" he asked. "This isn't a natural sleep."

"Sickle herb."

"That's creative. I'll have to remember that. It should keep him asleep for a while, but he'll wake soon enough. Try to keep that knife out of his reach when he does."

Aristos pressed his hands over Cal's heart, nodded, and then his pupils dilated as he started working. An hour passed, then another. Aristos's cheeks flushed red. Sweat rolled down his brow and dripped from his chin. In the middle of the third hour, Cal gasped and lurched upright. His thick hands clamped down around Aristos's wrists.

"You're hurting me," Aristos said, his voice calm, though Meaghan could sense his pain and fear. "I'm here to help you."

Cal twisted his fingers to tighten his grip. "You're a liar. I know every Healer in this kingdom. Who are you?"

"Aristos," he said. "Meaghan brought me."

Cal's gaze shot to Meaghan. "Tell me everything."

"There's no time, Cal. He's trying to heal you."

"Tell me."

"He's Garon's Healer," she said, and winced when Cal yanked on Aristos's arms. "I'm using my empath power to monitor him, Cal. Let him go."

Cal grunted and did as she asked. Aristos rubbed his wrists. Red welts forming along his skin made it clear he would need more than a light massage to ease his pain.

"What's Garon doing with a Healer like you, anyway?" Cal asked. "You don't exactly fit the image of his perfect Ærenden kingdom. Where are you from?"

"The Barren. Finnil's my father."

"Huh." Cal blinked several times, and then shook his head and lay back down. "If you're going to betray Meaghan, you'd better make sure you kill me first or you'll learn what it's like to eat your fingers. One at a time. Your toes will come after."

"I have no doubt," Aristos said, his fear no longer hidden. His hands shook as he placed them on Cal's leg. "This will take a while. Try to relax, okay?"

Cal slung an arm over his eyes. "Relax while an enemy is playing with my insides. That's a new one."

Time passed slowly for the next few hours. The fire dimmed. Laegoli alternated between stoking it and holding his stoic guard by the entrance. A mid-day sun outlined his body, casting a long shadow into the cave, and then faded as it chased the horizon. Cal groaned from his pain, but somehow kept from screaming. Aristos's breath grew labored. Meaghan brought him water, which he took without speaking. He resumed his task with the same singular focus. Sweat drenched his hair and plastered his shirt to his chest. When his arms shook and Meaghan felt certain he would not be able to work any longer, he lifted his hands from Cal's body.

"We're done," he said.

Cal sat up. He narrowed his eyes at Aristos, and then stood. His first step was tentative. The second had purpose. The third brought a broad smile to his lips. "Well, now. That feels a lot better."

When he returned to his spot, he lifted up his pant leg. The bright green tendrils had disappeared.

"Perfect," he said. "You should stay here tonight and regain your strength. The wild animals will turn you into a feast otherwise."

Aristos nodded. "I appreciate your trust."

"I don't," Laegoli said. "You're asking for trouble by letting him stay with you."

"He's not staying with us," Cal said. "We're leaving. I won't send the man who healed me out to get slaughtered, but I'm also not foolish enough to believe this place won't be crawling with Mardróch by morning."

"What?" Meaghan's gaze shot to the cave entrance. Black had begun to claim the sky again. A razor beast stretched lazily in the distance. "Cal, it's not safe. We have no place to go."

"Yup," Cal said with a lopsided grin. "Guess you should've thought of that before you saved my life."

CHAPTER NINETEEN

"I DON'T see why we couldn't have eaten before we left."
Meaghan crossed her arms over her chest and stared deeper into the
forest, trying to see anything remotely edible. She found nothing but
row upon row of stark green trees. The moon swelled overhead,
diving in and out of leaves with callous nonchalance. She sighed.
"I'm starving."

"I offered you worm root," Cal replied.

"And you told me it tastes like salty snot. I'm not interested."

"Then you aren't really hungry, are you?"

"Do you always talk to the queen this way?" Laegoli asked. He
guarded the back of their small line, his blade in his hand, as he had
for the last few hours. "It seems rather…insolent."

"No need to let her get too full of herself," Cal joked.

"Or full at all," Meaghan said. "I've had one meal over the last
two days. There must be something palatable around here."

"That depends on your definition of palatable. I happen to like
worm root." Cal plucked several leaves from a waist high bush and

handed them to her. "Give these a try."

Meaghan flattened the leaves against her palm. They looked no different from any other leaf—green, pointed, and uninteresting. "What is it?"

"Tamrin bush."

She frowned. "Nick said the leaves taste horrible and they're only edible when they're bearing nuts."

"He's right about the first part, not so much the second. They just taste worse off-season."

She dropped them to the ground. "I'll pass."

"Then stop whining. And don't sulk," he added when she glared at him.

Laegoli coughed and Meaghan grinned at his reaction. To an outsider, Cal's behavior looked disrespectful, but it helped Meaghan feel at ease. James, the man she had known as "Dad" on Earth, had been Cal's younger brother. She remembered dozens of conversations similar to this throughout her childhood, and each had ended the same way. Cal took a step back and looped an arm around her shoulders, mimicking his brother's familiar gesture.

"She knows I'm teasing," Cal said to Laegoli.

Laegoli nodded and pointed to a small tree a few yards in front of them. "If what I've heard about your secondary power is true, that should give you something to eat."

"What does it produce?" Meaghan asked. She approached the tree and ran her fingers through a cluster of orange leaves. They felt like velvet.

"Linnaeus flowers. They were named after the Gardener who first discovered them."

Meaghan focused on her revival power, moving it along her arm until it warmed her fingertips. She directed it into the tree. Dozens of yellow buds sprouted along its branches. One by one, the buds unfurled to reveal milky white petals striped with pink. She plucked one and set it on her tongue. It dissolved like spun sugar, though it tasted closer to pink bubble gum. A dozen more flowers stopped the ache in her stomach. Cal grabbed a handful for later and they continued toward Zeiihbu.

By morning, Cal had convinced Laegoli to leave them. He trekked north toward home, a letter in his pocket meant for Everel, Ed's cousin and leader of the former king's tribe. Cal and Meaghan planned to continue into Ærenden.

"Some of our villages along the border between Zeiihbu and Ærenden are still protected by Guardians," Cal said. "If we can find one, we might be able to reach Nick or May through them."

Meaghan had her doubts, but she could not think of a better idea, so she stretched her empath power and remained silent as she sensed for Mardróch.

Without wind or smoke, Cal could not easily use his power to search for enemies, so he muffled their footsteps by controlling the ground instead.

By the time the sun rose on the third day, Meaghan had grown tired of eating berries and nuts. She rubbed her eyes to rid them of sleep, and then blinked several times when they stumbled into a clearing. At its center, a hut stretched into the open sky. Meaghan grinned, but Cal responded to her joy with a frown.

"No lights," he said, pointing to the windows. He gestured at a squat chimney rising from the roof. "No smoke."

Meaghan nodded, understanding what he meant. No one was home. She tempered her excitement, but she still held out hope until they grew closer.

Zeiihbuans maintained their homes with meticulous attention. This hut showed no such pride. Its thatched roof had succumbed to rot and nesting animals. Paint peeled off in chunks along its outside walls. And shutters hung at odd angles, if they hung at all. The building reeked of musty abandonment.

Cal pushed open the door. It emitted a loud groan as it dragged a line through the dirt floor, and then came to a hard stop. He shoved his shoulder into it, but it refused to budge.

Meaghan wedged between him and the opening. Faint sunlight pierced the grimy windows, highlighting a wooden trunk that served well as a doorstop. She waved at Cal to follow her. He sucked in his stomach and wriggled through.

Little evidence remained of the house's former owner. Shattered earthenware and chipped bowls littered the shelves. Yellow mold crawled from a stone fireplace to the walls beside it. Several broken chairs occupied one corner. Their matching table lay in the center of the floor, upended and caked in mud.

Cal moved to the trunk and ran his fingers along one edge of it. Dust coated his fingertips, turning them ghost-white. "It's been a while, I think."

Meaghan joined him. "Anything useful in there?"

"Not likely," Cal said, but tugged open the lid anyway. It squealed in protest.

The odor of decomposing animal droppings accosted Meaghan's nose. Cal reached into the trunk. Piles of yellowing papers crumbled under his touch. He dug deeper, swirling his hand from one side of the trunk to the other, but found nothing else.

He moved to shut the trunk, but Meaghan grabbed his arm.

"The lid is flat inside," she said. "But the outside…"

Cal grinned. "It's a dome. Think there's a hidden compartment?"

"There's only one way to find out." She pushed it open again, and knocked on the flat portion of the lid. It jangled. She knocked a second time and got the same result.

"Yup, definitely something there," Cal said.

Meaghan slipped a blade from its sheath and jammed it between two boards. They split with a loud crack. Cal grabbed one of the damaged planks and yanked it away. Coins flowed through the hole he had created, disintegrating the paper at the bottom of the trunk. Meaghan dipped her hand into the pile and frowned at the silver and gold circles. Seated liberties, eagles, and regal busts stared at her. She picked up one and read the words stamped around its edge: *United States of America*. On the opposite side, *1840* declared its age.

Cal fingered another coin. "What's Britannia?"

"It's a place," Meaghan said and threw her coin back into the trunk. "On Earth."

"So these things would be…?"

"Money. Coins, actually. They're used for bartering."

"Oh," Cal let go of his coin. He shut the trunk. "Guess they're no good to us here."

"Not really," Meaghan said. Cal left the cabin and she followed him. "Do you have any idea why they're here?"

Cal grunted. "You should probably talk to Miles about that."

"Cal," she warned, using her best regal tone. "Miles isn't here. If you know something, you need to tell me."

"I have a theory," he admitted.

Meaghan waited for further explanation. When he remained silent, she pressed him. "Don't make me command you."

He ran his fingers through this beard and sighed. "There's probably a portal close to here. Some time ago the royal family had official Explorers."

"What exactly did they explore?"

"Earth, to borrow ideas mostly. The king and queen eventually decided it was costing us our heritage, so they stopped sending people. The Explorers' last report mentioned automatic carriages."

Meaghan raised an eyebrow. "You mean automobiles?"

"I guess." He shrugged. "No one used the portals again until Viv and James took you across."

"Why didn't you tell me this before? You had the chance when we met, when we talked about Earth."

"I didn't know then. The royal family swore the Explorers to secrecy. When they died, the Elders took over the portals."

The Elders had shared those secrets with Cal when he became one of them. Yet Meaghan's family had commissioned the Explorers and controlled the portals' secrets before the Elders. Why had they kept those secrets from her? The thought angered her more than she wanted to admit, and more than she cared to dwell on right now.

She stared up at the sky. White clouds painted images of flowers and horses across pristine blue. A light breeze tickled her hair, swirling it under her chin and she let it soothe her.

"Are we safe?" she asked. "We have wind, can you tell if there are any Mardróch around? I'd like to build a fire and cook something for lunch if we're able to."

Cal closed his eyes and recited a short rhyme under his breath. Meaghan had not heard him use the focusing technique in a while. It danced memories of their first meeting across her mind, when his disembodied voice had scared her with a similar song.

"No Mardróch," Cal muttered. His eyes popped open again. "But there's smoke. I was able to follow it to a torch."

"Why would anyone need a torch in the middle of the day?"

"Doesn't matter," Cal said. A grin stretched across his face. "This way. They aren't far."

"Who?" Meaghan asked. Her question bounced off Cal's back as he sprinted across the field. She forced out a breath of frustration and chased after him. "Cal!"

"Catch up," he said over his shoulder. "That is, if you want a nice feast by nightfall. I'm pretty sure Cadell won't mind lighting a bonfire. His men can protect us."

"I don't understand. What does Cadell—?"

Before she could finish her question, the answer came to her. Faillen's father had carried a torch to signal Cal. She let out a cry of joy and triumph. Anissa had received her message.

Cadell and his tribe had come to rescue them.

CHAPTER TWENTY

THEY ALL looked the same. Every village, every street, every house painted with bright colors. No matter how many times Nick tried to see the differences, they all blurred together.

The Village at Twin River Point was no exception. Years of neglect had dulled some of its paint and collapsed a few of its second stories. Mildew and dust had collected in grotesque shapes along walls, and weeds had found residence where humans had not. But after a month of hard labor, it would revert to its former state, a template built from every village that had come before it and donating to every one after. It made Nick ache for change.

He grew tired of the stamp the ancient kings and queens had replicated on the landscape. He wished they had been more creative, that they had designed buildings like the ones he had seen on Earth. Or rather, the ones he wished he had seen—the Eiffel Tower in Paris, the Colosseum in Rome, the Empire State Building in New York City. Each beckoned to him, unique works of art larger than anything the people of Ærenden could imagine.

He sighed. Earth had given him a taste of something else, something sweeter. It had coated his tongue and left him wanting more, though he knew what he craved came with a price. Just as a palate fed a steady diet of candy could no longer appreciate the purity of vegetables, an eye that feasted solely on spectacular sights no longer appreciated simple beauty.

Ærenden's smaller houses did not block the colors of a fall forest or the sharp sparkle of a clear night. They did not sprawl over the lands, replacing soft grass with concrete and delicate bird songs with the roar of traffic. They served a functional purpose.

Today, Nick did not care about function or natural beauty. He would rather be staring up at Big Ben or touring the Taj Mahal. He would rather be anywhere but here.

"You're awfully quiet today."

Nick jumped. How long had he been staring down the dirt-packed main road of the village? Ten minutes, at least. Clearing his throat, he offered a tight smile to his traveling companion. Edison's broad grin in return showed no grudge for Nick's distracted behavior. Nothing seemed to faze the man, though his age probably had something to do with that. Deep wrinkles worked grooves into his cheeks and white had taken over what little hair he had left. It ringed a smooth head Nick would describe as glistening rather than bald.

"The Elders said you'd been to this village before. That true?"

Nick nodded and tried not to let his mind wander again. The last time he had visited, he had been eleven. He remembered more about the birthday party the villagers had thrown for their Mayor than the layout of the streets. He doubted Edison would care about the best chocolate fruit tart Nick had ever eaten.

Edison raised one white, bushy eyebrow. It did not seem to separate from his deep gray eye. "And?"

"And what?" Nick asked.

"Do you know where it is?"

"Oh…yeah. This way." Nick pointed down a side street and hoped he had guessed right. Two turns later, they reached a dead end. He cursed.

"Too many of these streets look alike," Edison offered, though they both knew Nick's confusion had nothing to do with the streets. They had set up new villages four or five times in the last few months, improving their process each time until they could do the work in an afternoon. Most of today had already elapsed, in part because Nick had led them the wrong way in the beginning of the journey, and now because he could not seem to stay focused.

Edison did not ask for an explanation for his odd behavior. He knew the reason, as everyone who had been anywhere near Nick lately had known.

It had been weeks since Faillen's father had received the gildonae, weeks since the bird returned with confirmation that he had started his search for Cal and Meaghan. Yet they had not come home.

At night, Nick dreamed of battles and death. During the day, his mind revisited Earth. He wanted to undo the months since Vivian's and James's murders. He wanted to start over.

"Let's head to the village square and move out from there," Edison offered. "The building can't be that hard to find."

"Not at all," Nick said. "A building that looks like all the others should stand out easily enough."

Edison laughed, as amiable with Nick's sarcasm as he had been with his distraction, and led the way. Although Nick had been right about the house looking similar to all the others, the thin lines threading from its roof made it easy to spot. On Earth, he had come to understand the word *wires*. These translucent lines resembled strands of spun yarn rather than the heavy-gauge wire that had led to Aunt Vivian's house, but their purpose was the same. On cloudy days, these threads would be nearly impossible to spot. Today's late-afternoon sun had turned them into dancing rainbows against a blue sky. Dozens of them waved at him, each strand connecting this house to an adjacent roofline, then others beyond that, until Nick could no longer see their destinations.

He had helped string them in a new village as a teenager and had learned first-hand that they felt rougher than they appeared, closer to metal than any soft fiber.

"We could be in luck," Edison said, staring up at the threads. "None of the allumn appears to be broken. I'll know for certain once I get everything going again."

Nick hoped he was right. He wanted to sleep in his own bed before tomorrow dawned. Nick and Edison had two tasks to complete—assess safety and start electricity flowing again. No signs of Garon's army remained. By the dust and disrepair, Nick doubted they remembered the village existed. The second task belonged to Edison, one of the few Electrifiers still alive in the kingdom.

Edison pushed open the front door. Chips of red paint flaked off onto his boots as he stepped inside. Nick followed.

Some sunlight managed to filter in through the dirt-caked front windows, erasing the darkest shadows from Nick's sight, but his eyes still needed a minute to adjust. Despite its outside appearance, this house had no rooms and no second story. Its façade hid an energy stone.

The outline of the dark stone rose to twice Nick's height and its footprint commanded a third of the floor. Though he could not see them, experience told Nick the fine threads would stretch from the top of the stone to the roof's outline, feeding the lines he had seen outside.

Edison stepped forward. He placed his hands on the stone, and then looked back at Nick. "Shield yourself."

Nick cupped his hands over his eyes. Bright blue light filled the large room. Nick winced at the sudden volume of it, and then glanced sidelong at Edison as he worked. The power to create and control electricity had fascinated Nick since early childhood, when he had first accompanied Uncle James on his monthly rounds. Back then, nearly every village had access to electricity, instead of only the largest ones. James had replenished the stones, charging them the same way Edison did today.

Edison's entire body crackled as he surged blue energy into the stone. Nick backed against a wall, anticipating what would happen next. The stone pulsed, throbbing faster and faster until electricity exploded out and up, toward the roof.

With a sweeping gesture, Edison used his power to corral the excess energy, funneling it back into the stone. A tornado swirled around him, and then swallowed him within a dark cloud. Small lightning bolts snapped in the air, and Nick held his breath. Edison maintained control. The space surrounding Nick stayed still, though it warmed, drawing beads of sweat along his forehead.

Twenty minutes passed, then thirty. The cloud dissipated, revealing Edison's broad smile, then the tornado disappeared, almost as if the energy stone had absorbed it. The stone pulsed, its slow rhythm filling the house with a faint blue light.

Edison lowered his arms. "Now, let's test the electricity in these houses and get out of here."

§

BY THE time Nick crawled under the comforter on his own bed and closed his eyes, the rest of the village had started to rise. Children screamed outside his cottage, their morning excitement mixing with the sounds of wheels on cobblestones. Someone shared bread, he guessed, or fruit. Although his stomach would welcome either one, his mind demanded sleep. Five hours of walking through open fields at night, every muscle in his body tensed for a Mardróch attack, had left him exhausted. Even the noise outside his window could not keep him awake. It served as a reminder of his safety, soon lulling him into a dreamless slumber.

It did not last long. Less than an hour later, pounding on his door jarred him awake. He threw on clothes as he stumbled across the floor, then winced when he opened the door and welcomed sunlight into his room.

"You have to get out here."

Nick blinked several times, trying to clear the grogginess from his mind so he could focus on the person who had spoken. He knew the voice well, but it still took him a moment to place it within his sleep-addled mind.

"Max, what do you want? I just got back."

"This is serious, Nick."

Nick forced his eyes open fully. He had rarely heard Max use the word *serious*, let alone broadcast it in such a stiff tone. The worry Nick heard matched the concern turning Max's blue eyes into storm clouds.

"What's going on?"

"Just come on." Max grabbed his arm and dragged him from the cottage, nearly yanking him down the street before Nick righted his balance and pulled his arm from Max's grip.

"People are starting to stare," Nick said, though he kept running at Max's pace. "Where are we going?"

"To the edge of the village. The Elders are there already."

That statement jumped Nick's heart into his throat. The Elders had avoided him since the battle at Artair's village. Even his mother had kept their conversations short, though he had credited that to her care of Neiszhe's child. The infant had needed round-the-clock care until two days ago.

If they had asked for Nick, the situation was far worse than serious.

Nick charged down the last road, rounded the broad side of a barn, and then froze when he saw the field. Hundreds of Zeiihbuans gathered in groups of five and ten, talking in hushed voices. Not a dozen feet from where Nick stood, he spotted the Elders. Faillen stood with them, as did a man Nick did not recognize. The angular, long shape of his face held the same regal bearing as Faillen's and Nick did not have to guess his identity. Faillen's father, Cadell, had arrived.

Faillen glanced over his shoulder at Nick. A broad smile spread across his lips and he turned sideways so Nick could see what had triggered everyone's excitement.

Cal sat on a tree stump in front of the Elders. Behind him, almost completely hidden by Cal's broad shoulders, Nick found the woman that had haunted his dreams every night since she had left to rescue Caide.

Meaghan's copper eyes danced with joy. She stepped forward, her dark brown hair flowing with the movement. It beckoned him to touch it, to bury his face in it and hold her until time ended.

He wanted to run to her, to honor that need. His breath caught in his throat. She was here, finally. Aunt Vivian's prediction had come true.

Meaghan smiled. Gratitude and relief spread Nick's lips apart in response. When she took another step toward him, stronger emotions commanded his attention. He held his palm up, signaling for her to stop.

Her eyes widened, but he could not explain the anger he felt or the pain she had caused him. Not to her, and least of all to himself. Somehow, in the darkest shadows of his mind, he knew that if she came any closer, he would explode into a thousand pieces.

CHAPTER TWENTY-ONE

"NICK," CAL said, and his voice strained with the unasked question, *What is wrong with you?*

Lines furrowed along Cal's brow, and a frown disappeared within his full beard. He was not the only one who failed to hide his confusion. Faillen raised an eyebrow at his father. Miles and Sam shot Nick warning glances.

Nick's mother cleared her throat. She slung an arm across Meaghan's shoulders. "There'll be plenty of time to catch up later," she said. "I'm sure you're both ready for a nice bath right about now."

"That would be amazing," Meaghan said and wrinkled her nose. "I'm so tired of bathing in rivers. I'm sure my odor could peel paint off a door from ten feet away."

May chuckled. "Then let's get going before you wipe out all our hard work. It took weeks to paint the houses in this village." She nudged Cal from his seat. "I'll show you to your cabin on the way to mine. It's time for you to meet your son."

Cal flashed a smile so large it looked as if it would swallow his face. He bounded after May without any further prodding.

Once they had disappeared around a building, Miles cast a steely look in Nick's direction. "You're clearly not pleased she's home."

Nick shoved his hands into his pockets. "I don't wish to discuss it."

"Fine, then at least manage your behavior. You and Meaghan need to put up a unified front for the villagers. You're their leaders, not children."

Nick set his jaw, but he did not respond to the lecture. Anything he wanted to say would lead to an argument.

"You're not going to defend yourself?" Miles asked.

"I don't have to defend my actions, Miles. This has nothing to do with you."

"Of *course* it has something to do with me. It's my job—"

"Speaking of arguing in front of villagers," Cadell interrupted, his voice low and demanding. Nick blew out a breath and wished he could so easily portray the same command. Cadell nodded toward him and Nick wondered if the Zeiihbuan leader had interrupted to show support in his own way.

"I'm sure Zeiihbuans don't gossip any less than your villagers," Cadell continued. "Especially when they're hungry and tired. Where should I put them?"

"How should I know?" Miles snapped. "I'm not even sure why they're here. We asked you to rescue Cal, not bring your entire population into our village."

Cadell shrugged. "I didn't want to leave the queen unprotected.

Still, if you think this is all of my people, I welcome our next skirmish."

"That's enough, Dat," Faillen said. "You don't want the Elders to mistake your joking as a threat."

"I don't?" Cadell asked and rubbed his chin. Nick suppressed a laugh when he saw the twinkle in Cadell's eyes. The Zeiihbuan leader had definitely risen to Nick's defense. "Well, anyway, we can pitch camp in the field. We have the gear for it."

"And the Mardróch will be all over us by tomorrow," Sam said. "It will take us some time to extend the village's protection spell. Your people will need to stay within the boundaries until it's done."

"We need stronger powers to do that," Miles said.

"Good thing Meaghan and Cal are home," Nick said. "I'll have my mother send them. In the meantime, make sure the soldiers have food. We're low, but we can dispatch hunting parties in the morning."

"Thank you," Cadell said.

Nick nodded, and then turned, ignoring Miles's anger-flushed cheeks at the assigned task. For the moment, all he cared about was getting back to his bed so he could sleep.

No one else bothered him on his walk home. After dispatching a young neighbor girl to deliver the message to his mother, Nick opened his cottage door with a soft creak, and exhaled a loud breath when he found the single room inside empty. Meaghan had gone to his mother's place, as he had hoped, leaving him alone.

The urge to find her yanked at his heart again. He chased it away and flopped into bed. Meaghan's face danced inside his darkened vision, the pain his rejection had caused her fresh in her copper gaze.

He rolled onto his side and tried not to think about how thin she had appeared. Had food been scarce in her exile? What had she endured to survive? How often had her life been at risk?

The questions continued to hammer at him, despite his efforts to deny his need for answers. The more he pushed her from his mind, the more he wanted to hold her—not to soothe her pain, but to erase the sorrow that had owned him over the last few months.

He had missed her. He had mourned her. And he hated her for it.

He slammed a fist into his pillow, cursing when his knuckles crunched with the impact, then reached into the pillowcase to retrieve the Writer's book.

Miles had been right. Nick had been acting like a child. His anger had taken over and he would not give it free rein any longer. Tomorrow, he and Meaghan would talk. She might not like what he had to say, but she would hear it.

Nick tossed the book aside. It flipped open as it landed on the bed. Black print splashed across the page where only white had greeted him before. He leaned over to look at it and lost himself once more to a world that no longer existed.

§

ED FIRED arrow after arrow into his enemy. Rage hazed his vision. He focused past it, attacking with the speed of a dusk wolf. After he had reached for his last arrow, he tossed his bow aside and charged, ripping his best knife from his belt with the same ferocity that drove his feet.

He raised his arm, vengeance alive in his strike, and met resistance from another blade. Ed swiped right, his knife missing its target by inches when he realized who had attacked.

"Get out of my way," he growled.

"So you can continue mangling that tree?" Cal asked. "You'll dull your favorite blade, and then what?"

"I'll have it sharpened."

"That takes days. I'm not in the mood to stomach your complaining during that time."

Ed glared at his Guardian before sheathing his knife. "You need to respect me more. I am king after all."

"A title you hate," Cal responded with no hint of sarcasm or jest. "But it's because I respect you that I push you to become a better man. I don't waste my time with people I don't like."

"Lucky me."

"Yup, and don't you forget it."

Ed picked up his water bladder from the base of a tree and rolled his eyes. He had always found it impossible to stay mad at Cal, though in this instance, Cal had not been the target of his wrath. One man deserved that honor. Ed had pictured his face carved into the tree as he attacked it, wishing he could wage the battle for real.

It would never happen. In part, because he could not murder a man, not even one he loathed as much as Garon.

"Why are you out here?" he asked Cal. "I snuck out to be alone."

"It's my job to protect you."

Ed looked over his shoulder. The forest was empty, as it had been when he had started his tirade thirty minutes earlier. Not even a bird twittered in greeting. "From what, the trees?"

"From yourself. You have obligations in the castle soon. I know you don't like formal events, but you still have to do what's best for the kingdom."

"I don't see how putting on fancy clothes and pretending not to step on Adelina's feet is good for anyone."

"The people need to feel secure in their leaders. It's kind of like being a parent, really. If kids perceive weakness, they get scared. But you know that already, don't you?"

Ed did, though he hated to admit how much he had changed from his days leading his father's tribe. No matter how hard he tried, he could not shake the feeling the throne belonged solely to Adelina. His fights with Garon did not ease that belief.

"Adelina wants you here. The people love you. And if that doesn't matter to you, Meaghan should. She needs a good example."

Ed smiled as an image of his daughter's cherubic face flashed through his mind, the innocence in her copper eyes warming him in a way nothing else could. Within the confines of the royal apartment, while he and Adelina played with their two-year-old girl, he could believe this kingdom would be his someday. He had to take control of his destiny.

"You're right," he said. "I have a job to do, even if those closest to me don't always agree."

"I see." Cal scrubbed a hand through the short bristles of his black beard. "I should've guessed. What did Garon do this time?"

Ed shrugged. "It doesn't matter, does it? He and I can't agree on anything. Adelina plays peacekeeper with us almost daily."

"I take it you want to demote him."

"I don't know what I want, Cal. For the most part, he's a good advisor. He's just won't let go of his vendetta against Zeiihbu."

"He's not the only one in the kingdom who worries about them."

"Why? Because they're different?"

"It's enough for some people. For others, it's about the people the Zeiihbuans murdered in the war."

"Murdered?" Ed asked. "What exactly do you think we did? I saw fields littered with bodies from both sides of the border."

"They didn't win, Ed. History is written by the triumphant. It's polished by those who don't want to admit their faults."

"Then it's not history. It's fiction and I won't tolerate it, especially not from my advisor. Adelina and I are trying to build lasting peace. Garon is—"

"Doing his job. He's supposed to present all sides to you, even the unfavorable ones."

"Yeah, I guess. I just can't shake the feeling it's more than that. I heard his report to the Elders yesterday was rather scalding. They've asked to speak with Adelina about me."

"Because they're concerned. They want peace as much as you do."

Ed shook his head. He attached the water bladder to his belt and fingered his knife. "I visited the Pit yesterday. I wanted to see if my escape plan was still in place. You'd help me, wouldn't you, if I got thrown in there again?"

"They're not going to put you in jail."

"Just in case, can you make sure I get the cell I had when Adelina and I first met? You remember it, don't you?"

"It's hard to forget. You hid something behind the stone marked with an 'X', right?"

"Close," Ed said. "I marked it with my initials. It's in the farthest corner from the bars, on the outside wall."

"Whatever. You won't need it."

"I wish I could be so sure of that." He spun on his heels and launched his knife into the scarred bark of his Garon tree. Cal sighed, and the heavy sound brought a grin to Ed's face. "Guess you get a couple of days of complaining, after all."

CHAPTER TWENTY-TWO

A LATE sun cast long shadows across the cottage floor, turning piles of clothes and chairs into nefarious monsters. Nick blinked several times to clear a sticky fog from his mind, then threw off his blankets. Sweat collected on his arms. He could not recall falling asleep. After he had finished reading the latest story in the Writer's book, he had started reading from the beginning again. Then his mind went blank.

At first, he wondered if Miles had slipped him a potion, but he soon discarded his paranoia. No matter how much they fought, he could not doubt the Elder's loyalty. Exhaustion had claimed him. After working for two days straight and then dealing with the emotional impact of seeing Meaghan again, he had simply passed out.

For how long? Hours or days? He sat up and rolled his shoulders. Hours, by the grit still weighing down his eyes. The same dryness lined his tongue with sandpaper.

Standing, he turned in search of his water pitcher, and then froze when he saw Meaghan sitting at his small table, the Writer's book open between her hands. Shadows darkened her copper eyes with fear or weariness, he could not tell which. The same emotion held her body stiff. She did not even take a breath.

Nick said nothing as he continued his task, draining his water glass in three quick gulps. When he moved to the center of the room, she still watched him.

Another minute elapsed before she broke the silence. "Say something, please."

"What are you doing here?"

A frown dragged the shadows from her eyes to the rest of her face. She closed the book. "Your mom felt it would send the wrong message if I didn't stay with you."

"How long have you been here?"

"Not long. I've read my parent's wedding story a few times. It still amazes me that they were able to fall in love, despite their prophesied wedding."

"They aren't us, Meg."

"Meg," she echoed. "At least you're still using my nickname."

He could not deny her statement or the unspoken meaning behind it. His fury did not extend so deeply that he wanted to call her by her full name, the name she reserved for non-family. He turned to the fireplace and knelt in front of it.

"It's too hot for a fire," Meaghan said. Nick continued stacking logs within the hearth and she sighed. "Talk to me Nick. I know you're mad—"

"Mad?" Nick slammed a log down at his feet. It splintered. "Mad doesn't even begin to cover it. Do you have any idea what you did to me?" He spun on his heels to face her again, mindful to keep his voice low, to keep their fight from the neighboring villagers' ears, though he wanted to yell with every molecule of air in his lungs. He wanted to explode, as he had thought he might do when he saw her in the field. "Do you have any idea how much I've hated you over the last few months, how I've *mourned* you?"

Meaghan sucked in a sharp breath.

"You went off to die," he continued. "You welcomed it, even, without any regard for me, for how I felt about you. Why? I need to know why you care so little about me."

"I care a lot," she said.

"Your actions tell a different story."

"That's not fair." Tears swam in her eyes, but she did not let them fall. "I did it *because* I care. I didn't want you to get hurt."

"For someone so selfless, you can sure be selfish sometimes."

"Nick—"

"No. You listen to me for once. I'm tired of playing this game by your rules."

"I'm not playing a game."

"Aren't you? From the moment you climbed into my lap on Earth, from the moment you kissed me, told me you wanted me, it's been a game for you. I'm a toy. Your rock when you need someone. Your pawn when you don't."

"That's not even close to true." Her tears disappeared, dried up by a blazing fire. "You're the one who rejected me, remember?"

"And you'll punish me for that for the rest of my life."

Her lips turned white as she pressed them together. He turned back to the fireplace. "It isn't right what you did, Meg. If you didn't want to hurt me, you should've come home."

"I did come home, Nick. I'm here."

Nick's hand froze midway to another log. Through his rage, he had forgotten. She was alive. She was real. Not the ghost he had loathed over the last few months, but the woman he had wanted to hold.

The woman who had never returned his love.

He brought his gaze back to her. He still hated her and he felt shattered by that fact, torn into bits scattered along the floor. Meaghan crossed the room, her heels grinding those bits into dust.

"I'm sorry," she said and laid a palm against his cheek. He wanted to snap his head away from her touch. The warmth of her skin held him in place. He needed it more than he could admit. "It breaks my heart to realize what you must have gone through over the last few months. I didn't know it would turn out that way."

"No, you didn't. You thought you'd just march to your doom and I'd be okay with it."

"You have a right to be angry," she said. "I realize that. For the way I left and for the way I've treated you since our wedding."

Her hand slipped from his face and he captured it between his palms.

"Do you know what it's like to give everything to someone and have nothing in return?" he asked.

"Yes, I do." Meaghan's eyes met his. He saw no emotions within them. Her face remained relaxed, unremorseful.

He relinquished her hand. "I don't know how you manage to say so much with so few words. It destroys me to know you feel so little."

"You're not the one with an empath power," she said.

"I don't need one. You've made things very clear."

"Have I?" Her voice took on a passion he had not expected. Her eyes sparked again, and this time she let them blaze. "You're angry and you're hurt, more than you're letting on. I can sense that. But you have no right to tell me how I feel."

"And you have no right to use your power on me."

"Screw you."

Nick's temper boiled over. He glared at her, toying with the idea of walking out the door. The fire consuming her eyes stopped him. He pushed aside his anger for a moment to study her. She crossed her arms over her chest and stood her ground, stoic and unapologetic. Somehow, in the months she had been gone, she had changed. Certainty—no, self-assurance—held her body with purpose. He had failed to see it.

"Then tell me," he said. "Tell me how you feel."

"I love you, Nick."

He had never expected to hear those words from her, though he had always ached for them. Now that they had crossed her lips, he had trouble accepting them as truth. He wanted to reach for her, to fold her into his arms. He reached for the mantel behind him instead.

Her gaze did not waver as she stepped forward. She pressed her hands flat against his chest.

"There's more to it than that," he whispered. "There has to be. You've pushed me away for too long."

"It's complicated. It never should have been. What I felt for you on Earth—"

"Was a long time ago. I wish I could go back there, knowing what I know now. I wish I could do things differently. I keep thinking it might have changed everything."

Meaghan tilted her head. A small, almost seductive smile played across her lips. "What would you have done?"

"Whatever you wanted. You knew how I felt about you that night. You sensed it. I was afraid if I gave into it, it would destroy us both."

"I thought I knew what you felt, but I didn't understand my power then, so I couldn't be certain."

"I hurt you," Nick said and let go of the mantel to cup her cheek. Meaghan stepped closer. "I know I did. You thought you'd imagined everything and I embarrassed you when I pushed you away."

"Confused me," she corrected. "The physical aspects of your attraction were clear."

He chuckled, and then the moment turned serious again when he remembered where they stood—not in his cozy apartment on Earth, but afraid and desperate in Ærenden's war. "Saying no to you hurt more than I could let on. Your feelings for me changed that day and they changed more after we wed. Every night, I lay next to you in our cabin tortured by having your body so close and your heart so far. What happened, Meg?"

"I didn't know how to handle *this*." She swept her hand through the air, encompassing everything and nothing, and he realized she meant the kingdom beyond the cottage's four walls. "I didn't know how to handle us."

"You mean our wedding," he said. "The loss of control in your life."

She nodded and he understood all too well. On Earth, he had felt the same way. He had hated falling in love with a woman he could never have, and loathed the fact he could not control his desire. "I never should have let you leave that night," he told her.

"But you did," she said. "We can't change that. We can't go back. I'm not the same person I was then. I no longer have that innocence and neither do you."

He wanted to object, but he knew she was right. They were both different now. They had been through too much not to be. Despite it all, she looked at him with the same longing she had held for him that night. It smoldered in her eyes and in her touch when she pressed her lips to his chin. Her breath felt warm against his skin.

"We can't go back," she repeated. "But we can go forward. We have each other, Nick, if you can forgive me."

He closed his eyes, reopening them when Meaghan slipped her fingers between his. Something in him softened, easing the grief and panic that had kept him hostage over the last few months. She led him across the room to his bed and sat. He took the place beside her.

"I'm still mad at you," he said, though the words sounded empty, even to him.

She climbed into his lap, straddling him as she had the night of their first kiss. "It won't be the last time," she said and brought her lips to his. He pulled her tight against him, delving into her with raw urgency and a need corralled for too long. When they separated, she danced light kisses across his nose.

"I've never been able to control what I feel for you," she whispered. "But control is an illusion I no longer wish to harbor. I think it's time we gave into this. Don't you?"

"Yes." Nick grinned and flipped her onto the bed. His gaze held hers, binding her motionless as his fingers found her shirt and tugged on it. His mouth landed on hers once more. "Believe me, Meg. I won't make the mistake of saying no again."

CHAPTER TWENTY-THREE

"THAT'S QUITE an adventure," Nick said, though the awe in his voice belied the simple words he had chosen. Meaghan glanced at him. Sunlight streamed over his face, brightening his cheeks, and she leaned against him. He drew a hand up her thigh to her waistband and removed the corn husk doll she had hidden there before they left the cottage. He set it aside and brought his fingers back to rest on her hip. The doll stared back at Meaghan with unblinking black eyes, emotionless, though a full smile on its red lips gave it an air of happiness.

She had trouble taking anything seriously this morning. The world felt too perfect, calm and comfortable. She did not want to think it could ever change.

Sighing with contentment, she laid her head on Nick's shoulder. From their perch on his top step, she could see the village stretched in front of her, simple and silent. Not many people had begun their day. She doubted she would be awake already, if she had gone to bed.

He kissed her forehead, and then ran his hand up her back. He traced the chain for her mother's amulet with his fingers. "Do you think Stilgan's powers are still in here?" he asked.

"It's the only explanation I can come up with for why it feels heavier."

"You have a callous," he said, feathering the nape of her neck. The caress sent a shiver down her spine. "It's obviously weighing on you. Maybe you should take it off until we know exactly what's happening."

She felt for the spot he had indicated, surprised by the roughened skin. "I'd rather not. I feel safer having it in my protection."

"As you should," Cal's voice boomed from above them. Meaghan looked up. A smile overtook his face, flashing white through his full beard. "The last thing we need is that thing getting into Angus's hands."

"No one's heard from Meaghan's cousin since he disappeared at the old village," Nick told him.

"Doesn't mean he's not a threat," Cal said and dropped down onto the step next to Meaghan. "And I'm sure we'd hear from him plenty if he got ahold of that stone. But that's not worth worrying about right now. The morning is far too beautiful." He gestured toward the bright blue sky. "Not a cloud overhead. Not a Mardróch or razor beast in sight. We couldn't ask for better."

Meaghan raised an eyebrow. "You're in a good mood."

"It's hard not to be. I held my son and my wife last night. I slept on a bed that didn't have anything to do with rock and moss. I ate eggs and fresh toast this morning. I've never felt so alive. And it's all thanks to you."

He engulfed Meaghan in a rib-cracking hug, smothering her laugh in his shirt. "You look a lot better yourself," he said when he let her go. "There's a certain glow about you. I gather you two finally started acting like a wedded couple?"

Heat charged up Meaghan's cheeks. Cal's grin widened. It seemed as if it would split his face in two. "I'll take that as a yes. I'm glad. You've been through enough, both of you. You deserve to be happy. Especially you, lad," Cal slapped Nick's knee. "Don't forget that, and don't ever let her go again."

Nick wrapped an arm around Meaghan, firm enough that she wondered if he had taken the suggestion literally. He planted a loud kiss on her cheek. "I won't."

"That's more like it." Cal reached behind his seat to snag the doll from the step where Nick had left it. He touched an index finger to the doll's brown-thread hair. "Giving this a try again?"

Nick shrugged. "It can't hurt."

"So you think there's still a traitor here?"

"I'm fairly certain. The Shadow Guard must have learned about Viv's prophecy in the Writer's book or they wouldn't still be around."

"Neiszhe told me about that." Cal handed the doll to Meaghan. She tucked it into the back waistband of her pants. "Is our story still that Meaghan has to transfer her power to the doll to keep everyone's emotions from overwhelming her?"

"That's the idea."

"Then how do you explain her not needing it over the last three months?" Cal asked. "Or better yet, that she managed to travel with an army for two weeks without going insane?"

"We told everyone you were in seclusion before Cadell found you," Nick said. "As far as the rest, I filled Faillen and Cadell in on our plan. They've agreed to say the gildonae brought the doll to Cadell and he gave it to Meg."

Cal stood. "Works for me. It's a stretch, but like you said, it can't hurt. In the meantime, the other Elders asked me to come get you. Faillen filled me in on what's been happening, so I'm guessing this meeting won't be a welcome home party."

Nick stiffened. "Not even close."

"Well, we could get to it, or I could buy you two a little more private time. They won't know when I actually found you."

"How long?" Nick asked.

"Say…an hour?" Cal turned from them. "Get lost. I don't want to see you when I turn back around."

Without another sound, Nick grabbed Meaghan's hand and tugged her into the closest alleyway.

They ran over cobblestones and pebbled roads, through backyards and side streets, until they reached the grass field at the edge of town. Tents flapped in a steady breeze. A few of Cadell's soldiers brewed coffee in metal pots. No one seemed to notice when Nick led Meaghan around a dilapidated barn and out of sight. He sandwiched her between his body and the barn's red doors.

"We should've run into the cabin," he said. "I don't know what I was thinking."

Meaghan laughed. Something tickled her ankle and she looked down. Several yellow flowers waved back at her. She plucked one, and touched it to Nick's chin, watching as it glowed against his skin.

"This looks like a buttercup," she said.

"It essentially is." He ran a finger along the flower's stalk, then down her thumb. "We call them sunflakes."

She brought the flower to her nose and inhaled. Its perfume resembled apple blossoms and she closed her eyes to savor it.

Nick rested his hands on her shoulders. "There's so much I need to tell you," he said. "But I don't want to let go of this happiness."

Meaghan opened her eyes. "We control our happiness, Nick. No matter what else happens around us, we can control that. We can create it with each other."

Nick nodded and glanced to the side, at a garden overgrown with grass and weeds. "There's something you should see."

He waved a hand through the air and recited a counterspell she recognized. Laegoli had used it to reverse their invisibility in Garon's village. A five-sided stone appeared where tall grass had been.

Etchings marked each side of the stone. She recognized the lettering, though she could not read any of the words. "Ancient Æren," she said. "Is it a spell?"

Nick shook his head. "A prophecy."

Meaghan stared at the stone and knew, somehow, that this was not just any prophecy. This was the one she feared most. Her body felt cold, numb. Nick knelt in front of the stone.

"Read the last verse," she said.

"Meg—"

"Just read it, Nick. We can talk about it after."

"*In death's beyond, she'll find her way, until the day of dark,*" he began. She pressed the back of her hand to her mouth. He glanced up at her and continued. *"When sun and moon shall blend the lines, return the child to start. For in this place, where Æren sleeps, a Writer's history calls. Ancient words will bear the end; her Guard, at last, must fall."*

"No," she whispered. "No. Nick, we can't…" Her voice failed her as she stared at him. The last verse, the missing verse, meant more than her death. It meant her Guardian's, too. Cal filled that role now, but the Elders would give it back to Nick soon.

"It means nothing." Nick took her hands in his. "Little in this prophecy has made sense so far."

"It specifically says I'll die this time," she told him.

"So what? It's a prophecy with no context. It might as well be a bedtime story, for all we know about it. We can't keep living as if death waited for us around every corner."

Meaghan closed her eyes, and then buried her face in Nick's shirt. He folded her into his arms. "You went into Zeiihbu certain the prophecy meant you would die," he whispered. "We were wrong about it then. What makes you think we aren't now?"

She turned her head, pressing her ear to Nick's chest. His heart beat a slow, steady pace that confirmed his certainty. She listened to it, counting each thump until it calmed her fears. If death wanted her, it would take her no matter how hard she fought against it. If not, why send it a decorated invitation? The choice belonged to her. Believe in a prophecy she had no control over, no definition for, or take each step, each breath as if the prophecy never existed.

She peered up at Nick. "It's time we controlled our own destiny."

Nick grazed his lips across her forehead. "Your father said something similar in the Writer's book. Or rather, he thought it. You made him realize he had to control his destiny. You've done the same for me."

"Then it's settled," Meaghan told him. She recited the same spell Laegoli had used and the stone disappeared, she hoped forever.

"They're right over here," a voice broadcast across the field. Meaghan looked toward it in time to see one of the Zeiihbuans gesturing at her and Nick from his tent a few hundred yards away. Whoever had been looking for them must have gestured back an acknowledgement, because the soldier returned to his perch on an overturned log.

Nick sighed. "So much for an hour. Do you suppose it's the Elders?"

Before Meaghan could answer, Faillen and Caide rounded the corner. Meaghan's relief came short-lived when she realized both men had storm clouds weathered over their faces.

"The Elders?" Nick asked.

Faillen nodded. "It appears they've sent everyone out to find you and they've informed me that I'm not invited to this meeting."

"I can guess why."

"I can't," Meaghan said. "What happened?"

"I'll fill you in on the way," Nick told her. "The short version is they aren't happy about Cadell being here."

"They're going to be even less happy when you tell them the real reason for Dat's arrival," Faillen said.

"I'm looking forward to that."

"Be careful, Nick. You don't want to turn allies into enemies. You have enough of those already."

"I'll be diplomatic," Nick said.

Faillen's half-smile told Meaghan he doubted Nick's words.

"Caide," Nick addressed Faillen's son. "It's almost time for that spell I needed. Is it ready?"

"Close," Caide said. "I need to test it."

"Test it on your father. No one else can know."

Caide nodded. Nick took Meaghan's hand and they threaded their way through the village. The Elders waited for them in the center square. They offered only a few cordial greetings before escorting Meaghan and Nick into May's one-story house. The front room held a couch and several chairs. No one sat. They faced each other in a circle. Cal and May flanked Nick and Meaghan. Sam and Miles stood opposite them.

"I'm sure we can all agree that it's nice to have Cal and Meaghan back home," Miles said. His eyes coasted around the circle, then settled on Nick as the last of his words spilled from his mouth. "Most of us, anyway."

"I don't appreciate the insinuation," Nick told him. "Meaghan and I are fine."

"Glad to hear it. Your obligations—"

"I'm aware of my obligations."

Miles knitted his hands together in front of him. "I don't think you are. The royal family and Elders work in tandem, not against each other. Yet you consistently argue with us and go behind our backs."

"And you seem to relish in keeping information from us," Nick said. "I don't just mean what happened with Talea and Artair's village. Meaghan told me about the Explorers."

Miles's hot gaze shot to Cal, then back to Nick. "That has no bearing on this conversation."

"Doesn't it? You don't trust us. That has plenty of bearing. And you think you can make decisions without our input. Elders have say over Guardians, Miles, not the kingdom. Or did you intend to change that?"

"How dare you," Miles growled. He stepped forward, his face hard. "You're nothing more than a simpleminded mole worm if you think—"

May put a hand on Miles's shoulder to stop him. "Calm down. Nick didn't mean it that way."

"Yes, I did," Nick said. "We appreciate what you've done over the last fifteen years—"

"Our sacrifices you mean," Sam interrupted. "You appreciate our *sacrifices*, and there have been many. Our leadership over this kingdom began when you were a child, Nick. I taught you in school. Miles helped train you. Don't forget that."

"I don't," Nick said. "I remember well what you taught me, how you stressed the importance of keeping the leadership division intact, so no one would hold too much power. Have *you* forgotten?"

"Of course not," Sam said. "But we all have to agree to wage war. You can't decide that on your own, like you did at Talea's village."

"Right," Nick scoffed. "Because I prefer fighting an entire army with only three people. The Mardróch attacked us, not the other way around."

May sighed. "Look, Nick, you have to admit that you've been less than cooperative over the last few months."

"And you've been less than forthcoming. We're already at war, whether or not you agree to it. It's time to fight. It's time to reclaim the castle."

"I'd be willing to entertain the discussion," Miles said. "After all, we have plenty of time for the debate. Without commcrystals, we can't easily reach our villages. It'll take time to dispatch messengers and longer, still, to gather everyone. I'd say we're easily a month or two away from battle."

"This isn't a discussion."

Miles waved his hand through the air, dismissing Nick's anger with the gesture. "Semantics aside, you can't make things go any faster."

"I can and I have," Nick said, his voice cold. "I started sending marching orders using the gildonae months ago. We've contacted all of the villages. We meet the week after next."

"You did *what?*" May's cheeks flared red. "Nick, you know the Guardian army is at our command, not yours. You just said so yourself."

"I didn't send any messages to the Guardians. I sent them to the village leaders."

"So the Guardians are supposed to choose between abandoning their posts and disobeying our orders not to fight?" Sam asked.

"Guardians don't abandon their posts," Nick told him.

"Is that so?" Miles crossed his arms over his chest. "So you've turned this into a battle between the Elders and the crown. And you had the gall to accuse *me* of treason."

Nick took a step toward Miles, closing off the distance between them. He flexed his hand at his side and for a moment, Meaghan thought he might grab the Elder, but he maintained control. "My actions aren't treason. I'm the king, Miles, not you."

"Who do you think allowed that?" Miles shot back. "Kings and queens still have to be anointed by the Elders."

"That's only a formality and you know it," Cal said. "I watched the Elders flaunt that over Ed and Adelina for too long without saying anything and I won't do it again. The Elders can't prevent the royal line from ascending the throne any more than they can dictate when the moon hides behind a cloud. You're letting your authority blind you."

"Am I?" Miles rounded on Cal. "We've protected our people from Garon, kept them alive for over fifteen years, yet Nick thinks he can come in here and—"

"Do what he thinks is best for his people?" May asked. She kept her voice low and soft, but it sliced through Miles's protest anyway. "Isn't that what we wanted Nick and Meaghan to do? Isn't that their *job?*"

Miles shook his head. "It isn't time yet, May. They're too young, too inexperienced."

"You mean they aren't *you.*"

Miles pressed his lips into a thin line and glared at May. "Yes, perhaps."

"I understand," May told him. "It's hard to let go. You've been doing this a long time. You taught the kingdom how to hope when we had only blood and heartbreak to fill our days. You taught us how to rebuild when all we had were cracked foundations. You helped us find order, a real life again when we became trapped inside our own villages like prisoners. You're the reason most of us are still here. We know that and we're grateful, but if you stand in the way of this happening, you'll soon be the reason we all die."

"You can't be certain of that," Sam said. "Vivian said the prophecy applied to this war. It was right about the gildonae signaling our next move. We waited for the sign and Meaghan went into Zeiihbu when the time was right. If we hadn't waited, we'd likely be dead now."

Cal grunted. "Maybe. We can't be certain of that either."

"It worked out, didn't it?" Miles asked.

"Inaction is a form of action," Meaghan said. She had remained silent, watching as the fight brewed, but the moment had come for her to take the lead. This was her obligation, her kingdom, more so than Nick's. "The prophecy is murky. By choosing not to do anything, we might be going against what it wants us to do, too."

"I don't think the line we're waiting for can be misinterpreted," Sam said.

"Which one?" Cal asked.

"*Upon the loss of child's heart, freedom doth depend,*" Sam quoted.

"I see." Meaghan narrowed her eyes. "So why not take a knife to me if you think it's so important? Why not build an altar and make a sacrifice?"

"Don't be so dramatic," Miles said. "It may not be literal, but Sam's point is valid. The sign hasn't come."

Meaghan drew up to her full height. "We'll die before that

prophecy becomes clear," she said. "Either at Garon's hand or by old age. I'd rather die on my own terms than spend my life afraid to move because it might go against an incoherent prophecy. We *will* fight, with or without you. I want you at my side, but I won't sacrifice this opportunity. We're ready and we do our people a disservice by believing otherwise."

"What if you're wrong?"

"What if she's right?" Nick countered. "By waiting, we've given Garon control. We wait for him to attack and cower until he does. What sort of life is that, Miles?"

"One that isn't death. Or worse," Sam said. "Can you live with the guilt of knowing you handed our people over to Garon to become slaves? You don't understand—"

"No," Miles interrupted. His gaze held sadness when he fixed it on Sam. "We're the ones who no longer understand."

"Miles—"

Miles shook his head, silencing Sam's protest. "We made a pact in the beginning. Do you remember it? We promised we would do whatever it took to get the kingdom back. We promised to keep fighting no matter how long it took. When did we stop doing that?"

Sam looked down at his hands. They held the dark spots and wrinkles of a long life. Meaghan saw them tremble before he closed them into fists. "I don't know," he whispered and though tears coated his eyes, he held them back. "How do we know the traitors haven't already told Garon about our battle plans? We still don't know who they are. We could be marching into a trap."

"The villagers think they're being transferred to a new home,"

Nick told him. "For whatever reason, Garon has chosen not to attack up to this point. I doubt a move will change that."

"And when everyone arrives at the rendezvous point?" Miles asked. "What then? We'll have to tell them the truth."

"Don't worry. I have a plan."

Cal grinned. "Somehow, I knew that would be your answer."

CHAPTER TWENTY-FOUR

THEY TRICKLED in at first, by the dozens as people arrived from the smallest and closest villages, then by the hundreds when larger villages and those from the farthest reaches of the kingdom found their assigned meeting points.

Meaghan glanced past rows of bland green tents to the trees beyond them. Six camps had been set up like this one over the last few days. Each one was protected by fifty blue crystals the size of one of Meaghan's fists. The crystals hung from trees and wooden posts, enacted by the strongest powers in the kingdom.

A new group of villagers arrived at the base of a twisted, red oak tree in the middle of the clearing. Several horses trailed the first men and women in line, and Nick nodded toward them. "Equine Masters. Our cavalry comes from some of our remotest villages."

Villages Nick had trained to fight while Meaghan rescued Caide in Zeiihbu. Nick pointed to a young boy petting a skittish black roan. "That's Ambler. He tamed my horse, Equus."

Ambler turned his back on the tent village, unable to see it just as the other men and women he had traveled with could not. Meaghan squinted to focus on the boy. His angular body seemed to hold more bone than muscle.

"What is he…thirteen?"

"Unless he's had a birthday since I met him."

"He's not much more than a child, Nick. I thought children were supposed to stay behind."

"In most cases," Faillen said. "Those who are seventeen or older will fight. The younger Healers and Equine Masters will help us from the outskirts of the battle. Ambler will be invaluable in preparing the horses."

And he would learn the grisly realities of death at far too young an age. Meaghan watched Ambler laugh with the freedom of naïveté and felt weak from the realization.

"I'd better greet them," Nick said.

Faillen nodded. "I believe these are the last of the villagers for this location. I'll get Caide, and then it's on to our last stop."

§

BY THE time Meaghan stepped across the boundary line for their last camp, three traitors walked in tow behind her, bound with rope. This tent village, the largest, housed the villagers who had lived alongside Nick for months. Family and close friends would undergo the same scrutiny as strangers and Meaghan feared what would come of the interrogation. They had decided to make this their final stop for that reason.

The Elders met them in a secluded section of the woods, away from the curiosity of villagers and soldiers. Cal and Sam hung back while May and Miles approached. May hugged her son, though joy did not brighten her face when she stepped back from him and eyed the trio of prisoners.

"Dolan," she said, her voice heavy as she approached the oldest man in the center. Sunlight gleamed off his balding head, though his deep russet eyes appeared shadowed. He scowled, the gesture etching deeper wrinkles into his face. "I never would have thought you a traitor. I fought beside you when the Mardróch first attacked the castle. Your own sister was killed soon after by Garon's soldiers."

"My loyalty is to the kingdom as it always has been," Dolan said.

"Yet you spy for Garon, the worst threat to the kingdom's survival."

"He isn't the worst," Dolan said and his gaze coasted to Meaghan. "I've collected information. That's all. It isn't for Garon's ears."

May crossed her arms over her chest. "Then who is it for?"

"Not you," Dolan replied. May slipped a knife from her belt and took a step toward him. She pointed the blade at his throat. He did not flinch. "You aren't a murderer," he said. "I know you too well."

"And I don't know you at all, it appears," she said, though she sheathed her blade. She turned her attention to a white-haired woman at Dolan's right, and then a man around Nick's age on Dolan's left. "I don't know these other two," she said.

"I do," Miles said and nodded toward the woman. "Mysta wed a good friend of mine who was loyal to the crown. I'm certain of that, and I'm guessing he never knew about Mysta's duplicity or he wouldn't have fallen in love with her."

Mysta lifted her chin and stared straight ahead.

"She was assigned to one of our horse villages, which means Garon knows about our efforts with the cavalry. And this Guardian," Miles placed a hand on the younger man's shoulder, "is Phylline's nephew. I guess we now know who betrayed her."

"I didn't," the man said, then yelped when Miles tightened his grip. The tips of Miles's fingers turned white with the pressure.

"Don't lie to me, Paster. If it wasn't you, who was it?"

Paster shook his head. Like Mysta, he stared straight ahead, his chocolate brown eyes wide in unspoken denial.

"We're not going to get anything out of them," May said.

"No, we're not," Sam agreed. "At least not without help."

"Which is why we have Caide," Nick said. "I asked him to create a truth spell. It helped us find these three."

"No kidding?" Cal clapped Caide on the shoulder. The force of his impact sent the young Zeiihbuan forward a couple of inches. "I had no idea you'd gotten so strong."

"We've only asked basic yes or no questions so far," Caide said. "It may not work the way you want."

"It's worth a try," Miles said. "But it can wait an hour. Get settled in your tents. We'll reconvene before dinner. Some time with May as their guard should change their minds." Miles glared at Dolan. "You don't know her as well as you think, either."

At first, Meaghan believed Miles's words powered an empty threat. As she and Nick stepped into the clearing, she looked back over her shoulder, surprised to discover May had slipped her knife from her belt once more. Torture, it appeared, belonged to both sides in this war.

Meaghan followed Nick along a grassy path to their assigned tent. As soon as the tent flaps closed, her worry blossomed.

"Will your mother hurt them?" she asked.

Nick unpacked their few belongings without answering, though his pressed lips told her he debated the same question. He set a toothbrush and comb on a stump that served as their nightstand, then slipped the Writer's book into his pillowcase. When he handed her their clothes—one change each—she folded them and tucked them beneath her cot.

"I wish I could say no," he finally answered when she stretched out on top of her blanket. "The truth is I'm not certain. Mom could easily do it and hide the evidence by healing the traitors."

Meaghan ran an index finger over the corn husk doll tucked into the waistband of her pants. A few villagers had asked about it at the last two camps, expressing fascination at the idea of transferring power to an object. While Caide's spell would work faster at revealing their traitor than waiting for him or her to steal the doll, a backup plan never hurt. If both failed, May's tactic might be their only option.

"It's not right," she decided.

"It's war. We need the information."

Meaghan shifted onto her side, making room for Nick and he lay down beside her. His hand drifted underneath the hem of her shirt. She cushioned her body in his arms, and once more regretted the decision to deny her love for so long. Too much alone time had been wasted in their cabin. Now it seemed they had so little of it. Nick feathered kisses along her jaw. Chills raced down her spine.

"Are you scared?" she asked him.

"Yeah. You?"

She nodded and closed her eyes. His lips found her collarbone. "It feels like the next few days will bring the end of everything," she said. "I just don't know if it's the end of everything good or bad."

"Bad." Nick traced a hand through her hair, and then drew it down her back. "We'll defeat Garon. We have to believe that or no one else will."

"Do we have to pretend around each other?"

Nick rolled on top of her. "Never, Meg, but I do believe it. I refuse to think I can lose you again. You have to believe it, too. Promise me."

"I promise," she said and wrapped her arms around his neck, then drew his head down to hers. As soon as their kiss deepened, the sound of something bouncing across the floor broke Meaghan's concentration. She glanced down as a gray stone came to rest beside her cot, then refocused her gaze on the tent entrance. Another pebble launched through the seam of the closed flaps. It skidded across the floor, and then stopped at the base of the tree stump with a dull ping.

Max's voice followed the second rock. "Anyone home?"

Nick groaned and sat up. "Go away."

One of the tent flaps folded back and Max stuck his head inside. A lopsided grin gleamed white across his tanned skin. "Don't get mad at me. The Elders sent for you. They said your Mom's drawn a little too much blood."

"Figures," Nick muttered. "We'll be right there."

Max let the flap drift closed, but stuck around outside long enough to give Nick and Meaghan hugs before leaving them to their duties. They moved as quickly as they could, though not as quickly as they wanted. Friends of Nick's or villagers intent on meeting the queen stopped them often. Meaghan smiled and offered short greetings to avoid alarming anyone, but her anxiety grew with each delay.

When she and Nick finally reached the Elders, they caught May with a hand hovering over a cut on Paster's cheek. Nick cleared his throat, the unspoken accusation earning a glare from his mother.

"I didn't do it," she said. "He tripped over his rope trying to escape."

"Too bad," Cal said, showing up a step behind Nick. "I rather enjoyed the thought of you fileting our traitors."

Sam chuckled and Miles silenced him with a raised hand. Faillen and Caide waited beside the Head Elder.

"Let's get this over with," Miles said. "Caide, are you ready?"

Caide nodded. He took a deep breath and stepped forward. Meaghan released the control she held over her empath power, intending to use it on the spies. Caide's emotions caught her attention first. Fear emanated from him so strong that it stalled her breath. She had watched him perform this same spell dozens of times over the last few days. She had never once guessed it made him nervous. Faillen placed a hand on his son's shoulder.

"The strongest power in creation," Caide started reciting, *"the greatest gift of our relation—our self-control, our living will, the realities our minds fulfill. Removed within these words, this spell, in breath alone you each shall dwell. Utter*

not a word of lies; spill forth the truth, at last realized."

"Beautiful," Sam muttered. "The spell doesn't work like a truth potion. It doesn't force them to speak against their will. It removes their self-control so they want to do exactly what Caide asks of them. In this case, tell the truth."

Caide's hands shook and he tucked them into his pockets. Meaghan doubted anyone else had seen his slip, but it had been enough for her to understand his fear. Stilgan's mind control power had been Caide's inspiration for the truth spell. To change his command over those under the spell, he only had to alter the last line.

"Answer the Elders' questions," Caide instructed the traitors.

"Who brought you into the Shadow Guard?" Miles asked.

Mysta answered first. Her pale blue eyes now appeared vacant. "My father."

"Mine, as well," Dolan said.

"My grandmother," Paster added.

"That makes sense," Miles said. "Paster's parents were killed in a village raid several years ago. Estelle has raised him since."

"Isn't she the one who's caring for Phylline's children?" Nick asked.

Miles nodded. "Paster, did Estelle betray Phylline?"

"Aunt Phyl got too close to figuring out the truth."

"I see. We need to get the children away from her. Nick, did you leave someone in charge in each village, similar to Neiszhe's post in our village?"

"Yes," Nick said. "In this case, a non-Guardian named Varuca.

I'm not sure she's strong enough to go up against Estelle, though."

"I'll give her a binding spell," Miles said and glanced at Faillen. "Do you mind if we send a note using the gildonae?"

Faillen draped a cloak over his arm and held it out. A screech sliced the air, followed closely behind by a large raptor. It dove for Faillen, a blur of feathers and sharp talons, then it pulled up short to grip Faillen's arm like a perch. Gold glistened on the underside of the bird's wings as it settled them at its side.

"I guess that takes care of our first problem," Sam said as Faillen and Miles walked away from the group. Sam rubbed his hands together. "Let's see if we have any other issues. Answer May's question. How much have you three shared with Garon?"

"Nothing," Mysta said.

Cal crossed his arms over his chest. "Now why is it I have a hard time believing that?"

"It's true," Dolan told him. "Few people work directly with Garon. We tell the Tribunal and they decide what he gets to hear."

"The Tribunal," Cal said. "You mean the governing body of the Shadow Guard."

"Yes," Mysta confirmed.

"So what exactly do they know?"

Panic surged through Meaghan's power and she cast a glance over her shoulder. The emotion had come from behind them, not in front. Surprise eclipsed the first emotion. She thought she saw a shadow, but when the dark shape and emotions vanished, she brought her attention back to the traitors.

No one answered Cal's question.

"Dolan, tell us what they know," Sam said.

"*Let black eclipse your eyes*," Dolan began reciting instead. The vacancy had disappeared from his gaze. "*Rest at once until—*"

Sam extended his right hand and Dolan's voice ceased. "That's enough of that," Sam said. "You didn't think I'd recognize a sleep spell when I heard it?"

Dolan closed his mouth, frowned, and then opened it again. No noise passed his lips.

"My power," Sam told him. "I steal voices. I think I'll keep yours for a while." He gestured toward Mysta and Paster. "Yours, too, in case you get any ideas."

Mysta shook her head. Any protests she tried to vocalize came out as gasps of breath.

"I guess this means Caide's spell is over," May said.

"It shouldn't be," Caide told her. "They have to be released."

"Clearly they were," Cal said. "Intentionally or not, you let them go. My guess is you've overextended your power. Rest some more. We'll try again later."

"Okay," Caide conceded, though the doubt dragging lines down his face echoed Meaghan's own feeling. Something had gone wrong.

She reached for the top of the corn husk doll's head. Her fingers brushed cotton. A quick scan of her waistband confirmed that the doll had disappeared. Nick frowned at her when she looked up again. Too many people had greeted them after they left the tent. They would never be able to determine who had taken it in an effort to steal her empath power. They could confirm only one thing.

A traitor still lived among them, passing information to the

Tribunal and possibly Garon. Without Caide's spell, they would be a lot more than sitting ducks. They would be the center feast for Garon's celebration gala.

CHAPTER TWENTY-FIVE

CAIDE'S GAZE trailed over the line of green tents, from A-frame to A-frame as their soft sides rippled from an almost imperceptible breeze. One-by-one, the yellow glow leaking from the door flaps of each temporary home extinguished, marking the soldiers' journeys into slumber. Soon, the only light keeping night's black fingers at bay would be Caide's own. His father held conference with the king and queen. He would return soon. Caide did not want to be here when he did. Failure would shadow the flint color in his father's eyes, much as it darkened Caide's heart.

He ducked through the opening of his tent, shoved his pillow under his blanket to give the illusion of a sleeping body, and then snuffed out the candle resting on the stump between his cot and his father's. With any luck, his father would assume he slept and crawl into bed without using the light. It would give Caide time to think and maybe enough time to sort out what he had done wrong.

Threading his way through the densest part of the tent city, he held his breath and hoped no one would notice him. His luck held, and he moved into a cluster of trees that housed the outskirts of the camp. Only a few tents dotted this section. The king's closest friend, Max, had chosen one of these spots as his own, as had Cal. Both men wanted privacy for different reasons. Max had always preferred solitude, at least since Caide had known him. And Cal used this remote location to practice battle techniques with small tornadoes. Several saplings leaned sideways, a few others reached toward the moon with corkscrew trunks and Caide had to suppress a laugh at the sight of them. Cal's command over his power held equal parts art and skill.

The sides of Max's tent flickered from his candle. As Caide passed, the light disappeared. Cal's tent remained dark. The Elder attended the same meeting as Caide's father.

Beyond these last two tents, blue lights danced along the trees and circled the field, each serving as an end point for a line Caide dared not cross. No matter how much he wanted time alone, he would not risk the lives of everyone in this camp for that need. It only took one person to give away the camp's location to the Mardróch.

Caide traced the inner boundary of the crystals' power until he found a small pond. Although half the pond lay outside the protection, half remained within it. A tree trunk had fallen along the water's edge. Caide sat down on it, then took his shoes off and slid his feet into the night-chilled water. Circles rippled outward from where his ankles rose above the surface.

"Penny for your thoughts."

The voice interrupting his solitude would have startled Caide if he had not known it so well. It had comforted him nearly every day of his captivity, soothed him when pain gnawed at his body with razor fangs, and eased his torment after Stilgan had forced him to perform horrifying acts that still fed his nightmares. Emma had done more than heal his wounds. She had kept him sane by talking to him when he needed a friend most. Even when he could not see past the darkness, her voice had given him light.

He looked up at her. A warm smile danced across her lips. Moonlight cast a soft glow over her deep olive skin, and glistened over the satin strands of her black hair. Without waiting for an invitation, she sat next to him.

"Penny for your thoughts," she repeated.

Caide drew his brows together. "What's a penny?"

Emma giggled. The sound seemed to bounce across the water, echoing back like chimes in a summer breeze. "I have no idea. I heard Queen Meaghan say it to King Nick the other day. I think it's just a fun way of asking what's on your mind."

"Oh," Caide said. "I don't know. I'm just thinking, I guess."

Emma nudged him with her shoulder. "About?"

He shrugged. Her tone was light, playful, and he hated to drag down her mood with the weight of his own. "Nothing, really," he lied. "It's a nice night. I couldn't sleep with everything happening."

"The battle, you mean?" she asked, then cocked her head to the side as she studied him. "No, that's not it, is it? You're thinking about what happened today."

He frowned. "How could you possibly know that?"

"Because I know you. You feel responsible for everything."

Caide turned his attention back to the pond. "I *am* responsible.

Someday for Zeiihbu and for now…" He spread his hands out in front of him. "Do you realize how much this spell means to the king?"

"Of course," Emma said and took one of his hands into her own. The warmth of it softened his anger. "You put too much pressure on yourself. I don't expect anything from you, and I don't think anyone else does, either. Your power needs time to develop."

"That's the problem. I thought I had this spell. It worked at the other camps, but now it's failed twice. First when we needed information from the traitors and then after dinner when I tried to find the Shadow Guard member here. I can't figure out what happened. Cal thinks I'm tired."

"Are you?"

Caide shook his head. Although the spell had been complex, he had been careful not to let exhaustion overtake him. "I keep thinking that maybe I won't ever get it right. Not just this spell. Any of it."

"Why would you think that?"

Caide looked up at Emma, expecting to see judgment in her eyes. He found none. Her smile shared kindness he could not begin to measure.

He sighed. "I don't know, Emma. I sometimes wonder if what happened to me in Zeiihbu broke me to the point where I can't be fixed."

"You aren't broken."

"You can't know that. What if he—"

"You aren't," she insisted. "I can tell."

"How?"

"I've seen it before, in a survivor from one of the destroyed villages," she said, and released his hand. Her fingers trembled when she pushed them through her hair. "Sensing someone with my power is a lot like swimming through a river. This man felt like jumping across rocks. I could feel his pain, the presence of his injuries, but nothing connected. Pieces of him were missing."

"What happened to him?" Caide asked.

"We made him comfortable, healed his bones, but that's all we could do. His brain is a child's now."

Caide studied Emma's face and the shadows hiding her eyes. He wanted to reach out to her and offer comfort. He cleared his throat instead. "That doesn't mean I'm not broken. If I were at the beginning of my decline, I might not be bad enough for your power to sense it."

"No, it would. I can sense the smallest breaks. A few people in the village have them, but you don't. Maybe it's a miracle after what you went through, or maybe you're just stronger than you think."

"Maybe," he said, and let the night eclipse their conversation. Somewhere beyond the crystals, crickets chirped in symphonic greeting. Emma's hand found his once more.

"I thought I was broken, too, for a while," she told him. "I kept thinking I saw Mardróch in the alleys and shadows."

"I see Stilgan everywhere," Caide confessed.

Emma nodded and rested her head against his shoulder. "I was angry all the time. I dreamed about sneaking into the castle to kill Garon. I slaughtered every one of his Mardróch. Their blood covered me and filled my mouth. It tasted metallic and I *enjoyed* it. I woke up screaming for a long time after we moved to the village."

Caide closed his eyes and pressed his cheek to her forehead. "I still do," he said. "I want revenge, Emma."

"May says that's normal. Maybe it is, but it doesn't feel normal to me. It feels alive, like any moment it could consume me. It scares me."

"Me too."

"We won't let it, though. We can't. We didn't let Stilgan defeat us when he tortured us, when he killed people we loved. We can't let him start controlling us now."

Caide tightened his grip on her hand. "But he does, doesn't he? I froze when I faced a Mardróch. He could have killed the king and Max because of me, but I couldn't react. What if that happens again?"

Emma raised her head to look at him.

"What if I spend the rest of my life in fear, unable to truly use my power because of what Stilgan did to me?"

"And what if you don't?" she asked. "What if you keep trying until you get past your fear? He only wins if you give up."

A part of Caide knew she was right. Stilgan's death had released Caide from his grip. Yet another part of him wondered if Stilgan lived forever in the brands he had marked on Caide's mind. Emma had endured almost as much as he had, but she had not used her power for harm. She had not tasted the vileness of it, and the glorious freedom that came with removing every restraint. Anything he wanted could be his with the right words.

All it would cost him was his humanity.

"I'm not afraid of him, Emma," he whispered. "I'm afraid of me. I'm afraid of what I can do. Every time I write a spell, I long to let my spellmaster power explode, to unleash it again and feel the thrill that comes when it has no limits."

"And then what?"

"Then…" He hesitated. "Everything, I suppose. I could destroy Garon and his army. I could restore Ærenden to its good days."

Emma shrugged. "Okay. So why don't you then? If you could save us all, keep us from dying in battle, why would you wait?"

Caide stared at her, numbed by the callous way she welcomed mass destruction, and then jumped to his feet. The water ran from him in overlapping waves. "I wouldn't be able to stop, Emma. I'd be no better than those monsters. Do you really want that?"

She lifted an eyebrow in response, curious more than concerned. The gesture irritated him.

"Why are you here?" he demanded. "I came to be alone."

"You came to think," she said. "And you needed someone who understands what you're feeling. That's why I'm here. But to answer your first question, no. I don't want that."

"Then why encourage it? Don't you know what I'm capable of?"

"Of course I do. You forget. I was there. I watched Stilgan push you beyond your limits, force you to use your power in ways no one ever imagined. You surprised him."

"But not you," Caide said and the words tasted bitter. "You said you didn't expect anything of me. That's not true, is it? You want revenge as badly as I do."

"You're such an idiot," Emma said and stood, nudging him to

make room for her. "Of *course* you surprised me, and of *course* I'm not trying to encourage you to do those things. I'm trying to help you see how stupid you're being."

"Stop calling me names."

She rolled her eyes. "Fine, but you are being stupid. Think about this logically for a minute, okay? You're a good man, Caide. You couldn't do those things, not if it meant turning into a monster. But let's say the draw of your power was too much for you to overcome, you're not strong enough to kill an entire army. You looked tired after destroying our ceremonial hut."

"Stilgan had been torturing me."

"True, but I've noticed that powers have built-in controls. We grow tired for a reason. Can you honestly tell me you'd be capable of blowing up a castle without passing out?"

Caide had thought so at the start of this conversation. Now he was not as certain. If his power had no limits, why had Garon been able to kill the last Spellmaster? With a few words, Farrow could have ended Garon's life, yet he had met the same fate as too many with weaker powers.

Caide returned his attention to the glowing protection crystals, and then sought the surface of the pond. Tranquil water reflected dots of blue back at him, unerring in their clarity.

A spell could be just as difficult to wield as Cal's tornadoes. Cal had needed years of practice to manage a small funnel. Despite that experience, he rarely touched anything larger for fear it would destroy him as easily as it did his target.

The spell that gave the blue crystals their power had taken months or years to design. A spell with the destructive impact Emma had proposed would take Caide longer to write than the war would last. He might guess the right words sooner, as he had with his spell to shut off magic in Artair and Talea's village, but more likely than not, he would fail. A spell created with minimal thought had minimal impact.

Because powers had built-in controls. If a powerful spell came easily, a Spellmaster would not have enough time to analyze its repercussions. Even with every precaution, no one could fully predict a spell's outcome. It spread like ripples on the water, following nature's command rather than the Spellmaster's wishes.

Caide slipped a hand into his pocket. The scrap of paper Ella had given Nick hummed against Caide's skin. Farrow had to become a target of his own monsters to learn that lesson.

"You're right," Caide said.

"I'm always right," Emma joked, and the confidence lifting her tone warmed him. Years before, he had known her as a shy girl, almost timid. Apprenticing with the king's mother had helped her understand her own importance.

Caide hooked an arm around her shoulders and drew her against him in a playful hug. The moment her body pressed against his, he realized the gesture had been a mistake. Her breath danced across his neck, warming his blood and his desire. An image of Mycale's face shot through his mind and Caide set Emma back once more.

"We should get some sleep," he said.

"Yeah. Stay safe, okay?"

"You too."

She brushed a kiss across his cheek, and then retreated to the camp. He stared after her, watching as she disappeared among the trees. Caide's father had ordered Caide's return to the village, where its security would swaddle him like a child. Emma would be far from safe. As she saved soldiers on the outskirts of the battle, she would become a target for the unscrupulous Mardróch intent on weakening the army's ability to heal.

He wished he could be at her side.

CHAPTER TWENTY-SIX

NICK FOUND his tent more out of luck than knowledge. He knew the general direction he had to travel, but with only the moonlight to guide him, his tired eyes tricked him into missing stakes and pitch lines. Despite a few stumbles, he managed to avoid waking anyone in his near-blind meandering.

Once safely inside his tent, he lit a lantern and hung it from the center pole. Meaghan had stayed behind to talk to Faillen. She would return soon, if she decided to sleep. Nerves plagued all of them tonight.

Nick slid under his blanket and reached for the Writer's book. Underneath the plain brown cover, the story of King Ed and Queen Adelina's wedding stared back at him, deceptive in its simple black and white words. This one moment in history had started them all down the path they now traveled. Without Ed's interference, Garon might have been able to convince Adelina to try his tactics on the Zeiihbuans. Without their prophesied wedding, the Shadow Guard would still be hibernating. And without that moment in time, Nick would not have Meaghan.

He clutched the book tightly within his fingers. Meaghan would sacrifice her life to change the past if she could. Nick did not want to think of a world without her in it.

Flipping through the pages, he skimmed the story, and then turned each blank page following it with a deliberate eye, looking for anything to keep his mind off the upcoming battle. Toward the back of the book, new writing stopped his fingers from moving. Paragraphs appeared first, bleeding black into white, one line at a time. Then a title came into focus next. Unlike the other stories in the book, this one did not have a number, but a name: *The Final Chapter*.

Somehow, Nick knew he would not want to read it. He allowed the page to settle beneath his gaze anyway, and within a heartbeat, a past world enveloped him.

§

A FIRE snapped in the hearth, sending sparks cascading toward the screen in a bright yellow arc. Meaghan giggled and raced toward it, then squealed when Ed scooped her up and swung her through the air.

"Stop that," Adelina lectured, though the smile she attempted to hide behind her hand did little to add impact to her words. "You'll hurt her!"

Ed swung his little girl around again, mesmerized by her effortless joy. Each turn around the room brought a fresh round of giggles, punctuated by a single command, "Again, Daddy!"

"Come on, Ed," Adelina protested. She swatted at his arm. "Put her down."

"Not a chance." He shifted Meaghan to his hip, and then scooped Adelina against his other side with his free arm, spinning all three of them with the same momentum. "Not until we all fall down from dizziness."

"Ed!" Adelina tried to protest again. The objection dissolved in a fit of laughter. She gave into his motion, their twirling turning into an unsteady waltz. When they neared the back of their living room, Ed dipped both his wife and child into an awkward bow, delivering sloppy kisses to their faces before letting them go. Meaghan plopped down on the ground with the same enthusiastic squeal that had started the adventure. Adelina braced her arm against the wall, her crooked smile and sedate head shake no more a reprimand than her words had been. Before she could regain her balance, he stepped forward and swept her backward again, extending their kiss with more finesse and seduction than he had before.

"You get more wonderful every day," he told her.

"And you get more annoying," she teased.

"Give me time. I'll grow on you."

"Like sticky moss, maybe." She poked him in the ribs. "Even a good spell couldn't get rid of you."

"Not a chance," he said and pressed his lips to hers once more, savoring how easily their love flowed between them. Every moment like this reminded him why he stayed. Despite the politics, the headaches of trying to knit together a divided kingdom, and the constant battles with their advisor, his family had been worth the sacrifice.

He slid a hand down Adelina's side, caressing, then stepped back when small fingers tugged on his pant leg.

"Daddy!"

Ed glanced down at the tiny being his love with Adelina had created. Wide, copper eyes stared back at him.

"Yes, Meaghan?"

"Play."

Sweeping an arm in front of him, he bowed low. "Of course, my love. I am at your command."

Meaghan's giggle filled the room, bringing a smile to his face. Her hand slipped into his. Joy blossomed within Ed's heart, and then faded when he turned around.

A page stood in the door to their royal suite, the crisp preparation of his bright yellow tunic a stark contrast to pockmarks on his face. He stared ahead, his eyes unfocused as he tried not to witness the family scene before him. Ed wondered how long he had been waiting.

"What can we do for you, Degan?" Adelina asked, the breezy tone in her voice both forgiveness and welcome for the young boy. Ed doubted he could have managed such grace at the interruption.

"The Elders, my queen."

"What about them?"

"They," Degan's voice cracked. He cleared his throat. "I was told they wanted to speak to the king."

Adelina glanced toward Ed and shrugged. He doubted the page had caught her gesture, or the worry that flickered over her face. Ed knew her anxiety. Each meeting with the Elders brought him closer to being cast out, even years after he had arrived. Lately, he had managed to avoid them and the fights their meetings brought. It seemed luck no longer stood by his side.

"Let me get someone to watch Meaghan," Adelina said.

"Um…" The page glanced between Adelina and Ed. "They said just the king."

Ed raised an eyebrow, but gave into the request. If Adelina could avoid the drama, he would not argue against it. After all, the Guardian leaders loved her. Ed did not want to taint their favoritism.

He followed Degan out of the suite. A guard he did not recognize flanked the door, his arms at his sides in attention.

"Where's Cal?" Ed asked.

"Called away on duty, Sire," the man stated. He stared ahead, his gaze focused on a point over Ed's shoulder. Ed bit his tongue to keep from snapping at Cal's temporary replacement. Although the wrinkles at the corners of the man's dusky blue eyes placed him at Cal's age or a little older, angular cheekbones and a bony chin gave him a youthful appearance. Wisps of blonde hair circled around the stone gray beret of a castle guard's uniform—a sign he had been hand-chosen for the position due to his combat skills—and Ed decided not to mention the slip in protocol. The new Guardian should have made an introduction the minute he took over Cal's post.

Ed nodded, then followed the page down meandering stone hallways deep into the castle. The Guardian followed three steps behind and to the right, as his training dictated.

Ancient tapestries stood at attention as Ed passed, metallic threads winking at him from depictions of colorful forests and villages. Paintings honoring kings lined the walls between the tapestries. The men had held Ed's position before him and somehow, he felt camaraderie in their blank stares. The Elders could not have loved them all. Somewhere beneath their stoic expressions, he imagined a former king or two sharing a knowing groan for Ed's predicament.

At least he hoped so. The idea of being the only king in history who somehow had made an enemy of the Elders felt lonely otherwise.

Degan halted in front of a set of ornately carved red doors. They stood almost twice the boy's height, a symbol of the majestic space they guarded, and Ed wondered if the page had made a mistake. The Elders never met in the formal throne room. Ed and Adelina used it for ceremonies, and rare ones at that.

A swift knock at the door, followed by the click of a lock from inside the room allayed Ed's doubt. The page bowed, and then scurried back down the hallway.

Ed squared his shoulders, flattened a hand over a delicately carved leaf, and pushed the door out of his way. Sunlight streamed into the room in thick bands from a dozen tall windows to the left and right of the long room. Dusty rose quartz gleamed on the walls. Commanding black and white marble sparkled along the floor. Between the windows, two-story tall banners declared Adelina's heritage in interwoven threads of gray and yellow. Each held a symbol of her family's traits. A gold-colored rod with an amethyst crystal on top represented power, an onyx steed spoke of swift action, a faceless soldier holding a sword aloft represented their ability to fight, and a white nanny sparrow marked their kindness. The sparrow adopted other birds' orphaned young, even those chicks belonging to different species. At the end of the room, centered atop a one-foot high granite platform, two gilded thrones draped in royal blue velvet waited for the king and queen's presence. Ed hated using them almost as much as he hated presiding over the ceremonies hosted within this room.

Whoever had unlocked the door did not appear to be here any longer. Silence greeted Ed first, and then the echo of his footsteps surrounded him as he walked the length of the room. His temporary guard stood at attention beside the door. *Following protocol again,* Ed realized, and remembered why he had loathed Malven, his former Guardian. Cal's curiosity suited Ed much better. The empty room would have placed Cal at his side or even ahead of him as they walked.

Ed's gaze coasted from the walls to the thrones. Adelina's taller throne sat on the right. Ed's had been positioned to the left. A small book with a green cover lay centered on his gray cushion and he frowned as he picked it up. He had seen it too many times not to recognize it. The spell book belonged to Adelina's family. It should be in the royal safe, not left in the open for anyone to find. Many of these spells should not exist, let alone be cast.

"I see you've found my gift."

Ed's focus snapped from the book to the voice that had always made him cringe. Garon approached, walking down the center of the room along the path Ed had taken a moment before. A broad smile crested Garon's face, though it held no warmth. His eyes appeared bloodshot at first, and then his pupils took on a red tinge as he drew closer.

"I fail to see how this is a gift, Garon."

"Then you don't know its true worth."

"Where are the Elders?"

Garon's smile broadened. A few of his teeth looked sharper than normal, almost as if he had filed them into points. Ed took an instinctive step back as the advisor approached. Garon did not seem to notice. He ascended the platform, then turned and settled into Adelina's throne.

Ed set his jaw. "You have no right to—"

"Turn to page thirty," Garon interrupted. "You'll understand why we're here."

Ed debated walking out on Garon, but he knew the act would only create another division Adelina would have to mend. He suppressed a few swear words and found the page Garon had requested, flipping past several blackened pages that usually grabbed his curiosity. His annoyance would not allow a pause today.

When his eyes fell on the page Garon had mentioned, his stomach twisted. "Garon, this is a spell to kill Guardians."

"Just the ones whose names you insert into the third line," Garon corrected and the nonchalance in his tone sickened Ed. "It needs to be recited within a cave of rose quartz, which means you would need to travel to the southernmost parts of the kingdom. Or..." He gestured, indicating the throne room.

Ed followed Garon's gaze over the pale pink walls. The Guardian at the end of the hall remained unmoving, though Ed knew the acoustics in the room would have allowed him to hear the conversation.

"The throne room has always been the royal family's back-up plan in case the Elders tried to usurp power."

"And you think they are," Ed guessed.

Garon's fingers drummed on the throne's golden arms. "Don't you?"

Ed closed the book. "Not enough for this."

"And what if I told you it's you or them? They're deciding to banish you to the Barren as we speak. Do you really want to lose your adorable daughter, or your beautiful, yet naïve wife? She'll be given the choice of abdicating or losing you. Which do you think she'd pick?"

Ed glanced down at the book again. Its plain cover revealed no answers. Meaghan's face floated in front of his mind, her copper eyes staring up at him, as they had less than half an hour before. She was too young to lose her father, either to the Barren or to the wrong end of this decision. He could not become the monster Garon wished of him.

He tucked the book into the waistband of his pants. "They can face my family as they deliver their decision. I'm going back to my suite."

"Somehow, I thought that's what you'd say," Garon said, and this time his smile held genuine happiness. He gestured with two fingers and Ed realized he meant the motion for someone else.

He heard the sound of a sword leaving its scabbard and dropped to the ground. The weapon sliced through the air above his head.

Rolling to the side, he pulled a small knife from a hidden pocket in his boot. The blade would do little against his attacker, but he refused to give up without a fight. He sought the door and the help of his Guardian. A pair of black boots blocked his view.

He jumped to his feet, spun to avoid another attack, and then faced Garon's lackey. The man's gray cap fell to the floor. His angular cheeks left no mistake. Ed's guard would not be coming to his aid.

Ed dodged away from another strike, and then lunged with his knife, missing his mark by a foot. An elbow crashed into his temple. Stars scattered across his vision and a moment later, pain seared along his side. He lifted his arm to block the Guardian, but his small blade shattered from the force of his attacker's allestone sword. The weapon sliced down his arm. Warmth flowed from the wound, and then agony pierced his stomach. Hot pain filled every inch of his body, ripping the air from his lungs before he collapsed to the floor.

His muscles no longer obeyed him. Each shallow breath met his ears as an agonizing gasp. He saw only the black sparkle of the granite platform in front of him, and Garon's brown shoes on top of it. His advisor's voice sounded muffled.

"Did you kill him?"

"Not yet," the Guardian responded. "He'll bleed out soon enough."

"Finish the job," Garon said. "I don't want to risk a Healer discovering him."

"And the others?"

"Don't worry, Avilis. I'll keep my end of the bargain. The queen and her heir will be dead within the hour."

Adelina. Meaghan. Ed's wails remained trapped inside his body. His tears flowed, mixing with the red pooling on the floor.

Garon's feet disappeared. Footsteps echoed across the floor. The pair of voices grew distant, though Ed still heard the last of Garon's words. "Be sure to get the spell book."

Terror surged through Ed, giving him the strength to push the book away from his body, toward the platform. His hand slipped through the granite as his power made it fluid. The book disappeared. He drew his fingers back to his side, gasped one last breath, and then welcomed the painless dark.

§

WHEN NICK closed the Writer's book over the former king's last story, tears welled within his eyes. He ground his palms into them, unwilling to grieve Ed's tragic death. He had no other choice. The story had given him the name of their traitor. He had to get to the Elders.

Tucking the book under his arm, he shed his blankets and dashed out of the tent. He made it a handful of steps before a shadow blocked his path. Nick looked up. Max grinned, but the friendly gesture faded as soon as his eyes met Nick's. He tucked his hands into his pockets and nodded toward the book. "You read something important, didn't you?"

"Yeah, look, I have to go."

Nick stepped sideways and Max grabbed his arm. Burning seared Nick's skin and coursed through his blood. When Max let go, metal glinted in his palm. He held it up so Nick could see the needle.

"I've known you too long, Nick," he said. "You can't keep anything from me."

Nick shook his head. His vision hazed.

"What did it show you?" Max asked.

The book slipped from beneath Nick's arm and landed on the ground with a soft thud. Nick smiled. "A story," he said, though his words came out slurred.

"Of course it was, Nick. Don't make me hurt you."

"You already know, Max. It was a story about your father."

CHAPTER TWENTY-SEVEN

BREAKFAST DID nothing to kindle Meaghan's appetite. She stared at the boiled tamrin leaves piled on plates next to the fire and tried not to notice the sour smell wafting her way. She had woken this morning feeling queasy and the soggy mess did nothing to settle her stomach. She bypassed the meal, accepting a mug of sweet-berry tea from Cal instead, and stood as far away from the food as she could. May soon joined her.

"Have you seen Nick?" she asked.

Meaghan shook her head. Although Nick had not been in the tent when she returned to it a few hours before dawn, his choice not to sleep did not surprise her. The traitor weighed on his mind as much as it did hers.

"I expected him to show up by now," May said. "Are you planning on eating?"

"That sludge?" Meaghan laughed. "Not a chance."

"You need your strength if you plan to fight tomorrow. Nothing else grows here. You know that."

"Yeah, but I'd need to keep my breakfast down for it to make a difference. I'm already nauseous enough."

"Are you?" May brought a hand to Meaghan's shoulder, though the gesture did not convey compassion. She pursed her lips in concentration as she used her healing power to study Meaghan.

"I'm fine, May," Meaghan insisted. "I just need a little more sleep, that's all. It's been a rough week."

May's fingers tightened, and then she released her grip.

Meaghan put her mug down on a tree stump. "What did you sense?"

"Nothing much," May said, though her lips tightened. "You really should eat."

Meaghan tucked her tongue into her cheek, checking the impulse to call Nick's mother a liar. She did not get the chance to choose any other words before Cal sauntered up to them, a plate of tamrin leaves in one hand. Fluorescent yellow juice rolled along the plate's edge and dripped over the side. Meaghan swallowed hard to keep bile from charging up her throat.

He forced the plate into her hands. "The queen has to set a good example."

"Cal—"

"Nope, eat up. We have a lot to do today and no one's fainting on my watch. I'm still your Guardian until the Elders tell me otherwise."

He shoved a fork into the tamrin leaves. Meaghan scooped up a bite, wincing when the leaves oozed tan goo, and then pinched her nose closed and forced the food past her lips.

At first, the taste reminded her of the dandelion juice that had clung to her fingers as a child whenever she played in a field. Then sour turned to dirt, and dirt to rotten hay. She shuddered.

"Do that again, but with less revulsion," Cal instructed. "A few people are waiting to see how you fare before trying it themselves. We need our soldiers in top form."

She opened her eyes. Several people had stopped their activities to watch her. Many of them worked hard to suppress smiles and she could not shake the feeling Cal had pranked her.

Shoveling another forkful into her mouth, she swallowed it without chewing, and then followed that with a third portion. By the time she had forced a fourth bite past her teeth, her stomach felt as if it had hitched a ride on a storm-tossed sailboat. She handed Cal the plate, stood, and walked away from camp into the forest. When she felt certain no one could see her, she gagged out every bite of the revolting breakfast.

Sweat poured down her face. Above the smell of her sickness, the familiar scent of jicab drifted past her nose. Though she had always considered the tea the worst thing she had ever tasted, it now held second place.

She looked up. A tin mug floated in her vision. Behind it, a flash of red hair gave away its bearer.

"Thank you," Meaghan said, taking the mug from May. "I guess I might be coming down with something after all."

"It does seem that way," May said and looped an arm around Meaghan's shoulders. She walked them both to a fallen log and sat. Meaghan perched beside her.

"The tea will help," May said. "After you've had that, I'll give you my extra rations. I'm assuming you won't be convinced to stay behind tomorrow?"

"Never. This is my kingdom. I won't let others risk their lives if I'm not willing to do the same."

May moved Meaghan's hair off her forehead with an index finger. "Your mother would have said the same thing. She'd be proud of you, you know."

Meaghan stared into her mug. The brown liquid reflected her copper eyes back at her—eyes the same color as her mother's. Meaghan took a sip just to disturb the image.

"What was she like?" Meaghan asked. "I mean really like. I've read the stories in the book. That's not the same as knowing her."

"No, it isn't. She was kind and brave, wise and giving, sometimes to a fault. Garon used those traits against her, though I think if she had known the outcome, she wouldn't have allowed it to change her. At the core, she was one of the purest people I've ever met."

May had tears in her eyes when Meaghan looked up. "You considered her your friend, didn't you?" Meaghan asked.

"One of my closest. Losing her hurt almost as much as losing my own sister. I wonder sometimes if my relationship with Adelina set an example for Nick, made it easier for him to love you."

Meaghan's shoulders stiffened. "It wasn't as easy as you make it sound."

"Of course not," May said and tilted her head. Her emerald eyes did not blink as they focused on Meaghan. "Guardians are supposed to be detached."

"Cal said the same thing when we were in the wilderness."

"The same words, perhaps, with opposite meaning. He believes we could have saved them. I agree, but for different reasons. Because of my friendship with Adelina, she trusted me. Ed shared his concerns about Garon with me. I had some of the same worries. I never voiced them to him or Adelina because I wanted to remain detached. I was afraid to influence them in ways that would alter the course of our kingdom."

One side of May's mouth tilted up in a lopsided smile. "I'll never know, but that's the hard part about the past. We see so much of it, yet we can't change anything. We can only focus on the present. Nick's happy, Meaghan, just as I was from knowing your mother. You're a lot like her and I couldn't be prouder to have you in my family."

Meaghan did not know how to respond. Joy and bittersweet sorrow welled within her, but neither offered clarity. May seemed to understand and drew her into a hug. Contentment spread through Meaghan and she relaxed into the embrace.

When they parted, Meaghan saw Cal hiding in the shadows. Worry darkened his eyes and deepened the wrinkles etched along the sides of his face. He seemed to have aged a decade within minutes.

"Nick is missing," he said, stepping forward.

"What do you mean 'missing?' " May asked.

"I mean exactly what I said. We've checked everywhere. He's not within the boundary of the crystals."

"Then check beyond it. He wouldn't have gone far."

"We did that. You're his mother, May, and his Guardian still. You should be able to sense him."

May frowned. "I haven't sensed intense fear or pain from him. If he was in danger, I'd know it."

"What about his presence?" Cal asked. "Can you sense that?"

May closed her eyes. Color drained from her cheeks. "He's not here."

"You're certain?"

May nodded. "That doesn't make any sense. Where could he be?"

Cal glanced at Meaghan. His fear tugged on her empath power. "The doll's still gone, isn't it?" he asked.

"Someone took Nick," Meaghan realized, though the words fell heavy from her lips.

May stood. "Who else is missing?"

"I'm not sure," Cal responded. "But we'll find out soon enough."

Ten minutes passed before everyone in the camp had gathered around the cooking fire. The Elders tallied familiar faces, though Meaghan felt useless in the efforts. She knew too few people by sight and of those, all seemed to be present. Scanning the ocean of bodies once more, her heart stopped beating for a second when she realized she had made a drastic mistake. Not everyone she knew stared back at her. She grabbed Faillen's arm.

"Where's Caide?"

"With my father," Faillen said. "If you think he had—"

"Of course not. I need him to use the truth spell again."

"It didn't work yesterday, remember?"

"I think it will now."

Faillen snaked through the crowd, returning a moment later with his son in tow. The Elders followed close behind.

"What's going on?" Miles asked.

"Caide needs to recite the spell again."

Caide shook his head. "I haven't figured out—"

"Just do it," she commanded. "Cast it over everyone."

"But—" Caide started to protest, then shut his mouth when Faillen shook his head in warning. The spell rang through the air, loud with the force by which Caide projected it. After the last line faded, every villager and soldier stared ahead, their eyes as vacant as the traitors' had been the day before.

"Who here is a member of the Shadow Guard?" Meaghan demanded.

No one stepped forward. No voices pierced the silence weighing down the air.

"It's not working," Miles told her.

"It is," she said. "I wanted to confirm there was only one traitor."

"I don't understand," May said.

Meaghan did not respond. She raced across the field, focused on finding one of the tents on the outskirts of camp. Throwing open the flap, she crawled inside. Sunlight filtered through the thick canvas, casting a muted glow over the floor. Meaghan's gaze landed on the tent's single cot and she covered her mouth to keep from crying out.

Shredded yellow corn husk decorated a wool blanket in neat piles. On the top of one of those piles, a mangled doll's face stared up at her. Max had been the traitor the whole time. He knew everything.

And now he had Nick.

CHAPTER TWENTY-EIGHT

MEAGHAN PACED. The grass beneath her feet pushed to the side in deference to her worry, and then cowered flat when her steps became angry. She circled a tree and retraced the same route she had traveled over the last hour. Back and forth, she wandered while the Elders debated their next move. Always debating, always unsure what to do. It had been their pattern since she had known them.

Meaghan fingered one of the four battle knives attached to her belt. She wanted action and she wanted it now, but she could not figure out where to direct her energy. Nick could be anywhere. Since Max could teleport freely, that anywhere could be in the Barren or on a remote island no one else had discovered.

Inhaling a deep breath, she held it in her lungs, and then released it with slow control. She had no idea how she had missed the signs before. During the party at the Guardian village, she had lost hold on Nick's blocking power, leaving her vulnerable to the overwhelming emotions that had surrounded her. Max's weakener power had been the cause. She felt certain of that now. That same power also meant he was the shadow lurking in the forest when Caide's truth spell failed. She had felt surprise from him. He had believed she would not be able to sense him after he destroyed the doll.

"Do you think he's the one who let the Mardróch into the village?" Meaghan heard May ask.

"Yes, of course," Meaghan said, stopping to face her. "Who else could it be?"

"Abbott," Miles said. "We've already determined the Dreamer did it. After all, Max's wife was killed in that attack."

"You and Sam determined Abbot's guilt," May said. "I've always had my doubts."

"I have, too," Cal said. "We've already seen the Shadow Guard make hard sacrifices to get to Meaghan. Max couldn't have predicted Cissy's death, though he might've been willing to take the risk if he felt Meaghan would be part of those killed that night."

Sam grunted. "So kidnapping Nick is meant to lure Meaghan into the open?"

"We can't let her go," Miles said. "They'd slaughter her."

"We can't let Garon keep Nick, either," May protested. "There has to be a way. Maybe if we—"

"I'm sorry, May," Sam interrupted. "You can't be objective. You don't have a say in this."

"Neither do you." Meaghan turned on him. Fire raged within her, burning her cheeks. She felt as if she could breathe it over all of them in an instant. "You have no right to decide what I can and can't do."

Sam raised one hand in a gesture of submission. "I meant no disrespect. We're only trying to protect you and the future of the kingdom."

"I don't care about my safety. I care about Nick's and I will do whatever it takes to rescue him. If you stand in my way, I'll go through you. It's as simple as that."

Miles stepped forward. "We're not trying to stand in your way. We just need a little more time to figure something out. We don't even know where they're keeping him."

"Maybe not. I have a good idea where I can get the information though. Finish what we started. Manage the battle and if I don't return, the kingdom's yours. It seems like a win-win situation for you."

"Don't you think you're being a little ridiculous?" Miles asked.

"Enough talk." She pulled her knife and pointed it at him. "I'm leaving tonight. I don't want to see any of you again until this is over."

"Meg—" Cal protested. She turned from him and walked away. Although she had no targets, she kept the hilt of her knife tight within her grip. She had almost reached the other side of the clearing when Cal caught up to her.

"Nick's temper is starting to rub off on you."

She pressed her lips together and continued walking. Cal placed a hand on her shoulder. She shrugged it off.

"I'm not your enemy, lass. You know that. None of us are."

Meaghan stopped short and turned to glare at him. May stood a few steps behind him, though Meaghan barely registered her presence. "The Elders are going to let Nick die. I won't allow that, not without a fight."

"On your own?"

"No one else is going to help me. You've made up your minds already."

"Not all of us have," Cal corrected. "I joined the Elders to protect Nick. Do you really think I'd side with them if it meant losing him?"

Meaghan's gaze shifted to May. Shadows darkened her eyes.

"I lost my husband already," May said. "I won't lose my son."

"So you're not trying to stop me?" Meaghan asked.

May shook her head. "I would've done the same in your position, if I could have saved Nick's father."

"And I would've taken on the entire Mardróch army if it meant I had a chance of saving Alisen," Cal said. "But Meg, you need to realize it may already be too late. They don't need to keep him alive. They just need you to think he is."

Meaghan swallowed hard at the thought. Her heart felt as if Cal had crushed it in one large fist. She sheathed her knife. "I refuse to believe that."

"Somewhere deep down you do or you wouldn't be acting this way."

She looked away, focusing on the tents closest to them to keep her tears from forming. The army sparred with the Zeiihbuans at the edges of the protected boundary, leaving the camp devoid of its usual clamor.

"Meg, you may not want to face the truth—"

"Nick's death is not a given, Cal."

"Still, if it happens, you need to know that you can survive it. You may feel as if each step is agonizing and each breath is the worst torture, but you'll still take them. You have to believe that, or you'll make rash decisions, like I did. You have an obligation to your kingdom."

"I don't care about my obligations."

"Yeah, you do." A thick arm slipped around Meaghan's shoulders and she looked up at Cal. "As hard as those obligations can be sometimes, you'll always care about them, just as your parents did. And just like May and I did, you'll figure out how to put your life back together, and maybe you'll get some joy out of it in the end."

Cal's new family had brought him that joy, but Meaghan did not want to think about a family without Nick. She sought May's face. Nick's mother wiped moisture from her cheeks.

"We'll do everything we can to save him," she said. "But we won't sacrifice you in the process. If we're going to do this, you need to promise you won't take unnecessary risks."

Meaghan nodded.

"There's also something else you need to know. It's about your illness."

"Will it change my mind or weaken my ability to fight?"

"I doubt it."

"Then you can tell me after." Meaghan turned and continued on her original path. "If I'm still alive."

§

"WHAT INFORMATION do you think you can get from me?"

Meaghan rolled her knife between her palms. Sun glinted off the allestone blade, sparkling white through its dark gray. She watched the traitors over it with menace.

"You don't frighten me," Paster continued his mocking.

"She should," Cal muttered.

"Yes, she should," Dolan agreed.

"Why?" Paster scoffed. "We're already as good as dead. What can she do to us with her knife? Do you really think she'd torture us? She's not Garon."

"You never know what a woman will do for her loved ones," Mysta said.

"I'm less concerned with her knife than her power," Dolan said. "Max shared the truth with me."

"What did he say?" Meaghan demanded. When Dolan did not respond, she stepped forward and pressed the tip of her blade into his chest. "Tell me."

"Or what? Like Paster said, you aren't Garon. I don't believe you're capable of using that knife on me."

"My power…" she said and let her words hang in the air.

Dolan raised an eyebrow. "I have no doubt you'll be the downfall of this kingdom if the Shadow Guard doesn't succeed. I'd even wager you could use your power now if we angered you enough. By accident, anyway. But using it well enough to threaten me?" He shook his head. "You'd succumb to one of my spells first. You're defenseless without Sam."

Meaghan tightened her fingers on her knife, and then twisted it, slicing a ragged hole in Dolan's shirt. Before she had the chance to decide if she wanted to follow through on her threat, May's hand closed around hers. The blade left Meaghan's grip.

"This isn't you, Meaghan," May said. "You're a better person than that."

"Fine," Meaghan conceded, stepping back. "Let's get Caide. Maybe we can—"

May spun on one foot and plunged the knife into Dolan's shoulder. He screamed and collapsed to his knees. Blood flowed down the front of his shirt, turning the yellow material sick brown.

"I'm not, however, a better person," May said and yanked the knife from Dolan's body. He screamed in anguish. "You should've listened to Mysta, Dolan. I've lost too many people already. I'm not about to add my son to that list because of your fanatical beliefs. Where is he?"

Dolan shook his head. May flashed the blade through the air, her movement so quick that Meaghan did not realize what she had done until more blood spread across Dolan's chest. Red rolled down the blade and dripped over May's fingers.

"I...I..." Dolan gasped. May raised the knife once more. Dolan scrambled backward, scattering pebbles across the ground. "I don't know anything. I don't. I swear."

May narrowed her eyes. She stepped forward so she towered over him.

"He doesn't," Mysta said.

May swung the blade around, the threat obvious, though Mysta did not cower. She raised her hands, palms out in surrender. "I have something for you. It's hidden in my hair."

"You want us to let you reach for it?" Cal asked. "Do we look stupid?"

Paster snorted. Mysta kicked him in the ankle. "You're an idiot," she said. "Do you want to end up like Dolan?"

"The Elder will heal him," Paster said.

"And she'll make it the most painful experience he's ever had. Keep your mouth shut or I'll strangle you myself."

Paster's gaze fell to the ropes that connected the three traitors. He nodded.

"What do you have?" May asked.

"Max put a message for you in my braid," she said. "Last night, before he teleported with the king. It looks like a wooden stick."

"Get it," May instructed Cal. Stepping forward, Cal reached behind Mysta's head. He yanked the string from the end of her braid, unleashing her white hair so it cascaded around her shoulders. A silver stick fell to the ground at her feet. Cal picked it up. Two swift snaps revealed a hollow compartment inside that hid a rolled-up slip of paper. He brought it to Meaghan.

Her fingers shook as she unraveled it. Neat handwriting taunted her, ebony against dirty white.

> *I don't want to hurt Nick, but that's up to you.*
> *Your life for his.*
> *It ends where it began.*

CHAPTER TWENTY-NINE

THE FIRST rock broke into three pieces. The second exploded into gray shards. The third disintegrated into fine dust. Each became a distant memory in the shadow of Meaghan's fury. She launched a fourth at a large boulder, then a fifth, marking her hatred with white scars on the victimless landscape. Nick's oldest friend, the man he considered a brother, would kill him to get to her. Because somehow, he believed she would destroy the kingdom.

She tightened her hand into a fist and stared down at it. She imagined blood dripping from her nails and pooling next to Max's crumpled body on the ground. How had she not known? What good was her empath power if she could not sense the traitors closest to them?

She blew out a hot breath, then tugged a knife from her belt and shoved it forward, embedding it deep into the bark of the closest tree. Her forearm ached from the force. She yanked the blade out before driving it back into the same spot. Over and over, she attacked the tree. Tan bark splintered with each vengeful thrust.

The sun set behind her, casting black shadows into the forest and down her arms, encasing her in a chilling hug.

Shifting her hold on her blade, she swiped upward, gouging the imaginary faces of those she had turned her back on hours before, of those who had promised to protect Nick and now betrayed him in his absence. The Elders. Nick's mother. Cal. Each had voted not to attack the castle early.

A chunk of the tree flew away from her knife and bounced at her feet. Nick could be dead by the time they got to him. She would not allow that. Tonight, she would go to the castle. She would sneak past Garon's guard.

Then what? Knock on the front door and offer her life in exchange for Nick's, as Max had requested? Garon would laugh as he slaughtered them both.

A twig snapped behind her. She spun around, her grip tight on her weapon. The kindness brightening Faillen's flint-flecked eyes angered her more.

"What do you want?" she snarled. "If the Elders think sending you—"

"Calm down, Meaghan. I'm here as a friend."

"A friend would have stuck up for me. A *friend* would have figured out a way to convince the Elders to march today."

"No, a friend helps you succeed. Do you really think going into battle unprepared was the right course?"

She glared at him and sheathed her blade.

"I didn't think so. I know you're scared. I know you want to act now, but doing so without a plan is *re*acting. It's foolhardy."

"It's better than letting Nick die."

"They want you, Meaghan. They'll keep him alive until they have you."

And torture him, as they had done to Caide. Yet she had convinced Faillen to follow her plan and leave his son to the daily evils of Garon's worst Mardróch for a month. Guilt burned her cheeks and she turned from the Zeiihbuan leader. She could not think about the past right now. She had to focus on the future, and saving Nick..

"Please trust me," Faillen said. "We'll be ready to march tomorrow."

"Then what?" Meaghan asked. Her throat tightened the words into a whisper. "As you said, once they realize I've come, Nick is dead."

"Then we'll have to make sure they don't see you. There are many ways into that castle. And fortunately for you, the former king and queen's Guardians know them all."

§

"WE'LL CARRY the crystals with us," May said. "They should provide enough cover until we start the battle."

A fire blazed in front of Nick's mother, filling the campground with eerie yellow light. It turned her skin sallow and highlighted the gray shadows under her eyes. Meaghan hung back, clinging to her hiding place behind a tree as the Elders talked. Faillen pressed a hand into the small of her back, silently urging her to move forward. She refused to obey.

Cal glanced in her direction. As her Guardian, he had sensed her, though he did not divulge her presence to the rest of the group. He kicked dirt into the fire and Meaghan's gaze trailed from his foot to the shadows on the other side of the clearing. Artair stood beneath the canopy of a large oak, his black hair loose around his shoulders instead of bound in its usual ponytail. Though she could not make out his face in the advancing darkness, focusing her empath power in his direction yielded the reason for his hesitation. Confusion emanated from him. Beyond him, anger and fear came from someone Meaghan could not see. Neither person's emotions seemed to indicate a threat, so she allowed them their secrecy as Cal had allowed hers.

"We won't surprise Garon," Cadell told May. Faillen's father sat on a stump. He rolled his shoulders, his relaxed posture a stark contrast to those of the Elders. Sam worried a hand through his white hair as lines etched dark canyons along his forehead. Beside him, Miles paced. He gripped his fingers into five knots behind his back.

"I agree," Cal said. "Especially not with Max feeding him every last one of our secrets. We're waiting on…what? One village to arrive?"

"They won't be coming," Artair said, moving into the circle of firelight.

Cal raised an eyebrow. "What makes you say that, lad?"

"It's what I told him," a shaking voice responded from behind Artair. Branches rustled, and then a short woman appeared. Blood had dried to brown within her blonde hair and had stained her green tunic burgundy in spots. She clutched a burlap sack within her fists.

The bottom of it looked as if someone had dipped it in ink. Meaghan did not have to stretch her imagination to recognize blood within the red-black color.

"And who exactly are you?" Cal asked.

"Innelda. From the Village at Poplar Field."

Cal's eyes widened and shot to Meaghan's hiding place. Meaghan swallowed hard with her own recognition of the name. Talis had spoken it twice before he died. One of those times had been to confess his forbidden love for the non-Guardian.

"They're all gone," Innelda whispered. "The Mardróch attacked from everywhere. I thought I would die. Then *he* showed up. He said I had to live."

"Because of Talis?" Cal wondered aloud.

Innelda nodded. Tears spilled down her cheeks. "How could he possibly know?"

"I don't understand," Miles said.

Meaghan did. Bile churned in her throat. Max had told Garon Talis's secret. Garon had let Innelda live to torture her with more grief. How many friends had she lost in his newest attack? Did any of her loved ones remain?

"What does this have to do with Talis?" Miles prompted when no one answered him. "Who showed up?"

"I don't know his name," Innelda said, then swayed. Cal caught her before she crumpled to the ground and carried her to the closest log. She leaned against him while they sat.

May crouched down in front of them and pressed her fingers to Innelda's forehead. "You have a concussion. Can you continue?"

Innelda nodded.

"What did he look like?" Faillen asked, stepping out from his hiding place. Meaghan followed him, though no one seemed to notice.

"He was a man, I think, but his face looked as if it had changed into…I don't know. Something else."

"Something not quite human and not quite Mardróch," Meaghan guessed.

Innelda's focus snapped to Meaghan. Fear spiked harder against Meaghan's empath power.

"Yes. Yes, I think so. Have you seen him before?"

"Once. That's what Garon looked like before he took his potion."

"That doesn't make any sense," Sam said. "Why would Garon leave the castle just to attack one village?"

"Because he's taunting us," Cal said.

"Because he wanted to send us a message and he knew it would have the most impact if he delivered it himself," Faillen said, his voice firm with his certainty. He removed the burlap sack from Innelda's grip. "What else did he tell you?"

"Safe passage," Innelda said.

"Safe passage for what?" Cadell asked, though no one answered.

Meaghan held her breath. *Safe passage to the castle.* It had to be. Garon knew everything and he was offering them a chance to get to the castle, to prepare for battle.

"Anything else?" Cal asked.

"He told me not to look inside the bag, to bring it straight to you, but…" Innelda's eyelids fluttered closed. "I didn't want to bring you a trap."

"You looked," Faillen said and glanced into the bag. He quickly closed it again. His hand trembled when he passed it to Cal. "It's a blunt message, even for Garon."

"What is it?" May asked.

"A head," Faillen said. "I'm not sure whose. His skin isn't right for Ærenden. Or Zeiihbu for that matter."

"Oh no." Meaghan covered her mouth with her hand. "It couldn't be, could it?"

Cal's face paled, and then his gaze dropped to the bag. He looked inside. "Poor lad. Guess he was telling the truth."

"You knew him?" Miles asked.

"In a way. It's Garon's Healer." Cal's voice held no hint of emotion, but when Meaghan focused her power on him, she sensed the truth in the vacancy. Regret and guilt washed over her. "Guess Garon found out about him helping me."

It also explained why Garon had started his transformation into a Mardróch again. Without Aristos's potion, the monster would eventually take over.

"Did he say anything else?" Cal asked Innelda.

"Two days," she said. "He said 'in two days, we end this.' "

Faillen's gaze met Meaghan's and she understood. As they prepared, so did Garon.

"He told me…" A raspy exhale bubbled up Innelda's throat, and then silence followed.

Meaghan pressed a hand to Innelda's shoulder. "It's okay," she said. "You're safe now."

It sounded like a lie, even to Meaghan's ears. Innelda took a deep breath. The fear grabbing Meaghan's power turned to cold hatred.

"He said he's waiting."

CHAPTER THIRTY

THE ARMY marched on the castle, trudging through mud and forest underbrush, their bodies hidden by crystals and the sounds of their movements protected by the false security of a spell Garon knew all too well. It would take them a day to arrive at the castle. A long day of hours and minutes comprised of fear, tension, and happiness in those rare moments when they could find it. Before battle, the soldiers would tell stories of their ancestors, regale each other with memories of joyful moments and childhoods shared in distant villages they might never see again. The evening campfire would become a celebration of life, and a sacred feast to those who would fall.

And Caide would not witness it. He would be far away from his tribe, hidden alongside the children in his village because his father could not see him as the man he had become.

Anger blazed heat across his cheeks. He tightened his fists at his sides, resisting the urge to lash out at the Guardian who now escorted him across the wilderness.

Artair wisely remained in Caide's wake, silent as they plodded onward. By mid-day, Caide's steam had dissipated. He softened his fists and slipped his fingers into his pockets, seeking a now familiar slip of paper. Dry parchment greeted him and vibrated against his skin, its magic a kindred song only Caide could hear. He traced unseen words, reciting them under his breath as he had done nearly every waking moment since he first laid eyes on them. They called to him for closure, for completion. The last Spellmaster's power coursed through Caide, giving him fresh strength and a shadowy idea that grew more solid the closer he got to the village.

"I know this isn't what you want," Artair said. "But you have to see things from our perspective."

Caide grunted.

"Or you could continue to sulk."

Caide slid his eyes sideways. Artair now flanked him, his dark ponytail a blurred outline in the advancing night.

"I could help," Caide told him. "My power could make a difference in this battle."

"Or you could be captured," Artair said. "And forced to use that power against us. You could also be killed. Your power doesn't make you invincible."

"I never said it did, but it *is* stronger than almost everyone else's. What good does it do anyone holed up in some distant village?"

"A lot. If you live through this, the good you could do long-term, especially after your power gets stronger, would far outweigh the help you could offer now."

"You don't know that."

"Yeah, I do. Besides, we didn't send a team into Zeiihbu to rescue you only to have you die a few months later. More importantly, we didn't lose people on that mission to waste their sacrifices."

Talis.

The unspoken name hung in the air, a weight and noose around Caide's neck. Many had died rescuing Caide from Stilgan, but that one sacrifice mattered most to Artair and Caide knew it. Talis had been Talea's twin. Artair and Talis had been brothers, if only for a short time.

Caide chose to respond with silence. He could not prove what he knew in his heart. He could make a lasting difference in the battle and in the kingdom's future.

He pressed the paper against his palm and continued focusing on the words beckoning him.

"Do you ever wish you could do more?" he asked Artair.

"All the time."

"Then you understand why this matters to me."

"Of course I do, but your safety matters to everyone."

"So you're saying you'd just follow orders if you were me? If you knew you could make a difference, you'd do nothing?"

"I don't know if I can answer that question."

"You don't *want* to answer that question. You don't want to encourage me by admitting the truth."

"No. It doesn't matter what I believe and I'm not about to waste time debating hypothetical situations." Artair stopped short. "Look, whatever you're thinking of trying, don't. Just don't. We need you safe."

"What about what I need?" Caide faced Artair. Moonlight broke from behind a dark cloud. It highlighted the tight line of the Guardian's mouth. "I need to fight, Artair. I need to help defeat Garon. For my mother, for what he's done to Zeiihbu, for Talis."

Artair glanced away. He gave the slightest nod, and Caide found hope in his concession. "Help me, Artair. Please."

"Revenge is poison, Caide. It devours its host long before it destroys its intended victim. Don't let it blind you. You don't know for certain that you could help. If he caught you—"

"Then I would do more harm than good," Caide finished, the words bitter in his mouth. "You mentioned that already. As did my father before I left."

"Maybe you should listen to him. Come on, we need to get going." Artair started moving again, signaling the end of their conversation. This time, anger stiffened his shoulders and Caide could not fault him for the reaction. Caide had asked for too much. No Guardian would willingly put a charge in danger.

"I'm sorry," Caide said.

Artair glanced over his shoulder. "It's fine. I realize this is hard on you. I just can't support you in disobeying your father."

"I know."

"It will work out, Caide. You'll see."

"I know that, too."

And he did, but not for the reasons Artair thought.

The village appeared in the distance, toy houses silhouetted by tiny streetlights. The spell protecting it would not allow Artair to see it, but Caide used it as a beacon. It illuminated his resolve.

He counted his steps as they grew closer, as houses turned from toys to scale models. Children played in the packed dirt surrounding a one-story bungalow.

"Are we close?" Artair asked. "I can feel the protection spell pushing me away."

"We are." Caide gripped Artair's hand. "You are welcome here."

Artair's gaze coasted along the horizon, and then he smiled. "Great. I'll walk you to the border and leave you there. I want to join up with the army by morning."

"No. I need you to come with me to see Cal's wife."

"Neiszhe? Why?"

"Because if I don't show up, she'll report back to my father. And if I tell her I've been tasked to return to battle, she won't believe me. She'll believe you, though."

"Enough," Artair snapped. "I told you. There's no way I'm going to—"

"*The strongest power in creation,*" Caide recited.

Artair's eyes widened. "Caide—"

"*The greatest gift of our relation,*" Caide continued. "*Our self-control, our living will, the realities our minds fulfill. Removed within these words, this spell, in breath alone you now shall dwell.*"

"Caide," Artair begged. He took a step back, though both men knew he could not outrun Caide's spell. "Please don't do this."

Artair's desperation filled Caide's ears as he recited the last line to the truth spell, a new line that changed its purpose and dissolved the fear from Artair's face.

"*My commands alone you now shall heed, until I have no lasting need.*"

A child's laughter echoed toward them. Lights flickered to life within the windows of several houses. The moon hid behind a cloud once more, casting shadows over Artair's vacant stare.

Caide swallowed hard to ease the guilt tightening his throat. "Let's go," he said. "We have work to do."

CHAPTER THIRTY-ONE

"YOU LOOK like you could use some tea," Neiszhe said. Her hand shook as she tipped the kettle forward, splashing hot water into Artair's cup. Steaming droplets landed on the kitchen table between Caide and Artair. Neiszhe left them.

"Not as much as you do," Caide responded, somehow keeping his nerves from showing in the same way Neiszhe's did. Cal's wife suspected something. Distrust and confusion cast shadows beneath her eyes. She drew her fingers to the black bun at the base of her neck and fiddled with the clasp holding it in place.

"Any news of the battle?" she asked.

"It hasn't started yet," Artair said, his voice devoid of emotion.

"I see." Neiszhe pressed her lips together. "Caide, can I have a word with you?"

Caide followed Neiszhe from the room. They traipsed down a short hallway into the small living room. Neiszhe's infant son slept in a dark wooden bassinet. His plump pink lips parted in a murmur and Neiszhe placed a hand on his chest, soothing him.

"Do you want to tell me what's going on?" Neiszhe demanded. "Artair is acting strange."

"How do you mean?"

"He barely looks at me. His face has no emotion, and…" She hesitated. "He seems *off* somehow. Don't tell me you haven't noticed."

Caide wanted to say exactly that. Neiszhe's stern gaze quelled that instinct, more so than her words had.

"He's upset," Caide offered. "He's not happy that Cal asked him to babysit me."

"Perhaps, but my healing power isn't working either. I can't sense him. Or you, for that matter."

"Why would you need to sense us?" Caide asked, and knew immediately by Neiszhe's narrowed eyes that he had given the wrong reaction. At the least, he should have been surprised or worried that her power had stopped working.

"Because you've both been acting strange since you walked through my front door, and you know it. What have you done?"

He wanted to tell her the truth. He had cast a spell over Artair, and then used one on her to block her power—an adaptation of the same spell a traitor had convinced him never to cast again. Instead, he responded, "Nothing."

"Caide," Neiszhe warned.

The baby mewed and Caide looked down at him. His face held an innocent peace Caide wished he could still experience. The war and Stilgan's torment had taken it from him.

Neiszhe gripped his arm and he brought his attention back to her.

Kindness lightened her smoke gray eyes and it melted some of Caide's resolve.

"You can trust me," she told him. "You know that."

"I owe Cal everything," Caide said. "If it wasn't for me, he would have been here when your son was born. He wouldn't have been lost for months in the wilderness. He almost died."

Neiszhe's grip loosened. "All of that is Stilgan's fault, Caide, not yours. You shouldn't feel responsible."

Caide shook his head. "He went into Zeiihbu to rescue me."

"And he did so gladly, because that's who Cal is. He's a Guardian. He wanted to protect Nick and Meaghan. He wanted to help you."

"And I want to help him," Caide said. "I want to help my father, and the king and queen. I can't do that from here."

"So you have a plan," Neiszhe guessed. "What is it? And what does it have to do with Artair's strange behavior?"

"I want to fight," Caide confessed.

Neiszhe nodded. "Go on."

"My father refused my request."

"As he should have. You're too young."

"I'm a warrior. An adult by tribal rules," Caide countered.

"Yet you're here," Neiszhe said. "So…what? You cast a spell on Artair to get him to go along with you?"

Caide did not respond.

"And you cast a spell on me," Neiszhe continued. Caide remained silent and Neiszhe's tone hardened. "Is that really how you want to repay Cal? By manipulating his wife?"

Shame rushed heat over his cheeks. "I didn't think you'd allow me to go without Artair requesting it."

"I wouldn't have allowed you to go with it."

"You have to, Neiszhe. Please. They can't win this battle without my help."

Neiszhe crossed her arms over her chest. "You may be a warrior, Caide, and a brave one at that. But you can't single-handedly win a battle."

"I'm more than a warrior," Caide reminded her. "You know what I'm capable of doing with my spellmaster power."

"You've made that perfectly clear today," Neiszhe responded. "And by turning on your friends, your allies, you've also made it clear you aren't ready to handle your power."

Caide blew out a short breath and stepped away from the Healer. Her gaze followed him, as hot as her voice had been cold.

"I'm just trying to do what's best," he said. "You don't understand—"

"Don't I?" she countered. "I'm older than I look. I was around when the last Spellmaster began using that excuse."

"He was selfish. He wanted power. I'm not like that."

"Farrow didn't start out that way. He thought his spells were innocent. King Ed's tribe was a menace. They were robbers when he set a plague on them. It was justice. It was protecting others."

Caide's stomach pitched. He stiffened his spine. "His plague killed people. What I'm doing is different. I'm not hurting anyone."

"For now, maybe. But you're using people, Caide. What did you plan on doing when I said no?"

Caide looked away, down the hallway to the kitchen door that hid

Artair. Caide doubted the Guardian had moved since Caide and Neiszhe had left the room. He lacked the will.

Neiszhe's son whimpered. Neiszhe glanced at him, but did not turn her back on Caide. She did not trust him. Nor should she. Her son was the reason Caide had not cast the spell on her instead of Artair. Caide had feared she would forget to care for him.

He had a plan for that now.

"Caide, answer me."

Caide looked back at her and knew by the fear on her face that she had already guessed his answer. Her arms slipped to her sides.

"I'm sorry," he said. "I don't have a choice."

"You always have a choice, Caide."

"Not this time."

When he had finished reciting the spell, Neiszhe's face had lost all emotion.

"In fifteen minutes, you'll awake from the spell," he instructed. "You won't remember that I've been here. You won't think to report my absence to Cal until tomorrow."

She nodded. The baby cried in his bassinet behind her.

"Tend to your son," Caide told her. She sat down in an armchair and placed a lazy hand on the baby's bed, rocking gently as she stared forward. The baby settled.

Caide's stomach did not. He had fifteen minutes before he had to disappear from the village—fifteen minutes to find Aldin and betray everyone he ever loved.

It hardly seemed like enough time.

CHAPTER THIRTY-TWO

SHE GOT sick. Again. Meaghan could not think of anything worse than trying to maintain command while dodging behind trees to vomit. Except maybe doing so after every meal. She straightened up and ran the back of a shaky hand across her mouth. Even May's rations had not helped alleviate this illness, so she had stopped accepting them.

The gray edges of a dark shadow spread across the ground at her feet. Meaghan turned, expecting to see a Healer staring back at her with an air of boredom, sent by May to check on her. Instead, Innelda offered a bashful smile. A rose tinge replaced the gray that had painted her cheeks the day before, though dark circles still shadowed her eyes.

Talis's face flashed across Meaghan's mind. It tugged guilt along with it, and Meaghan released her empath power, bracing for the blame and hostility she knew Innelda must feel for the queen who had taken away her love. She found only compassion.

"That stuff is vile, isn't it?" Innelda asked.

Stuff. Few people wanted to think about the plant they choked down at meal times, let alone mention it by name. Meaghan unhooked a water bladder from her belt and rinsed out her mouth. "I'll survive."

Innelda's violet eyes glinted bright in the mid-day sunlight. "Then you're stronger than I am. I'd give away my shoes before entering a razor rock field if it meant avoiding tamrin leaves for the rest of my life."

Meaghan had never heard of a razor rock field, but she had a feeling a description would not help her nausea, so she did not ask for one. She reached into her pocket for a yellow candy and turned toward camp. Innelda fell in step beside her.

A strand of blonde hair drifted across Innelda's left eye as she nodded toward Meaghan's hand. "Do the melleu pebbles really help?" she asked.

Meaghan slipped the button-sized pebble into her mouth. It dissolved, coating her tongue with a light powder more reminiscent of mint than the lemon its color had indicated. She shrugged. "Some, I guess. It settles my stomach for a few hours, anyway. I'm hoping this illness passes soon."

"Will you be able to fight?"

Meaghan's gaze slid sideways. Although Innelda's sympathy struck Meaghan's empath power with a hard blow, she showed none of it on her face. Behind the emotion, anxiety prickled. Meaghan raised an eyebrow. "You don't need to be concerned about me."

"I…Oh." Innelda's cheeks flashed red. Embarrassment washed over Meaghan's power. "I'm sorry," Innelda said. "I just thought…"

"Thought what?" Meaghan prompted.

Innelda looked away. "It's not my place to say."

"That usually doesn't stop people. Try me."

"I thought maybe you should let your Guardians handle this one. With you being sick, you're not going to be able to fight as well. The kingdom needs you."

"And I need Nick." Meaghan pressed her lips together, and then sighed when Innelda squirmed under her gaze. "I can't ask anyone else to make a sacrifice I'm not willing to make."

"Even if that sacrifice is your life?"

"Even if."

They continued walking. Although Innelda's sympathy and embarrassment had faded, her anxiety remained. Meaghan waited, expecting Innelda to continue their conversation before they reached the outskirts of camp and Innelda did not disappoint her. Meaghan could hear canvas snapping in the breeze when Innelda placed a hand on her arm.

"Let me help," she said.

"You are helping. You're fighting alongside everyone else."

"No, I mean…" Innelda dropped her hand to her side. She blew out a heavy breath. "Let me help protect you. I want to make sure you get out safely."

Meaghan's instinct to reject the offer fell apart on her lips as the desperation in Innelda's request touched Meaghan's empath power. Behind it, raw grief throbbed. The ache enveloped Meaghan in a tight blanket. Innelda wanted to take Talis's place by Meaghan's side.

But Innelda had not been trained as a Guardian. She had barely received training as a village soldier. The chances of her coming out of the castle alive would amount to a lottery win. Yet her offer had been sincere. She wanted to protect her queen, to honor the man she loved.

Meaghan would have none of it. Too many people had died needlessly already.

"I can't let you do that," Meaghan said. "Talis loved you. He'd want me to keep you safe."

Innelda's shoulders slumped. "Does everyone know?"

"Only Cal and I know the truth," Meaghan said. "After you arrived, he made up a story so the Elders wouldn't suspect anything."

"Talis told you," she whispered. She passed a hand over her forehead. Gray colored her cheeks again. "He respected Cal. He trusted him."

"You can trust me, too."

Innelda nodded. "We decided not to do anything about what we felt. We couldn't take the chance."

Because doing so would have risked their powers wedding them, which would have weakened Talis and left him vulnerable to Garon's army. In the shadow of Talis's ghost, the cruelty of that decision became more apparent.

"I'm tired of not taking risks," Innelda said. "I hide behind invisible walls. I forego love to protect those I care about and in the end…" She spread her hands out, flat and empty. "I have nothing. At least if I help you and King Nick, I can make a difference."

Meaghan shook her head. "You're talking about suicide."

"I'm talking about living for once. I'm talking about taking back my life, making my *own* choices." She dropped her hands. "Besides, I have no one left. Garon took everyone from me."

"And you want to repay the favor," Meaghan said. "Revenge."

"The people I love are gone, but if you succeed, we all have a future again. We won't have to hide in villages or be afraid of losing those we care about. We won't have to worry about making friends because they might be traitors. It's what Talis wanted. It's why he fought and it's why I want to fight, too."

"I'll think about it," Meaghan promised. She wanted to trust the woman Talis had loved, but she could not let her attachment to him blind her. Innelda had never been subject to Caide's truth spell. Meaghan sensed no deceit in her, but she could not rely on her empath power to detect a traitor. Not any longer.

A gust of wind whipped past, carrying the scent of smoke with it and Meaghan trailed her eyes back toward camp and the fire she knew would mark the start of the dinner hour. They had not just stopped for the night. They had set up base in preparation for battle. Tomorrow began the end of Garon's reign. Either he would fall or they would all be dead.

§

NIGHT DRAPED a curtain over the sky, creating an ominous backdrop to the quiet tent city under Meaghan's rule. Most of the villagers had gone to bed, sleeping or pretending to as the hours disappeared behind them. They would mobilize before the sun rose and march straight for the castle. Meaghan and Cal planned to take a different route, under a more secretive schedule.

She closed her hand over a yawn and ducked behind a tree when she saw two shadows stretching across her path. A couple from one of the mountain villages strode past, hand-in-hand. Saying their goodbyes, Meaghan had no doubt. If they made it past tomorrow, there would be joyous hellos on the other end.

After the shadows had disappeared, Meaghan moved to step out of her hiding place and froze when a voice broke free from the forest.

"I don't know what to do."

May. Recognition carried along with the voice, though Meaghan had never heard Nick's mother sound so scared. Meaghan crept deeper into the woods. When she caught a glimpse of red hair, she pressed her body against the trunk of a white oak and peered around it.

May paced, treading between the shadows and moonlight with little care for either. The same moon cast silver over the face of her companion. Meaghan's surprise at seeing Miles soon dissolved beneath her worry. The Head Elder had lines etched deep into his forehead.

"I'm not ready for this, Miles."

The war, Meaghan thought, and then changed her mind when May turned. Tears streamed down May's cheeks. They glistened pure as diamonds.

"I can't lose him. I've always known it could happen, but I'm not ready."

"No one ever is," Miles said. He stepped forward and folded May into his arms. "We can prepare all we want, but we can't harden our hearts to reality when it strikes."

"I thought I could protect him," May said. "I failed."

"You haven't yet," Miles told her, though Meaghan struggled to hear the conviction in his voice. "Tomorrow still has promise."

May pressed her cheek into Miles's shoulder, turning her head so she faced Meaghan's hiding place. Meaghan took a step back out of instinct. She soon realized the move was not necessary. May had squeezed her eyes shut.

"It feels as if my world has died," May whispered.

Miles drew his hands up her back. "It will be okay."

"How?" She lifted her head. "If I lose him, how can it ever be okay again?"

Miles pulled her tight. Meaghan heard sobbing and backed away, leaving May to her grief, but she refused to shed her own tears.

Nick still lived. Meaghan was sure of it. After all, if the world had died, how could it still be spinning?

CHAPTER THIRTY-THREE

"YOUR FATHER and I used to spar here," Cal said, his voice barely a whisper on the still air.

Meaghan shifted in her spot to glance at Cal. Tall grass brushed her cheek, as much a hindrance to her and Cal's movement as it was their veil against Mardróch. Sometime after midnight, the wind had ceased and with it, Cal had lost the ability to carry information along the element. He parted the grass and pressed his hand into the dirt, though his attention remained on the horizon.

"Show me the truth, show me the lies. Show me what I can't see with my own eyes," he sang, using the short rhyme to focus his power. Meaghan followed his distant gaze, though she saw only an endless sea of green beneath the white face a full moon. No flowers, berries, or fruit broke the monotonous green of this forest. Garon had made sure of that. A spell kept anything edible from growing so close to the castle.

Rustling shook a tall bush and she dropped her hands to the blades at her waist, relaxing once again when a bird flitted into a tree.

"There are hundreds of Garon's soldiers waiting in the field surrounding the castle," Cal told her. "I'm able to jump from the ground to their camp fires. They're not saying much."

"Do you think they know you're listening?" Meaghan asked.

"Garon would be a fool to think I wouldn't be," Cal responded. "He's a lot of things, but he's never been that."

"I'm surprised he kept his word and didn't attack us on our way here," Meaghan said.

"The conversations I'm hearing may have revealed why. A large number of his female Mardróch aren't here yet. Garon had them posted somewhere in the Barren. They'll be one of his biggest assets in this fight."

"So if we attack first thing in the morning, we might not have to face them."

Cal stood. "They'll be arriving within the hour."

Meaghan tried not to think about the Mardróch who had fallen to his female counterpart's powers. "Does anyone know how to fight them?"

"Carefully," Cal said. "Or avoid them. Faillen feels his archers should be able to keep them occupied without too many casualties. Let's hope he's right." He gestured toward a white tree on their left. It seemed to sparkle within the shadows of the night. "That's a singing tree. Have you ever seen one before?"

Meaghan shook her head.

Cal made his way toward it, the grass parting in swift waves around his bulky form. He ran a finger down the tree's pale bark. It emitted a high pitch, like the peal of a copper bell. "This area used to be cleared. Your father and I sparred here."

"You said that already."

Cal grunted. "So I did. I didn't tell you that he would sneak off with your mother sometimes, so they could picnic here. She used to play these trees." He touched his thumb to a branch. It emitted a deeper tone, closer to a bass guitar than a bell. "It was like watching her direct a chorus. She never played the same song twice. I think she must've made them up as she went."

He withdrew his hand. "When we win this battle, I'll bring you back here and show you more. I don't want to risk the Mardróch hearing us."

Meaghan nodded at his back, though she knew he could not see her. He would not hear her, either, if she spoke, so she did not bother. His voice had taken on a distant, reminiscent quality. He belonged not to this moment, but to the past, to a time when he stood guard over a young king and queen who had spread a blanket over a manmade clearing and played sweet songs on a tree that represented the innocence of their time.

Cal dug his fingers into his thick beard. Gray and black whiskers danced across his chest. "Tomorrow's the day, friend," he whispered and flattened his palm on the tree. It echoed Meaghan's silence. "I promised I'd take care of you. I failed, but I'll make sure I succeed with your daughter."

"Cal…"

Cal cleared his throat. He glanced over his shoulder at Meaghan. A touch of embarrassment greeted her empath power, mixing with the grief that had flourished a moment before, and then both disappeared with the flash of Cal's lopsided grin.

"Well, I meant it. We'll get him this time. That castle belongs to your family."

Meaghan offered him a half-smile in return. She did not feel nearly as cocky about their prospects as Cal seemed. She reached for the thin metal strand of her mother's amulet and pulled it from beneath her shirt. The necklace chilled her palm. She curled her fingers around the amethyst glass that hid the Reaper Stone and surged her power through it, chasing the cold away. Contentment spread through her and she closed her eyes, allowing it to envelop her mind. Although she gained some solace from the heirloom, she wished she had the Writer's book instead. She wanted to visit the memories of her parents one more time, take comfort in their faces and voices, but the book had disappeared with Nick.

She stretched her empath power into the forest surrounding them. Undoubtedly, Cal's command over the elements would have shown him if an enemy hid under the cover of night, but she did not want to take any chances. Not when they were so close to the castle.

Her power brought no surprises. It rolled out and ebbed back undisturbed. She dropped the amulet and followed Cal as he continued toward the home she only remembered from fiery nightmares.

They walked single file, taking a southerly route. May and Sam approached from the north, seeking a hidden entrance that mirrored the tunnel Cal hoped to find.

Miles led the army alongside Faillen and Cadell. They would attack Garon's minions head-on before the sun met the middle of the sky.

Faillen had warned her that a battle this large could last days or weeks. Meaghan suspected it would be over in hours. They were outmatched. The closer she grew to her parents' place of death, the more her fears consumed her. Her fingers trembled and she tightened them into fists to keep her doubts from showing.

A breeze swirled past them, gentle in its pursuit of the night clouds. Half an hour passed, and then Cal extended an arm, stopping her with the force of a concrete pole. She bit her tongue to avoid yelping with the shock of it.

"A Mardróch," he hissed under his breath.

Meaghan nodded and refocused her power. The smell of rotten eggs assaulted her nose and she realized the monster hid close by. She would have noticed the horrible stench if she had not been so preoccupied with her own nerves.

Growling erupted from their right, a low throaty sound that held both anger and surprise. The odor of sulfur changed to decaying garbage. Blue lightning flashed through the trees. Several crickets chirped a song of panic in the distance. Then both the light and the noises faded.

Meaghan's power no longer translated the Mardróch emotion into rotten garbage and she realized it could mean only one thing.

"He's gone," Cal echoed her suspicion. "Teleported, do you think?"

Meaghan shook her head. "He saw us. I could sense his excitement. I doubt he would give up that easily."

"Maybe he wanted to alert Garon."

"Maybe," Meaghan conceded and frowned as another emotion

triggered her power. This one did not hold the putrid odor of a Mardróch. "There's someone else out there."

"Enemy or ally?"

"I'm not sure. Someone human though. I sense pride." Meaghan gestured for Cal to follow her this time. She made her way toward the emotion, focusing on it with her empath power.

Each step brought them deeper into the wilderness. Vines draped across bones of dead trees. Some slithered as Meaghan and Cal passed, and Meaghan kept a wary eye fixed overhead in case a creeper vine tried to attack.

Moss muffled their footsteps. More than once, when Meaghan thought she had lost Cal, she found him struggling with a patch of weeds behind her, his broad shoulders trapped by the spaces her slender body had passed through.

"You couldn't find an easier route?" he griped as he wrestled with a vine coated in white trumpet flowers.

Meaghan freed an allestone blade from its sheath and sliced the weeds in front of her, clearing a wider path for Cal. "Better?" she asked.

"Much."

Darkness settled heavily around them. Meaghan did not dare recite a light spell, afraid it would alert Mardróch. Instead, she moved slowly, memorizing the path in front of her whenever the moon danced between the leaves of the overlapping canopy.

The emotion continued to evade her, dodging outside her vision and at a pace a few steps faster than hers. At some point along the way, it had changed from pride to determination.

She halted when the path in front of her turned into a thick wall of thorny bushes.

"Did you lose him?" Cal asked.

Meaghan shook her head. "We can't get through. We can go around…" She hesitated, torn between following and going back.

"We don't have time," Cal said. "I don't like having someone know we're out here anymore than you do, but this could be a trap."

Meaghan narrowed her eyes, stretching her power's focus. She could sense nothing new from the person they chased. "Let's get back on course. I'll keep my power focused on him. If he comes closer, I'll know."

This time Cal took the lead, parting the sea of green with powerful forearms. The emotion followed them, maintaining a steady distance. Meaghan tapped Cal on the back to get his attention. She twirled her finger over her shoulder, gesturing that they had a tail. Cal nodded. When the forest gave way to a gravel road speckled with weeds, he nudged her toward the opposite side of the path. He hung back when she moved forward, and then disappeared from view, lost to the shadow of an old oak.

The emotion continued to follow. Meaghan scanned the tree line over her shoulder, expecting to see its owner emerge onto the road. Strong panic clawed at Meaghan's mind instead. She quelled the urge to run and shut off her power.

A few minutes later, Cal charged toward her. In one hand, he held an allestone sword Meaghan did not recognize. The other dragged their stalker.

"Innelda!" Meaghan exclaimed, anger mixing with her surprise.

The woman's cheeks flared bright red.

"Traitor?" Cal asked, shoving Innelda forward.

"Never," Innelda protested. Her gaze shot from Meaghan to Cal. Heat charged along it. "Garon took everything from me."

"It wouldn't be the first time someone sided with Garon over the people they loved."

Meaghan let her power roam free again. Innelda's rage seemed genuine. Grief swelled beneath it. Meaghan wanted to believe her, but her offer of aid and then subsequent refusal to obey Meaghan's command could just as easily mean she was a spy as it could she wanted to help.

"Did you take care of the Mardróch?" Meaghan asked.

Innelda lifted her chin. "I did. He had been following you for a while. He wasn't expecting me."

"I imagine not," Cal muttered. "We certainly weren't."

Shame eclipsed Innelda's other emotions. "I'm sorry," she said. "I thought it couldn't hurt to keep an eye on you."

"If you'd been seen, it would've hurt a lot," Cal told her. "You could've ruined our plans."

Innelda crossed her arms in defiance. "*You* were seen. If I hadn't come, that Mardróch would have reported you to Garon."

Cal grunted. "That's beside the point. We can't have you upsetting this mission. The army is marching this way. Hide until they get here."

"Fine." Innelda said and this time Meaghan felt deceit in her. She would continue to follow. Meaghan had no doubt. She also did not doubt Talis would have done the same.

"You and Talis butted heads a lot, didn't you?" Meaghan guessed.

"Maybe." Innelda shrugged. "It suited us."

"I imagine it did. It doesn't suit me, though. If you're going to follow us anyway, you might as well stick close so I can watch you. You'll do as I say, when I say it."

Innelda nodded and this time Meaghan knew she told the truth. Although she doubted Innelda posed any threat, Meaghan did not relish the idea of having another person slowing them down.

She soon realized she had no reason to worry. Innelda's movements were as quiet as Cal's, though he had to use the elements to muffle his footsteps. She had clearly spent time training. She moved with the stealth of one of Faillen's warriors and scanned the forest ahead of them with the vigilance of a Guardian. Even the way she gripped her broadsword spoke of a woman accustomed to handling weapons. Meaghan wondered if she had trained under Talis long before Nick had visited to teach her fellow villagers how to fight.

They broke through the forest into a vast field. The moon tickled silver fingers across hundreds of acres of green grass. Dotted along the green, thousands of simple brown tents fluttered in the breeze. Glowing embers hinted of campfires long forgotten. Innelda's fear washed over Meaghan, prompting her to mute her power.

"There are so many," Innelda whispered. "We don't have enough people."

"The camp you met us at isn't the only one we have command over," Cal told her. "We'll be evenly matched when the time comes. This way."

He turned and followed the edge of the forest until it intersected with a river, then walked along the bank. Meaghan took up the rear, counting Cal's large footprints and then Innelda's small ones as they sank into the mud and filled with pooling water.

The river bubbled in peaceful song while they traveled, then it babbled faster, an angry and urgent chant as the forest broke apart, yielding to large rocks and craggy boulders. Finally, it reached its apex, crashing over the side of a cliff and casting rainbows into a glistening pool below. Meaghan toed the rocky edge where river met waterfall and glanced down. A white-spotted deer stopped drinking to look up at her. Cal gripped one of her shoulders with a thick hand and turned her attention to the side.

From where she stood, the valley stretched unimpeded beneath a swollen moon. In the center of it, a castle rose steadfast and gray.

Meaghan caught her breath. Towers marked the corners of the massive structure, each a show of strength and ornate beauty. They rose into the sky, their allestone walls sparkling like crystal. A gray wall stretched in front of the castle, offering protection and a frame for vibrant gardens and slate courtyards. Meaghan had played among the fruit trees and rose bushes, danced on the grassy knolls, and swung from her father's arms next to the low stone benches.

And later, she had fallen inside her apartment with her mother when explosions crumbled the northernmost walls. Garon had left those walls as she remembered them—haphazard and black. Even the velvet green moss that grew wild over the scorched parts of the castle could not hide its ugliness. Her throat tightened. "How much farther?" she asked.

Cal lifted a hand. *"Illusion lifts, as sight I gift. For all who hear, let truth appear."*

A black hole opened in the ground a yard from Meaghan's feet. Cal recited another spell and a small orb floated over his hands, a magical flashlight that dashed ahead of him into the dark cavern.

"Shall we?" he asked.

Cal's calm belied the truth of what they intended to do. At the other side of this tunnel, they would enter the lair of the beast.

Meaghan could not shake the feeling he would eat them alive.

CHAPTER THIRTY-FOUR

DRIP. DRIP.

Nick pressed his face into his hands.

Drip. Drip. Drip.

He inhaled one deep breath, then another, each in time with the distant sound of water hitting stone. Every drop marked a second wasted, though he had lost count of how many seconds had passed, how many minutes and hours made up his time in the darkness.

Drip. Drip.

A mouse squeaked as it scurried outside his cell. Somewhere farther down the hallway an animal hissed. Nick pushed harder against the rock wall behind him, welcoming the pain each jagged edge delivered to his spine. Pain meant he still lived.

The animal yowled. Metal reverberated as something solid crashed into the bars, and then silence followed. A wild saber had made its nest in one of the dilapidated cells farther down the hall. Although the spike-haired rodent could fit within the palms of Nick's hands, he knew better than to mistake its stature for innocence. Each of its four front teeth extended the length of his index finger. A few swift bites could end his life if they landed in the right place.

Part of him welcomed the thought just to get out of this hell. It would be kinder than the torture he would suffer when Garon sent for him. Nick pushed up to standing, and then traced his hand along the rough stone, using it to guide him to the front of his cell.

He had seen his ungracious home a handful of times now, each for only a few minutes while a nameless guard deposited a tray of slop on the floor.

He reached the bars and started coasting along them, hand-over hand. They smelled of metal and rust. And maybe blood, though he credited that to his imagination. Several spots felt rough against his palms. His feet rustled what remained of his hay bed and mold permeated the air. He preferred to sleep on a cloak on the far side of the floor. At least Max had left him that.

"That's what friends are for, right?" Nick asked. His bitter sarcasm echoed back to him from the ceiling.

Chirping answered him. A pair of golden eyes floated down the hallway, stopped at his cell, and then continued onward. The saber had finished its meal. It would return in a few hours, as it always did.

Nick continued moving, too. He found the other side of his cell and turned to trace the wall. A dip in the bricks at chest-level marked a rectangular vent. He did not bother testing it for weaknesses. He had done that too many times already. Magic fused it to the stone and even if he knew the counterspell, only an arm would fit through.

It served no real purpose, from what he could tell. The royal family had installed it as an act of kindness. Criminals would have been able to talk to each other this way—commiserate before death met them in the form of exile.

No other prisoners remained in this hell now. No voices offered Nick companionship. Occasionally he heard whispers as the guards checked on him, though they had refused to acknowledge any of his questions.

Ammonia and pungent waste wafted in his direction, marking his approach to a back corner. Nick wrinkled his nose and skirted around the porcelain pot he had been using as a toilet. He followed the last wall back to the beginning, examining each contour with his fingertips, but found nothing new. The Pit was impenetrable. The royal family had ensured as much centuries before.

He would need tools to carve through the mortar between the stones. The closest he could come was a dull spoon from dinner. Spells had also proven useless. He had expected no less. Only a fool would build a prison without enacting binding spells to keep enemies from using magic.

In some cases, personal powers still worked. King Ed had proven that by walking through the bars of his own cell, but Nick's ability to prevent someone from sensing him did him little good. Garon already knew his whereabouts. Some of his Guardian powers also worked. He could sense danger. That power prickled for his attention every time a prison guard came close. But he had lost his ability to teleport. He could not travel from one end of the cell to the other, let alone outside the castle.

A yellow glow moved along the hall in the distance and Nick approached the bars once more. He received meals twice a day.

Breakfast had already arrived in the form of stale bread and rancid stone pear juice. It sat untouched in the corner. He had never had visitors in between. He did not have to think hard to guess who it would be.

Nick gripped the bars in his fists as Max rounded the corner. Nick's old friend lit two torches opposite Nick's cell, and then dropped the one in his hand into a wall bracket.

"Morning, Nick."

Nick did not respond. Max leaned against the wall and propped up one foot behind him, acting nonchalant as always. When he hooked his thumbs into his pockets, Nick imagined punching him between his blue eyes. An uppercut to the chin would follow and if Nick's aim was lucky, his so-called friend would split his head open on the rock wall. Dark red blood would do a nice job of messing up Max's neatly styled blonde hair.

"You look a little stormy today, pal," he said. "Imagining murdering me?"

Nick glared, as irritated by Max's humor as by his accurate assessment of Nick's thoughts. Months before, Max's ability to read Nick's face, and the childhood bond that had created it, would have made him smile. Today it made him sick.

"What do you want?"

"The chance to explain."

"Explain what?" Anger bubbled in Nick's veins. His cheeks flared hot. So did his voice. "You're a traitor, Max. That's all I need to know."

Max dropped his foot to the floor and stood up straight. "I was afraid you'd feel that way. You've always been too single-minded for your own good."

"Right, because it's better to keep my morals loose in case Garon offers a better deal."

"It's not as simple as that."

"Isn't it? Don't you feel anything for the lives you've taken? You grew up with the people in our village. You claimed to love Cissy."

"I did."

"You killed her."

Max cleared his throat and looked away. He slouched against the wall once more. "You make too many assumptions, Nick. It's not a good quality for a king."

"I'll be dead soon anyway. How long until Garon sends for me? I'm tired of waiting."

"He doesn't know you're here."

Nick shook his head. "The guards…"

"Shadow Guard members. As far as Garon's aware, you're still with Meaghan, preparing for battle. He laughs about that on a regular basis."

"Don't lie to me, Max."

"I'm not. Garon would've killed you by now if he knew you were here. He's afraid of you."

"He has no reason to be afraid of me."

"He does, actually. The Shadow Guard convinced him there's a prophecy that predicts you'll be his downfall."

"That's absurd. Why would you tell him that?"

"Because there is one." Max shrugged. "I think, anyway. It's a bit hard to decipher."

"Aren't they all?"

A smile tilted the corners of Max's lips. "That's the Nick I love. Some aren't as hard to decipher as others. Meaghan's a threat. I know you don't want to hear that, but it's true. I've seen the prophecy that warns us. Her power will kill everything."

"Nobody's seen that prophecy, Max. That's one thing the Shadow Guard members have all told us."

"Our foot soldiers haven't seen it. The Tribunal has. My father's one of them, Nick. I know everything he knows."

Nick shook his head again, trying to shake off his confusion. None of this made sense. Max's father had been a steady presence throughout Nick's childhood. He had been strict, but a loving role model. Nick never would have thought him capable of leading a group like the Shadow Guard. It took a ruthless mind to slaughter thousands of people just to get to one woman.

Yet he had seen Avilis murder Ed in the Writer's book. His face had held no remorse. Not long after, he had consoled Nick's mother on the loss of her charge. A loss he had orchestrated. Nick let go of the bars and stepped back, suddenly chilled by the truth.

"You've been using me this whole time," Nick said. "Was any of our friendship real or was it an assignment from the beginning?"

"My father encouraged it, sure, but it was real. It still is. I'm trying to protect you."

Nick glanced around his cell, from the cobwebs in one corner to the carcass of a long-dead rat in another. "You have an odd way of doing that."

"Trust me, you're much safer here. Meaghan's army will arrive at any moment. If I had let you try to protect her, you'd be dead before too long."

"So you're here to…what? Convince me it's all for the greater good, that someday I'll agree? I won't. I can't forgive you for this."

Shadows flickered over Max's face before he erased them with a chuckle. "You never change, do you? Always quick to judge. You'll understand eventually." He reached behind his back and produced a book. "I thought you might be bored so I brought you something to read."

He approached the bars. Nick retreated, and then froze halfway across the cell when he recognized the brown cover between Max's fingers. Max slipped the book through the bars and let go. Nick lunged forward to catch it before it hit the ground.

"I hope you don't mind me borrowing it," Max said. "I couldn't risk the Elders discovering my father's guilt. It looks like I didn't need to worry."

Nick flipped through the pages. Each one looked as if ink had never touched it.

"When the battle's over, I'll come back for you. You can't stay in Ærenden, not with Garon around, but we have a safe place for you in the Barren."

Max picked up his torch again, then turned and withdrew the way he had come. A moment before he rounded a bend in the hall, Nick asked the one question that had burned in his mind from the moment he realized Max's betrayal.

"Why?"

Max faced him again.

"Why did you do it, Max?"

"I told you already. Meaghan's power is dangerous."

"You know that's not true. You've seen everything she can do."

"No, I haven't, and neither have you. Our spy on Caide's rescue mission confirmed she has the reaper power. We can't allow it to exist."

"Reaper power," Nick echoed. Max retraced his steps to stand in front of the cell. "There's no such thing, Max. She reads emotions and helps plants grow. That's all."

"For now. I don't think this is a debate either one of us will concede, so you're just going to have to take my word for it."

Nick almost snarled a response along the lines of taking Max's words and shoving them in unpleasant places, but he checked the impulse. In the Writer's book, Adelina had once revealed that knowledge was the most important tool a ruler could have. Nick decided to heed her wisdom.

"All right," he said. "Let's assume you're correct about Meaghan. A Spellmaster's power is dangerous, too. Why isn't the Shadow Guard concerned about Caide or Aldin?"

"Some powers are too strong to be controlled."

"Like Ella's power, you mean? The Shadow Guard let her live."

Max's eyes flicked down. Nick cursed. "You used her to get to me, and then you rewarded her with death."

"I killed her out of sympathy. You must have seen how much her power tortured her."

"Tell yourself whatever you want."

Max shrugged. "I suppose it doesn't matter now. We weren't trying to get to you, though. We wanted Caide to have that spell."

"Why? What does it do?"

"I'm not sure. Only the Lead Tribune knows."

Nick waited. Max did not offer a name. "You killed innocent villagers just to get a slip of paper to Caide? Why didn't you sneak him the spell when he wasn't looking? You've had plenty of opportunity."

"It wasn't my call. The Tribunal wanted to test him, to see if he'd be a threat like Farrow."

Nick did not want to think about what would have happened if Caide had failed their test. Would Max have welcomed the Mardróch into the village? A shudder crept up Nick's spine.

"Please understand, Nick. I don't enjoy doing what I have to do, but I don't want to see the kingdom destroyed either."

"So you'll sacrifice anyone for your cause. It doesn't matter who they are."

"Leaders have to make difficult decisions. It's something my father taught me and something you'll learn soon enough. One life, one martyr can save the lives of many. Isn't that what we all signed up for when we began fighting this war?"

"I fight to make things better. Garon won't do that."

"My father will ensure he does. We won't let anyone's sacrifice be in vain."

Nick tightened his grip on the Writer's book. One corner bit into his flesh. He looked down at it. Two lives already had been lost in vain. The same two deaths had started this war. If the king and queen had lived, thousands would still be breathing, still be hugging their loved ones and cherishing new memories. Nick's father, Talis, James and Vivian—all of them were gone for the sake of defeating one unknown power. How many others would die before the Shadow Guard fulfilled their twisted purpose?

"Is that what you tell yourself every night?" he asked. "Does it help you sleep to think Cissy was a martyr and not a victim of your actions?"

Nick looked up. Max grasped one of the bars. His knuckles turned white.

"You let the Mardróch into our village. That decision killed dozens of innocent people, children, your own friends who trusted you and protected you in battle. You slaughtered them all. Does it give you peace to think it's all for a good cause in the end? Do you really think that matters?"

"It matters, Nick. It has to."

"Does it?" Nick stared into Max's face, into the eyes of the stranger who had shared most of his life. They looked stricken, and hollow. "Why, Max? No single power can do the damage the Shadow Guard has caused. You're the greatest threat to the kingdom, not Meaghan."

Max stared back at Nick, unblinking for a full minute, and then broke his trance with a hot breath. He turned away.

"You're wrong, Nick. It matters."

Nick did not respond. He saw no point in continuing the conversation. Max had been brainwashed from birth. Nick could get through to him about as well as he could convince a dranx monkey not to climb trees.

Max made his way back down the hallway, his pace slower than it had been before. He turned to exit, then hesitated and glanced over his shoulder.

"I only killed one person that night," he said. "I killed that Dreamer because he murdered Cissy. It matters, Nick, because *she's* the one who let the Mardróch into the village."

With those words echoing through the empty cells, Max disappeared into the darker recesses of the prison.

CHAPTER THIRTY-FIVE

NICK FELT as if sand grated his eyes. They burned from exhaustion, and his head throbbed from pent up fury. He rubbed his temples in an attempt to ease some of the ache. It did little to help.

At least Max had left the torches burning, though they offered no warmth and little comfort. Nick's temporary home ended this block, as he had learned from the few minutes a day the guards had delivered his food. More spiders claimed this space than he cared to count. That also was not new. One red arachnid the size of his palm hung above the grate between his cell and the next one. It dropped from its web, skittered down the bricks, and passed through to the other side.

Nick scanned the walls, careful to note every scratch and white scar that time had etched into the stone. Doodles from previous tenants covered the bricks. Intermingled among those, hash marks counted down days—until exile or trial, reminders of escape in one form or another. Nothing gave Nick hope.

Meaghan would be here soon. Max had told him as much and his former friend had no reason to lie about it. Nick would be powerless to stop her death while trapped in the Pit. The battle would resume, likely with Meaghan's insistence that they also try to rescue him. He would have no control over its outcome, no knowledge of who lived or died until smoke filled the castle and blood flooded the grounds.

Control is an illusion I no longer wish to harbor.

Meaghan's voice floated through Nick's mind and he tightened his fingers around the Writer's book. She had been talking about their love, but wisdom still echoed within her words. He had spent his life trying to control every aspect of it. All the effort had gained him was a list of wayward plans that mocked him from the shadows of his past. He ticked them off with disdain.

He had trained to be a protector of the royal family, not to be a member of it, yet he had become king in a nondescript cabin in the middle of an unchartered wilderness. The thought of leading people when he felt lost himself still kept him from sleeping well at night. He worried he would stumble and the whole kingdom would fall down with him.

He had also been woefully unprepared for his complicated relationship with Meaghan. Through most of his teenage years, he had pictured another woman sharing his life. He had loved Calia, had memorized the star-like freckles on the bridge of her nose, the twists of her flaxen hair, and the seductive curves of her hips. He had learned intimacy with her in the hayloft of a neighbor's barn and had planned for their wedding someday. It never came. No matter how many romantic dates and late evenings he spent with her, he could not keep them from drifting apart. He could not keep life from intervening. Nor could he control true love when it decided to grab him.

Finally, though he had closed off his heart from trusting—allowing only four people to earn his friendship—he could not control how easily those he trusted had hurt him. He squeezed his eyes shut as tears seeped through the sand. He had four close friends, and two of them had tried to kill him. They had both been members of the Shadow Guard.

Nick pushed out a long breath. It strained his throat and tightened the ache in his chest. He could not control his life. Not all of it, but he could control how he reacted to it. He could fight until his muscles no longer moved and his mind darkened with his last thought. Just as King Edáire had done.

He flipped open the book. Words greeted him, splashing across the pages line-by-line as if wiped into existence. The king and queen's wedding appeared first. Next came the profession of their love. Last, Ed's discussion with Cal about his distrust of Garon shimmered into view.

The other pages remained blank. Nick snapped the book closed and tossed it aside. He had wanted guidance, a new historical tale to give him a clue about escape. The book had only repeated the lessons Nick had already learned. He and Meaghan had shared the same prophesied wedding as her parents. They had learned to love each other in the same way. And like her parents, someone close to them had betrayed them. They had failed to see the truth until they could do nothing about it.

Nick pushed his fingers into his eyelids as an expression from

Earth rang through his memory. *Those who do not learn from history are doomed to repeat it.*

At least he was not the only king to have earned residence in this loathsome place.

Nick yanked open his eyes. He scrambled for the book. The same three stories stared back at him—three specific stories that held clues to King Edáire's time in the Pit.

When Nick had awoken in his cell the first time, he had not bothered to look for Ed's hiding place, because Max knew about it. Nick had told his friend every detail. He thought it would be foolish of the Shadow Guard to put him in the same cell. Yet the book always delivered the right stories in time of need. Nick held his breath as he looked at the words on the first page.

The book showed him the king and queen's first meeting. Nick followed Adelina down the winding halls of the Pit. He watched as she approached her future husband. Ed had been in the last cell, too. Although most of these sections looked the same, Nick felt the first spark of real hope enter his mind.

He broke his reading trance and flipped through the pages, but did not allow the story to pull him into it. He found Ed and Cal's earliest conversation in the woods. Before Ed and Adelina had confessed their love, the king had divulged his plan to escape the Pit.

"With a key. I stole one, and a knife... I hid them inside the wall of my cell."

Nick drew his gaze down the page, pausing when he found the second part of the conversation he needed.

"If you ever wind up in the cell, the spot on the wall is marked with my

initials."

Nick examined the graffiti-laden walls of his own cell and felt his hope sink. He would need days to separate Ed's initials from the thousands of scratches breaking the cell's uniformity.

But he still had one more clue buried within Ed and Cal's last conversation. He flipped straight to it.

"It's in the farthest corner from the bars, on the outside wall."

Nick vaulted from his seat. Although he had dozens of stones to read still, he had direction. He scanned each mark on the wall, looking for the king's initials. *E* for Ed, of course, though the king's secondary initial puzzled him. By the time he had finished a cursory look over the stones, he had more than two dozen possibilities. For a brief moment, he wished he were on Earth. There, at least, people had a set last name and they used it often. Here, the second initial represented a mother's name. Since everyone knew each other by sight within their close-knit villages, writing initials had become unnecessary.

Nick's initials were N/M for *Nick of Maiyhala.* Ed had never mentioned his mother in the Writer's book. If Nick had learned her name in his studies, he had forgotten it.

He tucked his fingers into the crevices of each potential stone, pulling and wiggling in an attempt to loosen the bricks. His efforts came up empty. None of the *"E"*'s stood for Ed.

Nick sank to his knees. He had been a fool to believe this could be Ed's cell, that Max had given him an escape.

He trailed his gaze toward the red spider's web. A fly writhed at the edge of the sticky silk, frantically trying to break free, and Nick felt empathy for the creature. The spider scurried back through the pass-through and pounced. Within seconds, it had cocooned the fly in white, saving it for dinner later.

Nick looked away. The torches had burned halfway down, marking the passage of time and the slow ebbing of his chance for survival. He set the book aside and glanced at the floor. Leftover hay from someone's bed had stuck to the bricks. Nick brushed a few strands from the wall, and cursed when brown goo coated the tips of his fingers. The scent of rot wafted under his nose. He rubbed the mess on his pants, and then quickly forgot about it when several new initials caught his attention. Dirt and hay had concealed them before.

The first three offered nothing worthwhile, but the last caught Nick's breath—E/É. Was Ed's sister, Élana, named after their mother?

At the top of the stone, a small chip led to a hairline crack that split white through the marbled gray. Nick wedged his index finger into the chip. Nothing moved. When he tugged harder, the front of the stone crumbled. Behind it, Ed had carved a small cavern into the wall. It would have taken many hours and a lot of strength, but he had had plenty of both. Within the cavern, Nick found a small blade, now dull, and a rusted yellow key.

He tucked the knife into his belt and palmed the key. Although he could not see the lock from inside his cell, he felt for it and inserted the key into the hole, then twisted. A click greeted his ears. The door opened with a loud creak. He held his breath. No guards rushed down the hallway in response.

He was free. Now he had to sneak past an enemy army and find his way through a castle labyrinth housing a ruler focused on killing him.

Adrenaline curved a smile over his lips. Now *this* is what he had trained to do.

CHAPTER THIRTY-SIX

"SOMEONE POKED holes in the sky."

Caide looked down at his younger brother and smiled, though it felt far from easy through the tension locking his jaw tight. They had been walking for hours, yet Aldin had not so much as yawned or spoken until this moment.

Aldin pointed at the stars. "See, holes. The sun is hiding behind the black. That's what makes the light."

Caide did not bother to correct him. The stars had already begun to fade. As they trudged onward, Aldin kept his focus glued on the sky with the wonder only a child could muster. The sun parted the black sea overhead. Warm rays danced over Aldin's soft face, brightening his olive skin and sparking light within his smoke-colored eyes. He stretched an arm up, mesmerized by a bird that coasted into a cloud, and Caide's attention drew to the tribal tattoo on the inside of his brother's forearm. It matched Caide's own, though it did more than instill a sense of pride within him. The two interlocking triangles served as a reminder of what mattered most in his life. The first represented the past, present and future. The second stood for nature, family, and honor. Between them, an open eye symbolized the wisdom of his tribe. It stared back at him, unblinking.

Caide mussed his brother's blonde hair. Aldin looked up at him with a grin so similar to their mother's that it brought tears to Caide's eyes. Caide would do anything to see her again and to get her guidance, but Garon had taken that chance from him.

He looked away from his brother, dismissing his pain and anger, and addressed the Guardian who continued to march in front of them in silence.

"Artair, stop."

Artair froze mid-step.

"The battle should be starting soon, if it hasn't already. I think it's safe to teleport."

Artair turned around, but remained silent as he approached. He placed one hand on Aldin's shoulder, the other on Caide's, then white eclipsed Caide's vision.

A forest solidified around him, starting first as the soft pastels of a watercolor painting, then darkening into the solid browns and greens of reality. Although Caide had heard of teleporting before—it had fascinated his father and grandfather since their days in the war—he had never experienced it until now. Few Zeiihbuans had. Their hatred of both the Ærenden people and their powers had ensured that.

Caide swallowed hard to quell his stomach, and then shook his head to clear it. His brain felt as if it sloshed within his skull. "I can't believe Guardians used to do this all the time," he said.

Artair did not respond. Caide chased away the guilt that chomped down on him with sharp teeth. Artair's blank stare reminded Caide of the frozen looks he had seen on his guards' faces in Zeiihbu. Each of them had been loyal to his grandfather before Stilgan manipulated them with his mind-control power.

But Stilgan had wanted to destroy the kingdom and everyone within it. Caide hoped to save them all.

Small fingers pressed into Caide's palm. Caide dropped his gaze from Artair's waxen skin to the innocent glow of his younger brother's face. Aldin's brow pinched together. "What's wrong with him?" he asked.

Caide squeezed Aldin's hand. He wanted to reassure his brother that everything would be fine, but he could not lie to him. Aldin had barely turned school age. The education he received today would change him.

If he lived through it.

The jaws of guilt tightened and Caide's stomach clenched in response. In this part of the forest, life seemed normal, peaceful and quiet. Too quiet, and that gave away their destination more than the distant clamor of voices and metal would. No animals rustled the leaves. No birds twittered in the trees. They hid in their nests or burrowed underground, protected and safe. They would live through the battle, if no one else did.

A high-pitched whistle arced over the trees, and then a flash of white and yellow exploded, momentarily outshining the sun. Aldin jumped, then whimpered, and Caide pulled him close.

"Artair," Caide said. "Report to battle. As soon as you see another soldier, you'll be released from the spell. You won't remember I'm here."

"Okay," Artair said. He turned and disappeared into the dense forest.

Caide's focus trailed to another errant bomb as it burst in the sky. By now, Neiszhe would have reported Caide's absence. He would need to be careful if he wanted to stay out of sight. He walked into the forest close behind where Artair had entered, but took a right where Artair would have taken a left. Caide did not want to find the field where lives were taken. He needed to find where they were saved. He needed to find a friend.

§

"**KEEP THEM** moving. Keep them moving!"

Caide hid behind a tree, watching a scene of carnage and salvation, of devastation and hope unfold before him. The sun streamed over a vast field teeming with fighters. Men and women—some with red tunics—fought hand-to-hand, power-to-power under the bright sunlight. Not a single cloud touched the clear blue sky. Beneath it, blood and mud saturated the green grass and bodies built hills on flat lands.

In the center of the chaos, standing tall and stoic against the onslaught, a castle waited to host the winners of the fight. Mardróch, their deep brown cloaks fluttering in the air with each sword strike, guarded the land closest to that prize. When their weapons no longer entertained them, they cast blue lightning bolts at the queen's army, blackening soldiers with each off-handed flick.

Farther afield, several horses charged a group of Mardróch. One woman in the cavalry took down a monster with her scythe. Another soldier launched three succinct arrows into the hoods of two other monsters, and then took aim at a third. No sooner had he pulled his elbow back than his arm shattered, spraying red over his feet. The man's agonizing howls echoed over the cacophony of noise, the loud clashes of weapons, and the hollers and weeping of fighters. Then it died as the rest of his body fragmented like his arm.

The woman turned her horse and attempted to escape, but she met the same fate. Bones and skin rained from the sky onto those soldiers nearest her. Caide gasped, then saw the source of the repulsive power—a female Mardróch dressed in clothing made from the same brown material as a Mardróch's impenetrable cloak. An arrow bounced off her shirt and she pressed her fingers to her temple, directing her attention toward the archer who had shot it.

Before she had the chance to murder again, Caide uttered the first spell that crossed his mind—one his brother had taught him after they had first met Queen Meaghan. Gray cascaded down the Mardróch's body, transforming her to stone and freezing her fingers at her temples for eternity.

"I said keep them moving!"

The stern voice drew Caide's attention back to the chaotic scene immediately in front of him. At the edge of the field, someone had cleared a section of forest. Smooth stumps of once grand burnwood trees served as evidence of a power Caide had never seen before. Between the stumps, boards formed makeshift cots for the injured and dying. People lay across them, their legs and arms hanging down. Gray and white faces, red fingers and black toes, limbs mangled or missing and pools of blood spoke of the limited time some of these men and women had left to live.

Healers scurried between them, laying hands on their wounds and declaring the order of their healing.

"This one needs acceleration," one young Healer yelled and a middle-aged man ran to her side. They covered the soldier's head with their hands and started working.

"This one can wait until later," a familiar voice said. Caide scanned the sea of faces for Mycale and spotted him kneeling over a young woman not much older than Caide. She held an awkwardly angled arm to her chest. "I'll give you some jicab root to dull the pain," Mycale told her. She nodded.

"Moving! Moving!" a loud male voice commanded. Caide trailed his focus to the source of it. A large man with a portly stomach continued barking out orders. "There are places to lay them down in the back. Pass them through the vetters so we don't miss any in dire need, and then keep moving them back. We have to clear the battlefield."

Several uninjured soldiers followed his direction, moving their fallen comrades down the line to a group of Healers who gave them a cursory look.

Caide held his breath when he recognized the man who had been barking the orders. They had met briefly after Caide's rescue, in the remnants of Caide's village. There, Mycale's father had followed Cal's leadership. Here, his demeanor made his command over the field hospital unquestionable. The thick white hair topping his head also alluded to his experience.

"Darvin!" a woman called out to him as she dashed between two trees. "I need help with an injured man."

Darvin flicked a finger at a muscular Healer. The Healer and the woman ran into the field. Darvin turned his head, scanning the hospital beds, and frowned when he saw Mycale move to a man with a wound in his stomach.

"What are you still doing here?" he snapped.

Mycale looked up, but did not flinch beneath his father's scowl. "You need hands, Dad. I'm helping."

"That's not your choice. I need hands that aren't exhausted. Take a break."

Mycale shook his head. Several red curls stuck to the sweat soaking his brow. Darvin's heavy sigh sounded closer to a growl.

"Where's Emma?"

"In the back, dealing with a head wound."

"I thought as much. She was supposed to have her break an hour ago. Grab some rations, then go get her and do as you're told or I'll send you back to the village."

Mycale pressed his hands into the injured man's stomach. "He needs immediate care."

"Who do you think taught you?" Darvin knelt beside Mycale and covered his son's hands with large palms. "There'll be plenty of lives to save when you get back, Mycale. I need you fresh."

Mycale puffed out an agitated breath. "Fine, but be careful, okay? The Shadow Guard still wants you dead."

"I know. Cal assigned me a Guardian." Darvin nodded toward a statuesque man Caide had not noticed before. The Guardian stood at attention under the shadow of an overgrown bird-nut tree, one hand tight around the hilt of a broadsword. The other held a small tornado.

Mycale laughed. "Leave it to Cal. I'll be back soon."

"Not too soon," Darvin said before Mycale disappeared into the back of the makeshift hospital. Caide threaded through the forest after him, pausing when Mycale stopped to collect Emma, and then followed them both as they moved farther into the woods, away from the battle.

They stopped in a small clearing Caide had found less than an hour before. Caide hid within a cluster of ebony trees and waited. Leaves rustled in a tree behind him. His gaze shot to the small form of his brother and he gestured for Aldin to stay put.

"I don't like not helping," Emma complained when she and Mycale took a seat on a fallen log. Mycale set a linen bag on his lap. He spread it open, revealing a hunk of cheese and a slice of dried mutton. Splitting the meat in two, he handed the larger piece to Emma.

"We can only ignore my father for so long before he gets insistent. He's still in command of the field hospital, after all."

"I know. I guess it's just…" She shrugged. "I hate this. I wish it was over."

"Me too."

They ate in silence. Caide waited for his chance to signal Emma without Mycale seeing. He did not get the opportunity before loud rustling filled the air from a tree overhead. It moved down the trunk and Caide issued a silent curse. He gestured for his brother to stay put again, but the attempt came too late. Mycale jumped to his feet, a knife in his hand.

"Whoever you are, get down here."

"It could be an animal," Emma said.

"Not a chance. I saw flesh." Mycale addressed the tree again. "You have until the count of three before I throw my blade."

Aldin whimpered.

"I warned you. One. Two—"

"Stop." Caide stepped away from his hiding place. "He's not going to hurt you."

"Caide?" Emma gasped. "What are you doing here?"

"Trying to find you."

Mycale sheathed his blade. "Well, you found her. Tell your man to get out of the tree."

Caide glanced up at his brother's hiding spot. "Come on down."

The rustling continued until Aldin dropped to his feet from the lowest branch. "I'm hungry," he said.

Mycale picked up the cheese and handed it to Aldin. "Forget telling us why you're here, Caide. What's *he* doing here?"

"It's a long story," Caide said.

"Shorten it. I'm about two breaths off from getting your father."

Caide's blood hammered in his veins. "Don't. Please. He'll ruin everything."

"Ruin what?" Emma asked.

"Does it matter?" Mycale gestured toward Caide. "Look at him, Emma. He's white. He's shaking. He brought a *child* to a battle. Whatever he's doing, we already know it isn't good."

"Give him a chance to respond."

Caide's mind spun. Lies and half-truths jumbled together, each more tangled than the last. For the briefest moment, he considered casting the willpower spell, but he knew Emma would never forgive him if he did.

"Forget it," Mycale said. "I'm getting Faillen."

Caide panicked and blurted out the first thing on his mind. The truth. "I need Aldin's help to stop the war."

"Are you serious?" Emma's eyes widened. "He's *four*."

"Five," Aldin corrected around a mouthful of cheese.

Mycale glanced down at Aldin and shook his head. "He shouldn't be here."

"What exactly do you think he could do?" Emma asked.

"Recite," Caide said. "I need him to cast a spell with me."

"What spell?" Caide did not answer. Emma planted her hands on her hips. "Please give us a reason not to report you."

Caide reached into his pocket to retrieve the paper he had kept there since his visit to Artair's village. "I haven't told anyone about this yet," he said. "I'm telling you now because I trust you."

"You trust us?" Mycale asked. "Or you don't feel you have any other choice?"

"Maybe a little of both. I trust Emma. I don't know you."

Mycale nodded. "That's fair. Go on."

The square paper sat flat on Caide's hand. He unfolded it with shaking fingers. It seemed so small, so inconsequential, yet the power it contained hummed through him like electricity. He could recall only three or four other spells with the same intensity.

"This spell isn't mine," he told them. "Not fully. Farrow started it before Garon killed him. I finished it."

"Okay," Emma said. "So what is it?"

"A Mardróch counterspell."

Emma's mouth dropped open.

"There's no way it would have survived this long," Mycale argued. "Not if Garon knew about it. I have a hard time believing he didn't."

"He did, but he couldn't get to it," Caide said, then hesitated at revealing the Shadow Guard's involvement. He did not want to make Mycale more suspicious.

"What do you mean?" Emma asked.

"Someone else got to it first. They kept it protected and I have it now. I have to cast the counterspell on the spot where Garon first used the original Mardróch spell. It won't work any other way."

"The first Mardróch came out of the Barren," Mycale said. "We learned that in school."

"You learned wrong. Those were failed experiments. Garon cast the first successful spell here, by the front gates of the castle. He used it on an unsuspecting guard. The first Mardróch wasn't a volunteer."

"How could you possibly know that?"

"It's part of my power. The spells tell me who wrote them, their intent, and sometimes details that matter to them."

"Details like where the Mardróch spell was first cast," Emma guessed.

"Exactly."

Mycale paced the ground in front of Caide. "Let me see if I can simplify what you're saying. You got ahold of a counterspell started by one of the most powerful Spellmasters in existence and you decided to finish it. A Spellmaster's power grows stronger each year, right?"

"Right."

"That means he was a lot stronger than you are now."

"Well, yes, but—"

"It took…what? Months for Farrow to complete the Mardróch spell?"

"Years," Caide conceded.

Mycale frowned. "Years, then. And he worked on this one for…what? Years again?"

Caide nodded.

"So you thought, in your young age, that you could complete it and cast it successfully on the Mardróch. That's insane."

"It's not insane."

"Yes, it is. And the fact that you don't think so makes you an absolute lunatic."

"Mycale," Emma warned.

Mycale faced her. "Do you really expect me to go along with this? There's no way it will work. On top of that, he's involved a five-year-old in his delusion."

Emma crossed her arms over her chest. "You're not helping."

"Fine. If he's not crazy, what is he?"

"Brave."

Mycale glanced over his shoulder at Caide. "I'd be willing to settle for stupid. Even if he could somehow complete that spell, he isn't as strong as the old Spellmaster. There's no way he could cast it."

"That's why my brother is here," Caide told him. "We can combine our powers. His is stronger than mine is. Together, we should be able to cast the spell."

"*Should*," Mycale stressed. "You're willing to risk your brother's life on *should*? And how can you be certain your brother will be able to cast the spell? I thought you had to write it down first. You're not strong enough to do that yet."

"It doesn't work that way for Spellmasters. He can recite it like he wrote it, just as I've been able to do with his statue spell."

"That statue spell isn't as complicated as a counterspell. Even if it did work that way, how do you know combining your powers will be enough? It's not like it's been done before."

Caide shrugged. "I just know."

Mycale shook his head and walked away. Emma remained on her spot, her stiff shoulders showing as much confidence as Mycale's dismissal.

"Emma, please believe me."

"I want to, Caide, but you have to understand our position."

"I know what I'm doing."

"Do you? You said yourself that you didn't even know the depth of your power until Stilgan made you stretch it, made you do unthinkable things."

"I know now. This spell is right, Emma. I could save a lot of lives if I could just get to the gate."

"With your brother, through a battlefield."

"Yeah." Caide glanced down at Aldin. His brother grinned. The innocent gesture stabbed deep into Caide's heart.

"Not to mention you've never tested the spell. What happens if it fails when you get up there?"

Caide chewed the inside of his cheek. "You're right. I'll take Aldin back—"

"We can blindfold him." Mycale's voice broke through the trees a moment before he returned to Emma's side.

Caide frowned. "I don't understand."

"Your brother. He doesn't need to see what's out there."

"You want to help me?"

"Maybe." Mycale shrugged. "Tell me the truth. Can you really pull it off?"

"I think so."

Mycale glanced at Emma. "Do you trust him?"

"I trust him as much as I trust you. But trust has nothing to do with this. No one can be certain it will work."

"If there's even the slightest chance it will, we have to try. Mardróch we can beat. The regular kind anyway, but the females…" Mycale grimaced. "We're all dead without this."

"The four of us might die earlier because of it," Emma pointed out.

Mycale nodded. "I know."

Emma fixed her gaze on Caide. Her eyes darkened, and he felt both comforted and unnerved by her intense scrutiny. "All right," she agreed. "I'm in, too. How are we going to get them to the gates?"

"With a lot of luck," Mycale said. "You just worry about finding Caide a weapon. It's going to take every bit of our strength to get to the front lines."

CHAPTER THIRTY-SEVEN

CAL SLAMMED his fist into the bars of the closest cell. Vibrating metal rang down the hallway, echoing louder than Meaghan would have preferred. Cal punched the bars a second time and a third, but stopped shy of hitting them a fourth time when Meaghan put a hand on his arm.

"Enough," she said. "We don't want to alert any more guards."

Cal nodded and shook his hands. Blood speckled his knuckles where his skin had cracked from the force of his punches. He did not seem to notice.

Meaghan slipped a knife from her belt in preparation for a fight. No one came running. Two guards lay on the floor of the first cell on this block, muffled by dirty handkerchiefs forgotten in the darkest corners of the Pit, and bound by old rope she and Cal had stolen from a guard stand when they had first entered the dungeon. They had searched dozens of cells since entering the castle. Each held remnants of their former occupants—putrid scents of rot and stench, moth-eaten clothes now resembling rags, blood dried brown and crusty on the walls—but none of them had shown any signs of Nick.

Innelda stepped aside as Cal pushed his way back down the hall. His mood had been sullen at best and Meaghan found Innelda's deference to it prudent.

"There should be more guards," he said. "Where are they?"

Meaghan sheathed her weapon. "I'm sure we'll run into them soon enough. Are there any other floors?"

"Just one," Cal said and led them down a flight of dreary stone stairs, the orb spell casting light ahead of him. The first corridor looked no different from the ones they had left. Cal stepped into a cell at the end and poked a toe into the crumbling remains of a stone. "This is promising," he said and nodded at a ceramic pot in the corner. Meaghan wrinkled her nose at the smells emanating from it. If Nick had not been here, someone else had called this jail home recently.

"If the king was here, where is he now?" Innelda asked. She stood in the doorway, but did not enter. Meaghan stretched her power toward the woman. Her frustration built with each word. "Where would they have moved him?"

Moved, because no one wanted to admit Nick's absence could mean something far more sinister. Meaghan frowned and kicked a black-speckled pile of hay. Mold exploded into the air and beneath it, a mouse shot from its hiding place. It slipped through the bars and scurried down the hallway. Steps before reaching the outside edge of the orb's light, it skidded to a stop. Bright gold flashed within the darkness, then grew closer. Meaghan recognized the almond eyes of a feline.

With a throaty growl, the cat pounced. A sickening shriek escaped from the mouse, and then crunching sounds followed as the cat chewed on its meal. Meaghan's stomach curdled. Innelda jumped into the cell and slammed the door shut behind her. Her fear pressed tight against Meaghan's power. Cal's joined it, though he tempered it with little effort.

"Can he get through the bars?" Innelda asked.

"She," Cal corrected. "Females are gold. Males are brown. And to answer your question, her head is too big. The royal family designed these cages to keep ilk like her out, not just to keep prisoners in."

"That's fortunate," Innelda muttered. Meaghan raised an eyebrow. Nothing about the feline appeared dangerous. Although the top of her head and the sides of her cheeks came to sharp points, Meaghan could easily have mistaken her for a favorite childhood pet. This cat even had the same white *"M"* in the center of her forehead that had marked Baxter's fur.

Meaghan removed a knife from her belt and waited. After the dranx monkey had nearly poisoned her and benign-looking cave moss had turned hallucinations into a near death experience, she had learned her lesson. Few things that looked safe in Ærenden actually were.

The cat finished her meal, and then licked the last scrap of gray fur from her left paw with a forked tongue before curling up and closing her eyes.

"Great," Innelda said. "We're stuck here now. We'll never be able to sneak past her."

"What is she?" Meaghan asked.

"An ospcat," Cal told her. "She and razor beasts have their claws in common, only ospcats move more quickly."

Meaghan raised her blade. "How quick is she? Faster than my aim if we opened the door?"

"You could say that. Those claws are backup weapons for her. She's full, so there's a good chance I could scare her off with a rock."

"Are you sure you want to try that?" Innelda asked. "We'd have some protection at the back of the cell, but you'd have to be close to the bars."

"Yeah, I know. We don't have much of a choice though. Are you ready?"

Innelda nodded. She put a hand on Meaghan's shoulder and pulled her over to the farthest wall, then flattened her back against it. Meaghan followed her lead. Cal picked up a small pebble from the floor and approached the bars. He slipped his arm through.

"Here goes," he said and tossed the rock. With a yowl, the cat jumped to her feet. Orange fur stood in tufted spikes as she arched her back. Turning bright orange eyes on Cal, she hissed. A stream of spit arced through the air, sizzling as it hit the bars and streamed halfway into the cell. Tendrils of smoke wafted up from the hay. Small pits formed where it hit rock. Black holes dotted Cal's pants and red welts bubbled up on his skin. His pain seared through Meaghan's power, though he did not scream. He puffed up his chest and hollered at the cat, "Go on, get lost!"

The ospcat relaxed. She circled in her spot and Meaghan thought she might go back to sleep, but she turned and sauntered into the dark. With one last flick of her golden tail, she lumbered toward the staircase the rescue party had used to enter the floor.

Cal drew his hand against his shirt. Meaghan counted three large burn marks and half a dozen smaller blisters on his arm.

"Those look like acid burns," she said.

Cal tore a strip of material from the bottom of his shirt and tied it around his hand. "They are. Fortunately, she was more annoyed than threatened by me. That was only a fraction of what she's capable of spraying. Let's give her a few minutes to find her way back home before we finish searching this floor."

Cal's pain continued to plague her power and she frowned. "Are you going to be okay with that injury?"

"I've fought in battles with worse," he responded. "During the Zeiihbu War, I had a three inch blade wedged in my shoulder for an hour before I found a Healer. At least this time I know one is coming."

"True," Meaghan said, though the words seemed equally as optimistic as the assumption Garon had moved Nick. May and Sam's tunnel had placed them closer to the king and queen's old apartment, on the other side of the castle. Making their way to the Pit meant more Mardróch, and more of Garon's thugs to get through in order to meet up with Meaghan and Cal. If they had succeeded, they would have been here long before now. A lump formed in Meaghan's throat. She stretched her power, sending it after the cat, though she could sense the animal about as well as she could sense the stone walls surrounding them. She could not seem to find the missing Elders either. Emotionless silence accosted her, cold and overpowering as an ice storm. She shivered.

"Those cats," she said, changing the subject. "Why are they here? You said the jail cells were designed to keep them out."

"Them, plus some other nasty creatures like them. The royal family used them to keep the mice population in check."

"But they're dangerous," Meaghan protested.

Cal shrugged. "Not really. They stay in hiding during the day. It's just at night you have to worry about them."

"When the prisoners were alone, you mean," Meaghan said.

"They learned to stay out of range."

Meaghan nodded at Cal's hand. "Or they paid the price, right?"

Cal ran his fingers through his beard. "I suppose. I have a hard time feeling bad for them, though. They were criminals, don't forget."

"My father was down here."

Cal grunted. "That's different. Even Ed admitted that some of the people in his dad's tribe deserved punishment for their crimes."

"But he didn't, unless you're advocating punishing the entire tribe for the deeds of a few."

Cal's gaze flicked away.

"Wasn't that Garon's argument at the beginning of the Zeiihbu War?" Meaghan pressed him. "Wasn't that why he felt the need to kill my parents, so he could persecute the Zeiihbuans?"

"With all due respect, Queen Meaghan," Innelda said. "I don't think it was that at all."

Embarrassment warmed Meaghan's cheeks as she faced Innelda. She had forgotten she had a witness to her debate with Cal.

"At least, not from what my parents told me," Innelda continued.

"People like Garon, they use fear and hatred to gain followers. But ultimately, it's about them wanting power."

"We're all to blame for allowing hate to fester, for not standing against it before it grows into a monster," Meaghan countered. "Without those of us willing to ignore our own atrocities, someone like Garon wouldn't be able to gain control. My father didn't deserve to be in here and even the criminals who did should have been treated with compassion. Our actions don't reflect on them. They reflect on us."

"I can't argue with that," Cal said. "But decisions are rarely as simple as they seem in hindsight. You'll soon find that out."

Meaghan glanced around the decrepit cell. Her father had spent a night in an unforgiving stone box similar to this, labeled a hopeless murderer, a threat to the kingdom. Little did his captors know his label would change to king less than twelve hours later.

That was the trouble with labels. They rarely stuck for long. It seemed wise not to read too much into them.

"Let's go," she said, and pushed open the cell door.

Half an hour later, they had cleared the rest of the dungeon and made their way back to the empty guard stand. Meaghan paced. The steady sounds of her shuffling bounced off the stone walls of the Pit.

"If the king's not here, where else could he be?" Innelda asked.

"Garon's quarters, maybe," Cal said. "The great hall, the throne room, the ceremony room—"

"Pretty much anywhere," Innelda interrupted. "This isn't a small castle. Searching every room could take days."

Meaghan blew out a frustrated breath, then turned a full circle in place, each step slow and calculated. They had no quick way of finding Nick. In the meantime, her army fought without her leadership, sacrificed while she remained in relative security, and died while she inhaled air bereft of dust from battle and copper from spilled blood. She could not take that long to finish her mission. That left one option.

She faced Cal again. "Where would Garon be hiding? I'm sure he's not brave enough to fight."

"The formal throne room, most likely. Do you think he has Nick with him?"

"I think he knows where Nick is. Maybe it's time we stopped avoiding him."

Cal cocked his head to the side. "You want to take the fight to him?"

Meaghan nodded and while Innelda's surprise surged across Meaghan's power, Cal greeted her with amusement.

"Why not?" he said. "He's not expecting us just yet."

"That's what I was thinking, but we can't exactly walk up to him and say 'hi.' He'll have guards posted everywhere."

"And Mardróch," Cal agreed. White teeth flashed pleasure through his thick beard. "That's why I intend to use the back door."

CHAPTER THIRTY-EIGHT

NICK HAD read once that a castle's best defense was its complexity. Rooms, hidden passages, dead ends—each architectural nuance created a maze meant to confound attackers. Castle Æren was no exception. Hallways seemed unending, long and devoid of direction. Dozens of doors led to rooms with no discernible purpose. Art provided landmarks, but after a while, it all blurred together. Nick felt hopelessly lost.

Garon had kept everything the royal family had cultivated—bright sculptures delivered by forest villages, clay figures carved with mountain tools known as knifepicks, even paintings gifted by Zeiihbuan tribal members. Nick touched the dark frame of a painting depicting the Zeiihbu treaty signing and frowned. Queen Adelina stood regal in her white ceremonial gown, a peaceful smile on her face and a gilded feather pen in her hand. At the least, Nick expected Garon to have burned this painting. It represented the moment he believed the kingdom had lost its way. Yet it hung in the same place Adelina had left it.

Nick straightened the painting next to it, a royal artist rendering of Queen Adelina and King Edáire's wedding, and decided Garon had not wandered through this section of the castle yet. Although he would relish in keeping the royal family's decorations, in walking in their footsteps and mocking the art that had made this castle their home, he would have happily destroyed any celebration of the king and queen's love, just as he had destroyed their lives.

Nick brushed his hand down a marble-lined wall, mesmerized by the varying cream tones. What would it have been like to grow up here? Would Adelina's parents have welcomed her laughter and tossed back the balls that she bounced along the rich stone? Or would they have expected her to maintain an air of regal silence as a mini-version of the queen they wanted her to become? Whatever her childhood had been like, Meaghan's would have mimicked, if Garon had not stolen that from her, too.

Footsteps broke the silence of this ominous wing and Nick ducked into an alcove until they passed and receded. He fingered one of the weapons he had slipped beneath his belt. He had managed to overcome two of Garon's soldiers soon after leaving the dungeon. Once he had hidden their bodies, he had traded his rusty knife for a small half-sword and an allestone blade, similar to the ones Meaghan carried. Since then, he had been able to avoid a fight. He had a feeling his luck would run out soon, especially if he reached his destination.

Stepping out of his hiding place, he jogged down the hallway and turned at the next intersection. This passage looked almost the same as the last, though these paintings and sculptures depicted steeds and their riders. Gifts from the horse villages, he had no doubt.

He turned down several more hallways, and then hit a dead end at a set of double doors painted in deep crimson. Carved within the center of each door's framed inner panel, a gray and golden crest bore the regal symbol of Meaghan's family—a black mare pawing the air in warning.

Nick gripped a brass handle tarnished by years of neglect and pushed. The door swung open, its mournful wails echoing into the room beyond. He tensed, expecting Mardróch to come running, but only silence followed. He quickly stepped over the threshold and closed the door behind him.

Sunlight seared his eyes instead of the dim light he had expected. A gaping hole consumed a portion of the roof and outer wall. The king and queen had lived on the top floor of the castle, allowing them to enjoy the beauty of their kingdom as it spread out below them, vast and green. Nick's view was far less serene. A wall surrounded the castle in a gray line. Beyond it, armies looked like small toys fighting in a child's playground.

Nick traced his gaze from the battle to the terrace outside the apartment. Its garden had been the royal family's oasis. It had once boasted vibrant flowers and meticulous lawns. Now it resembled a jungle. Vines and moss smothered statues. Weeds choked trees. Flowers wilted under the shade of wild bushes. Several straw nests balanced on piles of bricks that had once formed the outside wall for the royal suite.

Nick turned, scanning the room where he had seen Meaghan's parents in the Writer's book. Black stretched from one corner to the other, and clawed at what remained of the furniture. A table, half-ash and half-charcoal lay on its side in front of tangled springs that had once belonged to a couch. Chairs and picture frames resembled piles of kindling, and a candelabrum stood in the corner, twisted into a grinning, sidelong face.

Garon had removed Adelina's body, though Nick doubted he had buried her with the respect she deserved.

Nick crossed to the table, careful not to leave more footprints in the ash than necessary, and bent down to rest his hand on one wooden leg.

Meaghan had remembered this—the table as it had fallen after the explosion that had started the attack on the castle. She had also remembered where she saw her mother for the last time, splayed across the floor in death. He pressed his fingers to the spot where he imagined the young and frightened toddler had stroked her mother's hair.

A bird chirped overhead. Nick looked up in time to watch it descend toward the opening in the roof. It landed in mid-air before taking off again. His gaze coasted over the room once more. The king and queen's former apartment had withstood the last decade and a half with impossible grace. Exposure to rain in the spring and snow in the winter should have rotted the wood and bred mold on the walls, but fire had left the only evidence of destruction.

Nick stood. Slipping the short sword from his belt, he approached the door next to the fireplace. Flames had licked it, leaving ebony tongues behind. The bottom half had crumbled into gray dust, creating a hole that stretched into the bedroom beyond it.

Nick pressed his blade into the edge of that hole, attempting to force a splinter free from the weakened wood. It would not budge. He traced the sword along the soot-caked doorframe. The mark it left dissolved within seconds. Even his footprints had disappeared. Someone had cast a protection spell over this room, keeping it forever as a monument to the dead.

Or as a reminder of Garon's greatest accomplishment.

The thought chilled Nick's heart. He slipped the blade back under his belt and turned from the sadness that eclipsed him in this place. He had no time to mourn. From here, he knew exactly how to get where he needed to go. He had already walked the path with Ed in the Writer's book.

He only hoped he would not be tracing the same steps to a similar fate.

CHAPTER THIRTY-NINE

CAIDE STOOD on the edge of a boundless field. The sun flowed across the grass, kissing gold to green and cascading warmth over his cold skin. In front of him, men and women danced, their movements choreographed and grotesque, their weapons intertwined like limbs as they lunged and parried. The gray castle he had seen earlier looked like a clay model in the background. Caide reached for it, grasping its image as if he plucked a plum from the sky. He had witnessed only one battle before today. He had been at the center of it, captive and powerless, and he felt no more in control now. Worse, he felt equally afraid.

Turning away from the battle, he followed behind his companions as they traced the shadows outlining the forest. Emma led the way. Each step she chose with purpose, using trees as shields when skirmishes came too close. She glanced over her shoulder, signaled for him to stop when a Mardróch spotted them, and then planted her feet, a tri-blade knife in each hand. With a flick of her right wrist, Emma locked all three blades of the knife in a circle, and let it fly.

Pink and silver shayle metal glistened in sinister warning before the weapon found its mark. Emma collected her knife from the opening of the monster's brown hood, straightened the blades once more and kept moving. Mycale trailed several yards behind her, a scythe in his right hand, and Aldin propped on his left hip. Caide's younger brother wore a green hat to muffle his hearing and a black blindfold to block his sight. Caide brought up the rear. He would have preferred that Aldin remain at his side, but Caide's skill had always been best with a bow and arrow. He could protect Aldin better by watching him and picking off enemies as they approached.

A lightning bolt crashed into a tree in front of Emma. Caide fired an arrow at the Mardróch who had sent it, smiling with satisfaction when the monster fell. A second Mardróch stepped over his comrade's body, but ignored Caide in favor of a fight with a ginger-haired Guardian.

Caide recited the invisibility spell, hiding the four of them for the third time since they had set out on this path. Within moments, he felt the spell lift. Someone in Garon's army had recited the counterspell again.

A bomb blew a hole in the field behind them. Aldin whimpered. A second bomb went off, scattering bodies into the air and Caide scanned the battle for its source. A Zeiihbuan cupped her hands together. In her palms a ball formed, then spun faster and faster until it glowed. She threw it at an advancing squad of soldiers in red tunics and Caide relaxed his grip on his arrow. The explosion killed two enemies.

Emma ducked into an island of trees, moving away from a

Mardróch patrolling the outskirts of the grounds. Mycale followed and Caide raced to tighten the gap between them. He squinted as dim light blinded his view, then covered his eyes when another bomb burst overhead, showering the area with golden light.

Half a dozen Mardróch carpeted the ground in this section of forest, their limbs bent at odd angles, their cloaks spread out like wings, and their hoods blackened and charred. Another bomb highlighted similar damage to the trees. Caide ran a finger down the shredded leaf of a yellow honeyflower bush. They could not seek solace here, not if bombs continued to target the area.

Emma picked up the pace, moving deeper into the woods, then gestured for them to stop. Voices drifted between the trees. They tiptoed forward until they saw several horses sprawled out on the ground, motionless. Their riders were nowhere in sight. Two soldiers in red tunics picked through the saddlebags by the horses' feet.

"This'll do," said one, holding up three energy pearls. He popped one in his mouth and gave another to his friend. "You find anything useful?"

"A picture of some brat," came a woman's voice. She turned, facing Caide's group, though she did not see them. Wrinkles etched valleys beside her pale gray eyes. "A half-breed. I don't understand how anyone could willingly m with a Zeiihbuan."

Caide gritted his teeth. Anger tightened the back of his throat.

"What do you make of Astasia's suggestion?" the man asked.

"You mean breed the savages for sport like we do tusked pigs?" The elderly woman pressed her lips together and nodded. "Not bad, really. It's been too long since we've had some good entertainment.

Have them fight to the death. They're disposable."

Caide's arrow landed at the woman's feet before he realized he had fired it. Emma snapped her head around, a reprimand hard in her gaze.

The elderly soldier's smile cracked the wrinkles at the corners of her lips. She pulled a sword from a scabbard on her back and raced toward them, her body blurred by her speed.

She attacked Mycale first. He turned to shield Aldin and the blade bit into his shoulder. Blood seeped through his shirt. The woman raised her sword again and Emma rushed forward to deflect the blow. A third and fourth strike came with more force, then a fifth and sixth, each shaking Emma's balance. The older woman moved faster with each swing, catalyzed by an obvious power.

Caide tracked her with an arrow, his fingers ready to fire, but Emma needed no assistance. She snapped her blades into a circle and took the offense, her attack blinding until even Caide could not guess where her next assault would land. She blocked the sword one last time, and let a tri-blade fly. It sliced across the old woman's throat, then continued past her and stopped deep within her companion's chest. Both enemies fell.

Emma moved to Mycale's side to examine his wound. "It's not bad," she said. "I can do a partial heal to stop the bleeding. A full healing will have to wait."

Mycale nodded, then gritted his teeth when she placed her hands on his arm and surged her power into his skin. Caide had been subject to that power more times than he wanted to count when he and Emma had been Stilgan's prisoners. He understood the pain of the healing process and the necessity of it, but that knowledge never dulled the burning.

When she stood up again, she shot Caide a heated glare. "Do you want to tell me what that was about? They wouldn't have seen us if you hadn't done that."

"It was a mistake," he admitted. "I got mad."

She huffed out a short breath. "You're smarter than that, Caide. You almost got Mycale killed."

Her words hurt more than her healing power ever had. He had come to count on her friendship and support. Now she looked at him like the lunatic Mycale had claimed him to be. Caide crossed his arms over his chest. Although he realized his actions had been both foolish and dangerous, that knowledge did not temper his anger. "It was a mistake," he snapped. "But you don't have to worry about me making it twice. I'll do the rest of this on my own."

Emma shook her head. "You can't, and the four of us can't do it alone either. We need a better plan."

"Or any plan at all," Mycale muttered.

Caide did not know what he had been thinking when he came here. He had believed he would be able to muster a spell at the last minute, one that would allow him to walk across the field unaided. Yet every word he uttered fell from his lips like stones, bereft of magic and meaning.

"Forget it," he said. Stowing his bow, he picked up Aldin and walked off into the woods. He hoped Mycale and Emma would not follow and they fulfilled that wish with ominous silence.

The forest swallowed him. As he moved deeper, underbrush

tangled around his legs and leaves hugged his arms, slowing his progress. When he hit a wall of dead vines that blocked the small path he had managed to find, he turned back toward the battlefield. He still had no plan, no inspired words. He only knew what he had set out to do today was right.

"There is no shame in accepting help, Caide."

A chill ran across Caide's skin and he looked around the dim forest. His mother had spoken. He was certain of it. He saw no one.

"Mata," he whispered. "I need you."

She did not respond.

"Caide," Aldin whimpered and pulled off his blindfold. "I'm scared. I want to go home."

"Keep this on," Caide said and tugged the blindfold back over Aldin's eyes. He had been foolish to think his mother would appear to him here. Spirits sought peace, not a war zone.

He emerged onto the field again, and then ducked down behind a tree when he spotted several Zeiihbuan soldiers. One held a fireball an inch above her hands. Another aimed a crossbow in front of him. The third gripped an allestone sword.

"Asjia," Caide said, recognizing the last woman from his school, though she had finished the year he moved to Ærenden. Caide's closest friend had followed her around like a timid bullmouse, hoping to get her to spend an afternoon with him. He had never received more than a friendly hello.

Caide could not see their enemies, so he set Aldin down and crawled closer, using a cluster of pine shrubs to shelter him from sight. When he spotted two Mardróch, he froze. They circled the

Zeiihbuan soldiers. One tossed lightning bolts at the man's feet. The other swung a broadsword over his head. A grin split his webbed mouth and Caide realized that both monsters intended to toy with the Zeiihbuans before they fought in earnest.

One of the Mardróch cackled and Caide caught his breath. Stilgan's laugh had sounded similar. Caide's hands shook as he pressed them against the ground.

"I've always wanted to know what a Zeiihbuan tasted like," the Mardróch taunted. His sword sliced through the air, aimed at the older woman. She tossed her fireball at him. It bounced off his cloak and exploded in the dirt at his feet. His weapon kept falling. She jumped out of the way a moment before impact, and then dove to the ground when lightning grazed the grass at her side.

Before the first Mardróch could strike again, the man fired an arrow at him. It grazed the Mardróch's hand, drawing blood and a howl of pain. The Mardróch launched several electric bolts at the Zeiihbuan, narrowly missing with each attack.

"There's one too many of them," the second Mardróch growled. "Shall we take him out?"

"Nah," the first Mardróch said. He snapped his wrist, discharging another bolt at the man, though he missed by several feet this time. "I want to have more fun with him before I kill him." He nodded toward Asjia. "Kill the runt. I'll keep the others frozen."

The Mardróch cackled and descended on Asjia, his sword in front of him with a purpose he had not shown before. Asjia had been an able fighter in school, not the best, but strong enough to handle most of her sparring partners. This Mardróch would not be following sparring rules. He would fight blade-to-blade until he grew bored, then Asjia would have no defense against his lightning. Even now, blue sizzled at his fingertips and wrapped around the hilt of his sword with menacing foreboding.

"You have to help her."

Caide snapped his head around at his mother's voice. He saw only trees behind him. A crack of lightning sounded from the direction of the fight and he brought his focus back to it. Asjia had fallen to her knees, though she managed to dodge the lightning as it pierced the ground by her side.

Blue crackled within the Mardróch's hands. Asjia dove backward to avoid another bolt. A third set fire to her clothing. The scent of burning flesh permeated the air as she rolled to put out the flames.

Caide doubted she would live through another attack. He wanted to reach for his bow, but his arms refused to obey. The Mardróch laughed again and Stilgan's face flashed through Caide's mind. He closed his eyes.

"Open your eyes, Caide. Face your fears."

Asjia screamed.

"You almost got her," a guttural voice bellowed. "Let me show you how it's done."

"Now, son!"

Caide sprang into action. He yanked his bow around and shot an arrow at the Mardróch's back without thinking or aiming. It bounced off the monster's cloak. The Mardróch turned, and then signaled for his friend to do the same when he saw Caide.

"Look," he hissed. "Another Zeiihbuan toy."

"I'm nobody's toy," Caide said. His response elicited another gravelly laugh from one of the Mardróch. Stilgan's face danced in front of Caide's vision again. Caide held onto his mother's voice, her command, and dissolved his fear with an exhale.

Once the Mardróch became statues, their laughter would be a distant echo in his memory. He recited the spell his brother had taught him. Nothing happened. The Mardróch continued advancing. Caide retreated, stopping when he felt the bark of a tree pressing into his back. He recited the spell again. Once more, nothing happened. His power refused to budge. Terror welled within him.

In desperation, he fired a haphazard arrow at the closest Mardróch. The monster easily deflected it with his sword. Caide readied another arrow. Before he had time to use it, a fireball landed in the grass between him and the advancing Mardróch. Asjia followed close behind it. Her sword hit home, sinking deep into the shadows of the Mardróch's hood opening. The second Mardróch cast a lightning bolt at her. She jumped out of the way. This time, Caide's arrow met its mark. The Mardróch toppled over, coming to rest in a pool of mud.

Caide collapsed against a tree. His breath burned as he stared at the monsters. He wanted to flee, to run into the embracing darkness of the trees, but controlled the instinct when he saw someone watching him from behind Aldin.

His mother smiled, and then held out her arms in invitation.

CHAPTER FORTY

"**MATA,**" **CAIDE** whispered. He rubbed his eyes, but she remained.

"Caide?" Asjia's voice echoed to him from somewhere across a deep abyss. It carried little meaning. "Does your father know you're here?"

His mother dissolved into the shadows. Shock made Caide's steps tentative at first, and then he moved more quickly with the fear of losing her.

"Caide!"

Asjia's voice disappeared once Caide crossed the tree line. He had to find his mother. Her death had been real. He knew that. His father and his brother had witnessed it, suffered through the Healers' fruitless efforts to bring breath to a fire-consumed woman, wept when they could no longer deny her loss. They had buried her, too, beneath the bright pink flowers of a weeping rose tree. And Caide had missed it all while Stilgan held him prisoner in the remnants of Caide's childhood home.

His mother should not be here. Yet up ahead, the flash of her light olive skin kept him moving. Despite the screams of battle in the distance, despite the worry of losing control over his power, despite the pain of missing her, joy swelled within his heart. His mother's spirit had found him.

Branches scraped his cheeks. Thorns stung his hands. Underbrush choked the forest, making it almost impassable. He pushed on, buoyed by the occasional hint of his mother's silhouette. Her red hair flashed up ahead and he raced after it, breaking through a curtain of vines without caring if creepers hid within it. On the other side, sunlight blinded him. He shielded his eyes to look for her, but she was gone. In her place, a clearing teemed with Zeiihbuans. Caide dove back into the woods.

"Caide!" his grandfather's voice bellowed behind him.

He ran. The forest now tore at him in rage, gashing his skin with sharp teeth and battering his arms and legs with bruises. More than once, he fell, tangled in an aggressive root. Each time, he pushed back up, desperate to get away.

"Tell him the truth."

His mother's voice floated to him above the sounds of his own thrashing, the betrayal in it holding more of a sting than the sharpest nettles grabbing for him. She had led him there on purpose. She had wanted his grandfather to see him. She had wanted him to get caught. Now he would not be able to save the army. They would all die at the hands of the Mardróch.

"You take far too much responsibility, Caide."

This time his mother's voice came from in front of him. He

slowed, passing through the tree line and back into the clearing where he had fought the Mardróch. He found only the bodies of the monsters, piled together like discarded rags.

Caide counted the time by his heartbeats, fast at first, then slower as his fear tempered. He strained his ears to catch any sign of someone following him, the slightest rustle of a leaf or a soft footfall. He heard only sniffles.

No one had chased him. Maybe his grandfather had decided he had mistaken another soldier for Caide. Maybe an advancing attack had distracted his army. No matter how it had happened, Caide had escaped. He followed the sniffling to the spot where he had left his brother.

Aldin huddled at the base of the tree. Tears slipped down his cheeks from behind his blindfold, coursing tan rivers through the dirt caking his skin. Caide picked him up.

"You came back," Aldin said and wrapped his arms around Caide's neck. "I thought you left me."

"I'll always come back for you," Caide promised. "Did you see Mata?"

Aldin shook his head. "I miss Mata," he said and pressed his cheek into Caide's shoulder. Caide hugged his brother close as Mycale's words thundered in his mind. *If he's not crazy, what is he?*

Maybe he had been chasing an illusion, but it had given him hope. Beyond his grandfather's army, past the small clearing in the forest where his mother had led him, he had seen the castle gates.

He only needed to sneak around the Zeiihbuan army and thread through a nest of Mardróch to succeed.

Caide smiled as an old Zeiihbuan expression floated through his mind... *Every risk takes insanity as its dance partner.* If he really was crazy, he might as well embrace it.

He just had to be careful not to trip.

CHAPTER FORTY-ONE

MORE THAN a thousand years had passed since the royal family constructed their castle. Its age showed with deep grooves worn into the stone floors, and in delicate cracks that split the marble walls. Some paintings, like the ones Nick had seen of recent events, were infants compared to their elderly counterparts. Despite regular care by Curator powers, oils and pastels from centuries long gone had begun to crack and fade. Ancient queens looked down at Nick from the corridors, wisdom he could never know poised at the corners of their lips. Historical battles, peaceful celebrations, weddings, family portraits, and childhood moments all told tales of happier times.

He recognized the portraits King Ed had looked to for comfort and the sculptures of heroic Guardians Nick had studied in school. He tripped over hallway runners curling at the edges, cursed them, and then closed his mouth in respect when he realized talented artists had woven some of them hundreds of years before he had been born. They would remain hundreds of years after everyone forgot him.

When his gaze met the eyes of a portrait he recognized, he paused to take solace in it. The kind face had belonged to Meaghan's great-grandfather. Round, and some would say chubby, cheeks blazed red with humor. Brown eyes twinkled with understanding. And thin, pink lips held a half-smile that broadcast both demand and forgiveness. He had been a well-respected and well-loved musician before Adelina's great-grandmother had chosen him as her husband. His travels entertaining the kingdom had made him many friends. Those friendships had enabled the king and queen to expand the kingdom, building villages in areas where people had been afraid to travel before. Many of the towns along Zeiihbu's border had come from that era. In some ways, their actions had contributed to the Zeiihbu War, though they had not had conquest in mind.

Perhaps they had been the last true explorers in Ærenden. Since then, minds had grown smaller, fear had limited people to their villages, and close-fisted hate had replaced open hands of friendship. Nick had been guilty of that before he met Aldin. He had judged the Zeiihbuans based on his own prejudices and the limited stories of those who had lost battles in the Zeiihbu War. It took a small boy to show him a face behind his assumptions, and that face had been far from the savage he had expected.

He hoped his friendship with Aldin's father would teach the kingdom to open their minds and hands again.

Nick touched a finger to a corner of the picture. Rough paint brushed his skin. If they defeated Garon today, there would be paintings like this of Nick in the castle. His successors would walk by them every day and reflect on his legacy, both the good and bad. The realization made him feel inadequate, so he moved on, turning left into the last stairwell that led to the wing housing the throne room.

Dim light eclipsed his sight and he pulled his knife and short sword from his belt, holding them ready in front of him. Torches flickered in sconces every fifth step, casting wavering shadows around each twist of the spiral staircase. He turned his back to the wall and moved forward, glancing behind him as often as he looked ahead, though he realized his enemies would be upon him long before he saw them.

He controlled his breath and his movement, careful to shuffle each footstep to muffle sound. When he could see the outline of a wooden door, he quickened his pace, and then froze as a sense of urgency prickled in his mind, warning of danger. A low growl bounced along the walls above him. Below, the door creaked open and a soldier wearing a red tunic stepped into the stairwell. The soldier glanced up. Recognition widened his eyes, and then he snapped a crossbow in front of his face.

Nick dropped to his knees. An arrow bounced off the stone to his side and the growling grew louder. A Mardróch descended into view. Lightning cascaded along the ceiling, a warning for the soldier, though it came close enough to singe Nick's hair.

Nick counted seven steps between him and the monster. Eight separated him from the soldier below. Both enemies had weapons they could fire. Nick's blades would do him little good.

Blue charged along the Mardróch's fingertips as the soldier started climbing. Nick dove, crashing into the soldier and both of them tumbled down the last few steps.

Pain exploded in Nick's shoulder. The soldier landed on top of him and Nick grabbed his arms, flipping him over. The soldier's head smashed into the floor with a sickening crunch.

Lightning sizzled in the air and Nick jumped up, using the soldier as a shield. His red tunic caught fire. The smell of burning flesh permeated the stairwell, and then heat seared Nick's fingers. Nick bit back a scream and pushed the soldier forward, up the stairs to block the advancing Mardróch. He spun around and ran through the door.

"Over there," someone barked.

Nick did not look back. He turned down the next hallway, barely registering a loud bang when a door opened behind him. A howl erupted close by, signaling the Mardróch's continued pursuit and Nick cursed. He would never be able to outrun one of Garon's monsters. He needed a better weapon or a path of escape.

"This way!" a voice bellowed and lightning coursed along the floor to Nick's right. He veered at the next intersection, and then skidded around a corner into a long room with a heavy oak table. Twelve empty chairs surrounded it and dust caked the chandelier overhead. Allestone broad swords and gilded crossbows hung along the back wall, forming elaborate patterns. Beneath them, rose-colored arrows filled quivers decorated with bright coral shells. Redwood bows decorated the walls to the sides.

Nick sprinted down the length of the table and ripped a bow from its display. A crossbow arrow sank into a chair in front of him, but he kept his eyes focused on one of the quivers. Although his skin felt as if it would rip from his fingers where the fire had blackened it, he grasped a pearl-white quill, yanked it free, and spun around. He fired, hitting the attacking soldier between his eyes. Another soldier fell by his side, then a third. Bits of Nick's flesh ripped from his fingers. Blood made his bow slick, but he continued shooting until five soldiers and a Mardróch had piled up in the doorway.

The room grew silent. Nick prepped another arrow. He drew a ragged breath to control his near-blinding pain, and waited.

Minutes ticked by. No one crossed the threshold. Finally, Nick eased his grip on the bow and glanced around the corner into the hallway.

Three more soldiers lay sprawled out on the stone floor, their blood collecting in pools beneath them. Beside the closest soldier, a dark brown cloak lay crumpled in a haphazard pile. Several bony fingers reached out from beneath it. Those fingers did not move, but something else did.

Nick had an arrow ready to fire before his panic cleared and he recognized the man smiling back at him.

"You don't make it easy to track you down," Sam said, slipping a knife into his belt. "Next time stay put in the Pit, all right?"

Behind the Elder, Nick spotted a shock of red hair and almost wept at the sight of it.

"I think the idea is to avoid 'next time,' " his mother muttered, though Nick barely heard her words. He slumped against the wall. Her hands found his and her power surged through him, bringing relief in its wake.

§

"**YOU SHOULD** have left the second you got out."

Nick sighed as his mother paced the long floor of the formal dining room where they had hidden while she healed him. Sam held a crossbow at his side, an arrow ready if any soldiers discovered them. So far, his efforts had been unnecessary. Not a single footfall had echoed outside the closed doors.

Even if someone did wander past, no one would have a reason to look inside. Garon's soldiers and the two dead Mardróch formed a neat pile in a far corner of the room, next to a sideboard lined with dusty floral place settings and long-forgotten crystal goblets.

Nick pressed his back into a seat at the end of the table. "Believe me, Mom. You're not saying anything I haven't already told myself."

His mother glared at him. Her cheeks matched the red in her hair. "Then why are you still here?"

"Because I know where the royal spell book is hidden. I saw it in the Writer's book. Garon wanted Ed to use the Guardian murder spell, so Ed hid it. Garon won't hesitate to cast it himself if he ever finds it."

"And he won't hesitate to kill you if you try to claim it. Besides, if he could have found it, he would have by now."

"I can't take that risk."

May threw up her hands and began pacing again. Sam leaned against the door of an armoire and watched. Every few minutes he rubbed the short bristles of his white beard, the nervous gesture evidence of his opinion on the matter. Although Nick had never thought of him as an old man, his age showed on his face today, in the shadows dragging down his eyes and the lines cracking his cheeks. He had grown thinner since his daughter had died in the attack on their Guardian village, and paler since Nick had announced his intention to start this battle.

"You have an obligation to your people," Nick's mother tried again. "We need you out there, leading the army."

"Miles is perfectly capable."

"And this attack today was your idea, if you'll recall. I expect you to own up to it."

"I will, but getting kidnapped wasn't my idea. Since that got me into the castle, I'm not going to waste the opportunity." Nick stood. "The book is in the throne room. Do you want to help me or should we part ways now?"

"Mind your tone," May said. "I raised you to have more respect than that."

"You also raised me to do the right thing, no matter the cost. There will be survivors today, Mom. If Garon gets that book, no Guardian is safe. That includes Neiszhe and even her newborn son."

May huffed and turned to Sam. "Do you want to help me out here?"

Sam straightened. His steel blue eyes pierced through Nick before they found May. "You remember how to sneak into the throne room, don't you?"

"That's not the help I meant."

"Humor me."

May crossed her arms over her chest. "This is a waste of time. Garon knows all the hidden entrances."

"Not all of them. You and I guarded members of the royal family. We were privileged with knowledge even their advisor would have been blind to." Sam raised an eyebrow. "Do you remember them?"

"Of course I do. I'm not senile. Garon knows about the entrance through the butler's corridor and the one behind the armor. He would have used those to leave the throne room, just as Ed and Adelina did."

"And the others?"

"Stop testing me. There are four entrances." She ticked them off on her fingers. "The armor, the corridor, the one behind the banner of the nanny sparrow that leads to the library, and the one to the left of the main entrance that looked like a picture of Adelina's grandmother. The castle staff used it for events."

"Good memory, but you're not quite right. There are five." Sam addressed Nick. "Where's the book hidden?"

"Under the dais."

"Perfect. The last entrance leads from the royal quarters to a false pillar behind the thrones. It shouldn't take us more than a few minutes to get the book."

Nick glanced at his mother and waited.

She scowled at him, and then dropped her arms. "Fine, but if we don't make it out of there alive, I'll kill you myself."

Nick engulfed his mother in a hug. She laughed and for a moment, he felt as if they stood in her kitchen once more, relishing in the simplicity of a long-forged mother and son bond. If nothing else worked out today, he was glad she would be at his side until the end.

CHAPTER FORTY-TWO

MEAGHAN SKIDDED around a corner and ducked into an alcove half a breath before a bolt of lightning surged down the hallway, its blue glow overshadowing her sight before it dissolved in the air. She held her breath and waited.

"Hey, ugly!" Cal's voice boomed. "Try fighting this."

Meaghan risked a glance back in the direction she had come. Cal tossed a wall torch at the Mardróch who had been chasing her, then lifted his hands. Red flames raced under the Mardróch's brown cloak. A high-pitched wail echoed along the stone floors and smoke rolled across the ceiling as the Mardróch bounced from one wall to the next. Flames erupted from the opening in his hood. Pain met Meaghan's power as fetid garbage, mixing with the acrid smell of melting hair and she clamped her mouth closed over a surge of bile, then muted her power before the scent overwhelmed her.

A painting ignited when the Mardróch bumped into it, then a chair kindled farther down the hall. Innelda grabbed a tapestry and threw it over the chair, extinguishing the fire before it spread to a cabinet. The painting crashed to the floor, scorching the stone, then dimmed to an ember when Cal extended a hand toward it.

Behind him, Meaghan saw a shadow and the flash of a red tunic. She took aim and threw her knife. It sailed over Cal's shoulder, sinking into the soldier's neck as he readied his crossbow.

Cal raised an eyebrow at her. "Close call, don't you think?"

Meaghan rolled her eyes, but did not take the time to respond. They needed to get to the library. Before Garon's guards had spotted her, Cal had said they would find it down the next hallway that intersected with this one.

It might as well have been miles away. Two soldiers and a Mardróch advanced on Innelda. Her sword sliced through the air, decapitating one of the guards. A bolt of lightning shattered the stone at her feet, sending fine shrapnel into the air. Blood oozed through gashes in her pants. She swayed, then straightened again and swiped her sword at the monster.

The Mardróch grinned. He pressed his gray fingers together. Blue electricity formed a perfect sphere in the air.

Innelda raised her sword. "Come on. Let's get this done."

The Mardróch cackled. He lifted his arms, and Meaghan saw her chance. She took aim. Her knife sliced deep into the back of the Mardróch's hand. He howled and turned toward her. Meaghan's next blade disappeared into his hood.

Innelda screamed. Meaghan's gaze tore from the dead Mardróch. Blood pooled on the granite floor where Innelda had been standing and trailed into the next corridor.

Cal raced toward it, another torch blazing in his hand. Meaghan recovered her knives and followed him. A second scream shattered the air. She rounded the corner and tightened her grip on her weapons. A soldier used Innelda as a shield, a broadsword tight against her neck.

"Don't move," he yelled at Cal. Cal froze mid-step. "Put the fire down or she'll die with me."

Cal hesitated. Innelda hissed as the blade dug into her neck. Blood trickled along her collarbone.

"Kill him, Cal," she croaked.

"Shut up," the soldier said.

Cal set the torch on the ground. It dimmed to embers.

"You," the soldier said to Meaghan. "Tie him up. You're coming with me."

Meaghan released a tieback from a drape at the closest window. She approached Cal. Cal tightened his fists behind his back.

Meaghan held the rope up and in front of her, showing that she intended to do what the soldier asked. "Why go through this charade?" she asked. "Why not kill us? You're one of Garon's minions. We already know you don't value life."

"I'm not one of his," the soldier said. "I have other interests."

"The Shadow Guard," Meaghan guessed. "So the Tribunal spies on him, too."

The soldier said nothing.

"Right. You'll do anything to get me and my secret power. Well, you have me. Let her go."

"Once we teleport, she'll be free."

Innelda shifted her hand. Meaghan caught the subtle movement and stepped to Cal's side.

"I said tie him up or his death will be on your hands."

"We can work out a deal. I can see you don't like Garon either. Let us get to him—"

"No deals. Do as you're told."

Innelda slipped a knife from her waistband and drove it behind her, into the soldier's stomach. He howled, and then yanked on his sword. It sliced through Innelda's shoulder. She crumpled. Her knife clattered against the floor a foot away.

The soldier fell to his knees. He pressed one hand to the wound in his stomach. The other still held his sword. He raised it over Innelda.

"No!" Cal hollered and swept up Innelda's knife. He drove it into the soldier's heart.

Meaghan's breath stuck in her throat when she saw the blood soaking through Innelda's shirt. "Is she—?"

"Three doors down, to the right," Cal interrupted, lifting Innelda in his arms.

Meaghan ran ahead of him. A set of double mahogany doors rose to her side. She yanked them open, and then slammed them shut behind her once Cal had charged into the room. Bookcases lined every available wall. A quarter inch of dust covered the shelves in most places instead of books. Discarded bindings and shredded pages littered the floor.

"Hide the bodies in the hall," Cal instructed. "The burned things, too. Anything that might hint at our presence."

Meaghan's gaze fell on Innelda's face. It had turned waxy. "Cal, I can't leave—"

"Go," Cal said. "If someone finds those bodies, none of us stand a chance."

Meaghan followed his command, focusing on her task instead of her worry for Innelda. Blood stained her fingernails as she cleaned it from the stone. Drapes served as mops. Closets became crypts. Soon, bare walls that had once displayed a nature painting and the absence of a colorful tapestry served as the only evidence a fight had consumed this space.

She returned to the library. What she found robbed the breath from her lungs.

Dark green leaves covered Innelda's wound. Red and yellow spots speckled the green. Cal smoothed the leaves down with water, turning them into a makeshift bandage.

Although rags wrapped his hands instead of ambercat gloves, the scene felt surreal and too reminiscent of a time Meaghan did not want to remember.

"Prickle poison leaves," she whispered. "Cal—"

"I had no choice."

Meaghan glanced around the room. Nothing lived here, not even the wispy tendrils of a houseplant. "Where did you get them?"

"I've been carrying them in a leather pouch in my boot since…" He did not finish his thought, but Meaghan knew. He had kept them in his boot since Talis died, since they had used the leaves on his wound in an effort to save his life.

"We don't have a Healer," Meaghan said.

"I had no choice," Cal repeated. "Keep quiet, okay? It's not easy

357

trying to keep the poison from getting me, too."

He saturated the leaves with water, dipping his rags into a pitcher until rivers ran down Innelda's body. When he had emptied the pitcher, he handed it to Meaghan. "Get more," he said. "In the alcove behind you."

Meaghan blindly followed his instruction, turning to find a small room she had missed before. It held a cook stove and a sink, plus a few threadbare towels similar to the ones Cal used as rags.

She filled the pitcher and brought it back to him. Without a word, he continued his task until the leaves had turned translucent. Innelda's cheeks had regained some color, but her eyes appeared distant as she stared up at them.

"Am I going to die?" she asked.

Cal stood. "Not if I can help it. You have a few hours at least." He crossed the room to a bookshelf that looked no different from any of the others. This one still contained a few books, though bugs had chewed white holes in their spines. He traced his finger up a leather-bound book, and then tugged it forward. The bookcase swung open, revealing a tunnel behind it.

"We need to get going. Our best chance of finding a Healer is going through Garon."

"Innelda can't protect herself," Meaghan pointed out.

"Obviously not," Cal muttered. He planted his hands on the edge of a heavy oak table and pushed it in front of the double doors to block them. "That should do the trick, don't you think?"

Meaghan nodded and entered the tunnel, then turned to check on Innelda one last time. Innelda's chest heaved with the effort to breathe. Her eyes drifted closed and Meaghan's stomach sank.

"Stay strong," Cal told her. "We'll be back for you."

As the bookcase closed behind them, sealing them in darkness, Meaghan squeezed her hand around her knife and wished she could be certain Cal had spoken the truth.

CHAPTER FORTY-THREE

THEY WERE losing. Zeiihbuan and Ærenden bodies carpeted the grass. Mardróch and soldiers wearing red tunics had fallen beside them in far fewer numbers. The majority of the dead stacked up in front of the castle walls, three high in some places. Caide had seen few people kill Garon's female Mardróch. Talea had been one of those people, but she could not work fast enough to clear the front lines. At some point in the battle, Miles had commanded her to fall back, afraid she would become a target for Garon's army. Her power was too valuable to lose.

Several of the best Zeiihbuan archers had also taken down members of Astasia's legion, though they had been lost to a swarm of soldiers within hours of the first attack.

Caide recited his brother's spell once more, attempting to turn a soldier to stone. The words fell powerless onto the ground. He had successfully cast the spell a handful of times when he had first arrived, but he seemed to have lost the ability. The prospect of his power failing terrified him, so he clutched his brother closer to his side and dismissed the thought. He would make it work somehow—if he managed to get to the gate.

Garon's army outnumbered the Queen's by almost two to one. Soldiers wearing red tunics took commands from both Mardróch and officers. They swarmed the field, blocking escape routes and overwhelming Guardians until only bodies remained in their wake. Although some of the soldiers fought with confidence and skill, many of them looked as if they had never held a sword. Their weapons shook in their hands. They shot arrows far from their targets, and they caved at the slightest resistance. If they turned and fled, a Mardróch's lightning bolt warned others not to follow their example. They were expendable. When red tunics littered the ground, they became stepping-stones for their comrades.

Caide's grandfather battled farther up the field from where Caide hid in the tree line. He used his best fighters to sweep Garon's soldiers outward. When they had cleared a straight line, an Ærenden army of Guardians charged forward to attack a half-dozen female Mardróch. A small tornado managed to tear apart one of the monsters. A fireball engulfed another. One Mardróch pressed her fingers to her head, then another, and a third. The air rained blood.

Caide turned away. Aldin buried his head in Caide's shoulder. "Can we go home now?"

"Soon," Caide promised and tightened his brother's blindfold. Tears swam in Caide's eyes, but he refused to honor the weakness. He had to be stronger or everyone here would die.

"There's always hope, Caide."

He sucked in a breath and spun around. Tall pine trees and squat bristle bushes filled his view.

"Did you hear that?" he demanded of his brother. Aldin whimpered.

"You only have to find the right path."

His mother had sounded faint this time, but Caide no longer doubted he had heard her. He chased her into the woods.

"This way."

Her voice had come from the right this time. He ran toward it. Shadows filled the space where his mother should have been.

"Not much farther."

"Mata," he yelled. "Where are you?"

Silence responded. He crashed over thick underbrush, gritted his teeth against the bite of sticky thorn bushes, and forced his way through a patch of slime weeds. She no longer spoke to him. He doubled back to a cluster of purple rose trees, and then gave up on that route when creeper vines dropped to the ground in front of him. The last path led him into an empty clearing.

Angry, he spun around to retrace his steps. Emma stared back at him. She stood at the edge of the grass, blocking his path to his mother's voice.

"What do you want?" he snapped.

She raised an eyebrow. "Do you want to try asking that question again?"

He did not, but the hard set of her jaw told him he should reconsider. "I'm sorry," he said. "I need to get back to the battlefield."

"No, you need to listen. I've been looking for you everywhere.

I'm not about to let you walk away from me so easily."

He shifted his brother to his other hip. "You can't stop me, Emma. I'm stronger than you are."

"Are you sure about that?" she asked. She stepped forward and placed a palm on his chest. "You won't fight me. You'd have to hurt me and it's not in your nature."

Caide looked away, certain he could if he felt it necessary. It pained him to realize that.

"I'm just asking for a few minutes, okay? You can storm off again after, if you want."

"Fine."

"You can't do this alone, Caide. Mycale and I want to help you, but we'll all get killed if we go in there without a plan."

"I know."

"Okay, good." She dropped her hand. "King Edáire's former tribe has agreed to help us."

Caide's gaze snapped back to Emma's face. Hope danced copper through her dark chocolate eyes and he did not have the heart to tell her she had just doomed his mission.

"They know?" he asked.

"Not all of it. We told them you had a spell to kill the female Mardróch. That's partly true, anyway. They don't know about your brother, but if we hide him, it won't matter. They're going to surround you and get you to the front line."

"What do you mean 'hide him?'" Caide asked. He looked down at his younger brother. Aldin shook with fear. "How?"

Emma removed a cloak from behind her back and snapped it

open. The brown material reeked of blood and rotten flesh.

"You stole it from a Mardróch," he realized.

Emma shrugged. "It's the best I could find on short notice. Just leave the hood down, okay?"

Caide chuckled, despite the nerves jumping around his stomach. "Right. Because the last thing I need is someone mistaking me for a Mardróch. I think this might actually work."

"Of course it will," she said. She slipped the oversized cloak around his shoulders, and fastened it closed with a triangular metal clasp. Caide ran his thumb over the glass eye in the middle of it.

"My brother's," Emma said and adjusted the material so it billowed around Aldin's body. "There, that should do."

"Thane knows, too?"

"I trust him," she said, stepping back. "And you have to learn to trust me, Caide. I'm on your side."

§

"THIS WAY," Mycale said, plowing his way through the forest at a speed that would have made any Zeiihbuan warrior proud. The Healer had greeted Caide with a tone cold enough to freeze water. Caide had expected no less. Mycale's involvement in Caide's mission at this point had everything to do with Emma and nothing to do with Caide's spell. Caide had destroyed any good will Mycale had extended by storming away from them.

"We're going to run for the gate," Mycale continued. "We have to. The female Mardróch are pushing out from the castle. It won't be long before they start taking the offense instead of just defending the walls."

Mycale raised his scythe, broke through the tree line, and charged onto the field without changing his stride. Emma flanked him, her tri-blades ready in her hands. Warriors formed lines to their right and left, human walls against Garon's advancing army. Caide recognized none of them, but their skin gave away their identities. They looked as if they could be Caide's siblings, with olive skin tones not quite as dark as a Zeiihbuan's and not light enough to hold pure Ærenden heritage.

King Ed's tribe had come from the mountains separating the northern end of Zeiihbu from Ærenden. Long ago, their ancestors had traveled from both lands to form their nomadic community.

Caide slipped a knife from his belt, gripping it in front of him as he followed Emma. A white-haired man fell in step beside him. Although the man did not state his name, Caide already knew it. His bearing gave him away. Both Caide's father and grandfather held the same confidence in their shoulders and authority in their step. This was Everel, the former king's cousin and the tribe's leader. Although he had been part of the army that had rescued Caide, he had left before Caide had had the chance to meet him.

"Getting to the gates will take more skill and manpower than I have," Everel said.

"Look out!" someone screamed from behind them. Caide glanced up in time to see several arrows flying their way. He did not have time to escape, but he could protect his brother. He crouched down on the ground and curled up around the cloak hiding Aldin.

Everel placed a hand on his shoulder. "Keep moving. Our time is limited if we want this to work."

Caide glanced up at the leader, at the kind look on his long face and the calm in his water-blue eyes. The arrows hovered above him, parallel to the ground.

"As I said," Everel continued. "We needed help, so I called on an ally." He pointed past his men. Closer to the castle, Guardians amassed, using magical bombs, swords, arrows, even torrential water to keep an army of red tunics at bay. Within their numbers, Caide found a familiar face. Miles, the Head Elder, held his hand aloft. His shield had stopped the arrows from advancing.

"Quickly," Everel said and they started running.

Although Everel's men and women showed skill with their weapons, their tightly held lines wavered as Caide raced across the field. When two Mardróch breached the line with blue lightning, Everel left Caide's side to battle with them. Caide glanced over his shoulder once, to watch Everel pierce one of the monster's heads with his sword, then lost track of the leader when a group of red tunics pushed through the other side of the line and chased after him.

A man and a woman stepped out of formation to tackle the soldiers. The woman slapped one soldier on the back and he burst into flames. The man tossed his knife at another and missed. The knife halted mid-air, then turned and flew after the soldier, changing direction twice before it sliced into his neck.

Garon's army continued to gain ground. Caide threw his knife at the closest soldier. It sailed wide.

"Get down!"

Caide ducked as an electric orb flew over his head and exploded in the soldier's chest. A second orb showered dirt at another soldier's feet. Caide ran. He did not stand a chance if he continued fighting with a blade. He needed his bow, and he needed his friends' help to use it.

He scanned the battle for Emma and Mycale. They fought two Mardróch farther afield. Caide set Aldin down and released his bow from his back. In three swift moves, one of the Mardróch toppled over with an arrow in his face. Mycale finished the other with his blade, then he and Emma doubled back to meet Caide.

"I can't carry him and fight," Caide told them. "We need to protect him another way."

"Back-to-back," Emma said and without waiting for a response, she yanked Aldin between her and Mycale. They turned away from each other and stood guard over Aldin, deflecting blows from errant soldiers who spotted them.

Caide fired another arrow, taking down a Mardróch who chased Everel. Caide had made it halfway to the gate. Everel's army would not be able to get him any farther. Their lines had dissolved as skirmishes picked them off in handfuls of two and three. Guardians fought their way toward him. Miles's shield still held arrows at bay, though the Elder could not get any closer. No one could help in time.

"He's mine," a voice growled and Caide snapped his attention to the Mardróch who had spoken. He advanced on Caide. Blue lightning arced along his fingers in threat. Caide did not wait to see if he would cast it. He tore across the field, leading the monster away from Emma and his brother. Electricity bounced off the ground by his sides, too close for comfort, but far enough away that he knew the Mardróch had not aimed for him. He dodged around a fight between a woman with a scythe and a soldier with fire in his hand, and then doubled back to the woods. Two more bolts blasted dirt at his heels, and then the attack stopped.

Caide ripped an arrow from the quiver on his back and spun around. The Mardróch lay on the ground. Artair stepped over his body and extinguished an orb floating between his hands. Talea followed close behind, a curved blade held firmly in front of her.

"What are you doing here, Caide?" Artair asked.

Caide lowered his bow. He could not tell Artair the truth. Not now.

"I dropped you off with Neiszhe," he continued.

"No you didn't," Talea said. "That's why I came to find you. He didn't show up. Miles got a message from Neiszhe right before Everel talked to him."

Artair shook his head. "That can't be right. I remember—"

"There's no time," Caide said and looked away. "I have to get to the gate."

He lifted his bow again and fired at a soldier who approached from the left. Another soldier swung a scythe as he charged over the body of his fallen ally.

Talea pressed her lips together. The man clutched the sides of his head and fell to his knees. Rivers of blood flowed between his fingers and down his cheeks.

Talea sighed. "I hate my power."

"At the moment, I love it," Artair said, grazing a kiss across her cheek before addressing Caide. "Come on. Let's get you out of here."

"I can't go," Caide said.

"I'm not giving you—" Artair started, but Caide ignored him. He turned and raced toward Mycale and Emma. Aldin cowered between their legs, his blindfold collecting mud at his feet. Soldiers and Mardróch turned to stone, their gray figures dotting the field as Aldin recited the only harmful spell he knew. His small lips moved continuously as tears streamed down his face.

Guilt squeezed Caide's chest. Aldin stared at him with wide eyes, then broke free of his protectors and raced across the field toward Caide. The young boy did not see soldiers as they chased him down, or the monsters that bounced blue electricity along their fingertips with delight. Caide did. He fired arrow after arrow in Aldin's aid, trying to protect his young brother from those who recognized him. He had been a fool to bring Aldin here. They would not kill him. They would take him alive and raise him as their own.

When Caide reached for another arrow in his quiver and grasped air, he snatched a knife from the ground and charged toward his brother. A Mardróch pursued from his brother's left, floating with a speed no man could achieve.

Caide pushed his legs beyond aching. He had more than a yard to cover when the monster reached out a long, bony arm to grab Aldin. The Mardróch's fingers brushed Aldin's shirt, then his hand closed around air as Aldin squealed and ran faster. The Mardróch tried again. Seconds before grabbing Aldin's arm, he plowed headfirst into a wall. He howled, surged forward, and hit the invisible wall once more.

Aldin rushed into Caide's arms. From a distance, Caide could see

Miles watching him. Next to him, Caide's grandfather fought with his best soldiers. The Zeiihbuans made their way toward him.

Caide traded his knife for a sword he found beside a fallen body, and raced for the gate. Mycale fell in step beside him. Emma forged ahead. A woman charged toward them, a fireball poised in the palm of her hand. Before Emma had the chance to react, the woman fell to her knees, her hands clutching her head, and Caide realized he had gained a Guardian.

Artair drew up alongside him, though the scowl on his face told Caide he had not joined willingly.

"You're an idiot," Artair said.

"You're not the first to think so."

"If Garon gets ahold of a Spellmaster, especially your brother, we're doomed."

"I know," Caide said. "We have a plan."

"It had better be a good one." Artair halted, then turned and tossed an electrical orb at a Mardróch who floated up ahead. The Mardróch deflected the orb, but failed to see Emma's tri-blade. She collected it from the opening of his hood and kept moving.

They pushed forward, and then banked left to avoid several soldiers racing their way. The gate grew larger up ahead. In front of it, a dozen female Mardróch waited. One of the Zeiihbuan soldiers grew too close and exploded, showering bone and flesh across the grass.

"There," one of the Mardróch screeched, pointing toward Caide. The female Mardróch formed a line and marched on Caide's small group, pulling away from the gate. Arrows flew at them from the

Zeiihbuan army. Two Mardróch fell. The rest would need only a few minutes before they could destroy Caide with a thought.

"Fall back!" Caide commanded.

A shell horn blared behind them. Caide's attention snapped toward it. A young man with bright purple hair waved at him before sweeping his arm through the air. A wall of fire sprang up, stopping the Mardróch from advancing. Another wall erupted behind them, then two more to the side, trapping them. The man kept his arms elevated until the Zeiihbuan army had surrounded the fire, and then he dissolved the flames. The Zeiihbuans showered the female Mardróch with arrows.

More Mardróch charged on their location from other sections of the wall. The Zeiihbuan army pulled back, though their aid had been enough to clear Caide's way.

"Come on," he yelled and tore across the field. He whispered his spell into his brother's ear repeatedly until the words blended together. "Aldin," he said. "You need to remember this."

His brother whimpered.

"Say the spell," he commanded as he reached the gate. His brother shook in his arms, but when Caide started reciting, Aldin's quiet voice joined his.

As their words swelled, then disappeared into the cacophony of the battle, he waited. A minute elapsed, then another. The female Mardróch had almost reached them. Their male counterparts still murdered the queen's soldiers with blue lightning. Nothing had changed.

The spell had failed.

CHAPTER FORTY-FOUR

THE WRITER'S book had erased its stories again. Nick thumbed through the pages, then sighed and shut the cover. He should not have been surprised. The spell protecting the book worked on need. Nick's curiosity hardly qualified.

His mother lifted an eyebrow. "Anything important in there?"

"Not really," Nick replied. "I've been in this room before, when the book showed me a fight between Ed and Adelina."

"I'm afraid that doesn't narrow anything down for me," Sam said. "Fights were a common occurrence for them."

May's eyes lit with amusement. "They did seem to enjoy them a little more than most couples."

Nick smiled, though his heart did not hold the gesture. His mother and Sam shared fond memories of the king and queen. They used those to keep their spirits lifted while they surveyed the aftermath of Garon's treachery. Nick carried no such shield against the emotional onslaught. He had not expected to stand in the king and queen's former apartment again so soon, and he felt less prepared for it than he had the first time. When they had arrived, Sam had opened a door Nick had not seen before.

On one side of the doorway, the living room's destruction gripped Nick with sadness. On the other, a second bedroom showed little evidence of the flames that had destroyed the rest of the apartment. Smoke had caked the room in a thin layer of black. Beneath the film a short bureau, small bed and rocking chair waited for their owners to return. Yellow walls broke the black in places, shining warmth over gray rugs shaped like horses. Colorful books paraded single file on a tall bookcase, and toys dotted the floor. A doll here, blocks there, a ball that had lost its shape—these had been part of a joyful childhood.

Nick felt as if he straddled the threshold between life and death.

"I don't know how this room didn't burn," May said.

"The whole castle should have burned," Sam told her. "But what prize would that have left Garon? He has Firestarters at his command. I'm sure they put the fire out easily enough."

May nodded and picked up a rabbit figurine from the bureau. With a flick of her thumb, she rubbed soot from its back to reveal Meaghan's name etched in silver. "I gave this to her. This was her room."

"It was Ed's room before that," Nick said. "Right after he wed Adelina."

"The book may have shown you that," Sam said. "It wouldn't have shown you this." He crossed the room to the bookcase and pressed his index finger into the center of a flower carved at the top. The bookcase swung outward, creaking with the protest of an object unaccustomed to moving. Behind it, hand-chiseled sandstone bricks lined the opening for a tunnel.

"I'm not entirely certain Adelina knew about this passageway," Sam continued. "Her mother told me she had used it a few times to hide from her parents as a child. She didn't want Adelina emulating her, so she kept it a secret. Perhaps for too long. We should hurry."

Sam stepped forward and Nick followed. His mother removed a knife from her belt. She pressed her hand to Nick's shoulder, and then the bookshelf swung closed. Black swallowed Nick's vision.

"Mind your head," Sam said. He recited the light spell and a small orb floated ahead of them, revealing a drop in the floor. When they reached the cut off, they found a staircase. Deep red stone unlike any Nick had seen before formed its steps. A silver railing followed the slope down the wall. Sam gripped it and Nick followed his lead, grateful for the stability when he slipped on a patch of bright green moss. A damp, musty smell wafted upward, growing stronger as they descended. The moss increased with the stench. At the bottom, the tunnel split into two. Rocks and fragmented bricks blocked the section to the left.

Sam pointed at it. "If I remember correctly, that used to lead to the river east of here. It was supposed to be an escape route for the royal family, but it flooded too often so they sealed it. This way," he gestured to the right. This tunnel looked no different from the first, though it started to climb soon after they entered it. Cobwebs drifted across the ceiling. An occasional bug clicked as it scurried along the floor.

At the end of the tunnel, another set of stairs spiraled upward.

The walls narrowed as they climbed until they reached a short door at the top. Nick traced it with his fingers. It felt smooth and cold, like quartz. He would need to crawl to get through it.

Sam extinguished the light. Nick pushed closer to him. No one spoke. Although their Guardian sensing powers should have prickled with urgency if an enemy stood beyond the door, protocol required they verify their safety by sensing for magic. Nick focused his power on the room outside the pillar. It echoed back to him, a wave with no disruption, peaceful and rolling. Nick closed his eyes and focused harder. He received the same response. The room was empty. A soft click echoed in the stairwell as the door opened. Light filled the space.

"I'm going in," Nick said.

Sam did not move.

"Step aside."

Sam faced him, but did not clear the path. Nick tried to push past him and Sam stopped him with a hand to the chest.

"You're the king, Nick."

Temper rose into Nick's cheeks. "Precisely. Now get out of my way."

Sam removed his hand. "And you're a Guardian," he said. "Have you forgotten our purpose?"

Nick wanted to snap back a sarcastic response, but Sam's words had hit their mark. He stared past Sam's white hair—a symbol of both his age and the wisdom that had earned him his Elder status—and sought the throne room. He saw black and white marble glistening in the sunlight. His anger dissolved into nervousness. He needed that book. Every moment they delayed made the mission more dangerous.

Sam would not let him go first for that reason. Nick considered himself a Guardian foremost, but everyone else saw only the king. Especially the two Guardians who had joined him today, who had fought hard over the past fifteen years to ensure the royal line remained intact. Even his mother would consider his role as her son secondary to his position.

For once, Nick understood Meaghan's frustration when she first came to the kingdom. He had protected her in the same way Sam now protected him, and it made him feel coddled.

He was more than capable of fending off an attack, perhaps better than the Elder could. Yet he also understood Sam's position. Guardians did not protect their charges solely out of obligation. They *needed* to, and that need stemmed from their powers. He nodded. "Make sure the room's clear."

Sam crawled through the doorway. Nick pressed his back to the wall to let his mother pass next, and then he crouched down and followed.

The tunnel exited the room directly behind the gilded thrones where Meaghan's ancestors had presided over formal gatherings. The tallest throne belonged to the queen. Golden flowers curled around the chair's arms and legs. A painted version of the family crest Nick had seen on the royal apartment doors decorated the back, and amethyst jewels crusted two finials at the top. The king's seat on the left looked like a smaller copy of the first. Both thrones sat on an elevated platform constructed of black granite tiles.

Beyond the dais, a long room stretched before Nick. It had changed little from Queen Adelina's reign. Four banners hung between tall windows that washed the rose quartz walls with light. A golden rod with an amethyst crystal decorated one, an onyx steed commanded attention on another, a soldier holding a sword stared back at Nick from a third, and the white nanny sparrow that hid another secret entrance flew to his right. Each symbol represented Adelina's family. As with the paintings, it surprised Nick that Garon had chosen to keep them.

May pressed her fingers against the closest wall and drew them down. Hazy streaks darkened the quartz. "This room was always my favorite. I've never seen a stone quite so beautiful."

"And I'm sure you haven't seen one as deadly," Nick told her. "The spell to kill Guardians requires rose quartz. The royal family had this room built in case the Elders ever challenged them."

May's hand dropped from the wall. Her face lost its color. "I had no idea."

"I suspect there's a lot we didn't know about the royal family," Sam said. "But now's not the time to speculate. Where's the book, Nick?"

"Underneath the platform," Nick said. "Ed used his power to push it through the granite."

May nodded. "Okay. See if you can get it. Sam and I will stand Guard."

Sam fixed an arrow in his crossbow and moved halfway down the room. His mother took up a position next to the pillar, keeping her eye on their escape route. Nick circled the thrones and dropped to his knees in front of them. A master artisan had installed the tiles. Nick looked for a crack or chip that would give him a place to wiggle a tile free. He found nothing to interrupt the sheen of polished granite. Next, he traced his fingers down the seams, looking for weak points. Nothing budged. He slipped his knife from his belt, intent on pressing it into the groove where the platform met the floor, but froze when his sensing power prickled in warning. Danger approached. His gaze snapped to his mother. Her cheeks had turned white and he knew she had felt it, too.

Nick raced toward her. As he rounded the dais, the door at the end of the room creaked open. He swept his hand, directing his mother to hide. Sam disappeared behind a royal blue drape covering the closest window. His mother ducked into the small doorway hiding the tunnel. Nick hid behind the larger throne, then shrunk down and focused on his personal power. It had been weeks since he had felt the need to block others from sensing him, but it seemed more than prudent now.

"The Zeiihbuans have come, as you predicted."

Nick locked a fist around his knife at the sound of the voice. Although he had not heard it since the night of the attack on his village, he knew it well. Angus had been a regular part of Nick's life, until he betrayed them all in an effort to take the throne from Meaghan.

"Of course they have, Angus. I'm rarely wrong when it comes to predicting hubris."

The second voice seemed familiar, though Nick could not quite place it. It sounded like both a male tenor and a Mardróch rasp.

"It's a shame the Shadow Guard stole the royal spell book," Angus said. "We could have eliminated all of the Guardians by now."

Nick's blood chilled. Had Avilis recovered the book the day he killed Ed? If so, Nick had risked his mother's and Sam's lives for nothing. The thought terrified him until a second possibility crossed his mind. Avilis had not found the book and had lied to keep Garon from looking for it. If the Shadow Guard had had the spell to kill Guardians, Cissy's betrayal in their old village would not have been necessary.

"We don't need spells to win, Angus. Your cousin will be delivered to death today, I assure you."

"I'm greatly looking forward to that," Angus said. "The castle belongs in my line."

"If your mother had not been weak, it would still be within your line. I told her as much."

"I don't appreciate you talking about my mother that way."

"Somehow, I thought that's what you'd say."

Nick sucked in a breath as the line echoed one he had heard recently in the Writer's book. He pressed his stomach to the floor and risked a glance around the platform. Although Angus had his back to the thrones, Nick could see the face of his companion clearly.

Years ago, as Garon had appeared in the book, he had been handsome. Now his face had twisted into a grotesque sculpture of evil. Some of the man he had been remained as tufts of blonde hair mixed within the Mardróch black, but most of his features had transitioned into those of a monster. His cheeks had collapsed. Gray skin stretched across skeletal fingers. His mouth, though still framed by human lips, opened to reveal thick webbing at the corners. Pointed teeth flashed when he laughed. His red eyes flicked toward Angus and the former Elder's hands froze partway to straightening his cloak.

"Don't forget who I am, Angus. You'll remain in the castle, at Ærenden's helm, only as long as I feel it's appropriate. When this battle is over, I'll have these lands and Zeiihbu under my control, but there will be others. The kingdoms to the south are unsuspecting. The ones past the Barren are without magic. They'll fall in short time. They each need rulers to keep them in line, but those positions are powerless. All of this belongs to me. If you forget that, you'll be reminded how disposable you are."

A knock echoed through the room and Garon glanced toward the double doors at the front of the great hall. Angus's hands dropped to his sides.

"Step away from me," Garon growled.

Angus turned toward the dais and Nick shifted back to avoid being seen. The former Elder walked to Adelina's throne. Anger had turned his copper eyes into fire, but his composure remained as he sat. He crossed his legs and relaxed his lanky arms on the sides of the golden chair.

"Not there," Garon snarled. "You haven't earned it yet."

Though Angus swore under his breath, Garon did not seem to hear. Angus rose and crossed to the window opposite the one where Sam had hidden. Sunlight shone on his black beard, though it could not penetrate the thick whiskers.

Garon turned his attention back to the door. "Come in."

The door opened. A voice purred as it crossed the room. "It's a pleasure to see you looking so handsome, my Lord. Being a Mardróch agrees with you."

"I rather think so," Garon said. "I've come to prefer it. I'm certainly stronger anyway."

"And much smarter than the other male Mardróch."

"That's not a hard accomplishment."

Nick peered around the platform again. His stomach tightened when he saw the monster who had spoken. The Mardróch resembled her male counterparts in many ways. Gray skin framed a lanky skeleton. Sharp teeth lined a webbed mouth. Even her height topped Angus's by half a foot at least, though her eyes glinted with cold blue instead of red.

A black braid swayed across her back when she glanced at Angus. She frowned. "I see you've brought your lackey, my lord."

"Watch your words, Astasia," Angus said. "Garon won't be around to protect you forever."

"I hardly need protection. What exactly can you do with your little power? Toss me a few feet?"

"For starters." Angus raised a hand and flicked it in the air. Astasia flew backward into a pillar with a bone-bruising crunch. "I can do more."

"So can I," Astasia growled. She straightened her drab brown shirt and pants, and then pressed her fingers to her temples. "Let's see how you like my power."

"Enough," Garon barked. "We have more important things to discuss than your hatred of each other."

"Yes, my lord." Astasia dropped her hands. "This battle has made you tense. I can help with that."

Angus snorted. Astasia glared at him. "Your human inferiority is unbecoming," she said. "The king's new form permits him some joys that only my kind can give."

Nick switched his attention back to his task. He had to focus, and fast. He had no desire to watch a fight between strong powers, or worse, bear witness to a Mardróch mating ritual. He wedged his knife into a gap between two granite tiles and started digging.

"I'm a hybrid, Astasia," Garon said, his voice cold. "Neither man nor Mardróch. An evolution. You're not my equal any more than Angus is."

"Yes, my Lord. That is true, but I could make you happy."

"Or you could make me dead, as you did your brother. Your conniving nature does not escape me."

Her voice held the hint of a smile. "As it should not. It's a valuable trait, my lord, and one that has served you well. Farrow's misfortune was your fortune."

"I won't argue that point. I called you here for an update."

"One I'll gladly give. My legion is holding strong. A handful of them have perished, mostly at the hands of a dozen archers who are now dead, and a woman with the power to melt minds."

"Melting minds is far less impressive than exploding bodies."

"I intend to teach her that myself," Astasia said. "Though I'm disappointed it will be a short lesson. There are also two Spellmasters here. Zeiihbuans."

"Interesting. It appears their kind have no limits to their idiocy.

Go on."

"The traitorous villagers will be gone by morning," Astasia continued. "The Zeiihbuans fight well. Their stamina outlasts the rest, but their ruler is growing closer to the front lines and to my Mardróch's powers. Once he falls, the rest will disperse."

"Animals are lost without a pack leader," Garon agreed.

Nick glanced up. Through the gap between the thrones, he watched Angus pacing in front of Sam's hiding place.

"Anything more, my lord?" Astasia asked.

"Leave no survivors."

"Was there ever another option?"

Garon chuckled. "You may win me over yet. You're dismissed."

She nodded. "Of course, my lord. If I may ask one question, though…"

"What is it?"

"There's magic here I don't recognize. It's stronger than your own. Whose is it?"

"You're mistaken," Garon said. "There is no power stronger than mine here."

Astasia cocked her head to the side and sniffed loudly, then sniffed again, the action reminding Nick of his horse when she expressed displeasure at a strong odor. "The magic tries to hide from me, but I'm a good tracker. I'm certain of its presence."

Garon's gaze moved to Angus. "In my new form, I no longer hold my Guardian abilities. Have you sensed anything?"

Angus's lips turned white as he pressed them together. He stopped pacing. "I dulled my powers. I didn't think I needed to scan for enemies here."

"A foolish assumption," Garon snapped. "Don't make that mistake twice or your greatest danger will be from me."

Nick turned his focus back to the tile. He jammed the knife deeper into the gap and the mortar holding the black tile in place crumbled. He caught the granite before it hit the floor, and then reached under the platform. At first, he felt only cold air. He groped deeper under Adelina's throne and checked a shudder when something scurried across his hand.

Silence eclipsed the room and Nick realized Angus was using his sensing power to search for magic. Even though Astasia had been able to see past Nick's personal power, he felt confident Angus would not. That still left Sam and his mother vulnerable. Nick shoved his arm farther into the abyss.

"I don't sense anything as powerful as Astasia says, but there is someone here. There, by the window."

The tips of Nick's fingers brushed leather. He stretched deeper into the dark cavern and his palm hit paper. He closed his hand around what he guessed might be the edge of a spine, and tugged. The book slid into his grip. He withdrew his arm and backed away from the platform as footsteps rushed across the room.

"You!"

Nick did not have time to do more than glance at the green cover in his hand before he hid it under his shirt. He grabbed his short sword. Now that Garon had discovered Sam, Nick had two options. He and his mother could escape through the tunnel or they could rescue Sam and try to fight their way out of the room while a

Mardróch exploded their body parts.

Nick forced a smile and tightened his grip on his weapon. He had never enjoyed the easy route. He saw no need to start now.

CHAPTER FORTY-FIVE

MEAGHAN AND Cal fled through the tunnel, chasing a small orb as it bounced around winding corners and down narrow passageways. Bricks rounded out the ceiling over their heads. Paving stones lined the uneven terrain under their feet. Cobwebs danced like ghosts in the eerie glow of the light. Meaghan brushed them off her hair and shoulders more times than she wanted to count. Within minutes, sticky threads caught hold again. As the tunnel narrowed and began a steep incline, Cal dissolved the light.

"The entrance to the throne room is up ahead," he whispered. "Garon knows about this passage. He's taken it before."

He would be expecting them, if he had not closed off the tunnel already. Cal slowed their pace, and then put a hand on her shoulder to stop her.

"It's a trap," he said.

"How can you tell?" she asked. She could not see the whiskers on his chin, let alone the ground a foot in front of them.

"I'm a Guardian. I can sense magic, remember?"

Meaghan heard rustling, and then sparks shattered the darkness. She gasped and jumped back. "Cal? Are you—?"

"Just a rock," he said, reciting the light spell again. An orb formed in front of them. "Garon's using a force field." He pointed to a faint yellow light on the path up ahead. "A crystal. We need to find another way into the throne room."

"There's no time. Innelda might die if we don't get in now."

"Maybe, but we'll definitely die if we try to go through that."

Meaghan puffed out a breath in frustration, and then reached for her mother's amulet out of habit. It felt warm. The stone in it had not only grown heavier, it seemed to have gained life over the last few weeks. It hummed against her palm.

"The Reaper Stone," she said, thinking aloud.

"What about it?"

"It robs powers. Whoever enacted the crystal infused it with power, right? So that would mean the amulet could work against it."

Cal grunted and tugged on his beard. "We don't really know how the stone works, but you said it gets heavier every time you use it. Seems we ought to consider that a warning."

Meaghan drew her index finger down the glass casing that surrounded the stone. At the end of the day, her head throbbed from the strain of it. It was a dangerous weapon. Of that, she had no doubt, but they had run out of options.

"It's not much different than the prickle poison leaves," she said. "Sometimes we have to take risks because the alternative is worse."

Cal grunted again. This time the response sounded subdued, and Meaghan took it as agreement. She wrapped her fingers around the amulet and concentrated her power through it. It glowed in her hand. Amethyst light exploded from the stone and collided with the force field in a shower of sparks. The crystal faded.

She let go of the amulet. It tightened against her throat and she dug her fingers under the chain, pulling it away from her neck. "Looks like it worked," she said.

"Looks like it," Cal agreed. He picked up another stone. A series of pings echoed through the tunnel as the stone skipped across the ground where the force field had been.

"Let's go," Cal said, extinguishing the orb again. He took her hand and pulled her the rest of the way, stopping when two lines of light shone ahead of them, gaps created by whatever hung over the opening to the tunnel.

Cal pressed his back against the far wall so he could peer through one of the lines. Meaghan did the same at the other, and then rested her hand against the rough fibers of a heavy tapestry.

She spotted a large throne first, then a smaller one next to it. Two people spoke, though she could not see either of them. One voice she recognized well. Garon was here, as Cal had suspected. The other, a female voice, sounded both gravelly and coy.

A moment later, a crossbow and a knife slid across the floor. Sam followed them, tossed into the middle of the room by Angus. Someone rose from behind the thrones.

Nick, Meaghan realized and caught her breath. She gripped the edge of the tapestry, ready to dash into the room. Cal locked his fingers around her wrist to stop her.

"Wait," he whispered.

A hole opened in a pillar behind him and Nick's mother burst through it. Meaghan moved to Cal's side so she could see the rest of the room. The doors flew open. Half a dozen soldiers and Mardróch marched across the floor. Her attention snapped to Cal and he nodded. They were outnumbered and had little hope of survival, but they could not let their friends fight alone.

Grabbing a knife in each hand, she pushed the tapestry out of the way. Outside, a larger battle would decide the fate of the castle. But inside, the true war for Ærenden was about to begin.

CHAPTER FORTY-SIX

"CAIDE!"

The familiar command caught Caide's breath and he snapped his attention toward it. Beyond the line of advancing female Mardróch, past the red tunics fighting against Zeiihbuans, he saw the face he feared the most.

His father's cheeks blazed red as his gaze fell hard on Caide. He bellowed with a voice too loud to be real. It carried over the battlefield and filled Caide's ears as if his father stood beside him. A woman from Caide's village ran alongside his father and Caide realized she had the power of projection.

A soldier stepped in front of Faillen and met a lethal arrow. Another arrow flew into a female Mardróch and a third found a red tunic who strayed too close. The arrows charged furiously, their speed matching Faillen's anger.

The line of female Mardróch closed in, blocking Caide's view. Caide shrunk against the gate while Aldin sobbed in his arms. Caide wanted to join him. He closed his eyes to chase away his tears, and then yanked them back open when pain raced through his head. One of the female Mardróch winked at him. Her webbed mouth parted in a grotesque smile.

Caide recited the spell to turn her to stone. Nothing happened. His brother's soft voice repeated it and Caide's pain stopped. The Mardróch stood as a gray statue.

His brother changed a second Mardróch to stone, then a third. The rest of the Mardróch stopped advancing, though Caide realized the reprieve would not last long. He had to find a way to escape.

Clutching Aldin tightly, he jumped to the side as an arrow splintered the door next to his head. Another flew toward him. He ducked, but the arrow fell in midair. Miles approached from the left, using his shield to sweep arrows away from the gate. Caide's father broke through the line of red tunics on the right. Emma and Mycale fought with three soldiers farther afield.

"Caide!" his father thundered again, and in his anger, he failed to see the woman racing toward him. She did not wear a tunic, but Caide could not mistake the look of hatred on her face. She raised her arms.

"Behind you," Caide yelled, but without a projection power, his father could not hear the warning. The woman clapped her hands together. Three swords ripped from the closest Guardian's hands and slammed into Faillen's back. He collapsed to the ground.

"No!" Caide screamed. He felt as if a million needles tore him apart from the inside. He could not breathe. He could not see anything beyond the pain frozen on his father's face. Caide needed to get to him, but at least fifty Mardróch and soldiers separated him from his father's side.

An explosion reverberated from the far side of the field and Caide's attention snapped to it. A second explosion sent Mardróch flying into the sky.

Emma used the distraction to kill one of the soldiers attacking her. Mycale took down another, and the third met his fiery end by Artair's orb.

Emma raced toward Faillen. She dropped to her knees in the dirt and cradled his head in her hands, oblivious to a lightning bolt streaking her way. It crashed into an invisible barrier. Another met the same fate, then the Mardróch who had sent them screamed. He collapsed to the ground. Mycale joined Emma's side. Talea and Miles flanked him, standing guard over Faillen.

"All hands, attack!" Caide's grandfather boomed. His command came from everywhere, buoyed by the same power that had allowed Caide to hear his father.

Zeiihbuans surged forward, pushing from every direction. The line of female Mardróch turned away from Caide. Villagers exploded. Guardian blood soaked the grass.

Caide stumbled backward, and then collapsed in front of the gate. He had been certain he could rescue everyone, confident his power had no limits. He had never been more wrong.

His father was dead. Emma and Aldin would not survive long. Everyone Caide knew would draw their last breaths on this field, and he would live long enough to suffer with the knowledge he had failed them all.

"Have faith."

He closed his eyes, ignoring his mother's voice. Mycale and Artair had been right. Caide was not strong enough. He had been a fool to think he could make a difference.

"Have faith in yourself, my son."

Fingers lifted his chin and he opened his eyes. His mother stared back at him. A smile played on her bright pink lips.

"You're dead," he whispered. "I'm going crazy."

"You aren't. I'll always be here for my sons."

"Mata," Caide whispered and gripped her hand in his. "I miss you."

"I'm by your side, love. Use my strength. Trust who you are."

She pressed her lips to his cheeks, and then she was gone. The battle still waged in front of him. Emma and Mycale worked frantically on his father. Miles retreated as a female Mardróch stalked him, held at a safe distance by his shield. Caide grabbed his brother's hand and yanked him to his feet. Aldin whimpered.

"I want to go home," he cried. "I want Mata back."

Caide stared at him. "You saw her?"

Aldin sniffled and wiped a sleeve across his nose. "She visits me sometimes."

Caide's gaze shot back to the Elder, then to his father. He might not be able to save everyone, but he would save those who still lived. The scar on his shoulder prickled, and it fed into his determination. He had fought Garon's monsters before and won. He had withstood their torture in captivity. He would not let them defeat him now, not while he was free.

The Mardróch would fall.

"Look at me," Caide commanded. He gripped his brother's shoulders and turned him away from the battle. "Only me, okay?"

Aldin nodded.

"Focus on your words," Caide said, more to himself than Aldin. "Focus on your power. We can do this."

Aldin's eyes never left Caide's face as they recited the Mardróch counterspell once more.

Their words faded, and then silence followed. Caide's gaze searched the battlefield. Zeiihbuans still clashed with soldiers and lightning still arced through the air, but he could hear none of it. Heat coursed through him, an after effect of the spell's intensity. It numbed everything else. Then that, too, faded, and the screaming began.

Caide had never heard a more terrifying sound. It radiated out from the gate, until the Mardróch's collective shrieks drowned out all other noise. Aldin shook, but Caide could only smile.

For once, the monsters truly understood pain.

CHAPTER FORTY-SEVEN

"THE GIRL is mine," Garon roared as his soldiers and Mardróch surrounded him. "Punish the rest. If anyone dies too easily, you'll feel the pain they deserved."

The female Mardróch beside Garon hissed. Meaghan held her knives in front of her. Cal drew up beside Meaghan and slipped a blade from his belt.

Below Garon's sunken nose, a smile cracked his dry lips. "Astasia, start with the fool who calls himself the king."

"Yes, my lord," the Mardróch said. "My power will make quick work of him."

"But it would be far less fun," Garon told her. "Use a sword."

"As you wish." She pressed her fingers to her head. A soldier closest to her exploded. Flesh, blood, and bone rained down over the room. Meaghan shuddered as red misted her arms. She hastily wiped it off with her shirt.

Astasia picked up the soldier's fallen sword and swept toward Nick with the unnatural speed of her kind. In one hand, Nick brandished a knife. The other held a short sword. He raised both of them and stood his ground. His mother moved in front of him, her own blade ready in her hand.

"Nick's fine," Cal said when Meaghan took a step toward him. "We need to get Garon."

Meaghan nodded and followed Cal's lead, attacking a soldier who stood in their path. Cal sliced open the woman's arm, and then grunted when she twisted her wrist and sent him flying. She snapped her fingers and Meaghan's knives tore from her grip. Another snap and her legs collapsed beneath her. The soldier swung a crossbow around, and Meaghan scurried out of the way, grabbing a knife from her own belt and casting it at the woman. The blade shivered mid-air and dropped to the floor.

"Did you think I would be so easy to kill?" the soldier asked with a chuckle. She flicked her wrist and Meaghan crashed into a wall.

"Yep, I did," Cal answered from behind her as he drove his blade into her back. The soldier collapsed. "I hate that power," Cal muttered. "Hopefully no one else has it."

"Aside from Angus, you mean," Meaghan reminded him. She collected her knives and sought out Garon again. She found him halfway across the room, lobbing lightning bolts at Sam's feet as the Elder retreated, weaponless, toward a pillar.

Meaghan spotted Sam's crossbow a few feet away. A soldier blocked her access to it. "Come on," she gestured at Cal and sheathed her weapons. Cal nodded. He tackled the soldier. She swept up the crossbow and raced after Sam. Several yards from him, Garon turned and fired lightning bolts at the floor between them. Meaghan lifted the crossbow, but could not get a clean shot. Sam raised his hands and she threw the weapon to him.

He caught it and launched an arrow at Garon. It sailed wide. A second bounced off Garon's cloak. Garon growled and threw a bolt at the Elder. Sam dropped to the ground as electricity cascaded overhead, then scurried behind the pillar. One arrow remained in his crossbow. He let it fly. It struck a soldier and he claimed the soldier's scythe, swinging it around in time to prevent Garon's sword from slicing open his stomach.

Meaghan pulled a knife from her belt and charged toward Garon, but skidded to a stop when May cried out. Her attention snapped back to Nick. His mother crashed into a table.

"Angus," Cal barked. He plowed into the former Elder. They hit the ground and rolled. Cal came to a stop on top of Angus. He smashed one large fist under Angus's chin, another into his temple. Angus's head lolled to the side, and Cal jumped up in time to deflect a Mardróch's sword. He parried, sidestepped a second swing, and then drove his blade into the monster's hood.

Garon and Sam still fought around the pillar, their blades ringing with each strike. A Mardróch swept in from the side, and Meaghan raced toward him. She took a shot. Her knife hit his cloak and skidded across the floor. She grabbed it and another one from her belt, then drove both into the Mardróch's face.

Sam gestured at Nick before fending off another one of Garon's strikes. "Go, Meaghan. I've got this."

Meaghan detoured toward the dais. Nick and his mother circled Astasia, blocking strikes from her sword with their shorter blades.

Neither of them could get close enough to do any damage. Meaghan aimed a knife. Before she could throw it, she catapulted into a wall. Dazed, she stood and shook off the pain prickling behind her eyes. Cal hit the wall next to her.

"Guess Angus is awake," he muttered.

"Look out!" Nick hollered.

Lightning blew a chunk from a decorative table at Cal's side. Another bolt cascaded toward them. It exploded a chair to Meaghan's left. Cal grabbed Meaghan and tried to pull her down, but she shook him off and charged at the Mardróch who had assaulted them. Garon's claim on her life meant his monster would not harm her. Her knife disappeared into the opening of his hood. She spun around, looking for another soldier or Mardróch to fight, but none remained. Only Astasia, Garon, and Angus opposed them now.

Sam still held his ground in his fight with Garon, so she ran toward Nick. When she had almost reached him, her feet skidded to a stop. Angus grinned at her from across the room. She fingered her knife, but knew attacking her cousin would be useless. He was too far away.

Astasia laughed and Meaghan's attention snapped back to the dais. The Mardróch wielded her sword as if it were no heavier than vapor. Her strikes came swiftly at Nick's head. He blocked them each time, but they drove him back until she had pinned him into a corner. She knocked Nick's weapons from his hands with one solid blow, then raised her sword above her head and brought it down.

May jumped between them, stopping the blade with her knife. The force of the impact brought her to her knees. She swung one foot around, knocking Astasia's legs from beneath her, and stabbed her blade toward the Mardróch's face.

Astasia rolled out of the way, then vaulted to her feet and ran, leaving her weapon behind. Nick grabbed his short sword and chased after her. As they rounded the dais, she whipped around to face him, her fingers at her temples.

"Not another step," she hissed.

Nick halted. A chilling smile spread across Astasia's face, and Meaghan panicked. She yanked her mother's amulet from under her shirt and held it out. Heat charged through her as her power surged into the Reaper Stone. It flashed purple.

Angus gasped in surprise. He released his grip on her. She stumbled back and the stone slipped from her fingers, plowing into her chest like a brick.

Astasia howled. She lowered her hands, and then pressed them to her temple again. Her howls became wails of anguish. "What have you done?"

Nick drove his sword between her ice-blue eyes. She collapsed to the floor and Garon's rage filled the room as a guttural scream that thundered in Meaghan's ears. He shoved Sam away with the force of his wrath, sending the Elder skidding into a pillar.

"You!" Garon's fingers crackled blue as he faced Nick. "Your life ends now."

May joined her son. Meaghan wanted to do the same, but Cal called out for her. She swung around in time to see him crash into a table. He groaned and did not move again. Sam rushed to his side.

Garon cast lightning bolts at Nick and his mother, one after the other, shattering a side table, and setting fire to a tapestry. Meaghan reached for the amulet again. It floated out of her hand. She grabbed it from the air and tightened her fingers around it.

Angus gestured with one hand, twisting the chain around her neck. He pulled his hand back and Meaghan's vision grayed. She dug her fingers underneath the necklace, but she could not loosen it.

In desperation, she released the clasp. The stone sailed toward Angus. He grabbed it, and then screamed as a dagger sank into his forearm. The amulet fell to the ground.

Sam rushed past her. He stooped down to grab another dagger from a dead soldier's boot and threw it. Angus dodged out of the way.

Electricity sizzled across the room. Meaghan tore her attention from her cousin to Garon. He chased Nick with tendrils of blue lightning, the bolts leaving scarred marble close behind Nick's feet. Meaghan threw a knife at Garon. It ricocheted off the back of his cloak. Nick tossed a green book to his mother.

"Page thirty!" Nick commanded. She found the page as he skidded to a stop in front of her. They began reciting.

Meaghan lobbed two more blades in Garon's direction. They skipped across the marble at his feet. Her last knife grazed his hand. Blood trickled down his wrist. He ignored it. Blue electricity bounced along his fingertips. He held it in front of him in warning.

"The book," he growled. "Give it to me."

Nick and May kept reciting.

Garon spread his fingers wide, shooting lightning in all directions. One bolt cracked a pillar in two. Another hit the wall beside Angus.

Chunks of stone rained over the floor. Two more bolts cracked the marble tiles beside Nick and his mother. Garon fired a fifth blue streak, scorching the ceiling, and Meaghan realized he had missed intentionally. He did not want to destroy the book. Blue arced through the air as he raised his hands in threat again.

May and Nick did not flinch. They recited Garon's name, then one last line and slammed the book shut.

Meaghan held her breath, expecting Garon to explode or collapse. A cackle escaped his throat instead. "Angus, take care of the Healer."

With a snap of his fingers, Angus flipped May through the air. She slammed into a pillar on the other side of the room. She tried to stand, but her left leg crumpled beneath her weight.

The book shot from Nick's grip into Garon's outstretched hands. "I'm no longer a Guardian," he said. "That spell is useless on me. It won't be on you."

Garon began his incantation, his words heavy as gravel. Meaghan raced toward him. An invisible force yanked her back before she could get close. She came to rest at Angus's feet.

Garon said Nick's name and Meaghan grabbed blindly for any weapon that would help. One line more and Nick would be dead. She spotted the glint of a fine chain, almost completely buried beneath the pile of quartz Garon had blasted out of the wall. She grabbed for it and tugged. The amulet would not budge.

Angus chuckled. "It's time to watch your king die," he said.

Meaghan fought to rise, but Angus's power held her firm. Tears burned her eyes, then a movement caught her attention and she stopped struggling. Sam had snuck into position so he had a direct line of sight with Garon. He lifted his hand and snapped it closed.

Garon's mouth hung open. No words escaped it. When silence passed his lips a second time, he threw a lightning bolt at the dais. The king's throne exploded. Garon spun around and cast another bolt in Sam's direction. Sam jumped out of the way.

Angus relaxed his hold on Meaghan. He flicked his hands, pushing Sam closer to Garon.

Meaghan leaped at her cousin. Angus shoved her to the side with his power and fled across the room. Grabbing a sword from a dead soldier, Meaghan charged at Garon. Nick did the same. Their efforts came too late.

Two bolts converged at Sam's heels. Two hit by his side. As he tried to outrun another, Garon raised his hands and shot one last blue bolt in Sam's direction.

The Elder collapsed in a pile of black flesh and singed clothing. A sob escaped Meaghan's throat. Nick roared in grief. He spun around and hurled his sword at Garon.

Meaghan charged in Nick's direction. Angus's power yanked her back. She slammed into a wall, and her body launched upward. Invisible fingers choked her.

She clawed at her neck, her efforts useless against air. From here, a story and a half above the carnage, she could see everything. The door at the front of the room opened. Mardróch marched across the floor. They surrounded Nick, and then parted when Garon came through with his sword in hand. May hobbled toward her son, using a broken piece of wood as a cane. Cal stirred awake.

Meaghan struggled for breath, for hope, as she watched failure unfold before her. Garon looked up at her. His mouth spread open in a grotesque smile. He raised his sword.

Then he shrieked.

Mardróch fell, one-by-one, their agony washing through the room like a rainstorm. Those closest to the door collapsed first. The rest joined them in waves until only Garon remained standing. His anguish echoed from the walls. Flesh melted down his face and dripped from his swollen and bleeding fingers. Nick stole a blade from a writhing Mardróch. He brandished it in front of him, and Garon fled, escaping through the door behind the dais.

The edges of Meaghan's sight dimmed as Angus's hold tightened. Nick rushed toward him. A soldier rose up from the floor, a crossbow in her hand.

"Nick!" his mother screamed, and the soldier fired. Nick's eyes widened. He fell to his knees, gasped, then dropped down onto his chest.

May collapsed next to her son. She laid her hands on his back, around the arrow. Blood seeped through her fingers. She squeezed her eyes shut and pressed harder, though the sorrow on her face belied her efforts. She could not save Nick.

Heat consumed Meaghan in a flash of anger and hatred. For a moment, she thought her skin had succumbed to whatever had attacked Garon, but the thought disappeared within the molten lava heating her stomach and scorching her gaze. She pointed it at Angus.

Her breath escaped her mouth like steam. Burning consumed her heart. She allowed it to explode from her body until the fire had consumed every inch of her.

Angus's scream pierced Meaghan's ears. His hold over her released and she plummeted to the ground. Pain shattered her legs. She ignored it, and the haze still trying to claim her. She had to get to Nick.

She pulled herself across the room until she felt his hair at her fingertips. She grabbed a fistful of it and tugged his head around so she could see his face. His eyes stared blankly ahead.

"Nick, please," she whispered and pressed her lips to his. He did not respond. She drew her palm to his cheek. It felt like ice against her burning skin. "Please," she begged again and squeezed her eyes shut. "I can't lose you." The fire within her scorched her mind and she pushed it toward him, willing it to warm his body instead of hers. It flowed into her hands, and then drained from her until only darkness remained.

"Meg?"

Nick's voice floated past and she wondered if she had met him in the afterlife. Peace washed through her.

"It's not possible," May said. Her next words came faint as Meaghan's world faded. "Nick, you were dead."

CHAPTER FORTY-EIGHT

MEAGHAN STARTLED awake, though a hazy dream persisted, shadowing reality with fiction. Monsters grinned at her from the windows and dangled from the ceiling. She recoiled and reached for her knives, but grasped only the smooth cotton of a bedspread. As her grogginess faded, the monsters did too, leaving behind draperies and tan walls, a four-poster bed, and antique furniture she did not recognize.

She rubbed her eyes. The smell of lavender greeted her from newly washed sheets. Warm blankets wrapped her like a cocoon. Now that fright did not grip her, she felt refreshed, as if she had enjoyed a long night's sleep on Earth, safe from Garon's reach.

The thought tickled her memory and the battle came flooding back to her. *A soldier had shot Nick.* She bolted upright.

"Nick," she cried. No one responded. She threw back the covers.

A door swung open and Nick's mother crossed the room. She had cinched her red hair into a bun at the top of her head. The style only added to the stern look on her face. "Stay in bed," she said.

"You need rest."

"I need answers. What happened? I saw the arrow. It…" Meaghan lost her voice. "May, where's Nick?"

May pressed her lips together and sat down on the edge of the bed. She drew the covers back over Meaghan's legs.

"He's okay, dear."

"I thought he was dead."

"He was, or he was almost there. I couldn't save him."

"But he's okay?"

May raised an eyebrow. "Do you think I'd be so calm if he wasn't?"

Meaghan shook her head, more to clear her confusion than to answer. "What happened?"

"That's a bit complicated," May said. "And not mine to explain."

Meaghan sighed. "Fine, then at least tell me where I am and what I'm supposed to do now, *besides* stay in bed."

"The castle," a familiar voice said from the doorway. "And redecorate, I suppose. Garon left the place a mess."

Miles entered the room holding a tray laden with a teapot and cups. He set it down on a bureau and grinned. Before Meaghan could respond, Nick appeared behind him.

Meaghan caught her breath. He looked relaxed in a way she had never seen him. Even the dark circles under his eyes could not dampen the joy shining on his face.

Ignoring May's protests, Meaghan ran to him. Nick caught her and she buried her head in his shoulder, her body in his warmth, until she could no longer doubt his presence. He should not be alive, but somehow he was here.

May cleared her throat and Nick nudged Meaghan back to the bed. "There's a lot we need to talk about," he said. "And a lot we still need to figure out. I'm not sure where to start."

"The war," Miles told him.

Nick nodded. "It's over, Meg. The Mardróch are dead. Guardians are currently rounding up the last of Garon's followers."

They had won. Meaghan wanted to rejoice in their triumph, but the cost had been too high. Her heart felt heavy. "We lost Sam," she said. "Who else?"

"Many good men and women," Nick answered. "Cadell and Everel among them."

Meaghan closed her eyes. Everel, her father's cousin, had left a wife and three children. Cadell had helped her mother pioneer peace for Ærenden and Zeiihbu. Meaghan would mourn them both.

"Faillen almost didn't make it," Nick continued. "Emma and Mycale saved him. He's gone back to Zeiihbu with Caide and Aldin."

"What about Innelda?" she asked, turning to May for the answer.

May shook her head. "She's with Talis now."

Grief squeezed Meaghan's throat shut. Tears warmed her cheeks.

"We'll honor them at our coronation," Nick said and wrapped his arms around her. She pressed her face into his shirt. Something musky hovered on his skin, a scent of normalcy that seemed foreign to her after too many months fighting for the chance to breathe another day.

Meaghan drew her fingers up his back, searching for the spot where an arrow had almost taken his life. "You should have joined them," she said. "I remember it, Nick."

Nick reached behind him and took her hand in his. He brought it to his lips. "It seems the Shadow Guard told the truth about one thing. There's more to your power than we realized. Your ancestors explained some of it in the spell book. The revival power never existed. It was invented to hide the truth."

Bile rose in Meaghan's throat. "What truth?"

"You're a Reaper, Meg. Helping plants grow is a side effect of what you can do."

Nick did not need to say more. She had brought him back from the dead. "Angus," she realized. "I killed him."

May rested a hand on Meaghan's knee. "It was you or him. He left you no other choice."

"I know," Meaghan whispered. And she did, but that did not make the truth any easier. She held the power of life or death within her. Maybe the Shadow Guard had been honest about more than one thing.

"What do we do now?" she asked.

"Rebuild," May said. "Move forward. Garon escaped. Max, too. I doubt we'll ever see them again. We have a chance for peace in Ærenden."

"We have a chance for more than that," Miles said. "Someone cast a burn spell on the royal spell book. It blackened several of the pages—"

"I thought the book couldn't be destroyed," Meaghan interrupted. She turned her gaze on Nick. "Didn't you tell me that when we were in the old Spellmaster's house?"

"I did," Nick said. "Our guess is an attempt at destroying the book is why it's now protected. Let Miles finish."

The Head Elder pulled up a chair to Meaghan's bedside. "We were able to make out enough on one of the blackened pages to realize your ancestors put a curse on Guardians. They wanted to prevent your power from returning."

"That's why you lose your powers when you wed non-Guardians," Meaghan realized. "It was meant as a deterrent."

"There's a counterspell," Miles continued. "We'd like your permission to cast it."

"Of course. Why are you asking me?"

Miles glanced at May. She squeezed Meaghan's knee, and then let it go. "It seems the royal family and Guardians decided to cast the original spell together. We have to be in consensus to reverse it."

"Then we'll do it. There's no reason Guardians shouldn't be allowed to love whomever they wish."

May's gaze drifted to Miles again and lingered. Their faces held more emotion than Meaghan could read, so she released her empath power. Peace filled them, happiness, and relief. It spread through Meaghan, soothing her. They had struggled for more than fifteen years, terrified every day they would meet death. She wondered if they believed they would see the inside of the castle again.

Something else surged beneath their surface emotions and it lifted some of the sorrow from Meaghan's heart. She decided to keep her discovery silent for now and muted her power.

"How long have I been asleep?" she asked.

"A week," Nick told her. "By Mom's doing. You needed time to recover. There's something else you should know."

"It's about your illness," May said. Meaghan looked from May to Nick, then back again. Nerves danced over their faces.

"What is it?" she demanded. "I can handle it."

"I'm sure you can, dear. It turns out you and Nick will be giving the kingdom an heir."

Meaghan stared at May, and then shook her head in awe. Somehow, in the back of her mind, she had known. Her power had sensed contentment from her child. She sought the baby's emotion again. Peace filled her. It eclipsed her shock and warmed her heart. "That's what you wanted to tell me before the battle," she guessed. "That's why I was sick."

A smile hovered over May's lips. "A Healer's job has some perks. I had the pleasure of telling your mother, too."

Meaghan grinned in response. It felt right learning about this in the home where her parents had fallen in love and welcomed her into their arms. She leaned against Nick.

"Since my news is out," she said. "You might as well share yours."

May's eyes widened and flicked to Miles. The Head Elder stood. "I told you not to use your empath power to spy on us," he lectured. "We haven't even told Nick yet."

"You haven't told me what?"

May reached out and took Miles's hand. "We're wed. We have been since shortly after Meaghan left for Zeiihbu. We weren't sure how to tell you."

Nick stood and placed a hand on Miles's shoulder. "I'm glad," he said. "You're probably the only one brave enough to challenge my mother anyway."

Miles laughed and crossed the room to the tray he had left on the bureau. "I guess that settles it then. Tomorrow, we have a lot of work to do. Today is for recognizing what we've earned." He raised a cup. "A new beginning, a new queen and king, and the return of peace to Ærenden. I think our kingdom is about to enter its best era yet."

Meaghan stretched her hand over her stomach and chased away the questions still plaguing her about her power and the Shadow Guard. Time would reveal if Miles was right about his prediction for the future, but he *was* right about today. Finding answers could wait. For now, Meaghan intended to celebrate.

She had finally come home.

ABOUT THE AUTHOR

Born in Bangor, Maine, **Kristen Taber** spent her childhood at the feet of an Irish storytelling grandfather, learning to blend fact with fiction and imagination with reality. She lived within the realms of the worlds that captivated her, breathing life into characters and crafting stories even before she could read. Those stories have since turned into a wide range of short tales, poems, and manuscripts in both Young Adult and Adult genres. Currently, she is working on the Ærenden series from her home in the suburbs of Washington, D.C.

Learn more about Kristen and her work at www.kristentaber.com.